❧

The shapeless Mother Hubbard dress Rose wore did nothing for her curvaceous figure, but a man with his experience and imagination could guess what delights the calico material disguised.

"Are you listening to me, Your Grace? I asked if you were ready to try your hand at something else."

An interesting question, he thought. His hands itched to explore many things. . . . "I'm yours to command, my sweet Rose."

She blushed at the endearment. "No need to get flowery, Your Grace. We're only going to feed the hogs and slop out their pens. I doubt you'll be waxing poetic for long."

Rose rested the hoe against the side of the house, then marched off in the direction of the pig shed; Alexander followed two steps behind, and wondered what he'd done to deserve such punishment.

❧ ❧ ❧

*Please turn this page
for praise for
the Flowers of the West trilogy . . .*

PRAISE FOR
THE *FLOWERS OF THE WEST*

❧

"The first book in the Flowers of the West trilogy is a rousing success. . . . An excellent historical romance. . . . Criswell's creativity is in full bloom."
—*Affaire de Coeur*

❧

"I loved it! It was romantic, humorous, and fun to read."
—Karen Robards, author of *Hunter's Moon*

❧

"A charming, radiant romance that will lift and capture your spirit and your heart."
—*Romantic Times*

❧

"SWEET LAUREL is wonderful! You'll love this funny and touching romance! Millie Criswell writes a humorous, poignant love story with panache. A 'keeper' for sure!"
—Kathe Robin, *Romantic Times*

❧

"A delightful story full of humor, wit, and entertaining adventure that will leave you wanting more."
—*Rendezvous*

❧

"Nobody does a better Western romance with style and panache than Millie Criswell."
—Harriet Klausner, *Affaire de Coeur*

PRIM ROSE

BOOKS BY MILLIE CRISWELL

Flowers of the West Trilogy
Wild Heather
Sweet Laurel
Prim Rose

PUBLISHED BY
WARNER BOOKS

MILLIE CRISWELL

PRIM ROSE

WARNER BOOKS

A Time Warner Company

WARNER BOOKS EDITION

Cover design by Diane Luger
Hand lettering by Carl Dellacroce
Cover art by Ron Broda

Warner Books, Inc.
1271 Avenue of the Americas
New York, NY 10020

Visit our Web site at
http://pathfinder.com/twep

W A Time Warner Company

Printed in the United States of America

First Printing: December, 1996

10 9 8 7 6 5 4 3 2 1

For her support, encouragement, and kindness, for always taking the time to answer questions and provide solutions, and most important—for making me look good on paper—I dedicate this book to my editor, Jeanne Tiedge, and offer heartfelt thanks.

If I went West, I think I would go to Kansas.

—**Abraham Lincoln**

CHAPTER 1

Salina, Kansas, Late Summer 1883

"Damn, damn, and double damn!" Rose Elizabeth tapped her foot impatiently against the rotting boards of the railway platform as she waited with no small amount of dread for the arrival of the westbound train from New York City.

It was cursed hot, she was sweating like a pig, and there wasn't a cloud in the sky that held any promise of rain for relief.

"It's surely going to be something having a real live English duke living here in Salina," remarked Skeeter Purty, the station manager, scratching his whiskered chin. "I reckon it could put this here town on the map." The wad of chewing tobacco he spit missed its mark, landing just short of the brass spittoon near his rocker.

Rose jerked her head around, and with narrowed eyes she stared in disgust at the brown gooey mess on the platform, then at the old man himself, wondering if he'd been nipping at the bottle of corn liquor he kept hidden in his desk drawer

1

and thought no one knew about it. She had half a mind to turn the old fool in to the sheriff, though she doubted Morris Covington would do anything about it. Mo had a hollow leg himself when it came to drinking whiskey.

Liquor had been banned in Salina and elsewhere in Kansas for the past two years, though that hadn't stop old-timers like Skeeter and Morris from imbibing whenever they got a hankering, which was often.

"In case that feeble mind of yours ain't workin', Skeeter Purty, I am not one bit happy about that damned duke coming here, and I'm doubly damned unhappy that he's stealing my farm out from under me." She crossed her arms over her chest, and her foot went into double-time.

The old man rocked back and forth, and he spit twice more, unfazed by Rose's sharp tongue. Rose Elizabeth had about the sharpest tongue in the whole state of Kansas for someone of such tender years. Some folks said she could cut a man down to size without raising much of a sweat, her tongue was so keen.

The townsfolk had taken to calling her "Prim Rose" behind her back, because it reminded them of what she was and what she wasn't. Like her namesake, Rose was about as thorny as they came, and not the least bit prim and proper like a young lady should be.

"'Pears to me, Rose Elizabeth, that your sister wanted that farm sold off. Your pa, too. God rest his soul. 'Pears to me that you was lucky to have found a buyer so quick, and a rich one at that."

Rose felt her pocket for the cursed telegram that had arrived from the duke's English business factor, and she railed silently at the fates that had brought her to this day. Alexander James Warrick, the Duke of Moreland, would be arriving on the noon train. *"Please be prepared to greet his lordship, show him every possible courtesy, guide him to his new residence, and familiarize the duke with the estate,"* the telegram dictated, like she was one of his dukeship's royal flunkies.

"We'll just see about that!" No one dictated to Rose Elizabeth, except perhaps her older sister Heather, who, much to Rose's great dismay, had had the unerring good sense to insist that their local land broker, Mr. Walker, advertise their farm for sale in *The New York Times* and other large city newspapers.

Despite her bad luck that the duke's business factor had seen the ad for their land and had talked the stuffy old goat into buying it, Rose had absolutely no intention of following Heather's high-handed orders that she hightail it to Mrs. Caffrey's School for Young Ladies in Boston once she turned over the farm to the new owner.

She didn't need refining, and she certainly didn't intend to abandon Ma and Pa's graves to a total stranger—a damned Englishman, and a duke to boot!

Whatever could Heather have been thinking of? Rose knew perfectly well that it had been their pa's idea to sell the farm. Ezra Martin wanted better for his three girls.

But to cast them off to parts unknown . . .

To send them out into the cruel, strange world to seek husbands . . .

She shuddered. It was perhaps the most impractical idea Ezra had ever concocted, and he'd hatched some doozies in his lifetime. And for Heather and Laurel to have gone along with him was, in her opinion, even more ridiculous.

Just because Heather had a burning desire to illustrate for a big city newspaper, and Laurel, who had the voice of a tree frog on her best day, had taken it in her head to become an opera singer in Denver, was no reason that she, Rose Elizabeth, should be forced out of the home she loved, off the land that was so much a part of her, to travel to a dirty, depressing city so that she could get refined and become a schoolteacher.

Indeed, she couldn't think of a worse fate. Unless, of course, it was being hitched to some smelly old English coot like the Duke of Moreland.

He was probably short and squat and looked like a toad. And with that thought, she reached into her other pocket to make sure that Lester, her pet bullfrog, was all right.

The duke was probably a dandified gentleman who had absolutely no idea how to run a wheat farm, and he was probably so arrogant and mannered that the sound of a good belch and a few well-delivered curses would send him into a fit of the vapors.

Rose smiled at that notion, then glanced at the telegram again. *"Estate,"* it read. No doubt the duke was used to living high on the hog. He probably hadn't done a lick of work his entire life and was just looking forward to a holiday abroad.

Well, no stuffy Englishman was going to turn her respectable wheat farm into a playground for the rich, Rose Elizabeth vowed. Not if she had anything to say about it. And she would have plenty to say to the Duke of Moreland.

"Rose Elizabeth, praise the saints! Don't you have something better to wear than that old threadbare dress to greet the duke? Why, he's royalty, young lady."

Groaning at Euphemia Bloodsworth's high-pitched voice, Rose turned to cast Salina's most notorious gossip and resident spinster a thin smile. In fact, it was so thin you'd have been hard-pressed to find it, if your eyesight wasn't one hundred percent accurate. "Good afternoon to you, too, Miss Bloodsworth."

"Old Beaknose," which is how the Martin sisters had always referred to Euphemia behind her back, moved over to where Rose was standing.

"I don't mean to interfere, my dear," she said, as Rose rolled her eyes heavenward, "but I feel it's our duty to show his lordship that we aren't just a bunch of country bumpkins. As founder of the Salina Garden Club and Ladies Sewing Circle, I feel obligated to put our best foot forward." She smoothed the folds of her black taffeta gown and adjusted her white crocheted shawl. Euphemia supposedly had vinegar in her veins instead of blood, which explained how the woman could stand to wear such stifling garments in the summer heat.

"We *are* a bunch of bumpkins, Miss Bloodsworth," Rose replied. "And I don't think we should try to fool the duke into thinking any different. I certainly don't intend to put on airs and pretend to be something I'm not. My foot's staying firmly planted on good old Kansas soil."

Euphemia shook her head in disgust. "The other ladies of the welcoming committee will be joining me shortly, Rose Elizabeth. Perhaps the duke won't notice how provincial you look in that faded blue gingham gown. And really, Rose Elizabeth, you know how checks make a body look. . . . Well, you should take care to minimize your propensity to pudginess."

Rose's cheeks reddened in embarrassment, as they always did when someone had the insensitivity to comment that her figure wasn't as pleasing as her two sisters'. She'd been cursed with a curvaceous body, a "pleasingly plump figure," her ma had always called it. But though she'd been cursed, she wasn't about to starve herself or make herself into something God hadn't intended. As long as no one called her a "plump little partridge," which was the nickname her pa had always used, she could put up with just about any of their stupid remarks.

"Leave the girl alone, Euphemia." Skeeter rocked forward and rose to his feet. "Rose looks just fine. There ain't nothin' wrong with the way she's dressed, far as I can see."

Rose flashed the station manager a grateful smile, now firmly convinced that he had indeed been tippling at the whiskey bottle.

Skeeter and most of the other bachelors in Salina kept their distance from Miss Bloodsworth and did their best not to engage her in conversation if they could help it. Because to Euphemia Bloodsworth, conversation, no matter how innocent, no matter how mundane, was an indication of interest. And to a spinster of Miss Bloodsworth's years, an indication of interest was tantamount to a full-fledged proposal of marriage.

"Why, Mr. Purty," Euphemia advanced on the man, "how very gallant of you to come to Rose Elizabeth's defense. Though it was totally unnecessary." She pursed her lips into what was supposed to be a smile, which reminded Rose that she needed to pick up some lemons from the grocer while in town. "I'm sure Rose knows that I was only being motherly. Since she was orphaned at such a tender age, I've always done what I could to step in for dear departed Adelaide."

And she'd very nearly given poor Ezra a heart seizure every time he'd had the misfortune to run into the old windbag in town. The widower had been at the very top of Euphemia's eligible-husbands list until his demise last May.

Having absolutely no intention of placing his name under Ezra's scratched-out one, Skeeter stepped back. "I'd better mosey on in and check to see if there's been a telegram sent. Train shoulda been here by now." He clicked open his pocket watch and scratched his thinning hair in bewilderment. "Can't figure out what's causin' the delay." But he sure as hell was happy to have an excuse to leave for a spell.

Watching Skeeter depart, Rose Elizabeth had half a mind to run after him. Skeeter was, for all his shortcomings, her friend. And though he tried her patience on many occasions, he was kindhearted and harmless for the most part. Except when strong drink took hold of him. But even snockered, Skeeter was a better companion than Euphemia. Being alone with the spinster for any length of time was not an amusing prospect.

Where the hell was that damned train? Maybe his most royal pain in the butt wouldn't be as bad as Euphemia and her endless array of questions.

"You must be so excited to be entertaining a member of royalty." Euphemia's face flushed with pleasure.

"It gives me the runs just to think about it, Miss Bloodsworth. Why, my bowels have been in an uproar ever since I heard about the duke's arrival." At least that was the truth, Rose thought.

Gasping, Miss Bloodsworth's hand flew to the cameo brooch at her throat. "Really, Rose Elizabeth!" She drew herself rigidly erect. "Proper young ladies don't mention such things. It isn't seemly. I can see that your father and sister were justified in wanting to send you back East to attend finishing school. You've many tough edges to smooth out, my dear.

"You may not be aware of this, but I was a graduate of Mrs. Caffrey's. Though it wasn't called by that name back then. I guess you can see what proper guidance can do for a young lady."

Biting the tip of her tongue, Rose decided once and for all that she would never attend Mrs. Caffrey's, or any other finishing school for that matter. The prospect of turning out like Euphemia was enough to guarantee it.

"I don't see much use in finishing schools, Miss Bloodsworth. Aside from teaching a body to poop silently and cut an orange with a knife and fork, there's not much benefit in them." Rose Elizabeth chuckled inwardly at the choked sound the spinster made.

"I . . . I must go and see what's keeping the welcoming committee. Please don't let the duke leave without meeting all of us." Euphemia walked off the platform with more agility and speed than Rose had thought possible.

As the whine of a locomotive sounded in the distance, Rose's brown eyes sparkled with mischief, and her lips curved into a smile. Perhaps getting rid of his dukeship was going to be easier than she'd originally thought.

She had every intention, as the telegram requested, of showing his supreme portliness the lay of the "estate." She was certain that when she was finished with him, she'd also have shown him exactly which way the wind blew.

The welcome mat at the Martin farm was going to be just a **teensy bit smaller than the** Duke of Moreland likely expected.

The train pulled into the Salina Railway Station with screeching brakes and belching black smoke. A large number of curiosity seekers had gathered, eager to see what a real member of English nobility looked like.

Euphemia's welcoming committee included Sarah Ann Mellon, whose husband owned the mercantile, her daughter

Peggy, whose bustline matched her surname, and who "welcomed" just about anything with pants, and Abigail Stringfellow, wife of Horatio T. Stringfellow, mortician and sometime dentist. The four women waited anxiously for the duke to descend from his private Pullman car.

They were waving wildly at the train, grinning like hyenas, and, in Rose Elizabeth's opinion, making perfect fools of themselves. Why anyone in these United States would welcome British aristocracy with open arms, when it had taken this country so long to get rid of the pompous devils, was beyond her understanding. As her mama used to say, "There's just no accounting for taste."

Skeeter sidled up next to her, looking a mite perplexed by the turn of events. "I confess I was excited at the prospect of meeting the duke, but now I ain't so sure. 'Pears to me he's gonna be the center of attention for a right good while. The way them ladies are carrying on, don't know if that's such a good thing."

Rose looked into the crowd to find Marcella Tompkins waving as wildly as everyone else was. Folks in Salina knew that Skeeter had a crush on Marcella and was fixing to ask her to marry him someday. "I doubt Marcella will be interested in anyone as shallow as the duke, Skeeter," she reassured the older man, patting his arm. "He's sure to be as homely as my Lester, and not nearly as smart."

Slapping his knee, Skeeter let loose with a loud guffaw, and Rose Elizabeth followed suit. But her laughter died on her lips when her eyes fixed on the tall, incredibly handsome gentleman emerging from the train.

Impeccably dressed in a well-cut suit of black worsted wool, which contrasted dramatically with his snow-white shirt and flaxen-blond hair, he was surely the best-looking man Rose Elizabeth had ever laid eyes on. In fact, she was quite certain she'd never before seen such a fine specimen of a man. She knew damn well that there wasn't one like him in Salina, and probably not anywhere else in all of Kansas. A sinking feeling formed quickly in the pit of her stomach.

"Do you think that's him—the duke, I mean?" Skeeter asked, impressed in spite of himself, his complexion paling considerably. "I'd best go see how Marcella's faring. She might find this heat too unbearable, considering how delicate she is and all." In the blink of an eye he was gone, leaving Rose alone to face her fears and her worst nightmare.

Alexander James Warrick, the Duke of Moreland, was not the supreme portliness she'd been expecting. In fact, she doubted if he had a spare ounce of flesh on his muscular body.

"Damn, damn, and double damn!" She pasted on an uneasy smile as he approached.

"Miss Martin?" He held out a gloved hand to her, and she stared stupidly at it, as if it were some foreign object out to do her harm—it was definitely foreign—then she gazed up into his very aristocratic face, which was devoid of anything resembling a smile. "I'm Alexander Warrick, late of Sussex, England." His tone was imperious, and she knew without doubt that this man was used to issuing orders and having them obeyed.

Rose Elizabeth grasped his hand in what she hoped was a firm handshake. "I'm Rose Elizabeth Martin, presently of Salina, Kansas, of these United States of America," she mimicked, and several of the townsfolk laughed. "Where'd you stow your gear, your dukeship? We'd better get a move-on if we're going to reach the farm."

The duke glanced in bewilderment at the redheaded giant who appeared suddenly at his side.

"Now don't be selfish, Rose Elizabeth," Euphemia scolded with a silly giggle as she stood before the couple. "The rest of us would like to make his lordship's acquaintance."

The duke opened his mouth to speak, but Rose Elizabeth cut in, not allowing him the opportunity. "It's my responsibility to see that the duke gets settled in, Miss Bloodsworth . . . ladies." She smiled spitefully at Peggy, who she knew was in a perfect snit. They'd been rivals for years.

"Perhaps the duke will invite all of you out for tea and crumpets after he learns his way around *my* home." That shouldn't take him too long, Rose thought, considering that the soddy consisted of only three rooms, none of them very large. She couldn't wait to see the duke's expression when he saw his new "estate" for the first time.

Conveying his apologies to the group that had come to greet him, the duke issued orders to the man at his side, who Rose assumed was one of this servants, then clasped her upper arm rather firmly and led her off to the side of the platform where he could speak to her privately.

The duke's gaze slid over Rose Elizabeth, his blue eyes colder than a mountain stream, and it was obvious to her that he wasn't overly impressed by what he saw. She was taller than most women, and definitely a bit more well-rounded, and she did have a penchant for speaking her mind, but Rose considered these assets, not flaws.

"Don't ever presume to speak for me again, young woman," he said. "You've overstepped your bounds. You Americans are forever forgetting your place. Why, there is such a thing as simple courtesy, or are you so uncouth that you have forgotten that fact? Young women should learn to hold their tongues and speak only when spoken to."

He removed his leather gloves and slapped them against his left palm, and Rose had the distinct impression that Alexander James Warrick was trying to intimidate her. The arrogant, British jackanapes!

Fortunately, she wasn't easily dissuaded from her goals. And getting rid of Alexander Warrick was her top priority, however long it might take.

Swallowing all the vile things she wanted to say to him, she replied, "Custom dictates that I take charge, your royal highness," and was gratified to see the vein in his neck pulsing like oil gushing from a well.

"The telegram I received from your business factor stated that I was to greet and guide you to your new residence. If that's being presumptuous, your dukeship, then I guess I am." She smiled sweetly at him and was immediately rewarded with a dark scowl.

"Where is your conveyance, young woman? I'm tired, and I am in need of a bath and a hot meal."

"Really? Well, if you'll just follow me, your royalness, the farm wagon's out behind the station." She couldn't wait to see how he would manage to fit his rather well-sculpted backside into the old tin tub. No doubt he had a porcelain or even a gold one, back in England.

"I hope this wagon has a cover. It's deuced hot in this Kansas."

"This is nothing, your dukeship. Wait until the temperature really starts to sizzle. Why, you'll think your drawers are on fire for sure."

Alexander turned his attention to the young woman beside him, and his eyebrows arched up almost to his hairline. "If I didn't know better, Miss Martin, I would think you were trying to scare me off."

Rose shrugged. "Just trying to be honest about things. If you don't want to know the truth . . ."

"And are you a great teller of truths, Miss Martin?" Somehow, he thought not. Her lack of response proved only to confirm his opinion.

They had been riding in silence for almost two hours when Alexander mopped the sweat off his brow with a pristine linen handkerchief and said, "This is a strange land. I can't ever remember seeing anything so lacking in vegetation or so blasted flat." It was a harsh, unforgiving land, save for the fragrant wildflowers that bloomed in great profusion. Heat, wind, and miles and miles of nothingness stretched out before him. Windmills stood forlornly against the monotony of the azure sky, and tall prairie grass swayed gently in the breeze.

He cursed inwardly at his impulsive decision to flee England and purchase a country estate in America. But his fiancée's scandalous behavior, and his mother's harassing insistence that he marry posthaste, had made the trip a necessity. It was time to take leave of his problems, if only for a while. Once he had matters sorted out to his satisfaction, he would return to England and civilization. And to the responsibilities awaiting him there.

Adopting her best countrified accent, which she knew the duke would find appalling, Rose replied, "My pa used to say that if you stood at one end of Kansas, you could probably see all the way to the other. Of course he was just joshin'. Kansas ain't really that flat." Rose Elizabeth smiled at the memory, knowing that her father's love for the land flowed staunchly through her veins. "Pa also said that living here cultivates patience, a hide so thick you couldn't stick a knife through it, and a considerable sense of humor. Kansas ain't for everyone, that's true enough."

He winced at her fracturing of the English language. "I suppose not, but you seem quite taken with it."

"You've got to be born to this land to love it. Foreigners, such as yourself, don't usually fare well here."

"Indeed?"

She nodded. "Especially Englishmen. They're the worst of the lot, I'm afraid. With no great abundance of trees to speak of, no pretty green hills, no babbling brooks at every turn, like there is in England, Kansas is just too alien a place for most Englishmen to adjust to."

"You seem quite familiar with my ancestral homeland."

She clucked her tongue to prod the mules along. "I can read, your majesticness."

He cast her a glance of pure irritation. " 'Alexander' will do quite nicely, Miss Martin."

"I guess you might as well call me Rose Elizabeth, or Rose, if that's easier. That's my name."

"Ahh," he said. "That explains it then."

"Explains what?" she asked in confusion.

"Why, the thorns, of course." He smiled for the first time, and Rose's breath caught in her throat. Lordy be, he was a handsome devil. It was just plain sinful for a man to possess such long thick lashes and eyes the color of robins' eggs.

"On Richmond Hill there lives a lass more bright than

Mayday morn; whose charms all others maids' surpass—a rose without a thorn."

"Why, you're a poet, your imperial highness," Rose quipped to hide her embarrassment. "Let's hope you're as poetic about your new abode." Pulling the wagon to a halt at the end of the lane leading down to the sod hut, she waited for the duke to catch his first glimpse of his new home. His white-faced, eye-popping expression was everything Rose Elizabeth could have hoped for.

"Bloody hell! Bloody blasted hell!"

CHAPTER 2

That pile of dirt isn't a house, it's an abomination! The pulse at Alexander's temples hammered painfully as he stared openmouthed at his new residence.

Damn Phinneas Abbott! When he got his hands on his business factor . . .

Where was the grand country estate he'd envisioned, the blooded horses, the thick forest of trees and lush lawn-covered grounds? He'd come to Kansas for a holiday, not to be tortured and reduced to living like a common beggar. Or worse—a farmer!

"Welcome to your new home, your royalness. I hope you'll be very happy here." Rose almost let out the laughter bubbling up her throat. The Duke of Moreland looked as if he were about to have an apoplectic seizure, his face was so red. Actually it was closer to purple, she reconsidered.

He stared at her as if she'd gone quite mad, then back at the house, and finally shook his head. "This is a joke, am I correct? You are trying to dissuade me from staying here and have brought me to the storage shed." He gazed about, but he saw no other structure resembling a house.

"No need to be insulting, your highness. This is my home. And as you Englishmen are so fond of saying: A man's—or in this case, woman's—home is her castle."

This home she referred to was nothing more than a mass of earthen bricks. There was even grass growing out of the roof! There had been an attempt at civility—the clay pots of red geraniums beneath the two windows gave evidence to that— but this *home,* and he used the term loosely, was a hovel. Back in Sussex, he'd have been sorely pressed to board his horse in something as rustic.

"My pigs have a better abode than this." His upper lip curled disdainfully.

"Mine too, your majesticness," she replied matter-of-factly. "Pa took great pride in Elvira and Elmo. He planned to show them at the county fair this year." Come September, she'd be taking over that chore.

Jumping down off the wagon, the duke held out both arms to assist Rose, but she ignored the gesture and agilely descended on her own. "I'm used to doing for myself, your dukeship. You might as well know that from the onset."

"I thought it was decided that you would call me Alexander." He fought to keep the irritation out of his voice. The woman was as annoying as briars in a berry patch.

Alexander couldn't wait for them to part company, and he wondered what was taking his servant, Seamus O'Flynn, so long to purchase a few supplies. He should have arrived by now.

Once Seamus returned from town, Alexander had every intention of asking the Martin chit to vacate the premises. That comforting thought eased his frown into a semblance of a smile.

"Where is the staff, Miss Martin? I'll need a cook, a valet, and, of course, a housekeeper."

Rose's mouth dropped open, and she couldn't contain the grin that split her face. Unknown to Alexander Warrick, he'd just given her the perfect excuse to remain on the farm. She had no intention of vacating the premises and leaving the duke alone to ruin her family's farm. If she had to abase herself by doing his cooking and laundry chores, then so be it. It was worth any price she had to pay, no matter how humiliating, to hold on to her land.

" 'Fraid I'm it, your dukeship. This place ain't roomy enough for all those folks you're fixin' to hire. Besides, it ain't likely you'd be able to find anyone in town willing to work for you. Folks in these parts don't cotton much to foreigners, such as yourself."

"But . . . but I have a servant. Where will Mr. O'Flynn reside?"

She shrugged. "Guess he can sleep with you, your royalness, if you're so inclined."

Seamus Michael O'Flynn was at the moment engaged in what the Irish had called for centuries a brouhaha. In Seamus's humble opinion, there was nothing better than a good fair fight, and if that was in defense of a wee lass who'd been insulted, well then, that was even better.

"You scurvy dog!" Seamus yelled at his opponent, centering his fist squarely on the man's nose. "How dare you insult the lovely lass."

The woman in question was wringing her hands and shaking her head, praying that the altercation would cease before it drew attention to her. Fortunately, it was noon, the hottest time of the day, and most of Salina's residents had taken refuge indoors. "Please! You must stop this fighting at once."

Glancing at the bloodied face of his opponent, who was laid out cold and wouldn't be insulting anyone for quite a while, Seamus nodded in satisfaction. "I'll be doing that now, lass. But I couldn't let the lad's insult go unchallenged, now could I?"

Rebecca Heller cast a piteous look at the inanimate form on

the ground. She was used to insults; Hank Ferguson's were nothing new.

In a soft voice, she explained, "We don't believe in settling our differences with conflict, sir. We are Plain, and it goes against our doctrine to take up arms against our fellow man." She turned in the direction of the bakery she and her father had recently opened, praying that Jacob Heller was still resting in bed and had not observed the goings-on. She was sure to receive a stern lecture if he had.

Brushing a layer of dust off his gray-striped pants and righting his felt bowler hat, Seamus called after the woman. "Wait up, lass. You might be plain, though you don't appear that way to me, and I think you owe me at least a bit of gratitude. That man called you some rather rude names. We don't hold with talking to women like that where I come from."

The strangeness of the man's speech indicated that Rebecca's ardent defender wasn't from Kansas but rather from Ireland. His brogue, as thick as Mulligan stew, rolled off his tongue in a way that fascinated her.

Halting in midstride, she turned to face her redheaded rescuer, noting, despite her best intention not to, that his warm brown eyes were filled with kindness. "It wasn't my intention to be rude, sir. I appreciate your concern, but it wasn't necessary for you to come to my defense. I am perfectly capable of handling things on my own." Necessity dictated that she must.

"Well now, lass, it didn't appear to me that you were handling that scurvy scum. Not with himself shouting at the top of his lungs and raising his fist to ya, and you just standing there listening and not uttering a sound, like a poor defenseless lamb."

The beaten man had called the woman a witch and a heathen. Odd names for one so young and pretty. She was garbed rather strangely, dowdy even. Seamus noted the severity of her costume, like servant's clothing it was, and it didn't suit her at all. Her dress was gray, as was the large kerchief that covered her shoulders and disappeared into her trim waistband. Her hair was blond, judging from what he could see of the few strands peeking out from the front of her lace cap, which was housed in a small black bonnet. A white shawl and apron completed her attire.

Why she would call herself plain was a mystery to him. Seamus decided she was as comely a woman as he'd seen since reaching this blasted shore. Her alabaster complexion was near perfection, and she had the prettiest pair of green eyes, like shamrocks they were.

Rebecca looked about anxiously. If her father emerged from the bakery and saw her talking to this stranger . . .

Jacob Heller was devout in his Mennonite religion, and if he thought that his only daughter had been involved in anything unseemly or sordid, it would no doubt cause harm to his already failing health.

It had taken every bit of her powers of persuasion to get her father to abandon their Kansas farm which had proven ruinous to his health, and open the bakery. But with the bakery she could do most of the demanding chores, leaving her father to conserve the little strength he had left.

Farming in Kansas had proven itself far more difficult than tilling the rich, dark soil of Pennsylvania, from where they'd moved almost a year before. Rebecca wished they'd never traveled to this alien land of locusts and tornadoes. She'd lost her mother to typhoid on the journey, and now it appeared she might lose her father as well.

Rebecca could not afford to allow anyone to spoil all she had worked for. If this Irishman knew how long and hard she had pleaded with her father to leave the farm, to leave the security and companionship of his friends and community he would not be causing trouble for her now. She had to make him understand.

"You must go now, sir. It is not proper for me to be speaking with you. My papa would not like it."

"Where is this papa of yours? I can't believe any self-respecting man would let his daughter be spoken to like that scum spoke to you, and do nothing to avenge her honor."

Rebecca stiffened. "My papa is ill. And even if he were in robust health, he does not condone violence of any kind. We are peaceful people. We only want to be left alone to tend our business."

She hurried across the street, and Seamus followed, pulled by curiosity and a desire to know this woman better.

"Oh my God!"

The duke's horrified tone brought Rose's gaze about, and she bit the inside of her cheek to keep from laughing. Boomer, her six-month old, yellow-haired retriever, so named for his terror of thunderstorms, was using his majesticness's shiny black shoes as a urinal.

"Boomer!" she scolded halfheartedly. "Stop that, you naughty boy." She smiled apologetically at the duke, whose face was as red as the geraniums he stood near.

With a look of contempt, Alexander shook his foot in the dog's unrepentant face. "Is there not a speck of civility in this godforsaken place?" He removed a pristine white handkerchief from his coat pocket and mopped up the offensive liquid, then draped the damp linen over the edge of a wooden crate.

Boomer saw his chance and took it. Grasping the cloth between his teeth, he ran off in the direction of the wheat fields, ignoring the shouts from the angry nobleman.

"Come back here, you—"

"Civility? 'Fraid not, your royalness," Rose Elizabeth answered quickly, hoping to take his mind off her rambunctious puppy. Admittedly, Boomer's manners weren't the best.

"Now, if you'd like to proceed with the tour of the house . . ." She unlatched the front door and preceded him inside.

The first thing Alexander noticed upon entering the large front room was the tattered piece of canvas that covered the ceiling. (From it, a dead rat clung unceremoniously by its tail.) The duke grimaced at the thought of what else might reside in the frayed fabric.

The interior was much cooler than the temperature outside, owing, he surmised, to the two-foot-thick sod blocks of which the structure was built. The walls had been newly plastered and whitewashed, and there was homeyness about the place that surprised him.

Freshly baked loaves of bread stood atop the cast-iron stove; their yeasty aroma reminded him that it had been several hours since he'd last eaten.

A colorful bouquet of wildflowers graced the center of the scarred maple table; a pie safe, whose tin had rusted, stood near it. The red gingham curtains hanging limply at the windows matched the cushions on the rocker in the far corner. Various and sundry items decorated the walls, including pages from the Montgomery Ward Catalogue, a cracked mirror, and a calendar with a photograph of farm machinery.

The unusual objets d'art were a far cry from the Van Dyke's and Reynolds's that enhanced his home in England.

"It ain't much, your lordship, but it's all yours," Rose Elizabeth announced. "I suppose it's nothing like what you're used to, but I find it suits my needs quite well." When he didn't answer, she went on, hoping that the Duke of Moreland, who looked as if he'd just swallowed a whole bottle of castor oil, was about to have a change of heart concerning his newly acquired property.

"This is the main living area—the sitting room, we call it. The kitchen's yonder." She pointed to the opposite side of the room. "Through those doorways are the bedrooms. My pa slept in one, my two sisters and I in the other.

"The privy's out back. It's always best to hold it until morning during the winter, if you can, 'cause that frigid seat can stick to your bu— skin something fierce."

His eyebrow shot up, but he remained silent, nodding now and again to indicate that he was still listening. "You'll probably want to take over Pa's room, it being the larger of the two."

He moved toward the bedrooms, stuck his head through the doorways, mumbled something unintelligible, and returned to the sitting room. "I've never seen a grass house before," he finally admitted, then glanced at the ceiling and the heavy, wooden ridgepole supporting it.

Rose took her apron from the peg by the door and tied it around her waist. "It's called a soddy, your dukeness. It's made from what's known around these parts as Kansas brick. Buffalo grass is used mostly because of its toughness. If you ever plow the land, then you'll now what I'm talking about.

"Soddies are pretty common on the prairie, owing to the fact that there's not an abundance of timber for building the sort of house you're probably used to."

It was a far cry from Moreland House, that was for damned certain, Alexander thought. The stone and half-timbered structure had been in the Warrick family for years, containing some of the finest examples of Palladian windows in all of Sussex and quite possibly in all of England.

Turning toward the two crudely built windows, he noted the small clay pots of herbs on the sills, and sighed with something akin to regret. For all its beauty, pretentiousness, and wealth, Moreland House didn't contain an iota of the warmth that this three-room hovel possessed.

"Water's pumped up from the well by the windmill, but we're careful not to waste. The livestock use a great deal, as do the fruit trees and vegetable garden. I use coal for the stove, which I purchase or trade for in town. Wood's too dear, and I ain't partial to cow chips, or 'prairie coal,' as some call it. They give my bread and biscuits a peculiar flavor, if you get my meaning." She smiled inwardly at his horrified look.

The duke had a lot to learn about living on the prairie, and Rose Elizabeth was only too happy to see that he got sufficiently educated before hightailing it back to the civilized society whence he'd come.

* * *

"Why do you follow me, sir?" Rebecca paused before the bakery and cast the Irishman a look of pure annoyance, wishing he would leave before he got her in trouble.

Seamus smiled, and the two dimples that had impressed more than one young colleen deepened considerably. "Well now, lass, maybe I'm needing some bread. This is a bakery, isn't it?"

She nodded, looking anxiously toward the front window for some sign of her father, and was relieved when there was none. "Yes. My father and I own the bakery. But we are not open for business today. My papa took ill and I have been unable to find adequate help to assist me. I'm sorry, but you'll have to come back another time."

"What type of assistance do you require, if you don't mind me asking?"

"I do all the baking myself, but I'm unable to lift the heavy flour sacks and other supplies that are needed. And there are errands to run, ingredients to purchase. I'm not able to leave the bakery when goods are in the oven. And someone must be there to greet the customers."

Before Seamus could comment, the bakery door opened and an elderly man stepped out onto the sidewalk. The look of apprehension on the young woman's face told Seamus that this was her father.

He looked to be a stern old coot. He was dressed as oddly and severely as the woman herself, in black pants and a collarless coat. When he spoke, his accent was as strange as his appearance.

"Daughter, wot is wrong? Why do you not come inside? Who is dis stranger, and why do you speak to him on the street, like one who is common?"

Rebecca thought quickly as the questions were being fired at her, and though she knew she might be struck down for the telling of it, she fibbed, crossing her fingers behind her back as she'd done when she was a child. "Mr. O'Flynn is new in town, Papa, and is looking for work." She looked imploringly at the man, praying that he would back up her story.

"The name's Seamus O'Flynn. Like the lass says, I'm new in town."

Jacob gave the man a thorough once-over, then held out his hand and introduced himself. "Dis is my daughter, Rebecca. She forgets sometimes her manners. Come inside and we will talk. Perhaps my daughter will fix us tea and scones. She makes good scones, Rebecca does."

Her cheeks colored, and she hurried to the door, but not before saying, "Excuse my thoughtlessness, Mr. O'Flynn. Please come in. It is too hot to stand outside."

The sweat trickling down Seamus's neck gave credence to that, and he followed the Hellers into the bakery.

The interior was as plain and stark as their clothing. Nothing adorned the walls, and the only furniture was the long glass case that housed the baked goods, which now stood empty, and the sturdy, well-worn oak table used for preparing the dough.

But for all its plainness, the aroma of yeast and the spicy scents of cinnamon and clove lent a richness to the surroundings—a warmth that reminded Seamus of home and his mother.

"There's nothing like the smell of a bakery." The Irishman inhaled deeply. "Me blessed mother always says that the odor of freshly baked bread is far more enticing to a man than a gallon of French perfume. O'course, me mother isn't partial to the French."

Rebecca and her father exchanged puzzled looks before directing Seamus to follow them abovestairs to their living quarters.

Seated at the kitchen table, a plate of warm scones and a cup of tea before him, Seamus leaned back in his chair, his curiosity piqued by all he had observed. "Pardon my ignorance, Mr. Heller, but might you and your daughter be Quakers? I noticed you're dressed a bit differently than what I've seen since reaching America." He'd heard talk of the religious sect known as the Friends but had never actually seen one before.

Jacob's lips twitched at the man's directness. "You speak

your mind, Mr. O'Flynn. Dat is good, as long as the one listening takes no offense. *Wunnerfitsich,* we say. Don't be always so curious."

"I meant no disrespect, sir. It's just me natural curiosity getting the better of me unruly tongue."

The old man chuckled, and Rebecca breathed a sigh of relief, happy that her father had taken a liking to this man. Jacob Heller wasn't usually so friendly with outsiders.

"We are Mennonites, Mr. O'Flynn," Rebecca explained. "Our clothing and way of life, our very speech, are part of our religion. We are Plain."

"Plain?" Seamus's brow wrinkled in confusion. "So you said before."

Jacob nodded, and his white hair reflected the glow of the kerosene lantern. Dark green shades covered the windows, blocking out the bright sunlight.

"We are Plain, Mr. O'Flynn. Unworldly. Most of us are farmers descended from sturdy Swiss and German stock. We do not fight. We avoid worldly pleasures and worldly sin. We don't drink or smoke. We are Plain."

Seamus nodded as if he understood. But he didn't. In fact, he felt more confused than ever.

As if sensing the man's dilemma, Jacob added, "There are those who find us odd, Mr. O'Flynn. They condemn us for what they do not understand. We have suffered persecution for our beliefs, though we have done nothing to warrant it but worship in our own way.

"We are private, and we try to keep to ourselves and our own kind. My poor health forced us to move to town, away from others like us. I'm not sure we made such a wise decision." The old man's expression grew thoughtful.

Seamus thought of the loud mouthed man stretched out in the middle of the street and wondered the same thing. Some of Salina's good folk weren't too tolerant of those who were different, and he wondered if he would fit in. His brief stay in New York City upon his arrival from England had illustrated quite clearly the prejudice that existed against his own countrymen.

"We will do fine, Papa," Rebecca reassured her father, patting his gnarled, age-spotted hand. "You will see. Already your health improves. The land here is too harsh for farming, and baking bread is a good and honorable thing. Bread is the staff of life, like the good book says."

While Jacob reflected on his daughter's comments, Seamus took another bite of the flaky scone and made a sound of appreciation. "If Miss Heller bakes everything as good as these scones, then God has surely blessed her with a rare talent, I'm thinking."

Pleased by the unexpected compliment, Rebecca lowered her gaze and stared at the table. "Thank you, Mr. O'Flynn."

"What type of work do you look for, Mr. O'Flynn?" Jacob asked, staring intently at the stranger. He looked a bit *strubbly*. His hair and clothing were a mess, but he appeared to be a hard worker. Jacob could tell by the calluses on the man's hands that he put in a good day's work.

"We cannot pay money—our bakery has made little of it— but there is a room at the back of the store to sleep, and we can provide all the food you can eat." By the look of the Irishman, that was a sizable amount.

The hope in Jacob Heller's eyes struck a chord deep within Seamus. It was obvious that these people needed help, and he wished he were free to offer it. But his first loyalty was to the duke.

Seamus had worked for the Duke of Moreland for the past ten years, and he was paid a generous salary. Although he was more friend than servant—he and Alexander had shared many interesting exploits, some bordering on scandalous—he knew how to keep his place when the situation warranted.

Alexander was counting on him to help with the land he had recently purchased. And after observing the lovely, opinionated woman who had carted him off like so much unnecessary baggage, the duke was going to need all the help he could get. Seamus smiled to himself at that thought.

Still, it would be criminal to turn his back on these two lost lambs. It had been a long while since someone had really needed Seamus O'Flynn, as the Hellers apparently did.

When his mother had remarried six months ago, Seamus realized it was time to get on with his life, as she was getting on with hers.

Rebecca's soft green eyes drew him, and a well of protectiveness poured over him as he gazed into her lovely face. She wasn't like any woman he'd met before, and he found that not only enchanting but irresistible.

"I appreciate the offer, Mr. Heller," Seamus replied reluctantly, "but I was thinking about trying me hand at farming. But if that don't work out, then perhaps I'll come back."

" 'Tis no matter. We will get along. We always have. Isn't dat right, daughter?"

Rebecca nodded, and Seamus thought the young woman looked vastly relieved that he'd turned down the job. Her response was intriguing, and there was nothing Seamus enjoyed more than a good intrigue.

With Alexander James Warrick seated across the dining table from her, Rose had a difficult time concentrating on her fried chicken and biscuits with gravy. She was much too busy studying him beneath her lowered lashes.

The duke was as persnickety in his eating habits as he was in everything else. He didn't gnaw on a leg the way a man should, but picked at the meat, little by little, with those perfectly even white teeth. With him eating as slowly as he did, it was a wonder that he had managed to consume three breasts, four drumsticks, two wings, a pile of mashed potatoes, and six biscuits slathered with gravy.

The man had a huge appetite, and she couldn't help wondering what else that "appetite" might extend to.

She'd heard things about foreigners like the duke. They were decadent and prone to overstimulated sexual urges. She'd read about them in romantic novels. One, *Lord Lisle's*

Daughter, had particularly characterized the English as purveyors of perverse pleasure.

It was shocking! Shocking and terribly wicked. But oh so wonderfully intriguing to a woman of eighteen.

The duke licked the gravy off his fingertips, and Rose felt the oddest reaction in her midsection. Strange ripples, like waves of wheat swaying back and forth in the wind, tickled her innards. Hoping to quiet the unfamiliar, and certainly unwelcome, feeling, she gulped down the remainder of her cold apple cider and restrained the urge to belch. No doubt the duke would be horrified if she let loose with a good one, but she was tempted just the same.

"You are an excellent cook, Miss Martin. I quite think this chicken is the best I've ever tasted."

She blushed at the unexpected compliment. "Thank you. I've tried to make the most out of what God has given me."

"You like to cook and it shows."

Rose's lips thinned. "Is that comment directed at my figure, your majesticness? Because if it is . . ." She made to rise, but he motioned her back down, shaking his head in denial.

"I assure you, Miss Martin, I am too much of a gentleman ever to insult a lady."

She waited for him to add "to her face," but he didn't, and they resumed eating.

"Tell me, please, Miss Martin, why there is no wheat in the field. Shouldn't you be harvesting soon?"

She shook her head, and her sigh was one of pure exasperation, as if his question were the stupidest one she'd ever heard. "We plant Turkey Red here in Kansas, your grace. Unlike regular wheat, which is planted in spring and harvested in the fall, and doesn't hold up to our harsh winters, we plant in the fall and harvest in July. It's far more productive that way."

"I see," he replied, but by the blank look on his face, Rose Elizabeth knew that he didn't "see" at all. For all his wealth, breeding, and damnable good looks, his royalness, the Duke of Moreland, didn't know a thing about wheat or wheat farming, which didn't bode well for her plan to make the three-hundred-acre farm into the most productive and profitable in the state.

"Your cooking skills will be quite adequate for my needs, Miss Martin," he pronounced after another bite of chicken.

Rose was about to reply that she didn't give a tinker's damn about his opinion when the sound of wagon wheels on the drive halted her rejoinder.

"I do believe my man, Seamus O'Flynn, has arrived."

"Are you referring to that redheaded giant I saw you with in town this morning?" Rose Elizabeth didn't wait for an answer, but pushed back her chair and followed the duke to the open door.

"It's Seamus, all right." Alexander couldn't keep the relief out of his voice as he waved at his servant, and Rose Elizabeth felt like kicking him smack dab in his oh-so-very-proper posterior. It was obvious that the duke didn't enjoy her company nearly as much as his servant's.

"Seamus, my good man. What took you so long? I was beginning to think you had gotten lost."

The desperation in Alexander's voice made Seamus's smile widen into a grin. Apparently Alexander's first encounter with the comely American woman hadn't gone as planned. She didn't look particularly overjoyed with the duke's presence, either.

Alighting from the wagon, Seamus approached Rose Elizabeth and extended his hand in greeting. "I'm Seamus O'Flynn, Miss Martin. Pleased to make your very lovely acquaintance."

Rose took an immediate liking to the duke's "man" and returned his friendly smile with one of her own. Seamus O'Flynn appeared to be genuine and warm, and not the least bit condescending, like some others she could name.

"The pleasure's all mine, Mr. O'Flynn. Won't you come in and help yourself to some of my fried chicken? The duke's quite taken with it. Ain't you, your majesticness?"

Seamus swallowed his grin at the look of outrage on Alexander's face. The Duke of Moreland was not used to being addressed so impertinently. And he was definitely not used to encountering women who didn't fall head-over-heels over him, like those ladies at the train station this morning. That put Rose Elizabeth Martin high on his list, Seamus decided. It wouldn't hurt Alexander's inflated ego to shrink a wee bit.

"Thank you, lass, but I've already eaten. I've come with me baggage, and the remainder of his grace's, and the foodstuffs I purchased in town."

Alexander looked absolutely miserable as he pointed at the soddy. "This is my new home, Seamus. This is where I'll be residing for the time being, until I can construct an acceptable residence. But I'm afraid there isn't room for you to reside here. I'll acquire a room for you at the hotel in town.

"This hovel boasts only two small, very inadequate bed chambers"—he ignored Rose's gasp of outrage—"and Miss Martin will have to remain temporarily, until I can find suitable help."

Rose almost choked on her anger, but she kept silent, vowing somehow to get even with his lordship for his irreverence to the only home she had ever known—her ma and pa's home.

Seamus smiled apologetically at the young woman. "Excuse us for a moment, won't you please, Miss Martin," he said, leading Alexander toward a stand of spindly cottonwoods and hoping the duke's insensitive comment hadn't wounded the poor lass. The Duke of Moreland had never been known for his tact.

"I won't be needing a hotel room, Alexander. Since I won't be residing here on the farm with you, I'll offer my services to a family named Heller. They are looking for someone to help with their bakery."

"But you work for me, Seamus. Have you forgotten that fact?"

"No. I haven't forgotten. But the Hellers are desperately in need of my help. And you know perfectly well, Alexander, that you are capable of managing on your own. You've been doing it most of your life."

The truth of that made Alexander frown. He'd been boarded out to school at a young age, and had been brought home to live only when his mother became pregnant with her second child, his precious brother, Edward. She had finally decided to give up flitting about the Continent like a social butterfly and settle down to a semblance of normal family life. If you could call life at Moreland House normal.

With a staff of fifty, including an unending procession of governesses, tutors, doormen, and footmen, his home and childhood hadn't been conducive to intimacy and parental bonding. Even if his mother had possessed a measure of maternal instinct—which she had not, at least toward him—he had never been alone with her long enough for it to have made its presence known.

"I realize that my first loyalty rests with you, your grace, and I fully intend to help out with the farm. But I'd like your blessing in this matter of the Hellers. This is important to me." Seamus dragged the toe of his scuffed brogan back and forth in the dirt.

"No doubt there's a woman involved. There always is when it's important." At Seamus's grin, the duke sighed in defeat. "Very well. You may pursue your latest conquest. But I'll expect you to lend a hand here as well. I'm not cut out for manual labor, and I'll not be able to manage everything here by myself."

The two men walked back to the house, where Rose Elizabeth knelt in the doorway petting her overzealous hound. "Mr. O'Flynn is returning to town now, Miss Martin," Alexander stated in that imperious tone she was starting to detest. "You may withdraw and do whatever it is you do in the evenings. I shan't be needing your services until morning."

Rising to her feet, Rose crossed her arms over her ample bosom. "Let's get something straight, your royalness. I'm staying because I want to, not because you've ordered me to. You are obviously out of your element and wouldn't last an hour out here on the farm by yourself."

Alexander's mouth dropped open. "You are an impertinent

chit! Perhaps you had better depart with Seamus, Miss Martin. It is quite obvious that we don't suit at all. I will find other help."

"I refuse to leave. And you can forget about hiring anyone else, because no one would come out here to help you. Folks in these parts got their own families and farms to worry about, your dukeness."

"Are you insane, woman? Of course you are leaving. Now pack your bags and be off with you."

Seamus watched this exchange with amusement. Being a betting man, there was little doubt on whom he'd wager his money.

Digging her heels in like the most recalcitrant of mules, Rose Elizabeth shook her head emphatically. "I'm staying, your majesticness. This is as much my farm as it is yours, and I'm not leaving until I'm assured that you are totally capable of running this place by yourself. I'll not have my family's land turned into a playground for the idle rich."

His face reddened to apoplectic proportions. "Bloody hell! Bloody blasted hell!"

"My sentiments exactly, your dukeship," Rose said, before spinning on her heel and heading back into the house.

CHAPTER 3

Alexander slammed the door so hard that the petrified varmint dropped unceremoniously from the ceiling to land at his feet. He looked at it, then at the stubborn chit standing before him, and kicked the offensive creature out of his way.

Rose Elizabeth had the distinct impression that he would have liked to kick her as well.

"Are you out of your mind, madam? You most certainly are not going to stay here. I purchased this land. It is mine, legally and irrevocably, and I am asking you—no, I am telling you to vacate the premises immediately. I do not need, nor do I want, your help. I will instruct Seamus to find me a suitable housekeeper at once."

"Oh, don't get your drawers all into an uproar, your royalness. You know perfectly well that you don't know the first thing about farming wheat. And I know everything there is to know." That was a slight exaggeration. But then, Rose was very adapt at exaggerations, fibs, and downright lies, when the situation warranted. Which it did. She plopped down in her rocker and was soon into an easy rhythm.

"Madam, I insist that you leave at once. If we hurry, we can catch Seamus." He rushed to the door, hoping she would follow, but when he looked back she was still seated.

"I'm not leaving, your dukeship, so save your breath."

Alexander's sigh conveyed every bit of the frustration he felt. The woman was insane. Impossible. Irrational. He didn't want his holiday abroad spoiled by this crude, headstrong American woman, but if he didn't get rid of her, that's exactly what would happen.

He tried another tack. "Have you thought of the consequences of living with a man, a total stranger, without the benefit of marriage?" He hadn't wanted to be indelicate, but there it was. No decent woman in her right mind could argue with the logic.

The rocker didn't pause for a moment. "Lots of women live with total strangers every day. Why, you can't rent a room at a boardinghouse or hotel without living next to a stranger. And we have two bedrooms. I don't see what the difference would be."

Alexander rubbed the back of his neck, where a colossal headache was starting to form. "Miss Martin, I'm sure you have some sort of reputation to uphold in this community. Do you want to be considered loose or a fallen woman? You obviously haven't considered all the ramifications of your impulsive decision."

Rose jumped to her feet. "Oh, but I have, your royalness." Her voice was threaded with equal amounts of anger and pain. "I've thought of little else since last May, when my sister sold this farm out from under me. You see, I never had any intention of leaving this place. My parents are buried here. This is my home. You might own this land, your grace, but my parents' graves belong to me. And I'm not leaving them here with strangers . . . with foreigners." She spat the word, as if the very taste of it were bitter in her mouth.

"You aristocrats have plundered this land and killed the buffalo to near extinction. And all for the sport of it. I will not

leave my parents' graves for you to plow under like so much
fertilizer."

Alexander looked aghast. "I have never hunted buffalo."
He thought the sport, and the fact that the Kansas Pacific Railroad had contributed to the carnage, deplorable. "And I would
never desecrate a grave. What type of man do you think I
am?"

"A rich one, your grace. One who is used to getting his
way, giving orders and expecting them to be obeyed. Well, I
have news for you, Alexander James Warrick. I am not one of
your subjects to be ordered about. I will go where I please, do
what I please, and live where I please. And neither you nor
anyone else will tell me any different."

"Indeed?" A grudging respect flared in the duke's eyes, despite his irritation. Rose Elizabeth Martin had gumption. She
wasn't afraid to stand up for what she believed or what
she wanted. And apparently, for some unfathomable reason,
she wanted this pile of earthen bricks and the barren land that
went along with it.

"How would you get along here by yourself, your grace?"
Rose continued. "You don't cook. I bet you don't know the
first thing about tending a vegetable garden, milking cows,
feeding chickens. You had servants to do all that for you,
didn't you?"

He nodded. "Yes. A great many of them."

"Just as I thought." She flitted around the room, lighting
the kerosene lamps against the approaching darkness. "You're
not suited to this life, your grace. Perhaps you purchased this
farm as a lark, as some kind of amusement. But this is my
home. The only one I have ever known. And I won't sit back
and watch you destroy everything I've worked so hard to secure."

She had begun to pace back and forth across the colorful
braided rug, flinging her hands in the air while attempting to
make her point. Her eloquence and dramatic manner reminded Alexander of the performances he'd witnessed in the

House of Lords. Parliament could use a woman like Rose Elizabeth Martin, he decided.

"Please sit down, Miss Martin. You are giving me a pain in the neck with your marching about. I feel as if I'm at a tennis match."

"A what?"

He waved away the question. "Never mind. Just please sit and let's discuss this rationally. Surely you can understand that a man in my position can't allow negative public opinion and scandal to ruin his good name." Thank God she didn't know of the disgraceful episode he'd escaped back in England. He'd discovered, much to his consternation, that attempting to shoot one's fiancée and brother caused a bit of public outrage.

She plopped back in the rocker with a scornful expression. "So it's *your* reputation you're really worried about. I should have guessed." She snorted disdainfully. "And here I thought you were concerned for my welfare. Ha! That's a good one.

"But you needn't have worried in any case. Folks in this town gave up on trying to conform me to their ways." *Except Euphemia Bloodsworth,* she thought, *who'll hound me until the end of her days.* "I doubt anyone will be surprised to find out that I'm staying here. I made no bones about how I felt about you buying my land."

Alexander crossed to the window and looked out, hoping that the gentle breeze whispering through the cottonwoods and the steady chirping of the crickets would have a soothing effect on his nerves. He hadn't been this upset since finding his fiancée, Jessica, in bed with his weasel of a brother. Not that he loved the woman, for he didn't. But it had been damned humiliating and inconvenient to put up with the consequences of her actions.

Fleeing England and his mother's rage when she heard of his broken engagement had seemed the only course to save his sanity. Who could have known that coming to Kansas would prove far more aggravating and troublesome.

Turning to face Rose Elizabeth once again, he sighed in defeat. "I concede, Miss Martin, that I know little of farming wheat and the other tasks you mentioned. I also concede that since the hour is late and I am tired, there is little point in debating this topic further. I will take up residence in your father's old room, if that is agreeable. I trust you'll be sleeping in the other?"

Victory tasted sweet. Rose nodded. "That's correct, your dukeship. Your mattress has been aired, and the linens are fresh. I suggest that if you have a call of nature, you tend to it now. There's only a quarter moon tonight, and the path to the privy can be mighty treacherous in the dark to someone who's not familiar with it."

He bit his tongue to keep back the nasty retort teetering there. "Don't you think it would be advisable to repair it, Miss Martin? The path is used rather frequently, I warrant."

"Oh, there ain't nothing wrong with it. You won't break your leg or nothing like that. It's just that Boomer's taken it in his head to do his business there. It can get a bit messy if you don't watch where you're stepping."

Boomer again! How he would love to get his hands on that miserable hound and . . . He inhaled deeply. "Thank you for the warning, but you needn't concern yourself with me. I'll be perfectly fine. I have lived on this earth for thirty years and have managed quite adequately thus far."

Rose let loose a shrill whistle. "You're well preserved for someone your age, your grace, if you don't mind me saying so."

"Good night, Miss Martin," he said harshly, before swinging open the door and disappearing into the darkness.

Rose Elizabeth counted to twenty. That's how long it took to reach the privy, by her estimation.

"Oh my God!"

"Yep. Twenty's the number." She smiled, thinking about something her mama had always said: "A man's thickheadedness is usually in direct proportion to his ego."

In a fit of giggles, Rose headed off to bed.

*   *   *

"Papa, why did you ask Mr. O'Flynn if he was interested in working at the bakery? I do not think he would be right for the job."

Jacob's forkful of apple strudel paused in midair, and he looked questioningly at Rebecca. "And why not, daughter? He has a strong back and hands that are used to doing honest work. Wot do you find wrong with Mr. O'Flynn?"

Just one thing, Rebecca answered silently. And that was the problem. Seamus O'Flynn was handsome, kind, and considerate. But he wasn't Plain. He would never fit in to their way of life. "He's not one of us, Papa. He's not used to our ways."

"There is no one else, Rebecca. You know I am not in any condition to help you wid the chores right now. We need someone like Mr. O'Flynn to take the burden off you."

"But what will the brethren say, Papa? The elders are already upset that we left the farm. Surely hiring an outsider will not set well with them."

Pain filled Jacob's eyes. "Not one of dem has come to offer help. Dey have shunned us for our decision to leave. So be it. We do what we must. God will show us the way."

"I hope so, Papa. I feel guilty for taking you away from your friends and forcing you to move to town."

"You should know by now, daughter, that I could never be forced to do anything." He smiled, patting her cheek in a rare display of affection. "I am as stubborn as you, Rebecca. Where do you think you got such an unflattering trait? Not from Mama. She was calm and very patient wid others."

Rebecca had always wanted to be like her mama, but she knew that she didn't possess the strength of spirit to look the other way, as her mama had done so many times. Rebecca took things to heart, finding it difficult to forgive and forget, to turn the other cheek, as their faith dictated she must.

"You miss Mama a great deal, don't you, Papa?"

"Though it is a sin to admit such a thing, I will not be sorry to leave dis earth to join Esther in Heaven."

"Please don't talk that way, Papa. What would I do without you? I would be alone among strangers." She had thought about that a great deal since her father's health had failed, and it frightened her.

Jacob's eyes filled with determination. Rebecca would not remain alone if he had anything to say about it. She was twenty-four. Old enough to be married with children. But Rebecca needed a husband. Perhaps God would see fit to answer an old man's prayers.

As if by divine providence, a knock on the door interrupted their conversation. Rebecca glanced at the regulator clock on the wall. "It is late, Papa. Who could be calling at such an hour? I put the Closed sign in the window hours ago."

"Why not go downstairs and see for yourself, daughter. It is the only way to answer such a question, is it not?"

With a nod, Rebecca grabbed the kerosene lantern off the table and hurried downstairs. Peeking out the window, she recognized Seamus O'Flynn standing on the porch, and her heart gave a queer little lurch. She sucked in her breath before opening the door.

"Mr. O'Flynn. We were not expecting you back today." She hoped her voice was not as shaky as her knees.

Seamus's smile was full of apology. He hadn't been able to get Rebecca Heller out of his mind. The need to see her again had overwhelmed his manners and good judgment. "Sorry for the intrusion, Miss Heller, but I've decided to offer me services here at the bakery. The man I'm to work for has no room to board me, and your father mentioned something about room and board being included with the job. I figure I can manage both jobs with no problem."

Her eyes widened at the ramifications filling her brain. Seamus O'Flynn wanted to work at the bakery!

She fought to keep her composure. "Could this not have waited until morning, Mr. O'Flynn?"

"Your father said you had a room out back. I figured if I settled in tonight, I could get up extra early to help you with whatever it is you need help with."

"Who is it, Rebecca?" Jacob called out from upstairs.

With Seamus still wedged in the doorway, she answered. "It is Mr. O'Flynn, Papa. He's come to work at the bakery."

"I can come back tomorrow if it's inconvenient," Seamus offered, noting her pained expression.

"Dis is good. Show Mr. O'Flynn to the back room, daughter. We will begin teaching tomorrow."

Rebecca's heart fell, but she ushered Seamus into the bakery and locked the door behind him. Her father's word was law in their household, and she would offer no opposition. But his decision was sure to make things difficult. Mr. O'Flynn was not Plain.

Holding the kerosene lantern tightly, she indicated with a nod of her head that he should follow. "There is a small room at the back of the bakery. The bed is not so very large," she felt her cheeks grow warm, "but the bedding is clean. Come, I will show you."

The lantern cast golden reflections onto the ceiling and walls, and over Rebecca's creamy complexion and pleasing figure. Seamus felt his gut tighten as he watched the gentle sway of her hips. He'd never before reacted so strongly to a woman. Especially one he'd met just hours before.

When they reached the small but tidy room that would now be his sleeping quarters, he deposited his belongings on the bed, then turned abruptly, almost knocking into her. "Thank you for your hospitality, lass. You won't be sorry you hired Seamus O'Flynn. I do a good day's work."

As Rebecca stared at the formidable man before her, at the dimples that winked so rakishly in the lantern light and the full lips that were always turned up in a smile, she experienced the strangest fluttering in her stomach and hoped that Mr. O'Flynn would be right: She hoped she wouldn't be sorry.

The rooster's crow at five o'clock the next morning jarred Alexander awake. Forgetting for the moment where he was, he leaned toward what he thought was his bedside table to light the lamp and fell onto the floor with a thud.

"Blast it all to hell!"

He heard a strange grunting noise and groped his way back into bed, wondering if the pigs Rose Elizabeth had mentioned were residing outside his window. The grunt turned into a low growl as Alexander's fingers latched on to a fluffy ball of fur, then the growling subsided.

Something licked his hand, alerting Alexander to the fact that Boomer had been his sleeping companion for the night. Apparently the pup had decided to forgive Alexander's intrusion into his sleep.

Wondering if this nightmare would ever end, Alexander found the matches atop the nightstand and lighted the lamp next to the bed. In the glow he saw Boomer's happy expression. With his upper lip curled, the damn dog looked as if he were smiling, no doubt pleased that he had put one over on the man.

"I've no doubt your mistress had something to do with this." Alexander patted the dog brusquely on the head and received another wet lick for his kindness.

Reaching for his pants, which lay at the foot of the bed, he snapped open the watch inside the pocket and his eyes widened in disbelief. He looked out the window and saw that it was as black as Hades outside. Who in their right mind would awaken at this ungodly hour?

Then he reminded himself that Rose Elizabeth Martin was not of sound mind. Not in the least.

What kind of woman would want to remain on such a poor excuse for a farm, with nothing but animals for company when she could instead travel to faraway places and explore new and exciting vistas?

Only Rose Elizabeth Martin.

The object of his thoughts was at the moment stoking the banked fire in the stove and tossing in a few more pieces of coal she'd retrieved from the scuttle.

Rose Elizabeth always woke with the rooster's crow. There

were chores to be done, lots of chores, and it was best to get them done before the oppressive heat made the doing of them unbearable.

Winnie and Wynona, the milk cows, weren't likely to wait long for a slug-a-bed like the duke to awaken. They could bellow something fierce if they weren't tended to in time. Pa had called the cows "sore-titted bitches," but then Pa had never liked doing the milking, and the chore had fallen to Rose Elizabeth.

Setting the pan of cinnamon buns in the warming tray of the stove to rise, she pumped water into the sink and washed the flour from her hands, then began her preparations.

There were still three hams hanging in the root cellar, and some leftover slices in the icebox that she intended to fry up for breakfast, provided they weren't spoiled. Her neighbor had not been by this week with the ice delivery, so the icebox was far from being cold.

She cracked a couple of extra eggs into the blue splatterware bowl for good measure, remembering that the duke had a large appetite.

"Madam, do you normally prepare breakfast at this ungodly hour of the morning?"

Rose spun around so quickly that the bowl almost slipped to the floor. Her mouth unhinged as she stared at the duke, who was dressed in tight-fitting black pants that left little to the imagination and shiny black leather boots that went clear up to his knees. His white shirt was open at the throat, revealing an enticing glimpse of curly bronze hair.

She swallowed, trying hard to ignore the hornet's nest buzzing in her tummy. "Actually, your grace, I don't usually eat until after the chores are finished. But I figured you'd be hungry, seeing as how you're not used to the way things are done around here."

"Well, that is a relief to hear. When do you usually sup? Five-thirty? Six?" He didn't bother to mask his sarcasm, and Rose Elizabeth's face flushed with indignation.

"If you're going to live on a farm, your dukeship, then I

suggest you learn the lay of the land and the way things are done around here. This is not England. There are no servants to do for you. But there are cows that need milking first thing in the morning. Winnie and Wynona"—she ignored his raised eyebrows—"cannot wait until you are damn good and ready to service them. Eggs need to be gathered from the chicken coop. They don't magically appear in the bowl, your grace." She held it out for his inspection. "The pigs need tendin', and—"

Alexander knew he should set her straight about his intentions for the land. Playing at being a gentleman farmer and actually doing the work were two entirely separate things. But his pride, and the challenge shining in her eyes, kept him silent.

He held up his hand to forestall whatever she was about to say on that subject. "I get the picture, Miss Martin. There is work to be done before we can eat. How considerate that you bent your rules for me."

As she set the bowl on the table, Rose reconsidered. "Actually, your grace, since there's still time before breakfast is ready, why don't you grab that wicker basket by the door and go gather up some eggs. Boomer will show you where the chicken coop's located."

"You expect me, a lord of the realm, to engage in physical labor?" He shook his head. "That's out of the question."

"Only if you want to eat, your dukeship."

Boomer scratched at the door, obviously ready and eager to depart, and Alexander frowned.

"Speaking of that mangy animal, are you aware that he slept in my bed last night?"

Rose's eyes twinkled merrily. "He always sleeps with me. Old habits are hard to break, your grace. And I would think you'd welcome the company."

"I can think of better company to warm my bed than a flea-ridden dog." His eyes raked over her in an insulting manner, and Rose Elizabeth's cheeks filled with color.

"Kansas fleas are a mite more particular about who they feast on, your dukeship."

Rose turned back to the stove, ignoring the duke's angry glare, and was relieved when the front door finally slammed shut. She didn't want him to know that his comment had conjured up all sorts of sinful images.

Still a virgin, Rose Elizabeth had no firsthand experience of the lovemaking process. She knew only what she'd gleaned from watching the farm animals mate.

But there was no way on God's green earth that she would give the time of day or spare another thought to that arrogant . . . deliciously muscular . . . horribly rude . . . awfully handsome . . . irritating as hell Duke of Moreland.

CHAPTER 4

Rose Elizabeth stared at the basket of cracked eggs the duke handed her and started tapping her toe double-time. "I don't scramble the eggs before they're put into the bowl, your grace."

Alexander blushed under his day's growth of beard. "That damn dog kept jumping on my back each time I bent over to collect the eggs. How was I supposed to hang on to the bloody things!"

Boomer gave a mournful wail, as if offering an apology, and Rose Elizabeth patted his head. "Perhaps you'll have more of an affinity for milking the cows, your grace."

The duke rubbed his chin thoughtfully. "Who can tell? I've always had a great fondness for breasts." He stared at hers with undisguised interest, a naughty grin on his face.

Rose's cheeks flamed redder than the coals in the stove. "Cows don't have breasts, your denseness . . . I mean, your dukeness. They have udders."

"And teats. I remember my tutor telling me that."

"It's interesting, which lessons you choose to remember from childhood, your grace." Rose marched to the stove and

44

tossed the ham slices into the skillet, ignoring the duke's laughter, and the way the sound of it rippled along her spine.

Unfortunately, the milking of the cows wasn't proceeding any better than had the gathering of the eggs.

With far more patience than she thought his lordship deserved, Rose Elizabeth demonstrated the proper way to milk a cow, using Wynona as the subject. "Notice how I grasp the teats firmly with my fingers and squeeze gently." With an even pull, she showed him how easily and quickly the milk splashed into the pail. "It's a very simple procedure." She glanced over her shoulder at the duke, knowing darn well that it wouldn't be easy for him. "I'm sure even you will learn to milk in no time." The lie came easily to her lips.

The smell of fresh hay teased his senses, making Alexander realize how much he missed his daily rides on his favorite Thoroughbred. Comet was as fast as the wind and far more sweet-natured than his present companion—and he wasn't referring to the cow.

Rose and Alexander exchanged places, and Alexander seated himself on the short stool positioned near the cow's swollen udders. Wynona gave him a cursory glance, swished her tail once or twice, but offered no objection.

"I'm not without experience at this," he said with a cocky grin, grabbing hold of the cow's teats none too gently. Wynona mooed her disapproval loudly.

His remark surprised Rose, and her eyebrows lifted. "You've milked before? I wasn't aware . . ."

He shook his head, and the look he shot her was purely sensual, making her tingle in places she hadn't known existed. "I wasn't speaking of cows, Rose Elizabeth."

Doing her best not to incinerate right on the spot, though she could feel her cheeks burning, Rose hid her embarrassment behind a tight smile. "I think you'll find that cows are a mite different than women, your grace."

"Women are women, Rose. And I'm a—"

Before he could finish, Wynona gave a loud bellow of outrage, kicked out her left hind leg, and knocked Alexander off his stool and flat on his backside in a pile of cow manure. As a final insult, the milk pail upended on his lap, wetting him thoroughly.

Alexander's horrified expression brought torrents of laughter from Rose Elizabeth, who was having a difficult time getting herself under control. "I . . . I hope you treat women with a bit mo-more tenderness, your dukeness. Wynona, like most of her sex, requires a gentler touch."

"Perhaps you should stick to canned milk." She recited a popular slogan: " 'Carnation milk best in the lan', comes to you in a little red can. No tits to pull, no hay to pitch, jes punch a hole in the sonofabitch.' " She howled again, holding her sides, and Alexander shot her and the cow similarly outraged looks.

"I'll try to remember that."

"I'll finish milking Wynona, your grace. I doubt she'll let you get close to her again. Why don't you start on the vegetable garden. There're plenty of weeds that need hoeing."

A short time later, Rose Elizabeth found him bent over the rows of vegetables in the garden. Snap beans climbed tenaciously up wooden poles; tomatoes, ripe and ready for picking, were staked to keep them off the ground and away from pesky insects—not that that would do a lick of good if grasshoppers descended again this year; and firm heads of lettuce marched in military-straight columns.

Alexander sang an unfamiliar tune at the top of his lungs as he brandished the hoe like a weapon. It took only one horrified moment for Rose to realize that the inept nobleman wasn't swiping saberlike at the weeds.

"You're chopping my carrots, your grace!" She waved her hands wildly as she rushed into the garden. "Don't you know the difference between weeds and carrots?" She shook her head so hard that her long brown braid almost whipped her flushed cheeks.

Still smarting over Rose's earlier ridicule, Alexander shrugged. "Apparently not," he said, looking not the least bit apologetic.

Rose Elizabeth counted to ten, then counted to ten again, trying her damnedest to get her temper under control. It didn't work. "Dammit all to hell! Don't you know how long it takes carrots to grow?"

"Can't say that I do. I've always had servants to tend to these menial chores."

As if talking to a simpleton, which is exactly what Rose Elizabeth thought the duke to be, she grabbed the hoe from his hands. "These are the weeds." She demonstrated scraping the tip of the implement against the ragged plants. "Those are the tops of the carrots," she explained, pointing at the feathery green tops of the vegetables. "Please take care to learn the difference, your grace, or we won't be eating very well come winter."

Summer and fall fruits and vegetables were the mainstay of most Kansans' winter diets. Kept in dark, dank root cellars and covered with straw, the vegetables and fruits stayed relatively fresh. That is, if they were allowed to mature without being mutilated by inept aristocrats who didn't know their hind end from their head.

Alexander watched raptly as Rose Elizabeth hoed the dirt. His gaze riveted on her attractive backside, he was reminded of the saying that the size of the saddle was in direct proportion to the enjoyment of the ride.

The shapeless Mother Hubbard dress she wore did nothing for her curvaceous figure, but a man with his experience and imagination could guess what delights the calico disguised. At first he had thought her too tall, too plump, but the sight of her large breasts and pleasing derriere had altered his opinion.

Rose Elizabeth was a substantial woman, a little taller than he normally preferred. But when he thought of those voluptuous breasts pressed into his chest, into his palms . . . He shifted his feet uncomfortably. All that talk of teats had made him hornier than that damned frog Rose carted around with her.

"Are you listening to me, your grace? I asked if you were ready to try your hand at something else."

An interesting question. His hands itched to explore many

things, not the least of which were Rose's breasts. "I'm yours to command, my *sweet* Rose."

Not detecting the sarcasm in his tone, she blushed at the endearment. "No need to get flowery, your grace. We're only going to feed the hogs and slop out their pens. I doubt you'll be waxing poetic for long."

Rose rested the hoe against the side of the house, then marched off to the pig shed. Alexander followed two steps behind and wondered what he had done to deserve such punishment.

Rose lifted up the male piglet for the duke's inspection. The tiny creature squirmed in her hands, squealing his indignation. "Soon we'll have to castrate this little fellow," she explained, holding him upside down to display his tiny sex organ. "Since we have Elmo, we won't be needing any more boars."

Rose's words sent chills rushing through Alexander. He crossed his legs against the unwelcome image she evoked, feeling nothing but pity and a large measure of male empathy for the poor little creature. "Is that really necessary? It seems rather a drastic measure."

Rose Elizabeth wanted to laugh. The duke's reaction was so typically male. "Of course it's necessary, your grace. Barrows—castrated males—grow faster once their sex organs are removed. And since they're not going to be bred, but sent to market, it only makes good business sense to relieve them of their unnecessary equipment."

Staring at the defenseless creature, then at Rose, Alexander felt a sudden urge to rescue it from the clutches of the heartless woman. It wasn't difficult to imagine her castrating any male that didn't meet her rigid specifications, and it made the area between his legs ache.

"I don't see you castrating the girl pigs. I don't think it's quite fair."

"Castration without representation, your grace? Is that what you're saying?"

He ignored her laughter. "Your Patrick Henry would no doubt agree with me."

"I doubt Patrick Henry would have agreed with anything you English had to say, your dukeness."

Rose smiled at his indignation. Alexander's defense of the pig was quite unexpected. She would never have guessed that such a hardheaded stuffed shirt had a soft spot for animals, and that realization made the duke's character climb half a notch in her estimation.

"The females are called gilts before they give birth," Rose explained. "And no, we don't need to fix them like we do the males. Female pigs don't strut around the farm looking to get themselves into trouble, the way the males do. They're not territorial or prone to fighting. I guess that's why we call the males *bores*."

The Duke of Moreland stiffened, all prim and proper, a good indication that Rose's pun had scored a hit. And she could tell by the hostile look he cast her that he hadn't found her barnyard humor the least bit funny.

Her eyes twinkling with merriment, she handed him a shovel. "I guess it's time to muck out the pens, your highness."

By the time Rose Elizabeth and Alexander had finished with the pigs, the duke's shiny black shoes were dull brown with excrement, and Rose Elizabeth's dress was splattered in a like manner. Neither smelled fit for human company, but that is exactly what they received upon exiting the shed.

"Oh no!" Rose cried, shielding her eyes against the bright sunlight as she stared down the long lane leading to the house. Visitors were coming. Recognizing the two black buggies approaching, she knew Euphemia and her lady friends had wasted little time in taking her up on her earlier offer of calling on the duke. "Damn, damn, and double damn!"

Alexander sniffed the air several times, then glanced down at himself, unable to believe that he looked like a common fieldhand or laborer. It occurred to him that the dowager duchess would be quite appalled if she could see him now. An enticing thought, he decided.

"I doubt your friends will be staying overly long, Rose Elizabeth. We do not exactly smell like your namesake at the moment."

"That fact won't stop Euphemia, your dukeship. Once she gets her mind set on something, she's like a racehorse heading for the finish line, and she won't give a hoot and a holler who she tramples to get there."

Alexander thought Miss Bloodworth looked more like a sway-backed nag than a racehorse, but he neglected to voice his opinion.

"*Yoo-hoo!*" Euphemia called out, waving her handkerchief in the air to attract the duke's attention. "*Yoo-hoo*, your lordship."

Rose rested her case with a smug, lawyerlike smile.

With a groan, and a great deal of reluctance, Alexander waved back. The smile he wore as the ladies approached bespoke years of breeding and manners too ingrained to ignore. It was reflexive, polite, and pained.

Euphemia was accompanied by Peggy, Marcella, and Sarah Ann. They all looked horrified by the duke's and Rose Elizabeth's appearance.

"Sakes alive!" Euphemia declared, her hand clutching her throat. "What on earth have you done to the duke, Rose Elizabeth? You both look like you've been rolling around in the barn." Her expression was heavy with disapproval and her lips were so thinned that they practically disappeared. "I trust that's not the case."

"Actually, we've been rolling in pig manure, Euphemia." Rose ignored the older woman's gasp. "How nice of you to call, but I'm afraid you've caught us at a bad time. We haven't yet had a chance to clean up, and I'm afraid we smell worse than chicken droppings during a summer hot spell."

Obviously agreeing with that assessment, Sarah Ann wrinkled her nose in disgust at the foul odor, then covered it with a lace-edged handkerchief. "Why on earth are you still here, Rose Elizabeth? I'd have thought you would have departed for Mrs. Caffrey's by now." The hankie puffed out and retreated with Sarah Ann's every breath, confirming Rose's opinion that the woman was full of hot air.

"Yes, Rose Elizabeth," Peggy added with a spiteful smile. "Isn't it time you went and got yourself some manners and learned how to become a lady?"

Marcella's cheeks pinkened at Peggy's insensitive remark, but Rose, who was used to the young woman's snide comments, ignored it and winked reassuringly at her friend.

But what Rose couldn't ignore was the way Peggy had sidled up next to Alexander and was presenting him with her most engaging asset—her smile. Though she hated to admit it, Peggy Mellon's dimples were darn attractive. And by the way the duke was smiling down on her, all moony-eyed and solicitous, it was obvious that he'd noticed them, and no doubt her generous bosom as well.

"We've brought some lovely scones from Heller's Bakery. It seems they've reopened as of this morning," Sarah Ann informed her reluctant hostess, bringing forth a wicker basket.

The scones smelled divine, but they weren't as pleasing to Rose as the news that the Hellers had reopened their bakery. Though she didn't know Rebecca Heller well, Rose harbored a liking for the quiet, gentle woman, and she wished Rebecca and her father only the best.

Not everyone in Salina felt kindly toward the Mennonite family. Folks tended to fear what they didn't understand. But Rose knew that Salina, and the whole state of Kansas, for that matter, would be in an awful pickle if it hadn't been for the Mennonites. Those who had journeyed to America from Russia to escape religious persecution had brought with them the hardy strain of wheat known as Turkey Red, which had revolutionized the wheat farming industry. And she also knew that gratitude, not unkindness, was what the Mennonites deserved in great abundance for their contribution.

"It looks like Rebecca Heller finally found someone to help her out," Euphemia informed them. They were now standing beneath the stand of slender-stemmed cottonwoods near the corner of the house, enjoying the scones the ladies had brought and the cold apple cider Rose had grudgingly provided with a little urging from the duke.

"I saw a redheaded man I didn't recognize when I entered the bakery this morning."

Alexander's eyes widened at the spinster's announcement. The redheaded man was no doubt Seamus O'Flynn. Although Seamus had said that he planned to help out some people in town, the duke couldn't imagine the rough-and-tumble Irishman working in such dainty surroundings as a bakery. The man's temperament and size were far more suited to a boxing ring. In fact, Seamus had been quite the pugilist back in Ireland.

"Perhaps I'll take a trip to town soon and purchase more of these scones." There was a devilish gleam in the duke's eyes when he spoke. "They're really quite good."

Euphemia and Sarah Ann shared a pleased smile before the older woman said, "You must let us know when you're coming, your lordship. We'd just love to host a welcoming party for you. Most of the ladies in town are refined and genteel." She stared at Rose Elizabeth, indicating by her haughty expression that Rose was definitely not included in that description. "I'm sure you would enjoy meeting the rest of the Garden Club and Ladies Sewing Circle."

Peggy clasped the duke's arm, and there was a definite invitation in the smile she flashed him. "I'd be happy to show you around town, your grace. I know things that I'm sure you'd find just fascinating."

Rose snorted loudly. Peggy had been around the block a time or two, but it was doubtful that the Ladies Sewing Circle knew of her shocking behavior, or, if they had heard the rumors, believed them. Peggy had a way of explaining things away to suit herself.

Only a month ago she'd been caught in a compromising position in the hayloft of the livery with Wolf Turlock, the blacksmith, by none other than Tilde Turlock, Wolf's wife. The woman had been outraged to find the two of them together and had very nearly pulled out every one of Peggy's blond hairs. Of course, Peggy protested her innocence, blaming the entire incident on Wolf, and her mother and the others had believed her, for Wolf was a known womanizer in town.

Having had enough of Peggy's overtures and Euphemia's ingratiating manner for one day, Rose clapped her hands together in what was obviously a dismissive gesture. "Well, ladies, I hate to call an end to our lovely tea party, but the duke and I still have chores to finish. And we're obviously in need of a good scrubbing."

Taking the hint, goodbyes were made quickly, and the ladies departed. Rose couldn't contain her sigh of relief as she watched their buggies head down the lane.

It wasn't that Rose didn't like them, for she did. She even found Peggy tolerable on occasion. But like them or not, Rose knew that she would never fit in with their genteel, gossipy, feminine ways. She felt far more comfortable in their husbands' company, discussing crop production or the current market value of wheat, than she did debating the best remedy for colic or the latest fashions from the Montgomery Ward Catalogue.

Pa had always wanted a son; she guessed she was it.

"They really aren't that bad, Rose Elizabeth," Alexander stated with a great deal of censure. "I didn't see any reason for you to behave so rudely. Honestly, one would think that you didn't have any social graces whatsoever."

His barb struck, for Rose Elizabeth acknowledged, if only to herself, that she had indeed been rude. But she sure as heck didn't need a dandified duke to remind her of that fact.

"And what kind of social graces can you possess, your royal obtuseness, by making such a thoughtless remark?" With a toss of her braid, she headed toward the house, but not before adding, "I'll be using the tub first, so I'll thank you to stay outside until I'm finished bathing."

Alexander watched her drag the rusted tub through the doorway and slam the door shut behind it.

The woman was a definite puzzle, he thought, leaning against the trunk of a cottonwood and folding his arms across his chest. He'd seen the hurt in Rose's eyes when Peggy and Euphemia had made their callous remarks, though she'd done her best to mask it. He'd seen vulnerability in Rose Elizabeth today—vulnerability and insecurity that he hadn't known existed in the self-possessed woman.

Rose was possessed all right! Of many things, including an enticing body. Closing his eyes, he had no difficulty conjuring up an image of her naked in the bathtub, her full breasts floating atop the water, her pert nipples just skimming the surface of the scented liquid. . . .

An uncomfortable bulge pressed against Alexander's pants, and he swore viciously beneath his breath, disgusted with himself for thinking about that shrewish woman. Naked or not, Rose Elizabeth Martin was nothing but a pain in his backside and had been since he'd met her at the train depot yesterday.

Unable to believe that they had met only yesterday, he shook his head. It seemed as if he'd been living with her for months . . . years. . . .

There had to be a way to get rid of the woman. Unfortunately, however, for the time being, he needed her. She knew her way around the farm, while he was totally inept. Of course, a wheat farm and soddy were a far cry from the gentleman's estate he'd expected.

Damn that lying Phinneas Abbott's hide!

He gazed out over the harsh brown land and tried to envision how it would one day be. The stone farm house he'd wanted was out of the question, but a lovely two-story structure could be constructed. Craftsmen could be hired to build it, gardeners engaged to plan the landscaping and to plant trees and shrubs. And flowers, for God's sake!

How these Americans could live in such barren ugliness he couldn't fathom.

Well, he intended to change all that, and soon. He had no need for wheat and pigs, no need to sweat and toil like a peasant. He was a duke. And by all that was holy, he would have his gentleman's estate, come hell, high water, or Rose Elizabeth Martin.

The heat from the ovens made the bakery intolerable, and Rebecca swiped the back of her hand at the moisture collecting on her upper lip and brow. She pulled another batch of bread from the oven and smiled in satisfaction as she gazed at the perfect loaves. The golden brown, neatly formed rectangles emitted the tantalizing, yeasty scent that only freshly baked bread could produce.

Seamus O'Flynn had been correct in saying that the aroma of baked bread was better than expensive perfume. It was better, in Rebecca's opinion, than almost anything. Except, perhaps, the smell of an infant straight from his bath.

Rebecca adored the way babies smelled, cooed, felt when she held them in her arms. Back home in Lancaster, she'd had plenty of opportunity to cherish other people's children, and she hoped one day to have one of her own to cuddle to her breast, providing, of course, she found herself a husband.

Seamus O'Flynn's image came to mind, but she pushed it away and returned her attention to removing the loaves from their tins, unwilling to waste time on fanciful notions.

"They are perfect." Rebecca smiled proudly, knowing that if they hadn't been, she would have tossed them into the garbage without a second thought and started all over again. She didn't consider that waste, but necessity.

Perfection was something Rebecca expected of herself and her work, and she strove to achieve it, though she recognized the trait as a character flaw. Perfection went hand in hand with vanity, as her mama had told her so many times. Vanity was a sin. It was worldly and not Plain. Rebecca constantly tried to overcome her weakness, but to little avail.

But though she suspected her mama had been right, when she gazed at the loaves she had lovingly fashioned with her own two hands, she couldn't help the rush of pride she felt, sinful though it was.

Seamus paused in the doorway, admiring the view. Flushed from the heat, Rebecca's cheeks reminded him of pink rose blossoms, velvety soft and delicate. She was a beautiful woman, though he doubted she knew it. And that made her all the more appealing in his opinion.

"Where will you be wanting these sacks of flour, lass?"

Rebecca spun around so quickly that the muffin tin she held crashed loudly to the floor, the cornmeal batter splattering everywhere. *"Verdammte dunnerwetter!"* she cried. Then, horrified, she covered her mouth as she realized what she'd said. Though it translated only to "Jumping Jehoshaphat!" in Rebecca's mind it was a curse. Losing one's temper was not considered acceptable behavior.

"Excuse me, Mr. O'Flynn, but you have startled me. Please do not sneak up behind me again. We cannot afford to waste."

Lowering the heavy sack from his shoulder, Seamus set it near the rear wall. "I'd have thought your memory better. Don't you remember my arrival last evening, Rebecca?"

She ignored the familiarity, and the way the sound of her name on his lips made her feel all fidgety inside. "Of course I remember, Mr. O'Flynn. I am not simpleminded. But I thought you were still upstairs with Papa. He said he would show you the recipes."

It was doubtful that Rebecca could have forgotten Seamus O'Flynn's arrival last evening. He had been on her mind the entire night, and the knowledge that he slept nearby had made restful sleep impossible. It was little wonder that this morning her head resided in the clouds and her mind drifted to places it had no right to be.

"My apologies. I'll stamp my feet or whistle loudly next time I come in carrying a hundred-pound sack of flour."

His voice held a teasing note, and Rebecca's eyes twinkled in response. "You are funning with me, are you not, Mr. O'Flynn?"

"Call me Seamus. I'm not one to stand on formality. And yes, lass, I'm funning with you."

Though his dazzling smile was tempting, Rebecca chose once again to ignore the rush of awareness pouring over her. "There is work to be done, Mr. O'Flynn. Please, you will fill the barrels with flour and the canisters with the salt and spices. They are marked as to what goes where."

With patience—and patience was not one of Seamus's virtues—he attempted to tear down the barrier she had erected between them. "You've been working since sunrise, Rebecca. Don't you think it's time you took a break? It's nearly noon."

"Idle hands invite the devil, Mr. O'Flynn. And there is still much to do. I have no time to *dopple.*"

"I see no reason to kill yourself, lass. There's hardly been a rush of customers."

Disheartened, Rebecca sighed at the veracity of his words. "Aside from Miss Bloodsworth and her friend who purchased scones, we've had no one else come to buy. If we don't attract more customers soon, we'll be forced to shut down permanently."

"Perhaps few people know that the bakery has reopened for business. I'm thinking that you need to do a wee bit of advertising." Spying a large wicker backet hanging on the wall, Seamus retrieved it and handed it to the startled young woman. "Fill this with several loaves of the bread and some scones. I'll take it up and down the street and see if I can drum up a little business. Once they get a whiff of this bread, the good folks of Salina won't be able to resist buying some."

Her eyes bright with excitement, Rebecca placed the baked goods into the basket as Seamus directed, covering the bread and scones with a clean linen towel before handing the basket back to him. "Do you really think this will work, Mr. O'Flynn? I've never sold goods on the street before." Except at the farmers' market in Lancaster. But then, they mostly traded with friends and neighbors for the items they needed.

"It'll only work if you agree to call me Seamus, lass. Otherwise I cannot guarantee a sale." He flashed her a grin that set her pulse pounding.

Her cheeks filling with color, Rebecca lowered her gaze and stared self-consciously at her feet. "Seamus," she said, barely above a whisper.

CHAPTER 5

Smelling and feeling far better than she had an hour ago, Rose chopped diligently at the pile of potatoes and carrots, wondering if the duke had managed to fit himself into the bathtub. No doubt it was none too comfortable for him, him being as long and broad as he was.

She'd heard singing coming from his bedroom—the man was a regular songbird, it seemed—so Rose supposed he'd accomplished what he'd set out to do.

Rose had offered no help either in heating the water or in filling the tub for him, but instead had gone outside to bring in the wash from the line. When she'd passed by his window and noticed him standing with his back to it, she'd been unable to avert her gaze and had stared unashamedly, enraptured by his nakedness and the muscularity of his arms and back.

The instinct to see more had sorely tempted her to drag a wooden crate over and climb up onto it for a better view. It wasn't often—actually, it was never—that she got to see a naked man in his bath. It had only been Boomer's loud barking that had brought her to her senses.

Just as the water in the large black-iron kettle started to boil, Alexander stepped into the front room, smelling like exotic spices and looking more handsome than any man had a right to. He was dressed much as he had been this morning, but now his clothes were as sparkling clean as the rest of him. His wet, flaxen hair glistened in the sunlight streaming through the window, like dew-blessed wheat basking in the rays of the morning sun, and he had taken a razor to the day's growth of beard on his face.

"You're looking a mite better, your grace. I suppose you're feeling that way, too," Rose said by way of greeting.

Smiling, Alexander stepped toward the stove, sniffing the air appreciatively. "Something smells good. Is that our dinner? I'm starved. It must be all that hard work you insisted I do."

For his first day the duke had done all right, Rose admitted to herself. To him, she said, "It'll be supper as soon as I fetch the onions from the root cellar. 'Stew ain't stew without a proper amount of onions,' Mama always said."

He looked about, a curious expression on his face. "Where is this root cellar? I'll be happy to retrieve whatever it is you need."

No doubt it was his hunger that made him agreeable, and Rose wasn't about to look a gift horse in the mouth. Climbing down to the root cellar had never been her favorite thing. She'd ridden out too many cyclones and thunderstorms there.

"Outside the front door to your right, you'll see a trapdoor in the ground. The cellar's under the house. Once you pull open the doors, there'll be a lantern hanging near the top step. You'll need it to see your way down. It's very dark in the cellar. The onions, potatoes, and turnips are piled against the far right wall. Just sniff. You can't miss 'em."

He bowed with a flourish, and Rose's heart did a funny little flip. "Your wish is my command." He left the house, and Rose released the breath she hadn't known she'd been holding.

Returning her concentration to the boiling pot, she dumped

the potatoes and carrots into the water, then seasoned the bubbly mixture with a pinch of salt and a hardy sprinkling of pepper.

She sat in her rocker to wait for the duke's return, but when fifteen minutes had passed and he hadn't appeared, Rose knew something was wrong. It didn't take fifteen minutes to fetch onions. It hardly took that long to grow them!

She approached the cellar, noting that the trapdoor was still open. Peering down the darkened stairwell, she called out, "Hello? Alexander, are you still down there?"

Boomer's bark echoed up, filling Rose with dread, her worst suspicions confirmed.

"Of course I'm still down here," came the exasperated reply. "Where else would I be? This damn dog knocked the lantern over, and it's so black down here I can't see a bloody blasted thing."

Another bark, this time contrite.

Rose bit down on her lower lip to keep from laughing, thinking that perhaps Boomer might accomplish what she hadn't been able to: He might get rid of the duke. "Just a moment. I'll fetch another lantern and be right down."

She was back moments later, holding the lantern out in front of her as she made her way gingerly down the steps. The musty dankness of the cellar rose to greet her, as did the much nicer scent of Alexander's cologne.

She had descended halfway when the hem of her dress caught on a rusty nail protruding from the side wall. Cursing under her breath at the nail, and at the fact that she'd procrastinated fixing it, Rose set the lantern down to free the stubborn material, hoping she wouldn't rip it. She had neither time nor money to fashion new clothing.

Yanking impatiently several times, she worked the material loose. Just then a gust of wind came up and blew the cellar doors shut with a loud bang, extinguishing the lantern.

"Hell and damnation!"

"What's taking so long?" Alexander's impatient voice carried up the stairwell.

Her own patience growing thinner by the minute, Rose turned toward the exasperating voice, made a face, then muttered, "What the hell else can go wrong?"

Suddenly Boomer barked loudly, causing her to start. Her foot slipped on the tread, and she went hurtling headfirst down the steps with a bloodcurdling scream.

"Bloody hell!" was all Alexander had time to say before Rose collided into him, knocking him flat on his back. He made a whooshing sound as the breath went out of him.

"I'm not *that* heavy, your dukeness," Rose said rather indignantly when she realized where she had landed. "Thanks for breaking my fall," she added as an afterthought. "I'd forgotten what a long way down it is." She and her sisters used to jump off the cellar stairs for a lark, but that had been many years ago, when she'd been more of a daredevil and far more agile than she was now.

There were times when she missed those carefree days, when she had no responsibilities, other than doing her chores and keeping out of Heather's way so that she wouldn't be assigned any additional ones. She and Laurel had taken unfair advantage of their older sister, and she now realized that Heather had shouldered a heavy burden for a girl of fourteen.

At Rose's heartfelt sigh, Alexander's arms tightened around her waist. He could barely make out her face in the dark, but he could definitely discern her womanly shape. "You're not hurt, are you?" he inquired, resisting the urge to find out for himself.

They were nose to nose. Alexander's warm breath tickled her cheeks as he spoke, and Rose knew that if she leaned forward just a smidgen, their lips would touch. For an instant, she was tempted. Thinking about how soft his lips would feel pressed against her own, her nipples hardened into stiff peaks.

Apparently the duke was having similar thoughts, Rose decided, for there was definitely something long and hard pressing into her thigh, and she didn't think she had stumbled onto a carrot!

Quickly she righted herself, grateful for the darkness that

hid her burning cheeks. "My stew is probably boiling away, your grace. I'd best go back to the house and check on it."

Rose quickly located the lantern and relit it for the duke before escaping up the stairs.

Alexander smiled as he watched her scamper away like a frightened rabbit. She had felt his ardent response, just as surely as he had felt hers pressing into his chest, and she'd been embarrassed by it. Rose was no doubt inexperienced when it came to men.

That notion didn't displease him, nor did the thought that Rose Elizabeth was as hot as the stew she prepared, and probably tasted a damn sight better!

Sven Anderson clicked to the mules and hitched the reins as he guided the beasts down the dusty drive to the Martin residence. The wind gusted hard and hot, and he clutched at his flat-brimmed felt hat to keep it from flying off his head.

It was only eight in the morning, but already the sun was sizzling. That was the way it was in summer: heat, wind, and more heat.

Pulling his team to a halt in front of the soddy that wasn't so very different from his own, he announced his arrival in his thick Scandinavian accent, as he'd done every Sunday morning for the past few months without fail. "Rose Elizabet! Hurry! Ve vill be late for church."

His two young children, Peter and Wilhem, bounced excitedly in the back of the buckboard at the prospect of their weekly trip to town and the opportunity to visit friends their own age, chattering as noisily as the meadowlarks and robins soaring overhead.

Sven admonished his motherless brood with a sharp look, then shouted at the house again, and at the woman who he hoped would soon rectify that situation.

He and Rose Elizabeth had been keeping company, and he thought that she would soon be ready to accept his proposal of marriage. Theirs would be a good match. Rose Elizabeth

was strong and smart—the kind of wife a farmer needed—
and she would bear him many more sons.

"Rose Elizabet, vould you have us be late again? Pastor
Bergman vill use us as examples, as he did last week." *As he
does every week,* Sven amended silently.

The door opened and Rose Elizabeth stepped out, dressed
in a pretty pink floral gown, the hem of which dragged the
ground because she refused to wear the bustle that accompanied it. She smiled widely at the Anderson brood, tying the
pink satin ribbons of her straw bonnet under her chin.

Sven noticed that Rose Elizabeth was not alone. There was
a strange man with her—a fancy dresser—and the Swede's
brow furrowed. The stranger was probably that duke from
England that Rose Elizabeth had complained about so bit-
terly.

She wasn't complaining now, he noted unhappily.

"Good morning, Sven. Children." Rose winked at the two
boys, noting their impatience. She and her sisters had been the
same way at that age, always eager for a trip to town.

"Sorry I'm late, but the duke isn't used to getting up at the
crack of dawn like the rest of us." She gazed back over her
left shoulder and, ignoring Alexander's scowl, urged him forward to make the introductions.

"Sven Anderson, this is Alexander Warrick, the Duke of
Moreland."

His suspicions confirmed, Sven nodded perfunctorily but
said nothing to the impeccably attired nobleman.

Walking over to the buckboard, Alexander extended his
hand to the frowning man seated there. There was distrust in
Sven Anderson's light blue eyes. And wariness. With just a
hint of jealousy thrown in for good measure. It was obvious
to Alexander that the man hadn't expected to find Rose entertaining houseguests—male houseguests, to be precise.

"Hope you don't mind," Alexander informed him, not really caring whether he did, "but Rose said I could accompany
you both to town this morning. I thought after church service

I would check the livery for a suitable mount. I've missed my daily ride, and Rose Elizabeth's nag isn't up to the effort."

Noting the hostility lighting Rose Elizabeth's eyes, Sven felt momentarily appeased that she did not appear to be enamored of the duke. Swallowing his jealousy, he said, "You are velcome to come vid us, Alexander, but you vill have to ride in the back vid the children. There is no room for three on the bench."

And three is a crowd. Though Sven didn't utter that opinion, it came through loud and clear to Alexander.

Rose Elizabeth wanted to laugh at the displeasure on the duke's aristocratic face. Alexander wasn't used to taking a backseat to anyone. That was clearly evident by his pinched lips and rigid stance. But the duke had no alternative, unless, of course, he wanted to walk. Which would have been perfectly fine with Rose Elizabeth.

After their brief but disturbing encounter in the root cellar yesterday afternoon, Rose had become too aware of Alexander as a man. It was much easier to dislike him, ignore him, or make fun of him, so that she could distance herself and her feelings.

But yesterday her feelings had surged right through the material of her dress, had given her a sleepless night unlike any she'd ever had, and she wasn't at all pleased about it.

"That will be fine," Alexander finally said, eyeing the children cautiously before seating himself next to them in the back. He wasn't used to children and had no idea what to say or do around them. To the duke, children were like creatures from an unknown world. They talked strangely, acted even more strangely, and served no useful purpose in his opinion. Much like his younger brother, Edward, who was as useless as tits on a boar, as Rose Elizabeth was fond of saying.

Rose climbed up next to Sven and patted his thigh in a manner that Alexander thought very familiar and totally unnecessary, and that squashed his previous opinion about her inexperience with men. He frowned thoughtfully.

"How have you been, Sven? I haven't seen you for days. I

thought you would bring me some ice." Before the Swede could explain why he hadn't, Rose turned her head and said to Alexander, "The Andersons are my neighbors to the west. Sven and his boys own the land adjacent to mine."

"To mine, you mean?" Alexander took great delight in the angry flush now coloring Rose's cheeks.

The truth of his words stung like pinpricks, but Rose chose to ignore them. "Many Scandinavians came to America and settled in Kansas because of the severe drought in Norway and Sweden, which forced them from their homes. Isn't that right, Sven?"

"*Ja.* It was very bad there. The crops died in the fields and ve vent hungry. It is much better here."

"We like it here very much," Wilhem, the youngest boy, said politely. "Rose Elizabeth is very nice. She bakes cookies, and treats us like her own children. Do you have children, Mr. Duke?" Childish curiosity filled his eyes.

Pain filled Alexander's, and he winced at the shame of admitting his failure. "No. I have no children." And he never would, according to the doctor who had examined him. There would be no heir for the Duke of Moreland. The fall from his horse that had crushed his pelvis and left leg many years ago had also rendered him incapable of siring children. It had been a bitter pill to swallow, and one that his mother, the dowager duchess, had never allowed him to forget.

"You're like a gelded stallion, Alexander," the duchess had proclaimed cruelly, shortly after his accident. "You're less than a man. What use are you if you can't produce an heir to carry on the Warrick name?"

Alexander sucked in his breath, then expelled it along with the painful memory.

Rose turned to smile at Wilhem and caught the grief in Alexander's eyes. It registered as a dull ache in her chest, and she wondered what had caused him such sorrow. Grief was usually the result of death or great loss. She had experienced it herself after her father died, was still experiencing it to this day.

Ezra Martin had been more than just her beloved papa. He had been her closest friend. She had been her father's companion on more than one fishing expedition and weekly card game. They had made great plans concerning the farm and had talked about buying additional acreage and planting more wheat.

She missed him dreadfully. The cancer that had taken Ezra Martin had also eaten away part of the joy and contentment in her life.

Rose pushed aside her maudlin thoughts and forced a smile to her lips. "It's a perfectly glorious day, isn't it? What do you suppose our good pastor will preach about today, Sven?" Hell and damnation was the usual fare served up on Sundays. But to judge from the amount of sinning that still went on in Salina, such as drinking—even though the Rusty Nail Saloon had closed its doors—and gambling and fornicating, the rheumatoid old clergyman wasn't making much of an impression on the townsfolk.

"He vill say that I am late again and that I set a bad example for the children. That is vhat he vill say, Rose Elizabet."

Peter and Wilhem let loose with giggles. Alexander continued to frown.

Knowing the truth of Sven's words, and also knowing that she was usually the cause of his lateness, Rose Elizabeth patted his arm. "You can tell him it was my fault. Or better yet, tell him it was the duke's. I'm sure Alexander won't mind." She flashed him a smug smile, then turned quickly to look straight ahead. All the way into town she felt Alexander's annoyance boring into her back like bullets.

Alexander was not sorry to see the church service end. He'd never before heard such a zealous, despotic cleric as Pastor Bergman. The rector in Sussex had been a kind, soft-spoken chap, unlike the pastor, who shouted down fire and brimstone from his pulpit, as if he feared that every hard-working farmer, store clerk, and housewife would leave his church and proceed to break every single one of the Ten Commandments before the afternoon drew to an end.

The beginnings of a headache threatened and Alexander massaged his temples while smiling politely at the clergyman, who was now taking Rose Elizabeth to task for her failure to leave the farm. The aging pastor's sentiments mirrored his own, so Alexander kept silent, hoping the man would be able to talk some sense into the hardheaded woman.

"You bring great shame upon yourself, Rose Elizabeth," the clergyman counseled. "You are living in sin with a man who is not your husband."

She slid a look at her companion and found the duke paying close attention to the good pastor's admonishments, and no doubt wholeheartedly agreeing with them. Rose Elizabeth had to bite the inside of her cheek to keep from uttering the profanity that was on the tip of her tongue. Only the thought of another of the minister's lectures kept her from doing so.

"My situation is no different than yours, Pastor Bergman," she said, and both men's eyes widened. "You have Hermione Clinghoffer as your housekeeper, and the duke has me. I fail to see the difference."

The pastor's cheeks puffed out, not unlike Lester's, then his face reddened. She patted her pocket, reminding herself to leave Lester at home from now on. The frog had croaked four times during service today. Alexander shot Rose Elizabeth a scathing look.

"Young woman, Hermione Clinghoffer is a spinster of advanced years. Your situation is nothing like hers."

"Oh, but it is, Pastor Bergman. I'm unmarried, just as Miss Clinghoffer is, and many folks in Salina already consider me a spinster. There's nothing sinful, far as I can tell, about honest employment as a housekeeper. If there was, you'd have to kick poor Miss Clinghoffer out of your house. And you know what a wonderful cook she is."

Pastor Bergman patted his rotund stomach absently, giving credence to Rose's words, then looked in bewilderment at the duke, clearly taken aback by the woman's convoluted reasoning. "Is what Rose Elizabeth tells me true, your grace? You are not living in sin, and she is your housekeeper?"

Rose looped her arm through Alexander's and stared up at him with an innocent smile. But he didn't miss the hint of warning in her eyes that said she would make his life miserable if he gainsaid her words.

As if she could make me more miserable than I already am, he thought.

"We reside in separate rooms, Pastor. I am a gentleman and would never besmirch the young lady's honor.

"And let me assure you that I have counseled"—*shouted, begged, pleaded,* he wanted to say—"Miss Martin on the foolishness of her decision to remain on the farm, but she has chosen not to take my advice and is currently performing the duties of housekeeper. For how much longer, I am uncertain." He cast Rose a warning look of his own.

"Rose has always been the most headstrong of her sisters, I'm afraid, your grace," the pastor remarked, clearly dismayed by the young woman's independent streak. "Since Ezra died, and Heather's gone off to San Francisco and Laurel to Denver, she's become more difficult than ever. I worry for her spiritual well-being. Eternal damnation looms on the horizon." He pointed heavenward.

Rose sighed. "I doubt I'm going to be struck down anytime soon, Pastor Bergman, but I do thank you for looking out for my soul. Now, if you gentlemen will excuse me, I'd like to pay a call on a friend." With a curt nod, she extracted her hand from Alexander's arm, spun on her heel, and headed down the main street.

Alexander was no more sorry to see her go than he was to see the pastor occupied with one of his other parishoners. He quickly made his own departure, heading to the livery stable at the end of town.

Although Salina was situated in the middle of nowhere, it had an air of prosperity about it. The arrival of the railroad had increased its worth in the greater scheme of things, and as he made his way down the wooden sidewalk, Alexander noted that several new buildings were presently under construction or being remodeled.

Some were false-fronted, appearing substantial and imposing even if they were not. One, the Farmers' and Merchants' Bank, actually was, owing to the fact that it was one of the few buildings in town constructed of brick.

The hardware store displayed an assortment of rifles and hand tools and looked to have everything from ammunition to a large variety of boots and shoes, both men's and women's.

The butcher shop featured a plump turkey hanging in the window, while the milliner's next door proudly displayed a colorful array of ladies' hats.

As the duke passed Mellon's Mercantile, he wondered fleetingly if pretty Peggy Mellon was inside helping her father stock the dry goods. He fought the urge to see for himself. He hadn't missed the blatant invitation she had given him yesterday, or the way her large breasts had felt pressed into his arm.

Alexander had a weakness for large breasts, and he knew with a certainty that it would one day be his ruination.

Spotting the livery up ahead, he heaved a sigh of relief, relishing the opportunity to concentrate on four-legged beasts rather than plump breasts.

The heels of Rose Elizabeth's high-button shoes clicked along the sidewalk, the rapid staccato rhythm mirroring the anger pumping through her body as she made her way to Heller's Bakery.

The duke's veiled threat that she wouldn't be living at the farm much longer incensed her, making her even more determined to stay.

If that arrogant, pompous, self-inflated bag of wind thought he'd rid himself of her so easily, he had another think coming!

And he couldn't lie worth horse droppings. His face had actually blotched red when he'd told Pastor Bergman of their living arrangements and that he had no intention of besmirching her honor.

Besmirching. Who on God's earth used words like that!

By the way he had stared at her on occasion, as if he could see how she looked without her combination on, it was as obvious as the patrician nose on his aristocratic face that Alexander Warrick had every intention of doing some besmirching.

Not that Rose Elizabeth was totally opposed to that idea. She had given the duke's soft lips and naked body a great deal of consideration. And if she was truthful with herself, which she usually was, she had to admit that making love with Alexander Warrick was not an altogether displeasing notion.

However, displeasing or not, it would not be the smartest thing to do under the present circumstances—and Rose considered herself practical above all else—bearing in mind the fact that she wanted Alexander gone from her property and her life.

The bell over the door tinkled as Rose entered the bakery. Rebecca was nowhere in sight, but she recognized Seamus O'Flynn as he came forward to assist her, his smile widening as he recalled their previous acquaintance.

"Miss Martin, how nice to see you again. What brings you to town? Is Alexander—I mean, is the duke with you?"

She shook her head. "He's gone to buy a horse. Apparently he doesn't find Muriel to his liking."

"Muriel being your horse, I take it?" He smiled at her earnest expression.

"I admit she's a bit swaybacked and long in the tooth, but he was so darn rude about her. And she's been in the family for years. Thank goodness Muriel didn't overhear the duke's callous remarks. She's very sensitive about such things."

"You'll be needin' to excuse the duke on occasion, Miss Martin. For a man brimming over with social graces, sometimes he speaks without thinking. He's never had to mind what he says, him being a duke and all, and his tactless remarks tend to get him into trouble."

"Have you known Alexander long?" Rose found herself suddenly curious about the duke's personal life, and the Irishman evidently knew him well.

Seamus shrugged, coming around the side of the counter to stand beside Rose Elizabeth. "Long enough to know that he's not going to be changing his ways anytime soon. He's had all that nobility drilled into him since birth. He can't be helping it if he thinks he's a bit better than everyone else. It's what he's been told since he wore nappies."

Rose smiled, then looked about the room for some sign of her friend. "Is Rebecca here? I was hoping to pay my respects to her and Mr. Heller before I returned home. I'm so glad they were able to reopen the bakery."

"She's at prayer meeting with the old man. I'm not sure when they'll be returning."

"How do you like working here at the bakery instead of for the duke? I'm sure Alexander would rather have you living with him instead of me. We don't get on all that well."

Seamus threw back his head and laughed, a deep, hearty sound that Rose Elizabeth found quite infectious. "I don't doubt it, lass. Alexander isn't the easiest person to get along with. He's used to getting his own way, he is. But I cannot imagine him wanting to have a boring gent like meself living with him, instead of a bonny lass like you. And I'll be helping him out when the need arises. Besides, you're much prettier."

Rose's cheeks filled with color. She wanted to thank the kind Irishman, but before she could get the first word out, the bakery door slammed opened and Alexander came rushing in. He was breathing heavily, as if he'd just run a foot race.

"Quick! Pull down the shades. I don't want those crazed women to know where I've run off to."

Seamus went to the window and peered out, chuckling when he saw the group of women standing in the middle of the street. They were looking every which way in search of their prey, the Duke of Moreland. He pulled down the shades. "Your popularity knows no bounds, your grace."

Rose Elizabeth giggled. "I told you Euphemia was like a racehorse. Speaking of which: Did you buy your horse?"

Alexander appeared quite pleased with himself. "He's still at the livery. We'll need to pick him up before we leave, if Sven doesn't mind making a stop."

"I'm sure I can convince him, your grace." She tilted her head in a flirtatious manner.

Alexander's expression darkened. "No doubt. The man was practically drooling all over you on the way in to town. It was damned unseemly, if you ask me."

"Well, nobody did, your dukeship."

Seamus listened to this exchange with great interest and was inordinately pleased by the fact that Rose Elizabeth was no simpering miss. She gave the duke as good as she got, which was not setting well with Alexander.

"How's everything at the farm, your grace? Are you learning a great deal about farming?"

Rose let loose a loud guffaw, and the duke's cheeks crimsoned. "He's hopeless. He should hang up his fiddle and return to England before he gets himself maimed. The cow practically trampled him to death, and he's squeamish about pigs."

"She wants to castrate the damn things!" Alexander replied in disgust. "And only the males. Can you imagine, Seamus? The woman wants to castrate poor defenseless animals."

"It would be a wee bit difficult for her to castrate the females, your grace, seeing as how they're not suitably equipped." Seamus bit back his smile.

"Finally, someone who knows a little something about farming." Rose cast the duke a scathing look that said quite clearly that he didn't.

"I was raised on a farm, lass. But that was a long while ago. I doubt I'd be any more proficient now than Alexander."

She harrumphed. "That wouldn't take much, Mr. O'Flynn. Believe me."

"If you two are through discussing my failings, and if the

coast is clear, I think we had better depart, Rose Elizabeth. It's a long drive back to the farm."

"If you'd like to ride ahead on that fancy horse you purchased, feel free, your grace. Sven and I can manage quite nicely without you."

Though his smile was affable, Alexander's eyes were intent with purpose. "I wouldn't dream of leaving you and the Swede alone, Rose Elizabeth. It wouldn't be proper."

Rose's eyebrow arched. "Have you set yourself up as my chaperon, your grace? And have you forgotten that his children will be with us?"

"Pastor Bergman has entrusted you into my care, Rose Elizabeth. And since you're intent upon living under my roof, then I'm afraid as head of the household I must look out for your welfare. I intend to take my duties very seriously."

Rose chuckled, and Seamus grinned, but Alexander remained stone-faced.

"You're joshin' me, ain't you, your highness?" Rose laughed again. "You really had me going for a minute."

Taking Rose's arm firmly, he led her to the door. "I assure you, Rose, I've never been more serious about anything in my life."

CHAPTER 6

The old swing creaked, and the crickets chirped their strange mating call, filling the warm night air with comforting sound. Glittering stars blanketed the boundless heavens, and the swish of tall prairie grass whispered through the wind.

Kicking out with her bare foot, Rose pushed the swing into motion. She loved this time of evening, when the supper dishes were done and the most pressing chore she had was to decide how she would amuse herself.

Kansas really shone at night.

The state had its faults, there was no denying that. It was too hot, too dry, too flat, and too harsh on its inhabitants. But it was also beautiful in its simplicity and in the eerie vastness that surrounded those who lived there. She loved it.

"I don't believe I've seen a more serene look on your face."

Rose Elizabeth smiled up at the duke as he approached, then scooted over to make a place for him on the swing that her father had lovingly fashioned for his daughters so many years ago.

"I was just thinking about how much I love it here."

74

He gazed into the darkness, attempting to see what she saw, but he could not. "Perhaps you're right. Perhaps you do have to be born here to appreciate this land. I confess to missing aged oak trees, cooling rains, and acres and acres of green. The heat, the blasted mosquitoes"—he slapped at one of the pesky insects as it landed on his bare forearm—"make it deuced uncomfortable here in Kansas."

"The land grows on you, your grace. The wind blows through your body and you become one with it. The heat and the cold temper your soul until you can withstand just about anything the good Lord throws your way.

"Some days you wake up to find that hail has flattened your crop, or that fire is creeping through the grass, threatening all you have worked for, and you wonder if it's worth it, if you shouldn't just pack up and go somewhere else. But then you stand with your hand shielding your face from the scorching glare of the sun, staring out at ripened fields of golden wheat swaying gently in the breeze that never stops blowing, and you know you're here to stay."

There was a wistfulness in his voice as he said, "I envy your caring so much about something, Rose Elizabeth. I lost that capacity a long time ago."

She turned to study Alexander as he continued to look straight ahead, a thoughtful expression on his face, and she wondered if he was thinking about a woman. "Why is it you've never married? I'd have thought you would want an heir for your dukedom. Isn't that the way things go in England?"

"I was engaged to be married. But it died a natural death, as I wish my fiancée had."

She reached out to grasp his forearm in a gesture of consolation. "How dreadful! I'm so sorry."

Alexander thought to correct her misinterpretation but decided against it. Jessica was part of his past, and he wanted to leave her there. Besides, to talk of the circumstances surrounding his hasty departure from England would only reopen the wounds that were finally beginning to heal—wounds that would disappear only if his engagement was set aside.

It was a match doomed to failure from the onset. He and Jessica had never loved each other. But he had been pressured by his family to find a wife and enlarge the Warrick holdings, something both his father and grandfather had done. A bitter irony, he reflected, considering the fact of his sterility and his fiancée's penchant for mating with just about anything in pants.

Her dalliance with his brother, Edward, had been the final straw, and Alexander had been unable to look the other way. His pride and self-respect couldn't sustain such a blow, and so he had fled.

"I've learned to accept what cannot be changed," he finally replied.

"I was devastated when my pa died. He was very dear to me and my sisters, so I know how you feel."

"I doubt you do, but I thank you anyway for your kind sentiments." He noted the confusion on her face and quickly changed the subject. "Shall we talk of something more pleasant, like why you want to be a wheat farmer? It seems a hard life for a woman."

"Life's different here, your grace. Woman are free to own the land and work it. They're not dependent on their husbands or families for support. We were raised to make our own way in the world." That wasn't entirely true, but she doubted that the duke was acquainted with American custom, and she wanted him to think that independence was a God-given right, not something to be administered by the whim of man.

And she supposed that American women did have a great deal more freedom than their English counterparts. Western women certainly had more freedom and independence than did the ladies back East.

Her face grew animated as she warmed to her topic. "My two sisters are off doing just that. Heather's in San Francisco hoping to find a job as an illustrator for a magazine or newspaper, and Laurel's got it in her head to sing for a fancy opera

house. Of course, Laurel's not as talented as Heather and may
have a bit more difficulty finding a job."

Rose's sigh was pragmatic. "Both have the looks and figure that I was never blessed with, so I'm sure they'll do just
fine."

Alexander's eyes widened at Rose's disparaging opinion of
her attributes. "You're quite lovely, Rose. I can't believe you
think so little of yourself."

"I've always been the weed in the wildflower patch, your
dukeship, so you needn't bother with false flattery. I've
learned to live with the fact that I'm not as beautiful or talented as my sisters."

" 'A weed is no more than a flower in disguise,' " he said,
quoting the words of James Russell Lowell, then he placed a
warm kiss on her hand.

Rose blushed all the way to her tingling fingertips and
pulled back her hand self-consciously. "You've got the petti-
est way of speaking I've ever heard, your grace. Do you Englishmen practice all that flowery prose, or does it just come
natural?"

Alexander's eyes twinkled as he noted her embarrassment.
Though she continually tried to hide her reactions behind blis-
tering rejoinders, her bright red earlobes were a definite giveaway.

Rose was a study in contradiction. Extremely intelligent,
she was still as innocent and unworldly as a newborn babe
about so many things. He found her delightfully refreshing,
and not the least bit jaded as were the women of his acquaintance back in England, including his vain, calculating, deceitful fiancée. Alexander doubted that Rose possessed a
dishonest bone in her body.

"It comes from years of reading and being tutored by a suc-
cession of pompous bores," he finally responded. "Perhaps
you will allow me to read to you some evening. Poetry is
quite lovely, and it will help pass the time."

She considered his request for a moment. "Maybe. But
most evenings I stitch on my quilt, or prepare my bread dough

for the next morning. But I might be able to listen while I work."

"There's much to be said for idle pursuits, Rose."

"I've no doubt you've had plenty of those, your dukeness. Noblemen are not known for the calluses on their hands."

He picked up her hand again and stroked it softly, curious as to what her reaction would be. Seduction was an art form in his world, and he hadn't had much practice of late. And seducing Rose Elizabeth was very much on his mind. She was an enticing, lovely young woman, albeit a bit headstrong and challenging. And Alexander hadn't been challenged by anyone in a long, long while.

"Soft hands can bring much pleasure when applied to certain areas of the body, Rose Elizabeth." His finger traced up her arm, then her neck, and Rose thought she was going to dissolve into the swing and become one with it.

"I'd best be going in," she said in a voice she thought too shrill to possibly be her own. "It's late. And it's hotter than a fried rabbit out here. The house'll be much cooler."

"Pity. I was so enjoying our conversation."

Rose was pretty certain that some *besmirching* was going to enter into their conversation if she didn't hightail it into the house directly. "Tomorrow's another day, your grace."

Alexander smiled thoughtfully, realizing for the first time that he was happy she would be part of his tomorrows.

The rain had started shortly after midnight. It had begun as a soft drizzle against the windows, but now it lashed hard at the glass panes, driven by strong winds and a desire to quench the parched earth.

Snuggled beneath her covers and immune to nature's vagaries, Rose didn't hear the roar of the wind, but she did feel the first drop of rain splash onto her face.

With practiced ease, she bolted upright and snatched her wrapper all in one motion. A glance at the muslin sheeting that covered the ceiling confirmed her worst fears.

The duke's horrified scream confirmed his.

"Bloody hell! Help me! Oh my God, I'm drowning!"

She rushed to his room to find him still in his bed, buried beneath the wet muslin. The sudden downpour had eaten through the sod roof and collected in the sheeting. Gravity being what it was, the whole thing had collapsed in a heap onto the Duke of Moreland. He lay screeching epithets Rose had heard previously only at her father's poker games, as he flayed his legs and arms about, trying to escape his sodden prison.

Pulling hard on the muslin sheeting, she managed to free the outraged nobleman, who continued to sputter curse words and was covered with a goodly amount of dirt and debris.

If his expression hadn't been so pitiable, she would have burst out laughing. "Your grace!" She attempted to inflict just the right amount of alarm in her voice. "Are you all right?" She bit down hard on her lower lip at the fulminating look he cast her.

"Of course I'm not all right! I nearly drowned in my bed. What kind of home is this, where a man can't even rely on a roof over his head to protect him from the elements? I'm bloody cursed, that's what I am."

"I suggest you grab some dry woolies and meet me in the kitchen, your dukeness. Your surly attitude will no doubt improve once you've had a hot cup of coffee to warm your innards."

Alexander entered the main room moments later, but Rose could see from his dark scowl that his mood hadn't improved in the least. She gave silent thanks that the roof here seemed to be holding and was not in any danger of falling in, though it had in the past on numerous occasions.

Soddies could withstand fire and Indian arrows, but heavy downpours of rain were another matter.

The duke took a seat at the table, and she placed a steaming mug of coffee in front of him. "Feeling better? It's always hardest the first time."

He shot her a scathing look. "I am not a virgin, madam," he

said, and Rose blushed. "Nor am I a child to be placated. This humble abode of yours is unfit for human habitation; it's a disaster waiting to happen. We're like animals burrowing in the ground, and I am going to rectify that come morning."

His words caused panic to set in, and Rose paled. "What do you mean? Surely you have no intention of destroying the only home I have ever known. I was born in the bedroom where you sleep. This soddy was Ma and Pa's. It's all I have left of them."

Her attempt to cling to the past touched him, but he remained firm in his conviction. "I don't mean to be callous, Rose Elizabeth, but even you must admit that this is not a proper home for an Englishman ... or an American. I intend to build a fine new home, and I intend to begin preparations immediately." And he intended to level that blasted soddy to the ground from which it was built.

"Just because a little rain fell on your head is no reason to get all hysterical, your grace. We Kansans have learned to live with the elements, and so will you, in time."

"I prefer living in comfort, Rose Elizabeth. And if you don't care to witness progress in the making, then you are more than welcome to leave. After all, this is my home now, and I must make it fit to live in."

Her eyes sparked fury. "This is just another way to try and get rid of me, isn't it, your most deviousness? Well, it won't work. I have no intention of leaving here. If you insist on playing the role of tenderfoot and pilgrim, of a useless fancy-pants nobleman who can't withstand a little discomfort, then I'm going to be here to witness your humiliation.

"I thought you might be changing for the better, Alexander, but I can see that your neck is as stiff as ever."

The duke sighed as he watched Rose march out. With her sodden nightgown and wrapper trailing behind her, she looked like a regal countess making a grand exit, and he wondered if she knew how damn enticing she looked with her dark hair hanging about her shoulders in disarray, her wet clothing plastered to her body, outlining her rigid nipples and ample breasts.

His erect member pressed painfully against his pants; even the cold of the damp fabric couldn't lessen the effect Rose had on him. Though he played the role of seducer, he was the one being seduced.

If only his decision to build a new house would have forced her to leave . . .

If only he didn't have a burning desire to throw her down on the ground and make mad passionate love to her every time he saw her . . .

If only he wasn't such a bloody, blasted fool!

"I think you should go wid Seamus, daughter. The outing will do you good, and I can handle things here at the bakery."

"But, Papa . . ."

Rebecca paused at the determined look her father cast her. He obviously wanted her to drive out to the Martin farm with Seamus O'Flynn, but she had no idea why. It wasn't like him to send her off unchaperoned with a man. She didn't relish the idea of having to be in close proximity to Seamus for several hours, with nothing to do but talk and sit close to him.

Working with Seamus at the bakery was difficult enough, but at least there she could keep her distance, keep her hands busy, and keep her thoughts on something other than the Irishman's broad shoulders and infectious grin.

Rebecca was aware of Seamus O'Flynn as more than just an employee, and it frightened her. She tried again to reason with her father: "You have not been well, Papa, and there have been more customers of late. I don't think—"

"We won't be gone that long, lass," Seamus interrupted, having noted the frustration on the old man's face. "The duke wants me to bring supplies for the new house he's going to build. It'll be a quick trip out and back. If we leave now, we should be back before nightfall."

And if we aren't . . . ? Rebecca worried her lower lip at the possibility.

"Do not refuse me this, Rebecca. Your health is also important, and you have been working much too hard. Mr. O'Flynn's efforts to increase business have proven fruitful, and we have many new customers now. But you have been working long hours to accommodate their orders, and I won't have you falling ill, too."

An idea took hold, and Rebecca's face suddenly brightened as she thought of a way to see Rose Martin again without having to be alone with Seamus. "Perhaps you can come with us, Papa." She stared at Seamus for confirmation.

"You're more than welcome, Mr. Heller. We can put up the Closed sign for the remainder of the day. And I know the duke would enjoy meeting you."

The old man scoffed at the idea. "Young people need time alone to enjoy themselves. We get too soon old—und too late smart. Go. Visit wid your friends. I am old and would just be in the way. Besides, I look forward to a little time by myself without Rebecca hovering over me as if I am a small child."

The rest of Rebecca's arguments fell on deaf ears, and she soon found herself seated next to Seamus on the wagon seat, headed to the Martin farm.

The sun beat down hard and hot, and Rebecca's dark clothing seemed to absorb every smothering ray of it. She dabbed at her forehead with a handkerchief.

"Are you feeling uncomfortable, lass? I'm sorry that we have no shade to sit beneath. A buggy would have been nicer, but then I wouldn't have been able to haul them pieces of lumber Alexander wanted."

"I am fine. I do not wilt in the sun like a flower. Papa says we come from strong German stock. I guess that is so."

Seamus grinned. "You might not wilt, lass, but I'm thinking that I could melt right off this seat if we don't reach the farm soon. I'm not used to this hot weather. Back in Ireland it's cool. The breeze swirls about you like a mist. Everything's lovely and green as shamrocks, just like your eyes, lass."

Rebecca felt her cheeks warm, and it didn't have a thing to do with the scorching temperature. "Pennsylvania is green too, Seamus. I miss it very much."

"Why did you come here, lass? I hear there are many who practice your religion in Pennsylvania."

"We came for the land. We did not own the farm we worked at home. We were only tenants. The lure of free land was too much temptation for my father and others like him, so we came to Kansas to begin again."

Seamus nodded in understanding. "Aye, I know what it's like to farm the land for others, with nothing to show at year's end but a wee bit of money and a sore back. Owning your own place is far preferable, that's for certain."

A strong gust of wind nearly blew Rebecca's bonnet off, and she retied it before asking, "But you do not own your own land, Seamus. You are content to work for others. Why is that?"

He shrugged and flicked the reins, urging the horses to pick up their pace. "I was sick and tired of farming. Young men need adventure, and that's what I sought. I met Alexander at a boxing match in Dublin. We hit it off, so to speak, after I knocked him out in three rounds." He smiled at his pun, not noticing Rebecca's frown at the mention of the fight. "The duke offered me a chance to see the world and I took it. I've not regretted it, up until now."

"What has changed? Do you tire of the adventure?"

"I'm thinking that it's time for me to be settling down and having a brood of children. I've been yearning for a home and family of me own. I'm tired of wandering with no direction. It's time I put down roots."

Uncomfortable with the turn the conversation had taken, Rebecca squirmed in her seat. Seamus wanted the same things she did, but he was not one of her kind, did not share the same beliefs. That fact had just been made obvious again by his mention of the boxing match. Rebecca had heard of men who fought for money, but it was an alien, forbidden concept to her.

They were very different in so many ways, but even if they hadn't been, it was frowned upon to marry outside her religion. Of those who did it was said that they "went gay" and they were not welcomed among the Plain folk again.

Though she could see herself married to a man like Seamus O'Flynn, imagine herself in his bed and bearing his children, she could not give up the only identity she had ever known; she could not toss aside the teachings of her church, her family, for a lifetime of pleasure and happiness. Unless . . .

She stared at Seamus's strong profile beneath lowered lashes and heard herself ask, "What church do you attend, Seamus? I've noticed you haven't gone since coming to work for us."

"I was raised Catholic, lass. Most Irish are of that faith. But I haven't been what you would call faithful to my persuasion in the past few years. Me blessed mother would take a stick to me if she knew."

Rebecca's lips spread into a soft smile. "Mothers around the world are not so very different. I've had my share of switchings. Mama used to make me get the strongest hickory stick I could find and bring it to her."

"A pity, I'm thinkin', to mar an inch of that perfect flesh, lass." With a devilish grin, he winked at her.

"You are a flatterer, Seamus O'Flynn. Perhaps you have kissed that Blarney Stone I have read about."

Seamus threw back his head and laughed, and the sound of it echoed across the prairie for miles.

Seamus pulled the wagon to a halt. Across the yard, Rose Elizabeth was shouting obscenities at the duke and flailing her arms, and it looked to Seamus as if she might haul off and punch Alexander a good one at any moment.

"Oh, dear!" Rebecca's cheeks flamed at the vile words she heard Rose Elizabeth fling at the duke, and she cupped her face to still the heat. "I think we have come at the wrong time,

Seamus. Rose Elizabeth and the duke appear to be having a disagreement."

"There's no good time to avoid that, lass. Those two fight like gamecocks, circling and spitting at one another. I've never seen a more stubborn pair of people in my life." *Or two more suited,* he thought.

Rose Elizabeth's pronouncement that the Duke of Moreland was "a sad sack of horse manure" returned Seamus's attention to the sparing duo.

"That is the most ridiculous contraption I have ever laid eyes on, your denseness," Rose Elizabeth accused. "How on earth is one supposed to bathe standing up? It's ridiculous. Has the sun completely addled your brain?"

Alexander adjusted the wooden-plank door of the shower stall and smiled, quite pleased that he'd been able to construct a working shower with just a few pieces of leftover pipe and wood he'd discovered in the barn. No more sitting cramped in the tub for him, he thought.

"Once you've used the device, Rose Elizabeth, I promise you'll never go back to that rusted tub again. It's barbaric to have to fit one's backside into that confining piece of tin."

"You could have gone down to the river to bathe, if it was so disagreeable, your magesticness."

"And walk two miles to get there? No thank you. I much prefer to use my clever imagination and skill to construct a few modern conveniences, which, I might add, are sadly lacking here."

"You won't be happy until you change everything about this place, will you? You'll take everything good about the farm and alter it to your highfalutin ways."

The two combatants were oblivious to their visitors' presence, and Seamus could tell by the bright color staining Rebecca's cheeks that she was growing increasingly mortified by the minute. Deciding that something needed to be done, Seamus cleared his throat loudly.

Alexander turned, then grinned widely as he spied the couple. "We have guests, Rose Elizabeth."

Rose followed his gaze and ran forward to greet her friend. "Rebecca, how wonderful it is to see you again! You too, Seamus," she added, smiling at the Irishman.

"The duke neglected to tell me you were coming. I'd have prepared something a tad fancier than rabbit stew if he had." Though she knew Alexander would have been awfully disappointed if she hadn't prepared the stew. He'd been proud as a strutting peacock this morning when he'd returned home from his daily hunting expedition with two jackrabbits and a prairie chicken slung over his saddle. As he had explained on numerous occasions, the hunt was everything to an Englishman, even if there were no foxes to hound.

Rebecca returned Rose's hug, pleased by the unexpected display of affection, then introduced herself to the duke. "We cannot stay for your wonderful meal, Rose Elizabeth. My father is alone. He has not been feeling well, and I must return to the bakery as soon as Seamus is done delivering the supplies."

"Well, come inside with me and I'll fix something quick, so you and Seamus can eat before heading back to town. I've got ham left over from breakfast."

Rebecca presented a wicker basket. "I've brought some freshly baked bread, though I'm sure you have plenty of your own."

"I do. But there's nothing quite as good as eating food someone else has prepared." Rose winked at the thoughtful woman, then grabbed the basket and her hand in one deft motion and dragged her into the house.

Alexander watched the two women disappear and shook his head in disbelief. Rose's anger had dissipated as quickly as water on the sun-baked earth, and he wondered if he'd ever grow used to her volatile moods.

"I see you've upset the sprightly lass again," Seamus remarked as he removed the lumber from the rear of the wagon and stacked it beneath a stand of trees. "I take it Rose Elizabeth is none too happy about your plan to build a new house."

"I nearly drowned the other night in a storm because of the

deplorable condition of that soddy. It's bad enough that I've been reduced to performing manual labor on this wretched estate, but I'll not live like some common farmhand to suit Rose Elizabeth. Though no doubt she'd like nothing better than to see me brought down to her common level. Well, she is just going to have to get used to some changes around here. I'm determined to build us a fine new house."

"*Us,* is it? I thought you were intent on getting rid of the woman. Has she become indispensable to you, then?" Seamus delighted in the color filling the duke's cheeks.

"No woman is indispensable. But Rose is knowledgeable about the farm, and about farming wheat, and I'd be a fool not to admit that I can use her expertise in those matters." Though he'd die before admitting that to her.

"And will you be intent on using her for anything else, your grace?" The accusation hung heavily between them. "The lass is as green as this wood, and you're engaged to another. It wouldn't be right, taking advantage of her."

"I'm well aware of my responsibilities concerning both, and I don't need any reminders, Seamus." Nor did he want to be reminded that nothing permanent could come of a relationship with Rose Elizabeth. He would return to England one day to face the consequences of his actions. He would still have to marry and secure his place in society, if for no other reason than to make certain his younger, wastral of a brother, Edward, didn't usurp the duke's birthright. And even if Rose Elizabeth was willing to leave Kansas and her farm, which was extremely doubtful, he could never marry beneath his station, marry someone totally unsuited and unskilled in the ways of the nobility.

But knowing this did not lessen his desire for Rose Elizabeth, did not turn him away from his goal of bringing her to his bed.

Finally, he retorted, "And you would do well to reflect upon your own motives for working at the bakery, Seamus. I know you're not that fond of bread."

Seamus threw back his head and laughed. "No, your grace,

I'm not. But at least me intentions are honorable. Can you say the same?"

Guilt flushed the duke's face a deeper shade of red, and he stomped off toward the wagon without uttering the denial Seamus was hoping to hear.

"It's so wonderful to have a female to visit with," Rose told Rebecca as she set the ham and sliced bread on the gingham tablecloth. "It gets a mite tiring talking and arguing with the duke all the time. I've never met a more stubborn, bullheaded man in all my days."

"He seems very nice."

" 'Nice is as nice does,' Mama always said. And you just think he's nice because you've only just met him. Wait until you've been around Alexander for a while. I tell you the man is exasperating as all get-out."

"Mr. O'Flynn is not like that," Rebecca said softly, and Rose didn't miss the dreamy expression on her face. "He's very considerate and extremely helpful to me and my father."

"You make a fine-looking couple, Rebecca. A woman could do worse than that big hulking Irishman."

Rebecca's cheeks colored to match the curtains at the window, and she shook her head in denial. "Ours is not a romantic relationship, Rose Elizabeth. It could never be."

There was a wealth of regret in those words, which made Rose ask, "And why not? You're both healthy and strong. And as far as I know, Seamus O'Flynn is not married or engaged to anyone else."

"He's not Plain, Rose Elizabeth. It is not considered acceptable to marry outside of our faith."

Rose thought about that problem for a moment. "My mama always said that nothing worth having ever comes easy. All you need do is make Seamus O'Flynn Plain. How hard could that be?"

Rebecca plopped down onto a chair. "I have only recently thought the same thing, Rose Elizabeth. But Seamus has given no hint that he is interested in being more than friends. And he is of another faith. It wouldn't be right to make him change his beliefs for mine."

"There's only one God, as far as I can tell. What difference does it matter how you worship him, as long as you do? Mennonite, Catholic, Methodist—it's all the same. I don't see that there's a problem, unless you make one."

Rebecca envied Rose Elizabeth's pragmatism. To Rose, no problem was insurmountable, no situation too difficult to solve. *If only things were that simple,* Rebecca thought.

She tried to explain. "It would be like you trying to become an English noblewoman, Rose Elizabeth. Some people are not cut from the same cloth."

"Amen to that!" Rose agreed, thinking that she and the duke were cut from entirely different bolts. "But we're not talking about his lordship and me, we're talking about you and that handsome Irishman. You two are cut from the same cloth, Rebecca. Your clothing's just been sewn differently, that's all."

Rebecca looked clearly confused and not the least bit convinced, so Rose decided to clarify things once and for all. "Mama always said: 'A stone stops rollin' when it finds the kind of moss it wants to gather.' My mama was very rarely wrong, Rebecca."

CHAPTER 7

Sven arrived early the following morning, carting a hammer, a saw, and an odd assortment of tools in the back of his wagon. Alexander was in the barn, doing his best not to torture the cows while he attempted to milk them. He didn't observe the Swede's arrival, but Rose Elizabeth did as she stared out the kitchen window, wondering what was taking the duke so long and if her cows were surviving the ordeal of his milking them.

In the yard, Rose greeted Sven, who was dressed in his familiar denim bib overalls, but her welcoming smile melted when she noticed the hammer and saw he carried. "Just what do you think you're doing, Sven Anderson?" Her hands rode her hips indignantly and accusation flared bright in her eyes.

Puzzled by the woman's angry tone, Sven stepped forward cautiously. "I have come to help vid the house, Rose Elizabet. I hear the duke is building a new home, and he vill need some help."

"Don't you dare help him, Sven Anderson, or I will never speak to you again. The duke wants to tear down my home and build a fancy new one. If you're truly my friend, you won't help him do that." She had already put the word out in town that anyone offering assistance to the duke would not be looked upon kindly by her. Apparently, Sven had not been easily intimidated.

"It would be unneighborly of me not to offer my help, Rose Elizabet. And it is not like you to be so angry, or so strong in your feelings against someone who needs a helping hand. You are usually the first to offer support to a neighbor."

Sven's words made Rose feel sheepish and small, but she couldn't help how she felt. She tried to explain. "He's taking away my life, Sven. This is where I belong." She pointed to the soddy. "It's my home."

The blond man clasped her hand in his callused palm. "You could have a new life, Rose Elizabet. You could share mine and the boys'. You know that, don't you?"

Sven had made no secret of his wish to marry her. And Rose had honestly thought that one day they would. But things seemed different now—now that the duke had come.

"I know we've talked of joining our two farms, Sven, but now that is impossible."

"I want you for yourself, Rose Elizabet. Not for your land." His arm came about her shoulder, and he kissed her forehead, then her cheek. "I would make you a good husband. We could make many babies, *ja*?"

Alexander pulled up short, raw jealousy ripping through him at the sight of the Swede holding Rose Elizabeth close and kissing her, at the idea that Sven Anderson was capable of giving Rose Elizabeth a child and brazen enough to brag about it.

His hands clenched hard into fists. Too late he remembered the pail he held, which clattered noisily to the ground, spilling all the milk he'd worked so hard to get from the stingy cows.

"Good heavens, Alexander!" she cried at the sight of the white liquid blanketing the ground. "Watch what you're doing."

"I could suggest the same to you, madam."

A wealth of censure spiked his words, and Rose, whose dander was already up, responded to it. "Unlike you, your dukeness, I know perfectly well what I'm doing." She clasped Sven's arm, and Alexander's eyes darkened to cobalt.

In an effort to calm himself, he sucked in his breath and came forward, forcing a smile as he held out his hand to his neighbor. "Good morning, Sven. What brings you here so early in the day?" No doubt the Swede thought to play patty cake with Rose Elizabeth while his back was turned. No wonder she had given him so many unpleasant chores to do this morning. Her meeting with the Swede had probably been pre-arranged.

With an uneasy, sidelong glance at Rose, Sven replied, "I have heard you are making a new house, Alexander. I have come to help with the building of it."

Surprise touched Alexander's visage—surprise and a large measure of shame that warmed his face and neck. "That's generous of you, man. I welcome all the help I can get. It seems no one in town is the least bit interested in earning a wage. I'll have to hire laborers from the East to get the job done." He certainly wasn't going to get any help from Rose Elizabeth. She'd made that abundantly clear, even going so far as to suggest that she might sabotage his construction efforts, that his plans would be for naught.

Spying the lumber spread out on the ground to the left of the soddy and the round keg of nails, Sven scratched his head in bewilderment. "You have plenty of money, Alexander, so why did you not buy a mail-order house? It would have been much easier to construct."

"A mail-order house? I've never heard of such a thing."

"There's a man in Chicago—Lyman Bridges is his name. He makes houses with the parts already made. You just assemble everything once it arrives." He pulled a catalog from his back pocket and handed it to the duke, and Rose's frown deepened as the word *traitor* came to mind.

"This is where you can buy them."

As he studied the drawings of the various structures, which

included not only houses but churches as well, Alexander's eyes widened. One could purchase a three-bedroom home, complete with parlor, porch, dining room, and kitchen, for $1,850, and all hardware and materials were included. "This is incredible. I wish I had known."

"I've heard it takes several months to get everything," Sven said, "and you probably don't want to wait that long."

Ignoring Rose Elizabeth's rude snort, Alexander turned to look at the soddy. "Not one minute more than I have to, my good man, which is why I've decided not to wait for professional help. If I can learn to slop hogs," he smiled ferally at Rose Elizabeth, "I can bloody well learn to build a house. Shall we get to work?"

"I hear the duke's building a fine new house, Rose Elizabeth. I guess that means you'll be leaving for Mrs. Caffrey's School sooner than you expected."

Rose bit back the nasty retort on the tip of her tongue and looked around Mellon's Mercantile. She studied the rack of ready-made dresses on the far wall and the glass display case that held assorted handkerchiefs, combs, collars, and reticules. The farm implements hanging on the wall were nothing out of the ordinary, but she stared at those, too, then finally at the spiteful smile on Peggy Mellon's face, wishing she could seal those rosebud lips with glue.

"I'd like six yards of yellow gingham, please," she restated, a bit louder, just in case Peggy's hearing had suffered from listening to herself talk so much.

"My, my, aren't we touchy today," Peggy goaded, toying with the golden curls that cascaded over her right shoulder. "What's the matter? Hasn't the handsome duke been paying enough attention to you?"

"Unlike you, Peggy Mellon, I don't need the attention of every man in Salina, and that includes the Duke of Moreland."

"That's good. Because at Euphemia's welcoming party for

the duke next Saturday night, I intend to monopolize his lord-ship's time."

"What you do is your business. I couldn't care less. But I wouldn't be so smug about ensnaring Alexander Warrick. He isn't like the wet-behind-the-ears boys you're used to dallying with. I'd venture a guess that Alexander's taste runs a bit more refined."

"Which is probably why he hasn't gotten around to bed-ding you." Peggy punctuated her sharp reply by slapping the bolt of gingham down on the counter. "Any woman who'd live with a man, like you're living with the duke, and not take him to her bed, is a fool in my opinion."

Rose wondered for an instant whether she had VIRGIN stamped across her forehead in big bold letters.

"Isn't it fortunate that I have neither asked for nor desire your opinion. When I take a man to my bed it will be because I love him, not because I have the undying urge to rutt like a mare in heat, the way you do."

Peggy's eyes flashed blue lightning, but before she could utter another poisonous invective her father appeared from the back room, a friendly smile on his face.

The soiled apron around Tom Mellon's waist did little to disguise his rotund shape, and Rose Elizabeth was forced to remember one of the childish ditties she and her sisters used to sing about the portly shopkeeper: *"Mr. Mellon's belly shakes like apple jelly. When he sits down his big fat mound pours over his feet onto the ground."*

"Good day, Rose Elizabeth," he said. "Has Peggy taken care of all your needs?"

She smiled sweetly at her nemesis. "Actually, she hasn't, Mr. Mellon. I asked for six yards of the rose calico sitting on the back shelf, but Peggy keeps insisting on this horrible yel-low gingham."

Peggy gasped at the outright lie.

Like the true salesman he was, Tom Mellon *tsk*ed several times and wagged a chastising finger at his daughter. "Yellow is obviously not your color, Rose Elizabeth. Peggy should have known that right off. The calico is far more suitable. I'll cut it for you right away."

"That's what I kept trying to tell her, but she kept insisting on the gingham."

"What?" Peggy's eyes narrowed. "You—"

"Peggy!" the shopkeeper ordered, interrupting whatever his daughter was about to say. "Go in the back room and fetch the velvet ribbon that matches this material. It will look quite pretty with Rose Elizabeth's coloring." With one last hate-filled look at her rival, Peggy disappeared without another word.

Unfortunately for Rose Elizabeth, the ones Peggy had previously utttered had given her plenty to think about.

Sven paused, saw in one hand, and wiped the sweat from his brow with the other. "Where has Rose Elizabet been hiding herself, Alexander? I have not seen her all day."

Alexander moved his attention from the first-floor framing they had just completed and shrugged his shoulders. "She's like a woman possessed. All Rose has done from morning till night is sew on that flowered material she purchased a few days ago. I've hardly seen her myself, save for meals. And I can tell you, even those have suffered."

Sven arched a disbelieving brow. "Rose Elizabet is an excellent cook. She bakes bread for me and the boys in exchange for ice. I've never tasted better bread."

"She's a damned good cook," Alexander conceded. "But all we've had to eat all week is ham, cornmeal mush, and the like. What I wouldn't give for a taste of her fried chicken and those melt-in-your mouth biscuits."

"Rose Elizabet makes a dress for Miss Bloodsworth's party, *ja*?"

Alexander nodded. "It's all she can think about. I wasn't aware that she was enamored of Euphemia and the other ladies."

Bees droned noisily overhead, while two gray squirrels enjoyed a game of tag near the base of a tree. Sven ordered his children to quit playing with the dog and get into the back of the wagon.

"Rose Elizabet is a proud woman. She vorks hard on the dress so that she vill not be shamed by the ladies in town. They often make fun of her in their ignorance."

Alexander mulled over Sven's comments for a moment. "Rose acts as if she couldn't care less about what others think, but that is obviously a ruse." He stared at the soddy, wondering if she was still sewing her fingers to the bone. "I've heard some of Euphemia's comments." He frowned. "For such a small woman, she has a big mouth."

"The spinster is not cruel, just too opinionated for her own good. She likes to interfere in others' lives. Rose told me that she and her sisters never got along with the older woman."

"I wouldn't have agreed to attend that damn party if I'd known it would make Rose Elizabeth uncomfortable."

Sven squeezed the duke's shoulder in a gesture of comfort and companionship. "It is good for her to go. She vorks too hard and needs to enjoy herself once in a while. Besides, Rose Elizabeth has nothing to be ashamed of."

"You seem to know her well."

"I care for her," was the big man's reply, and that seemed to say it all. Though the duke couldn't fault Sven's loyalty to Rose, or even the fact that the man seemed to love her, Alexander didn't have to like it.

Thanking the man for another day of hard work, he waved him off and headed to the house.

"Boomer! You bad dog!"

Rose's screech became more distinct as Alexander drew closer to the house.

"Look what you've done to my new dress."

Alexander then observed Rose racing out of the house, hot on Boomer's trail. The back portion of her dress was partially missing. Boomer was definitely in trouble, and he felt almost sorry for the miserable dog.

"You stupid mutt!" Rose shouted, stopping her chase when Boomer disappeared around the side of the house. Bending over to retrieve the back panel of her gown, she winced at the sight of the half-chewed bow, which was to have been the crowning glory of her creation. "Damn, damn, and double damn!"

"I take it Boomer's been a naughty dog again?" Her look was so pitiable, he swallowed his smile.

She held out the panel and bow to Alexander. "He's ruined my dress for the party Saturday night. I won't be able to go."

"Nonsense. Of course you'll attend. You'll just repair what he's ruined."

She presented him her back, and Alexander got an enticing glimpse of Rose's underwear. "In case it's escaped your notice, your grace, a large portion of my dress is missing."

"Is there nothing you can do to fix it? Don't you have something else to wear?" He had no intention of going to Euphemia's party alone and placing himself in the middle of all those fawning biddies. Rose Elizabeth offered at least a modicum of protection, and he intended to have her there by his side.

"I'm not like those fancy ladies you're used to, your dukeness. My good dresses are limited to a few. They're fine for church, but I have nothing suitable for Euphemia's party, which is why I decided to sew a new one." It had become important to her to look as nice as Peggy always did in her store-bought gowns. She knew that Euphemia would be dressed in some gaudy creation, and the other ladies would likely follow her example in sheeplike fashion.

It continued to be a mystery to Rose Elizabeth how Euphemia had convinced the women of Salina that she was an arbiter of fashion and good taste.

Alexander rubbed his chin thoughtfully. Rose Elizabeth's plight was far different from that of his fiancée in England. Jessica would have had dozens of gowns to choose from in almost every color of the rainbow. And she was far less deserving than the hardworking woman who now stood before him looking so distraught.

"What time are you planning supper?" he asked, and Rose's eyes narrowed.

"Is eating all you can think about, your grace? I'm having a dire emergency and all you can think about is your stomach. How typically male." With one last, disgusted look, she stalked back into the house.

Alexander looked down at himself and cringed at the sight of his soiled garments. He was covered from head to toe with dust and sweat. Even to consider going to town in such a deplorable condition would have been unthinkable in Sussex.

But this was an emergency, as Rose had eloquently pointed out, so Alexander marched resolutely to the barn to retrieve his horse, without another thought to his slovenly appearance.

Rose paced angrily across the small confines of the sitting room, wondering where Alexander had ridden off to so many hours before. Darkness had settled over the land, and the fried chicken dinner she had worked so diligently to prepare was fast cooling on the stove. "Damn inconsiderate man!"

Hoofbeats sounded a few moments later, and she crossed to the window to look out, breathing a sigh of relief at the sight of Alexander riding into the yard.

She hurried to her rocker and settled there, so that he wouldn't think she'd been worried about him. A moment later, he entered.

"Well, it's about time, your grace. Here I went and fixed your favorite dinner, and it's practically ruined."

Rose sounded like an outraged wife, and Alexander had to bite back a smile as he shut the door behind him. Inhaling the enticing aroma of fried chicken, he cast an eager eye at the stove, his stomach rumbling in anticipation. "I won't be but a minute. I just need to wash off this grime."

"But where have you been? You've been gone for hours."

He shot her a cocky grin. "Miss me, did you?"

Rose Elizabeth fairly flew out of her rocking chair. "Certainly not! I hardly noticed you were gone. Except, of course, when it was time to do the chores. Then you were conspicuously absent."

He withdrew a wrapped parcel from behind his back and pressed it into her hands. "This is for you. I hope it will make up for my tardiness."

She looked at the package, then up at him. "What is it?"

"You'll have to open it to find out." He disappeared into his bedroom, leaving Rose staring at the unexpected gift.

With the eagerness of a child, she ripped off the twine and unwrapped the brown paper. Her eyes widened in disbelief as a mound of blue satin filled her hands. It felt sleek and smooth and was surely the most glorious thing she had ever touched in her life.

Awestruck, she held the dress out in front of her. It was a gown the likes of which she had never seen before. White lace edged the neckline, and a large blue satin bow graced the waist at the back and cascaded down upon the long flowing train, which, unfortunately, would require the wearing of a bustle.

Paused in the doorway, Alexander stared at the wonderment on her face, and his heart constricted in his chest. It was obvious that Rose had never before had such a fine garment as the one she held lovingly in her hands.

It hadn't been easy to persuade the dressmaker, Miss Fiona Pennypacker, to part with a gown she had created for another customer, but Alexander's generosity had won out.

"I take it from the rapturous expression on your face that you like the gown." She looked up, a brilliant smile lighting her face, and Alexander knew that his trip to town had been worth every tiring moment.

"It's the most beautiful creation I've ever laid eyes on. But you shouldn't have bought me such an expensive present, Alexander." Her smile faded a bit. "It isn't seemly for a woman to accept a gift from a man who is not her husband. Especially one as expensive as this must have been."

"Since when have you ever done what is seemly, Rose Elizabeth? I hesitate to point out that you wouldn't be living with a man who is not your husband if you were worried about what is or isn't seemly."

Rose held the dress to her and twirled around. "I don't know how I can ever thank you. I'll be able to go to Euphemia's party in grand style now. And no one will make . . ." She stopped herself from finishing, . . . *fun of me.*

Rose's uncertainty touched Alexander, and he stepped forward, drawing her into his arms. "You will be the most beautiful woman at the party, Rose. And no one would dare make a rude remark, for if they do, I will be there to smite them a mighty blow."

She laughed. "You're like one of those knights in shining armor that Heather used to read about to Laurel and me."

"My armor is only slightly tarnished, my lady," he quipped, pulling her close until he could smell the sweet lavender scent of her hair. "A knight would ride to the ends of the earth for a damsel in distress as lovely as you."

"I can't think clearly when you're holding me so tightly, Alexander. It makes me hot and cold at the same time. And I've got the strangest feeling in my stomach. Do you think it might be hunger?"

"No doubt, but not the kind you're thinking of." He pressed his lips to hers, savoring their sweetness.

As if they had a mind of their own, Rose's arms wrapped around Alexander's neck, the blue dress forgotten as it pooled at her feet. She pressed closer, moaning deep in her throat at the exquisite sensations his kiss elicited.

Alexander could feel her hard nipples boring into his chest. Desire, stronger than any he had ever felt before, poured over him, heating his blood, hardening more than his resolve. His hands molded her full, firm breasts, and he itched to tear away the clothing that prevented him from feeling her warm flesh, from exploring the rigid peaks of her mounds.

"Alexander," she murmured, opening her mouth to accommodate his tongue. Like a prairie fire out of control, Rose felt consumed with heat and longing. She had never experienced anything so wonderfully erotic as Alexander's kisses, as the sensation of his hands on her breasts, and she wanted that feeling never to stop.

But it did. And much sooner than she wished.

Alexander groaned. "We'd better put an end to this now, Rose, for if we do not, we soon won't be able to stop." His voice was thick with emotion as he got himself under control and set Rose from him.

Rose knew he was right—Alexander's kisses could become quite habit-forming—but she disliked his highhandedness in taking control of the situation, making decisions as if she were a child incapable of thinking on her own.

"You surely are full of yourself, your dukeness, to think that I would be unable to control myself after just a few of your kisses. Who do you think you are, Don Juan or something? I have been kissed before, you know." Though Sven's chaste kisses had never set her blood to boiling.

Rose's flippant attitude annoyed the hell out of Alexander, and he drew himself as rigidly erect as the male member pressing against his trousers. "We are not man and wife, as you so wisely pointed out a short while ago, Rose Elizabeth, and I thought it prudent to preserve your good reputation. What we just did would not be condoned by Pastor Bergman or the general populace of Salina."

She shrugged, as if the matter were of no importance, and picked up the dress off the floor, brushing it off, and his concerns as well. "I was merely thanking you for the gift of the dress, your grace. I wouldn't get your drawers all in an uproar over a few kisses. I'm not likely to besmirch your reputation. Besides," she said with a smirk, "I was hardly in any danger of losing my self-control."

He arched a disbelieving eyebrow. "That point is debatable, madam."

She tried her damnedest not to blush. "Well, it just so happens that I'm not in the mood to debate that point or any other at the moment, your grace. My chicken's turning cold, and I'm quite starved."

"Yes," he replied with a knowing smile. "You've already proven that. But I still don't think it's chicken that you hunger for, my sweet Rose." At her gasp of outrage, Alexander grinned and reached for a chicken leg.

CHAPTER 8

Fiddle and guitar music drifted into the street from the church hall. Rose Elizabeth's stomach clenched as tight as a balled fist as Alexander drew the wagon to a halt in front of the white clapboard building.

"I can't breathe in this damned corset," she whispered loud enough for him to hear. "You laced it too tight."

He smiled, remembering how getting Rose Elizabeth into her corset had been a singularly interesting experience, and one particular task that he'd never had the opportunity to perform before. He was far more adept at unlacing than lacing.

"You're going to have to suck in your breath, Rose Elizabeth, or I'm not going to be able to tie these strings tight enough," he'd ordered during the undertaking. Rose had been her usually uncooperative self.

"I am sucking it in, your royal denseness." She'd shot him a look of pure disgust. "Why in hell do you think my face is turning all red! I hate corsets. You should never have bought me this gown, and I should never have agreed to wear it."

"You're going to look lovely in it." The sight of her full

103

breasts overflowing the bodice of the garment had made his manhood stiffen and his fingers tingle in anticipation.

In fact, as he sat next to her on the wagon seat, he was still tingling. The need to make Rose Elizabeth his own had become overwhelming and frustrating as hell. Her kisses held the promise of what could be—he could still recall the taste, the feel of her mouth pressed to his own—but his damn honor dictated what could not.

"Just breathe normally, Rose, and you'll be fine. There's no need to suck in air like you're gasping for your last breath."

"Well I am! How would you like to be sitting on this damned wire bustle? It's unnatural putting women into such contraptions. I don't know why I ever agreed to come to this stupid party of Euphemia's. I'm going to be just miserable.

"Sven's boy Peter's come down sick, so Sven won't be able to attend, and it's you everyone's come to see anyway, Alexander."

He reached for her hand, which was clammy with fear, and gently squeezed it. "You're just nervous, but you shouldn't be. You're going to outshine every lady here tonight."

She gave him a skeptical look. "I doubt that. My dancing is atrocious. And I'm not very good at making small talk. I'm much better at slopping hogs than flattering old geezers like Sammy Balding, the barber, or telling Euphemia how splendid she looks in dresses that are usually so godawful bright that they're blinding."

Alexander climbed down from the wagon and came around to help her alight, noting that Rose didn't object this time. "My father used to counsel me at times like this. He always told me: 'Keep your chin up, your chest out, and walk in like you own the place.' "

"If my chest goes out any farther, your dukeness, it's going to spill clear down to the ground."

He eyed the large globes, which were indeed dangerously close to spilling over the top of her gown, and frowned deeply. Though Rose looked quite smashing, he didn't want other men ogling her. "Perhaps we should have purchased a shawl to go with your gown. I wouldn't want you to catch cold."

"It's still warmer than a Dutch oven outside, your grace, so I'm not likely to freeze to death. I'm just not used to showing so much bosom. That's more Peggy's style. She enjoys being the center of attention."

The strains of "Turkey in the Straw" grew louder when somebody opened the front door of the church hall.

"A crowd is beginning to gather at the entrance, Rose Elizabeth. If we don't enter soon, your friends will come out here to see what's the matter."

She turned toward the hall and glanced at the curious onlookers, the nosiest of whom was Euphemia Bloodsworth. Old Beaknose never missed a thing.

Rose gave a dispirited sigh. Formal social functions were definitely not her cup of tea. She much preferred a quilting bee with a few close friends, or a picnic down by the river. Dressed in her new finery, she felt like a turkey trussed up for Thanksgiving dinner and ready to be devoured.

"Rose Elizabeth?"

"Oh, very well. But as my official knight in shining armor, I'll expect you to come to my rescue if need be."

"Your wish is my command, my lady." He bowed with a courtly flourish and kissed her hand, and several of the ladies who observed his antics sighed.

Rose Elizabeth was suddenly grateful that Alexander Warrick was her companion for the evening. The man was class personified, a real gentleman . . . a real ladies' man. And he was hers for the evening, despite what that strumpet Peggy Mellon thought.

"Why, Rose Elizabeth! How very different you look this evening," Euphemia gushed, dropping into an exaggerated curtsy before the duke.

Rose offered a halfhearted smile at what she knew was a halfhearted compliment, and wished for a pair of tinted glasses to shade her eyes from the disturbing brilliance of Euphemia's orange gown. The sun had nothing on that dress, Rose decided.

"Rose Elizabeth looks absolutely smashing this evening," Alexander said, not allowing the spinster time to offer any disparaging comments about Rose's appearance. "I feel extremely fortunate to have been chosen as her escort."

Peggy strode forward and stopped before the duke. Her lemon silk dress was cut every bit as low as Rose had predicted and was so tight that it delineated every one of her ample curves.

"I wasn't aware there were any others in the running, your grace."

Like a she-wolf ready to strike, Rose Elizabeth bared her teeth, though it was supposed to have been a smile.

"Rose has never had to fight off the beaus," Peggy continued. "Not like her sisters. Laurel had men flocking to her feet, didn't she, Rose Elizabeth?"

"I'm sure she still does," Rose responded, suddenly reminded of the letter from Laurel that she hadn't read yet.

"If you'll excuse me, I see an old friend." With a curt nod at Peggy and an apologetic smile at Alexander, Rose lifted the skirt of her gown and sashayed across the large room, oblivious to the appreciative stares she received from the numerous gentlemen in attendance.

Wolf Turlock, the blacksmith, whose mouth fell open, received a sharp warning jab in the ribs from his wife, and he lowered his gaze to the floor; Sammy Balding, who gave credence to his name, for it was said that Sammy cut more hair in five minutes than he had on his entire head, nearly fell off the bench he was seated upon as he craned his neck to get a better look.

Skeeter Purty winked proudly at the girl whom, before tonight, everyone had considered an ugly duckling. "You surely are a sight for these tired old eyes, Rose Elizabeth," he remarked when she paused before him. "I had to blink several times just to make sure it was really you." No ugly duckling any longer, Rose Elizabeth had transformed herself into a graceful swan.

Wondering if Skeeter had been tippling at the whiskey bottle again, Rose smiled softly at the station manager, thanked him, then greeted his companion. "You're looking especially pretty tonight, Marcella. Is that a new dress?"

The older woman blushed pink to match her gown and nodded. "Skeeter brought me this wrist corsage." She held up her hand to show Rose the silk flowers. "Isn't it pretty? I just love roses."

"They were left over from the millinery shop," Skeeter thought to explain, lest anyone read more into the gesture than they ought to. "Sue Ellen Dobbyn fixed it for me and only charged me two bits."

"It's very pretty," Rose agreed, wondering when Skeeter was going to put himself out of his misery and ask Marcella to marry him. It was obvious that he loved the woman and she was equally enamored of him, but for some ridiculous reason Rose had never figured out, they both pretended not to be.

Rose glanced across the room and saw Alexander in conversation with Peggy. The woman was hanging on his arm and his every word, and he looked like he was enjoying her adoration and attention.

So much for knights in shining armor.

"Oh look!" Marcella pointed at the front door. "There's that sweet Rebecca Heller. I swear she bakes the best apple pies I've ever tasted, and I'm pretty proud of my own."

Rose followed her friend's gaze and saw Rebecca and Seamus paused in the doorway. Rebecca was scowling as if she'd just swallowed the tartest lemon, whole. Rose Elizabeth knew exactly how she felt.

"I don't think it's wise that we came, Seamus," Rebecca said. "I do not fit in among these people; they are all staring at me."

"They stare because you look so lovely, lass. Now quit your worrying. Remember, Jacob told you to have a good time tonight, and he made me promise to dance every dance with you." An easy assignment, Seamus thought, relishing the idea of holding Rebecca in his arms.

Jacob Heller had been acting very much out of character lately, and Rebecca wondered when her formerly conservative father had turned into such a social organizer. That he had insisted she attend a dance outside their own faith was inexplicable. Mennonites danced, but not at secular functions. And he had practically forced Seamus to escort her tonight. It had been horribly humiliating and quite confusing, to say the least.

"You will take Rebecca to the party tonight, Seamus." Jacob's request had sounded exactly like an order. "She's been working too hard at the bakery. Some fun will do her good. Dancing is not forbidden to us."

Of course, Seamus had agreed. What else could he have done? His employer had not offered any alternative, much to Rebecca's mortification.

"My father has not been well, Seamus, and I think his judgment has been impaired by his poor health. Perhaps he has been *ferhext*."

Knowing it was he who had been bewitched, Seamus grasped Rebecca's arm and led her farther into the gaily decorated room. Colorful buntings of blue and gold draped the ceiling, and against the rear wall, matching cloths covered three long tables laden with food and drink. The band, consisting of a fiddle, a guitar, a banjo, and a jew's harp, played on a makeshift bandstand.

"Your father told me that Mennonites dance. There's nothing wrong or sinful about you enjoying yourself this evening, Rebecca."

"But my clothing is all wrong for this party. Everyone is fancy-dressed in bright colors and silks. I look like a drab wren in my black dress."

Seamus's eyes twinkled at the purely feminine concern. Rebecca was usually oblivious to such matters. "*Tsk-tsk.* Vanity does not become you, lass."

She lowered her gaze, and two splotches of red dotted her

cheeks. "You are right, Seamus. It was wrong of me to say such a thing. It was worldly and prideful."

"Exactly. Besides, you have nothing to worry about. You look beautiful. Have you ever known an Irishman to lie?"

Suddenly Rebecca's eyes danced with amusement. "I don't think you want me to answer such a question, because I always tell the truth."

Seamus's bellowing laugh could be heard across the room, and Rose Elizabeth smiled at the sound of it. Seamus and Rebecca now seemed to be having a wonderful time, and she was glad that matters were progressing so well between them. The Irishman was good for Rebecca. She just hoped the insecure woman would accept the gift God had chosen for her.

"You're supposed to be having a good time, not looking so serious, Rose," Alexander said, sidling up next to her and handing her a glass of brown fizzy liquid.

Rose stared at the mysterious concoction. "What on earth is this?" She sipped the sweet drink, her eyes widening with pleasure. "It's very good."

"A man named Charles Hires invented it. It's called root beer. Apparently it was created to replace strong drink. An influence of the Women's Christian Temperance Movement, or so the good pastor informs me."

"It tickles." She wiggled her nose like a rabbit, making Alexander laugh.

"Champagne does the same thing. Perhaps I'll introduce you to it sometime. Would you honor me with this dance? I can never resist a waltz."

Panic assailed her. "I told you, your grace, I'm a terrible dancer. I'll probably step on your feet and scuff up your shiny black shoes."

"I'll take my chances."

Against her better judgment, and with a prayer that she wouldn't disgrace herself in front of the room full of people who knew how clumsy she was, Rose allowed herself to be led onto the dance floor.

"If you can count to three, you can waltz," Alexander explained. "Just follow my lead."

She did, and was soon moving in perfect harmony with his steps. "I neglected to tell you earlier that you look very duke-like this evening." Dressed in a dark blue pinstriped suit with a silver brocade vest—or waistcoat, as he called it—Alexander looked handsome indeed. His shirt was as white as lye soap and a washboard could get it, and he smelled of that spicy cologne he was so fond of wearing. The one that made her think naughty thoughts.

"Knowing how fond you are of nobility, I'm not sure I should take that as a compliment."

She grinned impishly. "You can. Just don't let your ego get any more inflated than it is already."

"With you around, my sweet Rose, that is quite impossible."

Peggy's eyes narrowed as she observed the laughing couple dance gracefully across the pine-plank dance floor. It wasn't fair that the Duke of Moreland had singled out Rose Elizabeth to receive his attention.

And that gown she was wearing had no doubt cost a fortune!

Rose was nothing more than a stupid farm girl. She had no social graces whatsoever, a biting tongue that was more masculine than was seemly, and a figure that bordered on bovine.

Peggy had always been the more popular of the two girls, certainly the better endowed, and she just didn't understand why the duke had not succumbed to her obvious flirtations. She'd given him signals even a blind man could have seen. There was no way he could doubt that she was willing to warm his bed, if he so desired.

And she certainly desired him.

He was everything she'd been looking for in a man. Handsome, rich, titled, Alexander Warrick would be her ticket out of this one-horse town.

There was no way Peggy Mellon was going to spend the remainder of her days cooped up in her father's run-down mercantile selling bits of thread and scraps of lace to ladies who had absolutely no class and didn't have sense enough to know it.

Her gaze landed on Euphemia, and she smirked. Euphemia Bloodsworth was the perfect example of someone who was always trying to rise above her station. If she only knew how ridiculous she looked in that bright orange brocade gown with its brown velvet trim.

Peggy had sold her the material and ribbon, telling the spinster that the color would be perfectly lovely with her pasty complexion. But rather than the ghostly apparition Peggy expected, Euphemia resembled a Halloween pumpkin—a big round Halloween pumpkin.

Rose waltzed by at that moment, and the look on her face could only have been called gloating. She waved airily at Peggy, laughed at something the duke whispered in her ear, and floated away on a cloud of contentment.

"Just you wait, Rose Elizabeth Martin," Peggy whispered beneath her breath, her eyes glowing with jealousy and hostility. "You might be laughing now, but when the Duke of Moreland is in my bed, you won't be laughing any longer."

Signaling to Wolf, who looked over his shoulder to make sure his wife wasn't anywhere to be seen before he came toward her, Peggy decided that the entire evening wouldn't go to waste.

Wolf might not be the most considerate man she had ever bedded, but he was inventive, and he did have the longest, hardest dick in all of Saline County.

Of course, she smiled to herself, she hadn't had the pleasure of testing out his lordship's yet.

But she would. Oh yes, she would.

"It was a wonderful evening, Seamus. I know it was my father's idea that you escort me to the party, but I thank you anyway. I had a very nice time."

Seamus stopped Rebecca in the middle of the street. "Now hold up, lass. No one tells Seamus O'Flynn what to do. And that goes for your father. I invited you to the dance because I wanted to spend time with you. In case you haven't noticed, lass, I'm very attracted to you."

Before she could protest, Seamus hauled Rebecca up against his chest and kissed her soundly on the lips, then he released her. "Do you think your father told me to do that, too, lass?"

Rebecca stared, speechless. Her heart was pounding like a blacksmith's hammer, and she was grateful for the darkness that hid her flaming cheeks. When she finally found her voice, she said with as much indignation as she could muster, "You should not have taken such a liberty, Mr. O'Flynn. *Knoatching* and *schmutzing* are not allowed. And I did not give you permission to kiss me."

Figuring that what she'd just said meant hugging and kissing, Seamus laughed and, ignoring her protestations, pulled her to him again. "I don't need your permission, lass, or your father's, for that matter. I follow me heart." He lowered his head again and with masterful persuasion captured her lips, kissing her until she grew weak in the knees and collapsed against him.

Rebecca thought she would faint. If Seamus hadn't been holding her at that very moment, she would no doubt have fallen facedown in the dirt.

She had never known such sinful pleasure, and she was sure she would be struck down for enjoying Seamus's kiss. But at that moment she didn't care. The feel of Seamus's lips upon her own was manna from Heaven. Nothing so wonderful could be sinful, she decided, almost protesting when he broke contact a moment later.

"There now, lass." He clasped her hand to lead her the short distance to the bakery. "Now that we've gotten that out of the way, I guess we should be heading back home."

Home. He made it sound as if he belonged there. As if they belonged together. But Rebecca knew that could never be.

"Why did you kiss me, Seamus O'Flynn? Did your heart really tell you to do such a thing?"

He smiled tenderly at the confusion he saw on her face and caressed her cheek. "Aye, lass, it did. I've been wanting to kiss you since the first time I laid eyes on you. A man can only restrain himself for so long. And I've never considered myself a very patient man. Tonight, when I saw you laughing so happily and having such a wonderful time, your green eyes glowing with pleasure, I knew that I was going to succumb to me hungers."

His words alarmed her, and she thought to reason with him. "It is not always possible to have what we want in life, Seamus. Sometimes we must let go of fanciful notions and do what is the most practical."

When they reached the front door of the bakery, Seamus stopped. Laughter from the church hall drifted into the street on a warm breeze. Crickets serenaded the two as they continued to stare at each other, lost in a multitude of thoughts and feelings.

Finally, Seamus spoke. "I realize you've had a different upbringing than me, lass, and I respect that. But when a man wants something, he don't let practicality stand in his way. I want you, Rebecca Heller, and it's best that you remember that. I'm giving you fair warning, lass."

Rebecca's heart pounded so hard in her chest, she thought it would explode. Seamus O'Flynn wanted her. But for what? And for how long?

It was on the tip of her tongue to ask him. She'd never before been reticent when wanting to know important details. But something held her back.

Perhaps it was the possibility that she wouldn't like his answer.

Or perhaps it was the possibility that she would.

Late the following afternoon, Rose Elizabeth found herself too tired to do more than sit on the swing, a glass of lemonade in her hand, and daydream about the events of the night before.

It had been a wonderful party, and for the first time in her life, she'd felt like the belle of the ball. Before, Heather and Laurel with their pretty faces and trim figures had received all the attention. Or Peggy, whose obvious attributes were always on display.

But last night it was Rose who had shone in her beautiful store-bought gown, who'd been the envy of every woman there as she waltzed about on the arm of the handsomest man in Salina. And quite possibly the world!

Leaning back in the swing, she smiled contentedly. The air was heavy with humidity; there would be rain or a thunderstorm before nightfall. Glancing at Boomer, who rested near her feet, she frowned. The dog was a pain in the butt during thunderstorms. He whined, he shook, he cowered beneath the bed like a frightened jackrabbit. It was pitiful for a dog to behave in such a despicable fashion.

She'd gotten Boomer when Abigail Stringfellow's dog had had puppies, deciding that since she would be living alone at the farm, she ought to have a watchdog. She smiled ruefully, thinking that she'd been wrong on both accounts: She was far from alone, and Boomer was definitely no watchdog.

Just as she'd predicted, the wispy clouds began to thicken into dark gray patches. She hoped Alexander would arrive home before the deluge started.

He had ridden over to the Anderson place to assist Sven with the building of a rabbit hutch. The duke wasn't adept at much when it came to farming, but he was quite skilled with a saw and hammer.

She glanced at the partially constructed house. It would be an improvement over the soddy, but she'd be damned if she'd admit that to Alexander. That house was going to remain a bone of contention between them as long as they continued living together. It represented everything that was different about them and the way they viewed life.

Rose didn't need creature comforts or material things to be

happy. She loved a new dress every once in a while. What woman didn't? But she didn't need fancy clothes and such to make her content. She derived her happiness from the farm, from the simple pleasures in life: a good apple cobbler, a litter of healthy piglets, an abundant wheat harvest.

Unfortunately, that wasn't the case with Alexander, who relished spending money needlessly, like buying that horse he was so proud of—Muriel was still brooding over that purchase!—or constructing the fancy house, complete with indoor bath, running water, and wraparound porch.

"You can't miss what you don't have," Pa had always said, mostly to appease Ma, Rose was sure. But he'd been right. The Martin women had never had a great many fancy things, but they'd made up for it with love—love for their parents and love for one another.

She wondered if Alexander could say the same. He never talked about his family, and she wondered if he had any brothers or sisters.

Reminded of the letter from Laurel, Rose reached into the pocket of her dress to extract the envelope and smiled as the lilac scent wafted up to greet her. Laurel had always liked perfumes and sachets, while Rose considered good old-fashioned soap and water more than sufficient.

Dearest Rose,

I thought it only fair to warn you that I have written to Heather about the fact that you're still living at the farm. No doubt you'll be hearing from her soon. I couldn't bring myself to lie to her as you requested. You're the one with the talent for fabrication, not I, sister dear. And Heather does worry so about the both of us.

Heather will no doubt be upset with me, too. My plans to find employment at an opera house have not yet materialized, and I have found it necessary to seek employment at a saloon called the Aurora Borealis.

Rose threw her head back and laughed heartily, unable to imagine her dainty, prissy sister working in such a place. "Well, Laurel, you do surprise me," she murmured.

> *Chance Rafferty, the owner, is a horrible man. And not a gentleman at all! I pray that my stay here will be brief. I have not abandoned my dream of singing opera one day.*
>
> *I hope things are going well on the farm, and that you have not been working too hard. How are you and the new owner getting along? I can't believe he is actually allowing you to live there. Are you sure that's legal? After all, you're not married.*

Although Laurel's naiveté did wear on a person, Rose missed her, just as she missed Heather.

Scanning the rest of the letter, she refolded it and placed it back inside the envelope. It would now be necessary to write Heather and explain about the duke and why she hadn't left the farm to attend Mrs. Caffrey's School for Young Ladies in Boston. That was one letter she absolutely dreaded writing.

But she didn't dread it nearly as much as the one she was sure to receive in response.

CHAPTER 9

Rose yanked the rope pull and a spray of cooling water washed over her. Grasping the container of homemade shampoo, which consisted of castor oil and whiskey scented with lavender, she lathered the soapy concoction into her hair and scrubbed vigorously until her scalp tingled.

While Alexander was in the barn grooming his stallion, she'd taken the opportunity to try out his new bathing invention, having been overcome by curiosity and the need to cool off from the sticky September heat.

She'd left on her combination for propriety's sake, just in case Alexander should happen to show up unexpectedly. It wouldn't do to have him see her buck naked, she'd decided, although it was a rather intriguing idea.

One final pull on the cord let out enough water to rinse off her hair. It was at that moment that Rose heard the duke's very unmistakable "Oh my God!" and knew immediately that something terrible had happened.

Praying it wasn't Boomer—that dog could get into more mischief than any animal on earth!—she finished rinsing as best she could and sprinted to the barn, unmindful of her wet underwear and dripping hair.

"Rose Elizabeth!" came the frantic shout. "Come quickly. Your pig is in trouble."

She entered the dimly lit barn to find Alexander crouched in front of the pigpen, looking white as Calumet baking powder. Elvira was making a horrendous wailing noise, and Elmo, in the adjoining pen, paced nervously in response to it.

"You *should* be concerned, you horny boar," she chastised the hog, shaking her finger at him before entering Elvira's pen.

Alexander glanced up, his eyes widening. Rose Elizabeth's hair was soaking wet, as was her nearly transparent linen undergarment. He swallowed the lump in his throat, which almost matched the one in his pants.

"I beg your pardon?"

"Elvira's about to have her babies, Alexander," she explained, kneeling next to him. "And I was just pointing out to Elmo that he's entirely at fault."

Sheer horror crossed his face. "You're not going to castrate him."

She laughed. "You men certainly do stick together, your grace. Hear that, Elmo? His lordship is worried over your privates." Leaning forward to check Elvira's progress, she said, "It won't be much longer. See how she's dilated? Those babies will be popping out before you know it."

"Shouldn't we do something?"

"I've already put in clean straw and fresh water. And it's plenty warm enough for the piglets once they arrive. I think the rest is up to Elvira." The pig looked sorrowfully at her, as if bemoaning the fate of all females.

"I feel so helpless. And so stupid not to have known what was ailing poor Elvira."

Rose leaned back against the post and smiled kindly. "You're learning, your grace. You can't expect to know everything there is to know about farming in the short time you've been here. Why don't you pet her? Like any woman, Elvira will welcome the attention."

Alexander decided that he'd much rather pet Rose Elizabeth than the pig. She looked a hundred times more enticing and smelled a hell of a lot better.

"Why are you all wet, Rose Elizabeth? Is it raining? And if I'm not being too presumptuous, may I ask why you're running about in your underwear?"

Aware for the first time that she was still in her combination, she crossed her arms over her chest and felt her cheeks warm at his probing stare. "I was washing my hair and didn't want to get my dress wet," she lied. "Besides, it's too darn hot to bother with clothes. And I figured that since you already saw me in my underwear when you cinched me into that corset and bustle, what's the difference?"

An eyebrow arched imperiously. "Where I come from, a woman would rather be caught dead than be caught in her underwear."

"Really? Well, that must make certain activities rather boring, wouldn't you say?"

At her bold reference to lovemaking, his hand stilled on the pig's rough hair. "You are an unusual woman, Rose Elizabeth. I guess it must be your farm upbringing."

"If you're trying to tell me that I have no class, your dukeness, then you're probably right. I was never schooled in the niceties, which is why Pa, God rest his soul, wanted to ship me off to a finishing school. He thought if I was refined, I might get a job as a schoolteacher, find a husband, and settle down."

With a body like hers, Alexander had no difficulty imagining Rose Elizabeth as a wife or even a courtesan. But a schoolteacher! That didn't enter into the realm of possibility—not with her short temper and colorful vocabulary.

"I wasn't referring to your lack of polish, Rose Elizabeth, but to the fact that you're earthy and honest. I find that enormously refreshing after all the womanly artifices I've had to endure most of my life."

"Do you have any family back in England, Alexander? I've never heard you speak of anyone, except your dead fiancée, of course."

Alexander turned his face away to conceal his embarrassment. Rose had obviously misconstrued his earlier comment about Jessica; yet, he saw no need to clarify the horrible mess for her. "My mother is still alive. And I have one brother, who may or may not be. The last time I checked, he was more alive than he deserved to be."

His reply surprised her, and it showed in the quick breath she drew. "I take it you're not close."

His laughter was bitter. "Edward's closeness was bestowed upon others, not myself."

"I couldn't imagine not being close with my sisters. Heather and Laurel are the most important people in the world to me. Don't get me wrong—we fight like all siblings tend to do—but deep down where it counts, we love one another. I'm sure you feel the same way about your brother."

Before Alexander could choke out an answer, Elvira let loose an anguished grunt, and the first piglet eased out onto the straw. Soon it was on its legs and running about.

Rose Elizabeth was too preoccupied to notice that Alexander had not bothered to respond.

"I don't see why we have to haul those pigs to the fair with us, Rose Elizabeth. I doubt Elvira's going to feel up to having people gawk at her. It's only been a week since she gave birth."

Rose looked at Alexander and sighed with pure exasperation. "It's pretty hard to show your pigs at the fair, your highness, when they're not there for the judges to see. They don't make house visits, you know. And Pa had already entered them in the competition. He had his heart set on winning that blue ribbon this year. I can't not take them."

He glanced skeptically at the wagon. "Are you sure it will hold all that weight with ours added to it? It's not exactly new or in very good condition." An understatement at best. The damn thing looked as if a good gust of wind could knock it over. He'd offered to purchase a new one, had even gone so far as to order it, but Rose Elizabeth had made such a fuss when she found out that he'd canceled the order.

"This wagon will be around long after you're gone, Alexander, which will be sooner than you think, if you don't move your ass and get those pigs out the chute and into the wagon."

"Your language leaves a lot to be desired, young woman. I think someone should have washed out your mouth with soap years ago."

Rose laughed. "Someone did. Many times." Heather used to chide her that if she didn't learn better behavior, her blood was going to bubble from all the soap she'd ingested. "I guess it didn't work. Now, are you going to help me with the pigs? The fair will be over by the time you're through arguing about this. I don't understand why you have to be so darn disagreeable about everything."

"Oh? Like you are about my new house? The framing's done and the roof is on, and you've yet to step inside to take a look."

She glanced at the structure and shrugged, indicating it was of little importance to her. Though it was an awfully handsome house, she thought. Or would be, when it was finished. "It's a house. I've seen houses before."

"You're just afraid that you might come to like it more than this miserable soddy you fondly call home."

With clenched fists, she opened her mouth to say something cutting, but Sven's arrival stilled her rebuttal. Instead, she smiled sweetly. "To take some of the weight off the wagon, since you're so worried about it, I'll ride into town with Sven and the boys, while you follow behind with the pigs. You can tie Percival to the rear of the wagon."

Percival! What kind of name was that for a stallion? The poor creature probably cringed every time he was summoned by the duke, Rose thought.

Turning to see the Swede pull into the yard, with Wilhem and Peter bouncing excitedly in the rear of the wagon, Alexander did his best to hold his temper, reminding himself that Sven wasn't to blame for his and Rose's latest disagreement. Nor was Sven to blame for the fact that Rose took great delight in throwing the Swede in his face.

"Sven doesn't talk to me like that, your dukeness."

"Sven knows the proper way to milk a cow, your ineptness."

"Sven knows how to speak four languages, your most graciousness."

Alexander could speak three himself, but that didn't seem to impress Rose Elizabeth, who reveled in being contrary and difficult.

"Fine," he finally told the impossible woman. "I'd just as soon have the pigs for company than you anyway. At least they're not so bloody opinionated."

"Fine," she retorted, stomping off to make good on her suggestion, and wondering why Alexander's impudent comment suddenly had the power to wound.

A sizeable crowd had gathered at the Saline County Fairgrounds by the time Rose and her party arrived later that morning. The pig judging would commence in a little over an hour, and the annual Salina Beautification Charity Horse Race, which Alexander had entered despite her protestations, was scheduled to begin after that.

Rose disliked horse racing. She thought it was cruel to push animals to the limits of their endurance just so that vain men could boast of their prowess afterward. She and Alexander had had words over his entering, as they did about almost everything, but he'd refused to give in, saying that racing was the sport of kings and had been so for centuries. As if that was supposed to make it all right!

Colorful patent-medicine wagons were lined up at the far

end of the grounds, their hawkers waiting to lure unsuspecting customers with promises of quick cures and remedies.

Ezra Martin had been a believer in Hostetter's Celebrated Stomach Bitters, but Rose suspected that was mostly because the medicine was almost fifty percent alcohol. Peruvian Syrup was supposed to cure everything from dyspepsia to liver disease by putting iron in the blood, but no one Rose knew had ever benefited from the stuff. And then there was Laurel, who had consumed so much Egyptian Regulator Tea, in an effort to increase the size of her bosom, that she had spent the better portion of a month holed up in the privy. Not that it had done a lick of good. Laurel's chest was still flatter than a flapjack.

With his arms propped on the fence rail, Sven leaned over to get a better look at Alexander's race competition. Horses of every size, breed, and description huddled together in the large corral.

"Those horses look to be pretty strong, Alexander. Do you think your horse can beat them?"

The duke smiled confidently. If there was one thing he knew, it was horseflesh, and Percival was a damn fine specimen. But more than that, Alexander was a damn fine rider.

"It's not so much the horse but the rider, my good man. Though Percival's a good mount, my equestrian experience will no doubt make the difference in the outcome of the race."

"Why do you race, Alexander? You know it vill upset Rose Elizabet. Perhaps that is why you do it, *ja*?"

"Everything I do upsets Rose Elizabeth." Too bad he knew more about horses than women, he mused. But then, women were a tad more complicated to figure out than horses. And a great deal more contentious.

He didn't know anyone who liked to argue more than Rose Elizabeth, who liked to voice her opinion as if it were the only one that mattered, then turn her nose up in the air as if you were the most doltish individual on the face of the earth for daring to disagree with her.

"A man's got to follow his conscience without always worrying about what a woman is going to say, Sven. Women are forever taking exception to the finer things in life." His mother had been the perfect example, always chiding his father for riding to hounds, or wasting his time and money on cockfights. "Maybe you should stand up to Rose Elizabeth instead of always giving in to her," Alexander suggested.

Sven rubbed his chin in contemplation. "Perhaps what you say is true. But what good is life without women? I much prefer Rose Elizabet's company to a horse. You can't kiss a horse, Alexander. And you can't take them to bed." With a laugh at the duke's shocked expression, Sven disappeared into the crowd, leaving Alexander staring after him.

"What did you put in your boxed lunch this year, Rose Elizabeth?" Marcella asked, and Abigail craned her neck to get a peek into the basket that was lined up with the others on the long wooden table. Everyone knew that Rose Elizabeth's baskets were hard to beat.

Rose smiled and tucked the blue gingham napkin more securely around the basket of fried chicken, biscuits, and chocolate cake. "Never you mind, ladies. You'll have to bid on my basket if you want to know what's in it."

Covering her mouth, Marcella giggled. "Don't be silly, Rose Elizabeth. You know only the single men can bid on the boxed lunches."

Rose wondered if Alexander would bid on hers after their little tiff this morning. She sincerely doubted it.

"Well, it smells just wonderful," Abigail said, her stomach grumbling. "I'm sure Horatio would rather eat what Rose fixed than what I brought. That man just hates my cooking."

"I'm sure that's not the case, Abby," Rose said in an effort to be kind, though she knew Abigail Stringfellow's skills did not lie in the kitchen. The woman burned more than half of everything she cooked, and her husband had learned early on in their marriage that if he wanted a decent supper, he had to dine out. Which is what he and Abigail did almost every night of the week.

Fortunately, being the town's only undertaker, Horatio could afford the extravagance. If there was one thing folks in Salina couldn't escape, it was dying.

"I'm hoping Skeeter will bid on my basket," Marcella confessed with a blush. "I tied that corsage he gave me to the handle of my basket, so he'd know it was mine."

Abigail shook her head and *tsk*ed in displeasure. "When are you going to up and marry that man, Marcella? Neither of you is getting any younger."

The petite woman's eyes filled with tears. "I know. But he hasn't asked me. I'm likely to die an old maid."

Rose wrapped her arm about the distraught woman's shoulder. "I know Skeeter's in love with you, Marcella. He's just an old bachelor who's set in his ways. I think what he needs is a little incentive to get him off his butt and into the church."

Marcella's mouth fell open, and Abigail's eyes widened as she asked, "Whatever do you intend to do, Rose Elizabeth? You've got the look of pure mischief on your face, and that doesn't bode well for poor Skeeter."

The older woman's hands flew to her cheeks. "Oh, dear!"

Rose smiled and gave the women a reassuring wink. "Just leave everything to me, ladies. By the time I get through with Skeeter Purty, he'll be making a beeline for the altar."

"Now you know what you're supposed to do, Sven?"

The big Swede nodded, but he didn't look any too happy about what Rose Elizabeth was asking of him. "*Ja.* I know, Rose Elizabet." He scraped the toe of his boot in the dirt, like a child who's just been punished. "But I do not want to eat supper with Miss Tompkins. I want to eat with you. Suppose she gets it in her head that I am interested in her?"

Rose swallowed her smile as she saw the miserable look on

his face. "She won't. I promise. All you have to do is outbid Skeeter for Marcella's basket, then have supper with her. It would mean a lot to me and to my friend Marcella if you'd agree to do this, Sven."

His frown disappearing, Sven's blue eyes suddenly twinkled. "And if I do, I'll be expecting you to give me a reward later."

Rose's hand flew to her throat as she gasped in mock outrage. "Sven Anderson, what a scandalous thing to say!"

He laughed and pinched her cheek. "I was only referring to a dance, Rose Elizabet. But I vill take the other, if you are offering."

Rose blushed clear down to her high-button shoes, wondering what had come over the usually shy Scandinavian. Then she remembered that Sven had been spending a lot of time with the duke lately, and it was obvious that Alexander's influence had not been good.

"You are beginning to sound like a rake and a scoundrel, Sven Anderson. You're beginning to sound like the Duke of Moreland. And that is not a compliment."

Not the least bit offended, Sven laughed. "Alexander thinks that I give in to you too easily. I think maybe he is right. You are a very bossy woman."

She pursed her lips in annoyance. "I think Alexander Warrick should mind his own damn business. The nerve of him, interfering in our relationship."

Sven grasped her hand, all traces of humor gone. "Do we have a relationship, Rose Elizabet? Lately you seem preoccupied, and I am beginning to wonder."

"And who wouldn't be preoccupied, with that horrible man living under the same roof with me."

"I told you, Rose Elizabet, you can live under my roof anytime you want."

Uncomfortable with the direction the conversation was taking, Rose sidestepped the proposal by saying, "All I want right now is for you to bid on Marcella Tompkins's basket. Can I count on you?"

"You can count on me for anything, Rose Elizabet. I want you to remember that, no matter what happens in the future."

She stared at his earnest expression, at the sadness in his eyes, and wondered what had brought on such a dire declaration. "You're a good friend, Sven."

Sighing deeply before kissing her cheek, he walked away, and Rose Elizabeth felt a chill of foreboding ripple down her spine.

Rose Elizabeth's pigs did not win a blue ribbon. When the judges came by her pen, Elvira lay down in the dirt and refused to budge.

Alexander did. And he flaunted the damn thing by wearing it on the lapel of his coat.

Marcella Tompkins ate supper with Sven Anderson, who'd outbid Skeeter Purty by six dollars, almost giving the older man an apoplectic seizure.

Sven complained of indigestion the entire way home.

Rose Elizabeth ate alone. No one bid on her basket because someone had switched napkins, and her blue gingham one had mysteriously ended up on top of Peggy's basket, which the duke had stupidly bidden on, thinking it was hers.

Alexander complained of indigestion the entire way home.

Small consolation, Rose decided, thinking back to yesterday's fair, which she considered the worst she had ever attended. If it hadn't been for the fact that Skeeter had danced every dance with Marcella after the picnic, the day would have been totally worthless.

"Sorry about the ribbons, Pa," Rose whispered, stirring the gravy, then adding a pinch more flour to thicken it. She had really wanted Elvira and Elmo to win a blue ribbon for her pa's sake. It had been one of Ezra's dying wishes.

The groaning wind almost drowned out the steady pounding of Alexander's hammer. Sven had not come by to help with the house today. His mare was about to foal, and something he'd eaten yesterday had given him the screamers, though he was a bit more discreet when referring to his stomach ailment.

The windowpane rattled loudly and Rose nearly jumped as the wind gusted harder. Setting aside the gravy pan, she rushed to the window and looked out.

The sky was darkening ominously, even though it was only midday. Immense black clouds had formed, and a streak of lightning suddenly forked through them.

Rose didn't need any of those fancy meteorological experts to tell her what was happening. And that knowledge scared her to death.

CHAPTER 10

Tornado!

The word sent chills down her spine, and Rose Elizabeth extinguished the fire in the stove, grabbed what candles and blankets she could, and hurried outside.

"Boomer!" she called out. When the dog failed to appear, her apprehension increased tenfold. "Boomer, you stupid dog! Where are you?"

Still nothing.

She ran toward the unfinished house, screaming the entire way. "Alexander! Alexander! Come quick. A twister's headed this way."

Sticking his head out of what was going to be an upstairs bedroom window, Alexander spotted Rose Elizabeth standing below, waving furiously at him and shouting for him to come down at once.

He gazed at the horizon, and shards of apprehension darted through him as he saw the funnel cloud forming in the distance. He had heard of American cyclones, had even read about them in the guidebooks he'd studied en route to Kansas, and now he was going to experience one.

"Bloody hell." He tossed his hammer aside and rushed out to where Rose was attempting to hold herself steady against the onslaught of wind.

"I saw the cloud," he said, pointing skyward. The funnel cloud was revolving violently in a counterclockwise direction.

"We must hurry to the root cellar. It's the only safe place now." Rose gave another quick glance around the yard, calling out again, "Boomer! Boomer! Here, Boomer!"

Another crack of lightning split the somber sky, and they ran to the cellar. Alexander held open the door while Rose Elizabeth made her way slowly down the stairs, still holding the supplies. He fastened the latch securely behind him, then followed her down.

"Over this way. There's a chest with supplies in it, and we can spread the blankets down on the ground to avoid the dampness of the soil."

Not about to argue, Alexander followed her lead, while Rose lighted one of the candles. As they huddled side by side on the blanket, Alexander wasn't sure which one of them was more afraid.

Rose Elizabeth had lived through tornadoes before and knew what to expect, though her trembling body didn't convey any acceptance of them. And though he considered himself a brave man, Alexander didn't mind admitting that he was concerned for their safety.

The roar of the wind grew deafening, and Rose Elizabeth clutched his arm for comfort. "Boomer's still out there somewhere," she said on a choked sob.

He put his arm around her shoulders to comfort her. "I'm sure he'll find refuge from the storm, Rose. Boomer's a pretty smart dog."

She nuzzled his neck, wetting it with her tears, and her voice was small when she said, "I hate tornadoes. They're destructive and cruel, and they never take into consideration how hard a body has to work to overcome the devastation they cause."

Twice before, tornadoes had flattened the wheat crop. The

barn had nearly been destroyed, and they'd lost a pair of lambs, which had been picked up by the gale and transported to parts unknown. Her concern for Boomer's safety was grounded in reality.

"I hope you're right about Boomer. He's just a pup, you know."

Alexander turned his head to offer words of comfort, but finding her mouth only inches from his own, he couldn't resist the temptation. Pressing his lips to hers, he heard her sharp intake of breath, then her sigh of pleasure, and deepened the kiss, sliding his tongue into her mouth.

Rose Elizabeth welcomed Alexander's kisses and the diversion his lovemaking created. Throwing caution to the howling wind, she joined her tongue with his in the strange mating game he initiated, surrendering to the exquisite feel of his hands now cupping her aching breasts. Shivers of desire raced through her with the same uncontrollable fury as the raging storm.

"Rose! Rose!" Her name was a sigh, a prayer, a litany of Alexander's longing.

"Kiss me again, Alexander. Your kisses make me feel so strange and wonderful."

He complied, gently easing her down on the blanket, his fingers making short work of the buttons running down the front of her dress, then the ribbons of her camisole.

Soon her satiny soft breasts filled his hands, and he plied questing fingers to the hardened tips of her nipples, reveling in her moan of pleasure.

"You're so very lovely, my sweet Rose."

Lowering his head, he captured one taut tip between his lips and rolled it gently, laving it with his tongue, then applied the same erotic touch to the other.

"Alexander!" Rose cried out in an awe-filled voice. "I . . ."

The innocence of her response intrigued and excited him, and he smothered her words with his lips, plunging his tongue into her mouth again and again, while his palm moved down to cup her womanhood. She arched her hips to greet him, as if searching for the fulfillment that eluded her.

Pleased with her eager response and determined to give her the pleasure she sought, he untied the tapes of her drawers, easing the material down her hips. Feasting his eyes on the dew-kissed flesh that was now revealed to him, he sucked in his breath. The candlelight flickered over her ivory skin in shadows of light and dark, teasing him, taunting him. Cupping her moist apex, he gently caressed the engorged bud with his finger.

Every nerve ending in Rose Elizabeth's body tingled, her heart felt as if it were beating in her throat, and she couldn't seem to draw a breath. "Stop! Please, Alexander. You're torturing me."

"But it's such delicious torture, my sweet Rose."

He kissed every inch of her exposed flesh, paying special attention to the underside of her breasts, then to the area just below her navel. As his head dipped lower to savor the musky sweetness there, she relaxed her legs, allowing him the access he sought.

Rose had never before experienced such wicked delights, had never even known such things existed. None of the novels she'd read had prepared her for so erotic a coupling, and she thought she would die from the sheer ecstasy of Alexander's touch.

A dog's insistent barking broke through her sensual haze. "Boomer," she whispered. Shaking her head, she pushed insistent palms against Alexander's chest, and with her last shred of self-control and a great deal of reluctance, she forced herself to a sitting position.

"Boomer's outside, Alexander. I can hear him."

"He'll be fine. Just relax," he reassured her, attempting to kiss her again, but Rose turned away. "Stop, Alexander! We must rescue Boomer. I hear him scratching against the hatch door."

With a groan of frustration and pain, Alexander released her, but not before taking one last longing look at what that damned dog prevented him from having. "Bloody damn dog!" he cursed. If only he could ease his throbbing member. Like lightning stabbing the ground outside, it was pushing determinedly against his trousers.

Putting her undergarments and dress to rights, Rose stood

and made her way up the stairs. "I'm coming, Boomer," she called out.

"I'm not." Alexander appeared inconsolable. *Bloody hell!*

A moment later the trapdoor slammed shut, and Boomer, wet and bedraggled, came bounding down the stairs, heading straight for Alexander.

Knowing the pain the dog was likely to cause if he jumped on his lap, the duke cried out, "Wait!" But Boomer didn't, and flattened Alexander back down, licking his face with excited kisses.

"Isn't it wonderful, Alexander?" Rose said when she saw the two romping together. "Boomer knew just where to find us."

"Madam," he said, pushing the dog away and rising to his feet with as much dignity as he could muster, considering that his member was sticking out like a tent pole. "It's probably escaped your attention, but you and that damned dog have miserable timing."

Her face flushed at the implication. "Boomer's safety is far more important than our satisfaction, Alexander. I'm sure you realize that. Besides, we were getting a bit carried away because of the storm and the fright we were experiencing."

"We were experiencing a bit more than fright, Rose Elizabeth." He sighed with exasperation. "We were about to experience sexual gratification before that stupid hound ruined everything."

Her eyes widened to the size of saucers. "Just because we were kissing and touching, Alexander, is no reason for you to think that we would . . . Well, we're not married, and *that* would be a sin. Pastor Bergman is very clear about fornication being a one-way ticket to hell."

"Madam," he replied coldly, "you were as close to Heaven as any woman I've ever seen. Do you deny it?"

Her look communicated that she thought he was being ridiculous and unreasonable. "Of course I don't deny it. I thought what we did was simply wonderful. But you have to admit that it would probably be considered a sin for a woman such as myself to be touched so intimately by a man who is not her husband."

"It's a bit late for you to be making that argument. You certainly didn't voice any objections when my head was pressed between your thighs."

She gasped, blushing furiously. "Don't be crude, your highness. I realize that I allowed things to get out of control, but that's no reason to forget the fact that you're a gentleman, and I'm supposed to be a lady."

" 'Supposed to' being the operative words."

"Well, if I were the strumpet you're implying, Alexander Warrick, you'd be standing there with a huge grin on your face at this very moment, instead of that horrible pained scowl. Isn't that so?"

"Why in hell do I bother to argue with your convoluted logic, woman?" He stalked back to the blanket and resumed his seat, folding his arms across his chest.

"I really don't know, Alexander. But I think it would be safer for me and Boomer to sit on the step while we ride out this storm."

But Boomer had other ideas and went to lie down beside Alexander on the blanket, resting his head in the duke's lap, much to the duke's very great disgust and Rose Elizabeth's annoyance.

"You have wreaked havoc in my life since the first day I met you, Rose Elizabeth. I think it would be best if we keep our distance from each other until you come to your senses and move into town. I think you'll agree that it isn't safe for you to remain living in the soddy with me after what just happened."

His words wounded, but she wasn't about to let him know that. "Feel free to leave anytime, your dukeness, because I have no intention of doing so. But I do think you're correct in saying that we should keep our distance from each other. Obviously there is some kind of strange attraction between us." That was probably the understatement of the century. But there was no way she'd let this arrogant blue blood know how much she desired him.

"That strange attraction you refer to is called man and woman. Maybe you've heard of it. But yes, I'll be only to happy to keep my distance."

However, when the storm abated and they ventured back to

the soddy, it was to find that the room previously occupied by the duke was no longer standing. That portion of the roof had caved in under the onslaught of the wind and driving rain. Alexander and Rose just stood there staring at what used to be his bedroom and knowing full well the complications they now faced.

Lester had apparently not fared as well as Boomer, for there was no sign of the frog, and Rose gave a silent prayer for him.

Wiping the rain from her face with a dish towel, Rose clucked her tongue in false pity. "I guess this means you'll be leaving after all, your royalness, since your room has been destroyed."

His look was incredulous. "Like hell it does. Once I've finished the new house, I'll be moving in there. And in case you've forgotten, Rose Elizabeth, the room you're presently sleeping in is by all rights mine. Since my bed has been destroyed, I guess you'll have to share yours." His grin was deliciously wicked, and Rose sucked in her breath.

"But . . . we're not married, Alexander. What if someone were to find out?"

He shrugged. "I've given up worrying about your reputation, Rose Elizabeth. It's obvious you haven't given it much concern. But if you're truly worried, I guess you can always move into town. I'll be happy to put you up at the hotel and pay all your expenses."

With a full head of steam, she marched into the main room and plopped down on her rocker. But rather than the expression of defeat Alexander expected to see when he entered, Rose was smiling with such confidence that it scared him.

"You've probably forgotten, Alexander, but it's nearly time to begin planting this year's wheat crop. I don't suppose you know how to accomplish that, do you?"

Her words hit him like a lightning bolt, and he shook his head, feeling inept as ever. "You know I don't know the first thing about planting wheat, but I suppose I could get a book from the library."

"I suppose you could. Thelma Tucker would be only too happy to assist you, especially after that huge donation you made to the library fund." Thelma had been the duke's latest conquest in his efforts to win over the entire town. Pastor Bergman had received a sizeable donation to complete construction of the church addition, and the Salina Primary School now boasted a shiny brass bell with which to call its students to class, thanks to Alexander's largesse.

Money talked. And the Duke of Moreland's voice was louder than most.

"Maybe while you're there," she added, "you could check out books on cooking, sewing, hog production. . . ."

Alexander reconsidered. If she left, he'd definitely miss her cooking. He couldn't boil water worth a damn.

And though he'd paid attention and tried his best to milk those cows, he still hadn't gotten the hang of it. Wynona had never forgiven him for his first, botched effort and hated the very sight of him.

And though he'd made every effort to gather the eggs in a responsible fashion, he still broke more than he admitted, burying them in the garden to hide them.

And the garden! He wouldn't try to convince himself that he knew a carrot from a turnip or a turnip from a weed. He'd be lucky to have enough vegetables to get himself halfway through the winter.

Having spent his life being waited on hand and foot, and never enduring physical labor such as he'd experienced since coming to Kansas, Alexander now admitted that his eyes had been opened and his opinions changed about these midwestern farmers. He now respected their independent, self-reliant ways.

Rose Elizabeth had done a superb job of deflating an English ego that had gotten "too swell-headed," as she was fond of pointing out.

He sighed in defeat.

Rose smiled. "I guess we can share the same bed. Rebecca told me about a Mennonite practice called bundling, where you put a board or stack some pillows between two people who are courting. I guess we could try that."

His laughter was self-deprecating. "'Courting'! That's rich. We're far beyond the courting stage, my sweet Rose. We've been living in this miserable abode like man and wife. I put up with your constant nagging, while you put up with my unwanted attentions. It's exactly like a real marriage, but without the finest part. Of course, we could remedy that. You could become my mistress."

She stared at him for a moment, her mouth open, then she shot out of her chair. "Your mistress! Hell will freeze over before I become any man's mistress."

"Those who have shared that position have been quite content. I'm very generous. You would never want for anything."

"I don't want for anything now, your highness, including you. In case you've forgotten, you're not the only man who's made his interest known. But at least Sven is honorable. He wants to marry me."

Alexander's face whitened, though the news of the Swede's declaration came as no surprise. Sven had been courting Rose for months, at a snail's pace. He needed a wife to help him with the farm and to be a mother for his two children; Rose Elizabeth was the likely candidate. But Alexander had a difficult time imagining Rose in anyone's bed but his own.

"If you were in love with Sven, you would have accepted his proposal by now."

Rose's lips thinned. "What goes on between Sven and myself is none of your affair. But since you're so set on knowing my business, you might as well know that I'm not ready for marriage. I've got things I want to accomplish that have nothing to do with Sven, or marriage in general."

Alexander suspected that Rose Elizabeth's reluctance to marry had more to do with keeping her land than with maintaining her independence. Of course, she'd forgotten an important fact: He owned the land. And if that obstacle was keeping her from marrying the Swede, then it had been a worthwhile purchase after all.

"Are you going to make supper soon? I'm starved."

"You're always starved for something, Alexander. But then, it's common knowledge that Englishmen suffer from overblown appetites and overinflated egos. It's certainly no wonder that you lost the colonies during the Revolution. King George's madness must have extended to the entire *bloody* kingdom."

He stiffened in proper British outrage. "Madam, I will not stand here and listen while you malign my country."

"Fine. Then go out to the chicken coop and kill us a hen for supper. I'm planning to fix chicken and dumplings tonight."

He blanched. "You want me to kill a chicken?"

"It's time you learned how, your dukeness. Just wring its neck." She demonstrated with the dish towel still in her hand. "Make it quick and clean, and the bird will feel no pain." But Alexander was certainly going to, if his expression was any indication. She'd never met a man so squeamish about such things.

On leaden legs, Alexander ventured to the door, but he paused and looked back before opening it. "This is your way of getting back at me for what I said earlier, isn't it? You're angry because I asked you to become my mistress."

Rose's innocent sweet smile was her only reply.

Taking a seat on the edge of the bed, Rebecca reached for her father's gnarled, clammy hand. In the last few days his condition had worsened. He was feverish, his skin ashen, and Rebecca worried that he was too frail to fight off the malady he had contracted.

"Papa," she whispered. "How are you feeling today? I have brought you some rich chicken broth."

The old man opened his eyes and shook his head. "Just the sight of you makes me feel better, daughter. I don't want to eat anything right now. My stomach is not too good."

"But you must eat to keep up your strength. I have baked strudel. You know how much you love my strudel."

"It is better than your mama's," he conceded, "but I would never have told Esther dat." He attempted a smile. "You have been a good daughter, Rebecca. I will miss you when I am gone."

Tears filled her eyes. "You mustn't talk like that, Papa. You will get better. I'm going to summon the doctor. He will come and make you well."

"I don't want no English treating me. I would rather die first."

"You are a stubborn old man, and I will not let you die. Perhaps there is medicine that can make you well. We won't know unless we try."

"When God calls me I will go, Rebecca. Until then, I will stay with you. Now tell me, wot have you and Seamus been doing? I miss coming downstairs to watch the two of you argue."

Knowing that to disagree would only sap her father's strength, Rebecca chose to placate him. "The Irishman thinks that after only a few weeks he can make the recipes as well as I. His bread is like stone, and his piecrust is so tough even Mrs. Flannery's dog from next door will not eat it."

Jacob's lips twitched. "Where is Seamus now?"

"He has gone to the mill to fetch more flour. The rain has made business slow, so I closed early."

"Seamus has been a big help to you, has he not? He seems a quick learner. And I know he's a very hard worker. I don't know wot we would have done if he hadn't happened along. God's providence. Dat's wot it was."

Rebecca thought back to the night of the dance, and her cheeks filled with color. Though Seamus hadn't tried to kiss her again, she knew it was just a matter of time before he would. He had promised as much. And she didn't have the strength of will to resist him. God's providence, as her father had put it, had made for some very serious problems.

She chewed her lower lip thoughtfully for a moment. "I have something to confess to you, Papa. I hope that you will not be too disappointed in me."

"Wot is this serious look you are giving me? Surely nothing can be as bad as all that, daughter."

"You remember the night when Seamus and I went to the dance? The one you insisted he take me to?"

Jacob nodded. "You said you had a wonderful time. So wot could be so wrong with that? You are young. You should have good times."

Rebecca swallowed with some difficulty. "Seamus kissed me, Papa." Though she expected many reactions—anger, disappointment, contempt—the soft chuckle that escaped his frail chest was not one of them.

"So? This is wot you are so worried about? Because a man finds you attractive and wants to *schmutz? Schmutzing* is not forbidden. If it was, you would not have been born." He smiled, remembering the many nights he and Esther had spent behind her father's barn, kissing and hugging and making plans for their future.

"It was different with you and Mama, Papa. You were of the same faith. Seamus and I are too different. I am Plain, and he is not. He has fought, Papa, with his hands. For money. That type of behavior goes against everything we believe in."

Jacob patted his daughter's hand. "I can see the love shining in your eyes when you speak of him, Rebecca, and it gladdens my heart, despite all the problems you and Seamus might face. True love can even out many differences."

"But, Papa . . ."

He closed his eyes, his strength depleted. "I am weary now, daughter. And you must make these decisions for yourself. No one can tell you who you should or should not love. Only God can give you the answer you seek. Pray to him, Rebecca. Ask for his guidance and blessing. You already have mine."

Her eyes widened and she sucked in her breath. Rebecca knew her father liked and admired Seamus for his strength of character and intelligence, but she had never thought he would accept him as a son-in-law.

"Seamus is a fine man, Rebecca, and he will make you a good husband. I only wish I could be here to see my first grandchild."

Unable to fathom why God in his greatness would take one good man away from her and replace him with another, Rebecca laid her head on Jacob's chest and cried.

CHAPTER 11

Heather's letter arrived on the first day of planting. Sven had delivered it, along with a block of ice. Though there was a nip to the crisp autumn air, Rose didn't think the gooseflesh on her arms was caused by it, but rather by the knowledge that her sister was probably furious with her. The first paragraph confirmed her fears.

My Dear Sister Rose,

Though I was happy to have finally received word from you, I can't tell you how disappointed I was to discover that you still remain on the farm and have not gone on to Mrs. Caffrey's as promised.

I'm sure the Duke of Moreland can't possibly be as inept as your letter indicated.

Rose rolled her eyes heavenward, then stared out at the wheat field where Alexander was attempting to push the breaking plow through the hard-packed earth, and laughed aloud. At the rate he was progressing, the first furrow would be finished sometime around Christmas.

But she didn't want to be too hard on him about his lack of skill with the plow. The tornado had ripped off the roof of the new house and he'd taken the loss somewhat badly. She didn't think his temperament was up to ridicule right now. With a sigh, she continued reading.

> And I'm further certain that someone so refined and mannered, as the duke surely must be, would not cause any harm to our parents' graves. Therefore, I must insist that you turn the farm over to this "Duke of Disaster," as you unkindly refer to him, and leave for Boston at once.
>
> I don't have to tell you of the notoriety your staying there will cause. No doubt Miss Bloodsworth's mouth has been moving a mile a minute to discredit your good name!

Rose managed a smile. She missed both her sisters something awful, but she had no intention of following Heather's order that she leave. Even though the next sentence did cause her a bit of concern.

> I hope you realize that the duke's money has already been deposited in our bank account, and that we cannot afford, nor do I intend, to return it to him. That money has been earmarked for our future.
>
> Things are proceeding here as well as can be expected. The children in my charge are delightful, though their father is extremely unreasonable and hardheaded, and takes great pleasure in ordering me about and exerting his authority. Brandon Montgomery is arrogant

*and opinionated, but I will not break under his com-
mand. I am still determined to become an illustrator, and
this is just a minor setback, in my opinion.*

The rest of the letter was filled with more criticisms of Mr.
Montgomery and reasons why Rose should leave the farm,
and Rose wondered how Heather could possibly live under
the same roof with a man who was as bossy as she was.

Stuffing the letter into the pocket of her denim overalls,
which she always wore during planting season, she filled a
jug with cold water and headed back out to the field.

Alexander wiped the sweat from his brow with the back of
his hand and gulped down the cold water greedily. Plowing
was much harder work than he'd anticipated, and though he'd
suggested to Rose only this morning that he would be happy
to hire additional laborers for the chore, she wouldn't hear of
it, saying that if he was going to be a wheat farmer, he had to
learn the hard way.

It seemed Rose's way was always the hard way. The stupid
thing was, his pride had gotten in the way of his common
sense, and now he wanted to prove to her that he was capable
of handling whatever task she set before him.

He recalled the saying, "Pride goeth before the fall," and
knew he was going down fast!

"This sod is difficult to plow, Rose Elizabeth," he admitted,
staring at the closely knit grass. "Perhaps we need a bigger
plow."

"Perhaps we need a stronger plowman," she suggested with
a wink. Then she explained, "The moldboard plow you're
using is the best one made for the job. The roots of the sod are
deep, which is why we sometimes allow half the land to lay
fallow for a year to accumulate additional moisture from the
rain. Unfortunately, I didn't have that luxury this year, so the
plowing is a bit more difficult. I can spell you, if you'd like."

"I don't like. Any more than I like you parading around

dressed like a man." His gaze lingered on her costume. "Ladies don't behave in such a fashion."

"Ladies don't sleep in the same bed with a man who is not their husband, either," she reminded him. "So I guess that means I'm not a lady." She shrugged. "I'd rather be practical and comfortable than be fashionable."

The denim material hugged her buttocks and thighs, leaving no doubt that Rose was every inch a woman and Alexander felt the familiar stirring at his groin. It had been pure hell sleeping next to her every night, even with that damn board she insisted on placing between them.

Smelling the lavender scent of her hair, listening to her steady breathing while she slept, knowing that she lay just inches from him, played havoc with his emotions.

If he couldn't push the damn plow, it was most likely because he hadn't slept much this past week. But he'd rather be tied to the back of the plow from morning until night than admit that to her.

It rankled him that Rose Elizabeth didn't seem to be having the least bit of problem with the sleeping arrangement. She acted as if having him in her bed were no different from having that damned dog sleeping with her. It was deuced hard on a man's ego and bloody difficult on a man's privates. And it made him more determined than ever to show her just what she was missing.

What had started out as a simple seduction had turned into a quest to conquer, to prove to Rose Elizabeth and to himself that he was the man she wanted, the man he wanted to be.

"Dawdling ain't going to get that furrow plowed, your dukeness," Rose reminded him, and Alexander grimaced. "I'll tug on the mules' harness. It might make the going easier if I lead them."

A hawk dipped its wing and cried out, as if mocking him, and Alexander wondered how Rose managed to put the invisible ring through his nose by which she now led him around.

Leaning in to the plow, he put his back to the task, and

prayed for deliverance from overbearing, opinionated, head-strong women.

"It says here in the newspaper that William F. Cody has opened his Wild West Show in Omaha, Nebraska." Alexander's voice grew animated. "What I wouldn't give to see something like that. Cowboys, Indians, the sharpshooter Annie Oakley . . ." He'd read about them in the London newspapers and had grown fascinated with the prospect of experiencing the real West, as recommended by New York City newspaper editor Horace Greeley. Now the opportunity was at hand.

Rose Elizabeth paused, wet dish in hand, and shook her head at Alexander's childlike exuberance. Foreigners were always so impressed with what they thought was the real Wild West. They didn't realize that here in Salina, folks were living that reality every day.

"Buffalo Bill was a frequent visitor to Salina years ago," she explained, setting the dish aside and picking up another. "He was master of ceremonies at several of our holiday celebrations. I guess he grew soft and decided to become a showman. Now he exploits the very things he nearly exterminated: buffalo, Indians. . . ."

"Nevertheless, I would still like to see his show." He set down the paper. "Why don't we travel to Omaha and see it for ourselves. It'll be my treat." If he thought she'd be grateful or excited, he was wrong. Rose stared at him as if he'd lost his mind.

"It may have escaped your notice, your royalness, but we are still in the midst of planting a wheat crop. After the plowing is done, we have to seed, fertilize, then harvest. We can't just run off to seek our pleasures and forget about what's important. What kind of responsibility were you taught back in England?"

He stiffened in his seat, and his voice was cold as he said, "I've had responsibility heaped on me since I was a small child. I had to learn my place, live up to my father's expectations, which was next to impossible, and assume the duties of nobility, whether I wanted to or not. I can assure you, Rose Elizabeth, that when it came to responsibility I more than adequately shouldered it. Perhaps I am tired of it weighing so heavily upon me now."

She listened with rapt interest. It wasn't often that Alexander offered such insight into his past. It couldn't have been easy, she realized, for him to grow up as heir to a dukedom, to have a title thrust upon him that perhaps he'd never wanted.

"Why don't you go to Omaha, Alexander? I can run things here until you get back. It will be a good diversion for you. You've been working very hard." *Not accomplishing a great deal, but working hard just the same*, she added silently.

He was bloody tempted. Going to Omaha would mean satisfying the sexual yearning that had been building inside him for months and was ready to explode. If he didn't do something soon to alleviate his frustration, he wasn't certain he'd be able to control himself with Rose Elizabeth.

And he never wanted to do anything to hurt her. For despite all their disagreements, their cultural differences, and her dictatorial ways, he cared for Rose more than he wanted to admit. And far more than he should.

"You're sure you'd be able to handle things here?"

His eagerness to leave disappointed her, though she knew she should be happy. With him gone, she'd be able to sort out all those strange feelings she'd been having, all those torrid dreams that haunted her at night.

"I handled things before you arrived, your dukeness. I'm sure your departure won't offer any hardship."

"I can have Seamus stop by and lend you a hand. He is still in my employ, though he seems to have forgotten that fact."

"I don't want to take Seamus away from the bakery. With Mr. Heller as sick as he is, Rebecca will need him more than ever."

"Are you the only one who needs no one, Rose Elizabeth?"

His voice was strained and filled with hurt. "Doesn't it get lonely being an island unto yourself?"

The dish she was wiping slipped from her fingers and crashed to the floor, and she jumped back, startled. Alexander's question had disrupted her composure quite effectively.

She was lonely. But then, she felt that way even in a crowd of people. Her insecurities had made her so. Her fear of failure, of not living up to her father's dreams, had made her a hard taskmaster on herself and on others.

Alexander was too perceptive for his own good; right now she hated him for it. "At least when I'm by myself, I'm never disappointed."

Her barb, razor sharp and pointed, poked a large hole in his ego, and he replied, "High expectations have a way of crumbling, Rose Elizabeth. I hope you're not caught under them when they do." He rose from his chair. "I'll be leaving for Omaha first thing in the morning. Until then, I bid you good night."

As she watched him walk away, a great feeling of despair washed over her. Alexander hadn't left yet and she already missed him.

"Bloody hell!" she whispered, mimicking his favorite phrase.

When had he crawled beneath her skin?

When had he burrowed into her heart?

When had she fallen in love with him?

Spread along the western bank of the Missouri River like branches of a massive oak tree and reaching up to the nearby hills, Omaha was the cultural center of Nebraska and the hub of the cattle industry. Thanks to the multitude of railroad lines, livestock markets and meatpacking houses abounded there.

But for all its good fortune, Alexander found the streets dirty and unpaved, and the shops, which bore German names from the settlers who emigrated there, not much better than those in Salina.

The one thing it did have was a decent hotel. The Grand Central, a large, imposing brick edifice, stood smack in the middle of the main street and attracted an unusual clientele. Cowboys fresh off the trail with several months' pay mingled with avaricious businessmen eager to lighten their purses, and fancy-dressed ladies of dubious reputation consorted with homespun-garbed farm wives eager for a day in town.

Alexander entered the hotel's large dining room his first morning there to find it crowded and noisy. The clatter of glassware and dishes added to the steady drone of conversation, and he wondered if he shouldn't just have had a tray sent up to his suite.

With his face buried in his menu, and trying to decide between the steak and eggs or the ham, he didn't notice the couple two tables over who tried desperately to attract his attention. But the distinctive scent of gardenia soon drifted toward him, drawing his attention, and he glanced up to see a smiling Peggy Mellon and her father standing by his table.

"Well, this is quite a coincidence, your grace." Tom Mellon held out his hand. "We sure didn't expect to find you in Omaha, did we, Peggy girl?"

The young woman shook her head, then glanced quickly about the room, as if looking for someone. "Did Rose Elizabeth come with you, Alexander?"

Alexander rose to his feet, a stunned look on his face. "No. No, she didn't. I've come to see the Wild West Show. Is that why you're here?"

"May we join you?" Peggy asked, glancing down at the two empty chairs and trying to keep her excitement under control. Alexander Warrick wouldn't be alone for long, if she had anything to say about it. Rose Elizabeth was a fool for allowing the duke out of her sight. But then, Rose had never been very smart when it came to men.

"We can have the waiter bring our food over to here," she suggested.

"Of course. Where are my manners?" Alexander shook his head, as if clearing his thoughts. "I'm just surprised to see both of you. Delighted, but surprised," he added smoothly, not knowing quite how to feel about this unexpected turn of events.

"We're here on a buying trip, your grace. Peggy often accompanies me on these trips. Sarah Ann's not much for traveling, and they help to ease Peggy's restlessness. You know how young women can get."

If that predatory smile was any indication, Alexander sincerely doubted that a trip to Omaha would alleviate Peggy's restlessness. Though, he thought, smiling to himself, it could very well alleviate his, if that smoldering look in her eyes was indicative of her desire.

He flashed her a grin. "There's much to do here, or so I'm told. What is it that piques your interest, my dear?"

"Clothes and the like, your grace," Tom answered for his daughter. "It's no use trying to deny her. Peggy throws an awful fit if she don't get her way." Since the first time she'd looked up at him from her cradle and smiled, Tom Mellon had indulged his daughter's every whim.

A slight blush touched the young woman's cheeks, but despite the maidenly show of protestation, Alexander suspected that Tom was right. Peggy seemed every bit as tenacious as a bull terrier—not unlike another woman of his acquaintance.

Alexander decided that it must be the Kansas water.

"Papa, what an awful thing to say. The duke is going to think that I'm terribly spoiled."

"On the contrary. I admire a woman who knows what she wants and how to get it."

"Well, that definitely describes me, Alexander." His name rolled off her tongue like a caress. She turned to her father. "Papa, isn't that Harry Townsend, the salesman you've been trying to meet these past two days?" She pointed at the heavy-set man at the corner table by the window.

"I'll be damned if it isn't. Will you excuse me, your grace?

That man's slippery as an eel, and he owes me two cases of bone buttons. I won't be a minute."

Elated as she watched her father walk away, Peggy scooted her chair closer to the duke's. "What a wonderful coincidence that we're both in Omaha at the same time, Alexander. It might prove very interesting for both of us."

The woman was as much a tart as Rose Elizabeth had indicated, and Alexander felt guilty as hell for what he was about to do. But he needed a tart right now, and Peggy Mellon was handy, extremely willing, and very well endowed. Big bosoms, he reminded himself, would one day be his ruination.

"I'm always interested in diversions, my dear. What do you have in mind?"

With practiced ease, Peggy placed her hand on his thigh, rubbing his leg in a slow, circular motion, and Alexander felt himself harden. Her seductive smile was full of self-confidence when she noticed his response.

"I think we both have the same thing in mind, your grace. Why don't we spend the day together? If we're still of a like mind by evening, I'll get rid of my father and we'll act accordingly."

He found her boldness exciting, somewhat distasteful, and too damn tempting to ignore. "As I said, I admire a woman who knows what she wants."

Her tongue traced her lower lip in a slow, sensual motion, and she squeezed his leg again. "It's no secret that I want you, Alexander. I'm getting wet just thinking about how it's going to be between us."

And it was going to give her a great deal of satisfaction to present Rose Elizabeth with a detailed account of her encounter with the Duke of Moreland.

Rose pulled the wagon to a halt in front of Mellon's Mercantile and sighed. She was not in the mood to spar with Peggy today. In fact, if she hadn't run out of quilting thread, wild horses couldn't have dragged her into town.

"Hello, Sarah Ann," she said when she entered the store, surprised by the woman's presence. Sarah Ann was not fond of working in her husband's store. It was no secret that the former Sarah Ann Baxter of Fairfax, Virginia, who had been the belle of the county, felt that working in a mercantile was beneath her, as was living in a rustic farming community like Salina.

"It's certainly quiet in town today."

Sarah Ann shrugged her bony shoulders. "It's quiet in this tomb of a town every day. Why, back home we had barbecues and balls to attend. It was always so festive; there was always something to do." A faraway look entered her eyes, and Rose Elizabeth almost felt sorry for the woman.

Some folks thought that the grass would be greener elsewhere, but Rose knew that grass was grass, and the same old color, no matter what side of the fence it grew on.

"Have you ever gone home to visit, Sarah Ann? Perhaps a trip back to Virginia would do you good."

Sarah Ann made a great pretense of straightening the gloves in the glass case. "I guess there's nothing left for me there anymore," she said, her voice melancholy. "My parents are both dead, and I have no other family. Besides, Tom says we can't afford to be taking any trips right now." Her lips pinched into a frown. "Of course, that doesn't include him and Peggy. They've gone off to Omaha, leaving me here alone to fend for myself. And I can tell you——"

"Peggy and Mr. Mellon went to Omaha?" Rose's stomach suddenly soured. "When did they leave?"

"A few days ago. Tom goes on buying trips every once in a while, and he prefers to take Peggy with him rather than me. He says I whine too much. And maybe I do, but then, I have plenty to complain about."

Rose wondered if Alexander had known that Peggy would be in Omaha. Perhaps that was the reason for his sudden desire to go there.

"You look downright peaked, Rose Elizabeth. Can I fix you a cup of hot tea or something?" Sarah Ann's gaze drifted to the window. "There's definitely a chill in the air today. Won't be long before winter is upon us again, and I dread the prospect. This store gets as drafty as an old barn."

Rose pasted on a smile. "I'm fine." She held out a sample of the thread she needed. "My quilt's nearly done and I ran out of thread. Do you have anything resembling this cherry-red color?"

"I'm sure I do. Just let me run to the back room and take a peek."

She returned moments later and handed the spool of thread to Rose. "How are things out at the farm? Has that handsome duke adjusted yet?" She chuckled. "I can still remember how horrible you two smelled that day we came to visit."

Rose remembered that day, and all the days since, and her heart ached at the void Alexander's departure had made. "Alexander's gone to Omaha to see Bill Cody's Wild West Show."

Sarah's eyes widened and a calculating smile curved her lips. It wasn't hard for Rose Elizabeth to figure out what the woman was thinking.

"Well, isn't that just the strangest coincidence? Perhaps my Peggy will have the opportunity to visit with the duke while he's there. Peggy always was one to socialize, if you recall. I guess she's just like her mother."

Rose sincerely doubted that. Sarah Ann, for all her affectations, was at least a lady—something Peggy could never hope to be.

She smiled politely at the woman. "Omaha's a big city. Perhaps they won't run into each other."

"Oh, I'm sure Peggy will find the duke if he's there. She can smell money a mile away. And you have to agree, the Duke of Moreland would be an excellent catch for my girl. Peggy doesn't belong in this godforsaken town any more than I do."

Rose Elizabeth paid for her purchase, thanked the woman, and hurried out of the store without further comment. But that didn't keep her from worrying the entire way home.

*   *   *

Alexander was so delighted to see Rose Elizabeth when he arrived home two days later that he picked her up, swung her around, and gave her a peck on the cheek before setting her down in front of the coal stove.

He'd missed her. And that realization had played havoc with his composure the entire trip home.

"Alexander, for heaven's sake! What's gotten into you?" He looked a little too chipper for Rose Elizabeth's liking, and she had to bite her tongue to keep from asking what was uppermost on her mind: Had he been with Peggy Mellon?

"Aren't you happy to see me?" There was genuine disappointment in his voice, reminding Rose of a small boy.

"Of course I am. In all honesty, I missed you." A mischievous smile curved her lips. "It got quite boring around here without having you to boss around."

Her admission pleased him, and he chuckled before seating himself at the table. From behind his back he brought forth a brightly wrapped package and set it at her place. "I brought you a little something from Omaha."

She spooned rabbit stew into two bowls and set them on the table, eyeing the gift and wondering if it was meant to salve a guilty conscience. "You shouldn't have spent more of your money on me, Alexander. Did you have a good time? Did you see the Wild West Show?"

"Yes to both questions. Now open your present."

Seating herself, she carefully unwrapped the package and found a small, intricately carved wooden box. Lifting the lid, she squealed in delight as a snappy rendition of "Buffalo Gals" burst forth. "Oh, thank you so much, Alexander. I love it. Wherever did you find such a pretty thing? I've always wanted a music box."

"At the Wild West Show. It seems Mr. Cody is quite the entrepreneur. He had all kinds of souvenirs and items for sale, but this was by far the nicest one. And the sassy tune reminded me of you."

She leaned over to kiss his cheek. "For this I will give you a double helping of apple pie tonight."

His smile softened. "I've decided I much prefer apple pie to tarts, Rose Elizabeth. Tarts tend to leave a bitter taste in your mouth."

She looked at him curiously. "What on earth kind of tarts did you eat, Alexander? It must have been some type of berry that wasn't ripe."

His sigh was full of disgust, directed mostly at himself. "It was ripe all right. Too ripe. But bitter just the same." Though he'd never consummated his relationship with Peggy, the memory of her hands caressing his body, of her lips pressed eagerly to his, still nauseated him.

Even as desperate as he thought he was for a woman, Peggy Mellon was just not the right woman, and he hadn't been able to bring himself to make love to her. To assuage her hurt feelings, he had embellished the story of his fall off his horse, leading her to believe that he was incapable of consummating the sex act. She had laughed in his face before storming out of his room.

Alexander had only to glance at Rose Elizabeth to belie what he'd told Peggy. He got hard just thinking about her. In fact, he'd been hard as a brick the entire trip home on the train because all he could think about was Rose Elizabeth's sweet, smiling face.

"By the way, where's that mangy mutt of yours? I found myself missing him, though not quite as much as I missed you."

Heat splashed her cheeks with color and infused her entire body at the admission. But the niggling suspicion about Peggy still festered, and she had to know. "I hear Peggy and her father were in Omaha the same time as you." She studied him, noting the slight flush to his cheeks, and her heart sank.

"Yes. They were there. I saw them briefly."

A tense moment hung between them, then Rose pushed back her chair and stood. "I'll go find Boomer. He's probably bothering the pigs again."

"Shall I come with you?"

She shook her head. "No need. I'll only be a few minutes."

Grabbing her shawl off the hook by the door, she hurried outside into the cool evening air, welcoming the chance to escape.

Rose needed time to think, and she couldn't do it with Alexander around. Being with him confused her, put her thoughts all in a jumble. She had thought that while he was in Omaha, she'd be able to sort out her feelings for him and decide what to do.

And she had. Sort of.

She had come to the decision that they would continue the platonic aspect of their relationship and keep things uncomplicated, until Alexander decided it was time for him to leave.

Rose had no doubt that he would someday. Alexander was a duke. He had responsibilities back in England. His sojourn to America was only a temporary diversion, a respite from his responsibilities, like attending the Wild West Show had been.

Though she loved Alexander, she was practical enough to know that a romantic relationship with him was an impossibility. She didn't want to be a temporary diversion, a fling for a bored aristocrat.

When she gave her heart to a man, she wanted it to be forever. She wanted to sink her roots in, like she did with the land, and make something beautiful grow.

That's who she was. That was how it had to be.

CHAPTER 12

On a wet October morning Jacob Heller was laid to rest in the small cemetery at the outskirts of town. None of the brethren from the Mennonite church had been summoned to his passing, nor had any of Pastor Bergman's congregation. Rebecca wanted it that way.

Those who had ignored Jacob Heller in life would not get a chance to atone for it at his death.

Seamus was there to speak kind words over the body and to pray for Jacob's departed soul. Though the words had been memorized from the Catholic Bible, they'd been spoken from the heart, and Rebecca realized that what Rose Elizabeth had told her those many weeks ago was true: It wasn't a man's religion that mattered, but only what was in his heart.

Seamus had a good heart, and Rebecca had come to love him for it.

How many times had he sat with her at Jacob's bedside to offer words of comfort, to bathe her father's frail body when she was too exhausted, and he had never wavered in his devotion to either of them. He'd been more of a friend to Jacob than those so-called men of religion who had turned their backs so long ago and abandoned them in righteous indignation.

Rebecca stared at the wooden casket now sunk deep in the ground, then glanced first at Seamus, then at Alexander and Rose Elizabeth. Untying the strings of her bonnet, she removed it and her lace cap and tossed them into the grave. The decision had not been easy, but it had been necessary.

"This part of my life I bury with you, Papa," she whispered, tears streaming down her face.

Believing that this was a Mennonite burial ritual, Alexander and Rose Elizabeth exchanged puzzled looks as they huddled under the umbrella. The rain was falling harder now, like crystal tears from Heaven, mourning the loss of a true believer.

Seamus stared at the woman he'd grown to love and wondered at her odd behavior. Rebecca had never before uncovered her glorious hair in public. It was considered a vain gesture, something a Plain woman would never do.

When the last shovel of dirt had been placed on the mound and the wooden marker, carved by Seamus's own hand, set in place, Rebecca turned to the small gathering. "My father would have been greatly touched to know that you traveled so far to wish him well on his journey. I thank you from the bottom of my heart."

Her tears starting anew, Rose stepped forward to grasp her friend's hand. "If you need anything at all, Rebecca, you let us know. It's difficult losing a pa. I know."

Alexander took Seamus aside. "Like Rose Elizabeth says, if you need anything . . ."

Seamus shook his head. "It's all been taken care of. Jacob started putting money away when he first took sick. He told me he didn't want to be a burden to his daughter." Tears filled the big man's eyes. "Jacob was kind, and I'll miss him." He'd grown to love the old man like a second father. The baker had shared with him not only his recipes for baking but his recipes for life.

"Do not wish time away," he'd said to Seamus one day when the Irishman had grown impatient about something. "Time is something we can never get back. Once it is gone, it is gone for good. Enjoy each minute to the fullest and the hours will take care of themselves."

But it had been the promise that Jacob had extracted from Seamus right before he'd died that had had the most impact. "Take care of my daughter, Seamus. She will need your strength once I am gone. You love her, do you not?"

He'd been so taken aback by the question, he could only stammer at first, but then he'd smiled and said, "I love the lass more than I ever thought possible, Jacob. She'll never want for anything as long as I'm around."

"She's stubborn, Rebecca is. Don't let her *grexin'* put you off. A woman needs to complain every once in a while."

"She could never be as mule-headed as me, Jacob."

The old man had clutched Seamus's hand and squeezed it, though there hadn't been much strength in the gesture. "Promise me you will always love my Rebecca, Seamus. It will not be an easy road for you to travel because you are both so very different, but it will be worth it at journey's end."

Seamus had given Jacob his word, and now as he stared at the woman before him, with her blond hair whipping about her cheeks and her sad eyes filled with tears, he knew it was a promise he would keep.

Death always made Alexander uneasy. It reminded him of things best not remembered, like his father's dying declaration that Alexander would succeed him as duke and make him proud; like old Will Farris, Moreland's stablehand, who'd been a great friend and counselor to a young boy starved for love and attention; like the kind old man they'd just buried six feet under.

Alexander gazed thoughtfully at his companion asleep on the wagon bench beside him, and though the deluge continued, Rose Elizabeth slept the sleep of the innocent.

The mules plodded along at their own rate, and Alexander was content to let them. It gave him time to think, to sort out the conflicting emotions he'd been experiencing of late.

Guilt was certainly one of them. Guilt for what he'd almost done with Peggy, for what he *had* done. And guilt for wanting to make love with Rose Elizabeth so desperately that his whole body ached with need.

He had no right to feel this way—he'd told himself that a hundred times or more. He wasn't a free man. He had no legal means to do right by Rose Elizabeth. And even if he had the means, marriage to Rose would be impossible.

His title and position, and all the miserable pomp and circumstance that went with it, dictated who he was, who he must marry, and how he should behave in any given situation.

His education at Eaton had trained him to be a leader. He'd been taught that composure in the face of mortal danger was the hallmark of a true gentleman.

But no one had taught him about loving the wrong woman. No one had taught him how to turn off his feelings, to harden his emotions, to ignore the dictates of his heart.

His mother had tried. She'd warned him about love, about the unsuitability of some women, about wearing his heart on his sleeve, and the foolishness of young men's desires.

But, starved for attention, Alexander had ignored her, pursuing one young bit of fluff after another, making promises he knew he could never keep, searching out the warmth that had been missing from his life.

And now that he'd finally found it, it was out of his reach. Rose Elizabeth would never fit into his orderly world of rules and decorum. The pretense and confinement of his life would kill her soul, as it had damaged his.

And he could never give her the child he knew she wanted.

Alexander had seen the yearning in Rose's eyes whenever she gazed at a baby. Despite her protestations to the contrary, Rose Elizabeth was destined for marriage and family. She had a nurturing spirit and gave of herself unselfishly. It would be criminal to deprive her of such joy and fulfillment.

Her head lolled over to rest on his shoulder, and a large lump formed in his throat. He loved this strange woman-child. Loved her with all his heart.

If only . . .

He shook his head. *If only*s were for commoners and unencumbered souls. They weren't for men of noble birth . . . for affianced men of any birth.

"Good God, lass, have you lost whatever sense the good Lord gave ye?"

Smoothing the folds of her new green calico dress as she entered the kitchen the morning after her father's funeral, Rebecca shook her head, hoping her cheeks weren't as red as they felt. "My senses are perfectly intact, Seamus. I have decided that I will no longer be Plain."

His eyes widened, and his mouth dropped open. "You cannot change who you are, Rebecca. You were born Plain, raised to be that way. You cannot change at this late date. It would be like me trying to change the fact that I'm Irish." A purely sinful thought, he decided.

Tying a pristine white apron around her middle, she went to the windows to lift the shades. Bright sunlight poured into the room. "I have decided that Plain does not suit me anymore. I honored my parents' wishes to be like them, but in my heart I know that I am not. I am prideful. Sometimes vain. And I cannot help that." Nor could she help the sinful feelings she had toward a man who was not her husband. She wanted Seamus as husband, as lover, as father of her children, and if she had to forsake all else to have him, then so be it.

"You are just experiencing some sort of shock because of your father's passing, lass. In time you'll return to your true nature." When she stubbornly refused to listen and turned toward the stove, he added, "And are ye forgettin' that you just buried Jacob yesterday? You should still be wearing the colors of mourning. And where did you get that dress anyway?"

"My papa knew that I loved him, Seamus, and in my opinion it is not necessary to wear black or gray, though others may be convinced of it.

"I purchased this dress a week before my father died. I decided that if Papa did not survive his illness, that if God took away such a wonderful, kind man, I would be Plain no more.

"Now, shall we begin with the bread or the crullers this morning?"

Seamus stepped forward and took her hand. "Your faith has been tested, lass, and it's come up short in your opinion. But that's no reason to throw away a lifetime of teaching and turn your back on the only religion and way of life you have ever known. Trying to be something you're not will eat away at you and make you miserably unhappy."

She studied his face, which was filled with compassion and tenderness, and she knew he was speaking from his heart. "Have you tried to be something you are not, Seamus? Is that why you feel so strongly about what I am doing?"

He crossed to the stove, filled two ceramic cups with coffee, then seated himself at the work table, indicating that Rebecca should follow. "It's not me I'm talking about, lass, but Alexander Warrick."

Her eyes widened. "But the duke has great wealth and a title. Why would he be discontented?"

"Alexander's not a happy man. He's lived his whole life trying to please others. First his father, then his mother, then his fi—" He took a deep breath at the blunder he'd almost made. "Alexander is no more cut out to be the Duke of Moreland than I am fit to be King of England.

"The smothering confinements of his role go against the grain of the man himself. To the outside world he embodies everything that is noble and suited to his role as duke. On the inside, he's like a bird who's eager to fly and experience new things—only he's had his wings clipped, so to speak."

"The duke and I are not so very different, Seamus. There were things I wanted to do while growing up, but I was not permitted. Things my parents would have considered worldly."

"Such as?"

She touched the crown of her braided hair, a wistful look on her face. "I've always wanted to wear my hair down like the other girls I would see on their way to school. Some wore ringlets, or braids, and some just let their hair fly loose in the wind. I was so envious of those girls.

"And there were times when we'd go into town and I'd watch the other children buy licorice or hair ribbons, and I'd feel so left out because everything I had was homemade, from the clothes we wore to the food we ate."

"But look at the fine craft you've learned, Rebecca. There's no other woman in this town who can bake as good as you, and I've no doubt that you have your Mennonite upbringing to thank for that."

She set down her cup and stared pensively into the dark liquid. "Perhaps that is true. I was taught to cook when I was very young. While others my age were playing with dolls, I was learning to knead bread dough."

"Do ye resent your upbringing, then?"

She sighed. "I do not resent anything my parents did, for I know that it was done out of love and a sense of duty to their beliefs. But when I look at Rose Elizabeth, who is so carefree and bold, I sometimes wish I had grown up with such freedom. There is much to admire about a woman like Rose Elizabeth."

Seamus smiled. "Aye. The sprightly lass is a kind, caring woman."

"She would be a good marriage partner for the duke."

"I've thought the very same thing, lass. But I know how Alexander feels about love, romance, and the like. He won't be talking marriage."

Before Rebecca could lose her nerve, she stared the Irishman straight in the eye, sucked in her breath, and asked, "And what about you, Seamus O'Flynn? Will you be talking marriage?"

*   *   *

"Just come inside and take a look around. I know you're going to love it once you've seen it."

Rose stood obstinately on the step leading to the almost finished wraparound porch of Alexander's new house and held out the lunch basket she'd prepared. "I've no desire to see your fancy house, Alexander. And besides, it isn't even a house yet. There're no walls inside, and no glass in the window frames."

"The glass has been ordered, and the interior walls will be going up this week."

She peeked around his legs to see a splendid walnut staircase leading to the second floor. She counted thirteen steps, an unlucky number if ever there was one.

"Another time. I've got chores to do. Some of us are not free to indulge ourselves."

His eyes narrowed. Rose Elizabeth had nothing on either of her mules when it came to being recalcitrant. "You're just afraid that you're going to like this house, Rose Elizabeth. Afraid that it's going to put that hovel of yours to shame. Why don't you admit it?" He took a step down, and so did she.

"Since I'm not a blue blood, such as yourself, your dukeness, I don't need to be puttin' on airs. I'm perfectly content with my soddy. If it was good enough for Ma and Pa, then it's good enough for me."

"I wonder what you'll do, then, when it's no longer standing. When this house is finished I intend to knock that miserable hovel the rest of the way down and construct a horse paddock in place of it."

She yanked the lunch basket back just as he reached for it, and her nostrils flared like those of a bull ready to do battle. "You most certainly will not! I intend to continue living there after you're gone."

"What makes you think I'm going anywhere, except to move across the yard to this house?"

"Because you're a duke. And dukes don't farm wheat in Kansas. They have other obligations."

The truth of her words made him wince. "At the present

time, my obligation is to this farm, and to this house. I intend to give them both my undivided attention."

He'd already placed advertisements in several eastern newspapers to acquire a staff to care for things in his absence, for Rose was correct: He would have to leave. But he had every intention of returning. And when he did he wanted Rose Elizabeth to be waiting for him.

With her knowledge of farming and household matters, she would make an excellent manager for his property, and he intended to suggest just that when the time was right.

Her bosom heaved, but it wasn't with indignation. Rose Elizabeth wondered what it would be like to experience Alexander's undivided attention. Her gaze drifted up his long muscular legs, past the manly bulge outlined by his tight trousers, to his rock-hard abdomen, then to his tanned chest, visible beneath the open shirt front. She swallowed with a great deal of difficulty.

"I . . ." She cleared her voice, which sounded far too high, and began again. "I'm not gonna let you tear down my house, no matter what I have to do to stop you."

His smile was rakish. "Are you threatening me with bodily harm, Rose, or are you offering a more interesting incentive for me to change my mind?"

"I'm willing to barter."

"I doubt you'd like my terms."

"Why don't you try me?"

His grin widened. "Sweet Rose, that's what I was hoping to hear you say."

She blushed as red as the gingham napkin covering the cold chicken. "I meant—I'm willing to hear your offer."

"I made one once and you soundly rejected it," he reminded her.

Now her ears grew red. "I told you, I won't be any man's mistress."

"If you're holding out for marriage, I'm not in a position to offer that."

"I wouldn't marry you, Alexander Warrick, if you were the

last man on the face of this earth. Just the thought of spending a lifetime with you gives me hives."

He laughed. "Just what type of bartering did you have in mind?"

"I thought I could do your chores—you know how much you detest milking the cows—and perhaps I could sew curtains and such for the new house."

He rubbed his chin as if contemplating the offer. "A tempting proposition, but not as tempting as what I'm thinking about."

She stiffened, hands clenched tight around the lunch basket. "You Englishmen are all rakes and scoundrels."

He stepped down until he was standing on the same step with her, his body so close that she could feel his heat radiating toward her. "And you American women are exciting and provocative. Is it any wonder that you bring out the worst in us poor foreigners? We're not used to so much combustible material."

She poked his chest. "You just leave my *bust* out of this, your highness."

He threw back his head and laughed, ignoring her annoyance, and pulled her into his arms. The basket slipped from her hands to the ground. "I want nothing from you, Rose Elizabeth, except to remove that stupid board you've put between us in bed. I want to hold you in my arms at night, kiss you until you can't think straight, and make mad, passionate love to you until the wee hours of the morning."

She couldn't think straight now. The blood rushing to her brain made it impossible. "I . . . I told you I won't be your mistress."

"I'm not asking for that. All I want is one night. One night of making love to you. And in the morning everything will go back to the way it was. Unless, of course, you decide that you like my lovemaking and want it to continue."

"But I won't be a virgin any longer."

"That's true." His seductive gaze raked her from head to toe. "On that count you can rest assured, my sweet Rose."

Her cheeks flamed redder than the reddest of ripe cherries. "And if I consent to this one night, you'll let me live in the soddy? You won't tear it down?"

He nodded. "Providing you agree to one stipulation."

She grew wary. "What's that?"

"I want you to manage this property during my absences to England."

The gall of the man! He wanted her to be an overseer, an estate foreman, an employee who would live on *his* property and manage *his* estates, and she could just toss in her virginity on top of it.

She swallowed her anger, knowing that she had no choice but to agree to his terms if she wanted to remain on the land. And it wasn't as if she was saving herself for anyone else. . . .

"All right. I'll do it. I'll give myself to you, and agree to manage things here, if you consent to let me live in the soddy for as long as I desire."

Unable to believe she had agreed to his outlandish proposal, Alexander's eyes widened. "You would surrender your virginity in exchange for your soddy? It's hardly an equal wager."

"You're the one who set the terms, your royal dukeness. Are you reneging on your offer? I thought you were a gentleman. Gentlemen don't break their word. It has something to do with honor, doesn't it?"

Honor could hardly be brought into this situation. Merely to consider such a despicable wager would be highly ungentlemanly. He was still engaged to another; he would be leaving to return to England. . . .

"Under the circumstances, I don't think it would be wise to . . ."

Before common sense convinced her that she was making the biggest mistake of her life, she held out her hand, telling herself that she had to lose her virginity sometime, and that it was unlikely that she would ever marry. And if she did, she could always make up some excuse about falling off a horse or something.

"Shall we shake on our agreement?"

He shook his head, clearly taken aback by her decision. "Rose . . ."

"One night of lovemaking for my living in the soddy as long as I like. Is it a deal?"

"Are you sure you want to surrender your virginity for something as meaningless as that sod hut you call home?"

"It might be meaningless to you, Alexander, but I put a great store by it. It's more important to me than expensive jewels or store-bought gowns. It's a reflection of my roots, my family, all I hold dear."

He stared at her outstretched hand, which shook slightly, an indication of her nervousness. Then he was surprised to discover that she wasn't the only one who felt vulnerable.

"Once we shake on it, you won't be able to change your mind, Rose Elizabeth, for we'll be consummating more than this agreement."

"A Martin always holds to her word." She swallowed, wondering how on earth she could ever go through with the outlandish bargain she'd concocted. "Is it a deal then?"

He gazed up at the sky as if hoping for divine intervention. When none came, he sighed. "God help me, but it is."

CHAPTER 13

"Marriage!" Seamus's eyes widened, then he broke into a grin and jumped to his feet, pulling Rebecca up with him. "Are you proposing to me, lass? Is that what you're saying?"

Her hands flying to her burning cheeks, Rebecca turned away, unable to face the Irishman. If he mocked her, made fun of what she was about to say, she would curl up and die a thousand deaths. "I would marry you, Seamus O'Flynn, if you were of similar mind."

He spun her around to face him, disbelief etched clearly on his face. "You would? But you've never given me the slightest indication."

She couldn't confess that she loved him. Though he'd kissed her, acted as if he cared, he was a man, and men were often prone to such behavior. And he might not love her in return. That thought pained like no other.

"It would be very practical for us to get married, Seamus. With my father gone, it wouldn't be proper for you to continue living in the same residence with me. People would talk.

And . . . well, you've worked hard here at the bakery. It would become half yours upon our marriage."

Her unromantic, practical confession didn't come close to what he'd hoped to hear, and it rankled. "So you want to marry me as a business arrangement and for no other reason?"

"Of course I care for you, Seamus. You've become part of the family, like an older brother. Papa was very fond of you too. It was his idea—about sharing the bakery with you."

Jacob's generosity forgotten, he shouted, "A brother! You care for me like a brother?" His look was at first incredulous, then disbelieving. "You might have convinced yourself of that, lass, but I've tasted your lips, felt your response, and it was far from sisterly." He pulled her hard against him, grinding his lips over hers to prove his point, then gentled his touch as his tongue traced the contours of her mouth before plunging deep inside.

It was at that moment that the front door opened. The bell tinkled, followed by a loud gasp of scandalized outrage.

"Merciful heavens! What is going on here?" Euphemia Bloodsworth pinned the couple with a searing, condemning gaze, waiting with crossed arms for an explanation. Her black-booted foot tapped impatiently on the floorboards.

Red-faced and appalled, Rebecca broke out of Seamus's embrace and rushed to the counter. Never in her life had she been in such a compromising situation. She thought that her father would surely roll over in his grave if he knew.

"Miss Bloodsworth, how nice to see you again."

Like the pendulum of a clock, Euphemia's index finger swung back and forth in the young woman's face. "You should be ashamed, Rebecca Heller. Your father has just been laid to rest, and I find you consorting with the hired help." She cast the redheaded giant a disdainful look.

Stricken, Rebecca covered her face in mortification, while Seamus stepped forward angrily and placed his hand on the spinster's shoulder. "You have jumped to the wrong conclusion, Miss Bloodsworth. Rebecca and I are to be married. We were merely sealing our engagement with a kiss. It's an old Irish custom."

Rebecca swallowed her gasp and turned to stare at him.

Her outraged sensibilities forgotten, Euphemia clapped her hands and smiled widely at Seamus. "I couldn't be more delighted. Allow me to hold a party in your honor." There was a weighty pause before she added, "Otherwise there might be talk. You know how some folks like to carry tales."

Seamus knew exactly, and his eyes narrowed. He'd have liked nothing more than to rip out the old biddy's tongue, but he wouldn't allow the loose-lipped spinster to sully Rebecca's reputation.

He smiled politely, hugging Rebecca close. "That's generous of you, Miss Bloodsworth. Isn't it, lass?"

Stunned and tongue-tied up until now, Rebecca cleared her throat nervously. "Yes . . . Yes, it is. But it is not necessary for you to give us a party. And I do not think it would be proper. As you say, Miss Bloodsworth, my father has just been laid to rest."

Not one to let mourning interfere with a social function, especially one of her planning, Euphemia brushed off the excuse with a wave of her handkerchief. "Nonsense, my dear. Jacob Heller was a practical man. I'm sure he'd understand the necessity of our plan. Every father wants his daughter to be accepted into society with a spotless reputation. And I know he would want you to have a proper engagement party."

Appalled at the idea, Rebecca shook her head. "It isn't our way. I don't think—"

"Of course it is, lass. Don't you remember? You decided to cast convention aside and try something new. Well, here's your chance. Miss Bloodsworth's party is just the thing to try out your new role."

Euphemia was clearly perplexed. "I'm afraid I don't understand."

"Rebecca's decided to embrace a different way of life. One that's not so confining," Seamus explained.

"But . . ." Rebecca protested, wondering why Seamus was

now in agreement with her plan to change, when only minutes before he'd been chastising her for it.

"Excellent!" Euphemia declared, practically gushing at the idea. "You'll need an entirely new wardrobe, my dear. Something bright and smashing for our . . . your party. And of course you'll want to join the Garden Club and Ladies Sewing circle. Your new life is going to be so totally fulfilling, you'll hardly be able to stand it."

Truer words have never been spoken, Rebecca thought, a sick feeling growing in the pit of her stomach.

Seamus saw the consternation on his fiancée's face and smiled inwardly. What he hadn't been able to convince Rebecca of, Miss Bloodsworth surely would.

Rose Elizabeth pulled the hairbrush through her long sable tresses, unable to meet the duke's eyes in the mirror. He leaned back against the headboard of the bed, devouring her with those compelling blue orbs, waiting like a wolf eager to pounce, the consummation of their bargain not far from his mind.

"You've been brushing your hair for over twenty minutes, Rose Elizabeth. Don't you think you've gotten the tangles out by now?"

She set down the silver-handled brush that had been her mother's and turned to find Alexander removing the bundling board that divided the bed in two. She attempted to swallow the lump in her throat, but it wouldn't budge.

"Just because we've decided on a bargain, Alexander, doesn't mean we'll be consummating it tonight. I need time to adjust to the idea. And why have you removed the board? I didn't give you permission to do that."

Alexander continued to stare at Rose and thought that a more enticing woman had never been born. Though her full figure was hidden by her pristine flannel nightgown, he knew what delights it concealed. Her lustrous hair shone like a mantle of brown velvet, and his fingers itched to lose themselves in the thickness of it.

He pulled the quilt over his lap to conceal his eagerness. "It sounds as if you're the one who is reneging on our agreement, Rose Elizabeth. I thought you were so anxious to have this done with, so you could remain in the soddy."

She twisted the folds of her nightgown between sweaty fingers, staring first at the empty space on the bed where she was to lie, then at Alexander, who looked as if he was enjoying her discomfort immensely. "I do not intend to renege on our agreement. But I need more time to prepare myself for such an undertaking."

He laughed at her naiveté. "We are not going to climb Pike's Peak, my sweet Rose. We are merely going to make love. I assure you it is not an 'undertaking,' or quite the ordeal you are making it out to be." He pulled back the covers on her side of the bed. "Why don't you join me and find out for yourself?"

She tried to move forward, but her feet seemed rooted to the floor. "As you've probably guessed," she said, her cheeks crimson, "I haven't done this sort of thing before. I need time to grow used to the idea of losing my virginity."

Virgins were a complicated lot, which is why he'd made it a hard and fast rule to stay away from them. Of course, like any rule, there was always that one exception. "Very well. But I will not put that blasted board between us again. If I agree to your terms, you must allow me to hold you in my arms and sample just a few of your charms."

His smoldering look alarmed her, as did the nakedness of his chest, and she wondered how much else of him was unclothed. "How few?" she asked.

He shrugged. "Some kisses and hugs. Perhaps a peek at your breasts."

Her face flamed again, and her nipples swelled at the thought of him seeing her unclothed body again. "I see," she choked out.

Alexander patted the space next to him. "I'm waiting, Rose Elizabeth."

She studied his long outline beneath the covers, then blurted, "Are you completely naked under that quilt?"

"Come and see for yourself."

She shook her head. "It wouldn't be proper for you to be completely naked, your dukeness. I'm told even married couples do not sleep in the altogether."

His eyebrow shot up. "Who told you that bit of rubbish?"

"I don't remember." But she did, and quite distinctly. It was at a quilting bee last winter at Abigail Stringfellow's house. Abigail and Sarah Ann had indulged themselves with three glasses each of port wine and proceeded to debate the propriety of nakedness in the marriage bed. Their conversation had grown quite ribald, as she recalled.

Shocked clear down to her drawers, and on the verge of the vapors, Euphemia had taken both women to task, threatening to inform Pastor Bergman of their disreputable behavior. It had been decided then and there that nakedness had no place in the marriage bed.

Alexander snorted disdainfully. "No doubt it was that opinionated, man-hating spinster, who wouldn't know what to do with a man in her bed, naked or not, if her life depended on it. I trust that you don't wish to end up a dried-up old crone like Euphemia Bloodsworth."

That image was enough to propel Rose Elizabeth toward the bed.

"To set your mind at rest, Rose, I still have on my drawers."

She slid beneath the covers and lay stiffly beside him. "I have no desire to become like Euphemia," she admitted finally.

Alexander scooted closer and drew her rigid body into his arms. "Relax. It's not as if we haven't kissed or been close before. And we've been sleeping in the same bed for weeks."

"But . . . this is different. This time it might lead to something more."

"We'll take it slowly. I promise. But only if you'll allow

yourself to relax. You're as stiff as that damned board I threw out of here."

She took a deep breath and expelled it slowly, feeling herself relax as Alexander's hand made circular motions against her back. "Aren't you going to turn off the lamp?" His warm breath tickled her ear, and she felt gooseflesh rise over her arms and legs.

"I want to look at your lovely body, my sweet Rose. I can't see the fullness of your breasts, the rosy hue of your delectable nipples, without the light on."

She held her breath as his fingers went to the buttons of her nightgown. She had thought she'd be safe and secure in the plain, faded flannel, but she was wrong. More than her body would be laid bare and vulnerable.

Alexander pushed back the parted edged of the gown and gazed reverently at her bosoms. "You are perfection, my sweet Rose." His hand came up to cup one breast, his thumb circling the sensitive, swollen nipple. "I have seen many breasts in my lifetime, but none as lovely as yours."

"Thank . . . thank you."

He smiled, then kissed the tip of her nose and said, "You're welcome," before lowering his mouth to take first one protruding bud, then the other, between his lips.

Instantly, heat flooded Rose Elizabeth's thighs and she grew wet. Never before had she wanted someone to kiss her as she wanted to feel Alexander's lips upon her own. Grasping his head between her hands, she drew it to her mouth.

Their kiss was sweet and hot, and Rose lost herself in the sheer ecstasy of it. Then she had to forcibly remind herself that, as sweet as it was, it held the promise of what would happen if she did not put an end to it now.

Before she could pull back and voice her fears, a familiar croaking sound ensued.

Ribet . . . ribet . . . ribet . . .

Alexander stopped and turned his head, looking none too pleased by the interruption. "What the hell was that?"

A huge smile of relief lit Rose Elizabeth's face. Lester had survived! He was back. "Just Lester. He sleeps under the bed."

Ribet . . . ribet . . . ribet . . . The croaking sound grew louder.

The duke's eyes widened. "Has that damned frog been sleeping under this bed all the while?"

Rose smiled impishly, happy to be back in control of her emotions, her body, if only for the moment. "Lester disappeared during the tornado, but now he's back. And he's always slept under the bed. He's usually quiet and hardly ever croaks at night, but I guess our activity disturbed him."

"Well, isn't that just too damned bad!" Alexander leaned over the side of the bed and peered beneath it, scowling. A bloat-faced frog with bulging eyes stared back at him.

Ribet . . . ribet . . . ribet

"Oh my God!"

At that moment Boomer burst through the doorway and leaped onto the bed, showering Alexander's face with wet kisses.

"Now look what you've done, Alexander. Your shouting woke the dog."

Wiping his cheeks with the back of his hand, he whipped about to look at Rose. "It was not I, madam, who turned this bedroom into a menagerie. Animals should be kept outside, where they belong."

Boomer barked his disgust.

Lester croaked his contempt.

Alexander fell back down on his pillow and pulled the covers up over his face.

Rose Elizabeth petted the dog and breathed a sigh of relief. She'd been granted a reprieve tonight. But the piper still had to be paid.

Alexander took another bite of his ham sandwich and looked askance at Seamus, who had arrived a short while ago and was now standing at the bottom of the stairs looking rather sheepish. "What do you mean you're engaged to be married? You've only been here a couple of months."

"Time cannot dictate the workings of the heart, Alexander. I'm planning to marry Rebecca as soon as we can get everything arranged."

Alexander suspected that Seamus's heart was not nearly as involved as his groin, but he didn't voice his opinion, not wishing to have his face rearranged by the pugilist. "Rebecca's father has only been dead a week, Seamus. How will it look to everyone if she marries so quickly?"

"How will it look if I'm living in her house and we're not married? People will talk. Euphemia Bloodsworth has assured me of that, your grace. And I'll have no one staining the lass's honor." He told Alexander about the incident at the bakery and Euphemia's plans for an engagement party to be held next Saturday evening.

"That old hen's got a mouth bigger than the Atlantic Ocean." Having lost his appetite, Alexander stuffed the remainder of his sandwich back into the wicker basket. "I guess this means you'll be staying here in Kansas permanently."

"Aye. And I'm thinking that I'll be liking that just fine. There's nothing left for me in Ireland. Me mother's found a husband, and opportunities for a man like me are nil. Once Rebecca and I are married, I'll be granted half ownership of the bakery. It's more than I would ever have back home."

"But what of her religion, her way of life? It's so alien to you, man. Are you going to adopt her ways, then?"

With the palm of his hand, Seamus braced himself against a post on the newly constructed porch. The crisp autumn breeze felt good against his face. "I don't know right now what will come of all that. Rebecca's got it in her head to toss aside the teachings of her upbringing. Her father's death hit her pretty hard. It's made her face things she cannot understand or accept."

With a sigh, Alexander rose to his feet and faced his friend. "I'll miss your companionship, Seamus. You've been a good friend to me all these years. I'd probably be in prison right now if you hadn't stopped me from shooting Jessica and Edward."

"You were drunk. It wasn't too difficult to intercede, as I recall. Though I'm not sure to this day that the two fools didn't deserve to be shot. I just didn't want you to be the one doing the shooting."

"It's a debt I can never repay."

Uncomfortable with the duke's praise, Seamus changed the subject. " 'Tis a fine house you're building, Alexander. Have you convinced the sprightly lass to be moving in here with ye?"

Alexander didn't attempt to hide his disgust. "She's determined to stay put in that miserable soddy."

"Is that so?" Seamus's brow lifted. "And how did she convince you of that? Last time we spoke, you were determined to tear down the place. 'Chop it into little pieces,' if I recall correctly."

A flush crept slowly over Alexander's face. "We've struck a bargain of sorts."

"And does this bargain have anything to do with the lass becoming your mistress?"

The duke shook his head. "Rose has flatly refused that offer. Beyond that, I will not discuss our personal affairs."

The Irishman's tone grew as serious as his expression. "You must tread carefully, your grace. Rose Elizabeth is a loving woman. Once she gives her heart away, she's not likely to take it back. And one day you'll be leaving."

"Her heart is not involved, Seamus. Trust me. Despite the fact that we're living together, Rose still views me as the enemy. She cares only for this land, that miserable pile of earthen bricks, and a profitable wheat crop."

"For an educated man, you're not very smart, Alexander. One has only to look at the lass to see that she's smitten."

"You're wrong, I tell you."

"And what about you? You're in love with the woman and don't even know it."

"You're wrong, there too, Seamus. I do know it. And it

tears at me every single day. But there's nothing I can do. You know as well as I that I'm not free to commit myself. And even if I were, can you see Rose Elizabeth as a duchess? Can you picture her in a formal drawing room, seated across from my dour-faced mother, pouring tea out of a porcelain pot and making idle chit-chat with vapid women who've never had thoughts beyond what dress to wear or what ball to attend?

"She would hate it. And then she would grow to hate me."

Alexander looked so miserable that Seamus felt compelled to comfort him. Clasping the duke's shoulder, he squeezed it affectionately. "Rose Elizabeth is a strong, determined, intelligent woman. I think she could adapt to almost any situation, if she put her mind to it. You shouldn't sell her short, Alexander. If you love her, then make it work."

He would have loved nothing more than to believe his friend's words, but Alexander knew that love was not the panacea the Irishman thought it to be. "Spoken like a man in the throes of an all-consuming love."

Seamus laughed. " 'Tis true. I love the lass something fierce, and nothing and no one will stop me from possessing her."

"Spoken like a man who does not already have a fiancée."

"Aye. You're in quite a pickle, your grace. But you've got the means to end it."

"It's not as easy as you make it out to be, Seamus. Not only do I have the dowager duchess to contend with"—he grimaced at the thought—"but there's also the matter of Edward. He's still my brother, despite everything that's happened. I'm not certain what action to take against him."

"Castration would be a good start, your grace."

Alexander smiled at the Irishman's jest. There was no love lost between Seamus and Edward. They had hated each other on sight. Alexander had often wondered if it was Edward's unreasonable jealousy of the Irishman—of Seamus and Alexander's close friendship—that had led his brother to Jessica's bed.

"In order to set aside my engagement, Seamus, I must return to England. I'm not ready to do that yet. There's the house to finish, the wheat crop to harvest. . . ." His voice trailed off as he stared at the fields, at the green shoots sprouting up, and felt a great sense of accomplishment at what he'd done with his own hands.

"The longer you stay, the harder it will be to leave."

"Maybe I won't leave. Maybe I'll just live out the remainder of my days as a Kansas wheat farmer."

Both men knew that this was only wishful thinking. As much as he might want to, Alexander couldn't change what he was: a nobleman, an English duke, a man committed to more than an unfaithful woman. And most of all, he was a man determined not to see his brother squander the fortune it had taken his family several generations to amass.

CHAPTER 14

"I've decided that it's time."

Alexander stared down the ladder he was perched on and saw Rose Elizabeth gazing up at him. Though it was the middle of the afternoon, she was dressed in a nightgown and wrapper. Odd behavior, even for her.

Removing the small finishing nails from his mouth, he said, "I've just finished dinner, so I know it cannot be time for supper yet."

"It's time," she repeated, pleating and repleating the folds of her wrapper. "You know. Time to . . ."

The scent of lavender drifted up to him, and it was then he noticed that her hair was loose and hanging to her waist. She looked ready for bed, but it was only the middle of the day. "Are you sick? Is that why you're in your nightclothes?"

Her nervousness made her tongue sharp. "Honestly, your denseness!" She shook her head, amazed that any man could be so obtuse. "It's time to meet our agreement, I've decided."

His mouth dropped open, and the ladder started to wobble. "What?" He shook his head as if to clear it. He'd been waiting days for Rose Elizabeth to get adjusted to the "undertaking," as she called it. And now, in the middle of the day, while he was trying to complete the interior walls, she strolled into the unfinished house to announce that she was finally ready!

To make sure he'd heard her correctly, he leaned down and asked, "You're finally ready to meet our bargain?"

"Are you deaf? I said yes, I'm ready."

Her response so unnerved him that his foothold began to slip, then he came crashing down the ladder and fell at her feet, which were bare, he noted.

Alarmed, Rose dropped to her knees beside his still body. "Alexander! Are you all right?" She performed a cursory examination, assessing his arms, legs, and ribs. Nothing seemed to be broken, and she let out a deep sigh of relief.

As if reading her mind, he said, "I've broken my pride, madam. Nothing more." He rolled slowly to his feet, rubbing the small of his back, which felt stiff and sore. "Your announcement took me a bit by surprise."

"I don't know why. I said I wouldn't renege. Are you ready?"

Now that she'd finally made up her mind, she was as eager as a racehorse at the starting gate. "Rose Elizabeth, as much as I would like to make love to you—have dreamed of little else these past nights—I have just fallen off a ladder and will need some time to get my muscles back in working order."

Her eyes widening, she stared directly at his crotch. "Oh! I didn't realize that you had injured yourself in such a manner. Elmo had a similar problem once."

He straightened up, and was immediately sorry as the pain in his back intensified. "I can assure you, madam, that *all* of my working parts are in order. Alexander Warrick can always rise to the occasion. And I take umbrage at being compared to a pig."

She found his indignation extremely amusing. The male gender was prideful to a fault. Even Elmo had sulked for days on end when his equipment had failed to function.

"Come to the house and I'll rub some liniment on your back. It'll help ease the soreness out of the muscles."

"Is it that same smelly liniment you use on the pigs and mules?" His nose wrinkled in disgust. The only thing more malodorous was Percival's droppings.

"The very same. But it works. And you're not in a position to be choosy."

"I'll need to take a shower first. I'm sweaty and dirty from working on the house. The interior walls are nearly finished," he said proudly, but she ignored the pronouncement and sniffed the air like a bloodhound.

"So I noticed. But it's a bit chilly to be bathing outside in cold water. Why not let me fill the tin tub with hot water, and you can soak in it awhile. It'll loosen up those muscles real quick."

An erotic look crossed his face. "I'm beginning to like the sound of this more and more."

"Well, I hope that by the time you're done bathing and complaining about your various ailments, I don't change my mind about the agreement. I had to work up to coming out here, and now I'm fixin' to change my mind again."

Rose started to walk away, but Alexander reached out and grasped her hand, pulling her to him. "Before you go, let me give you a little incentive to get your courage back up." Pressing his lips to hers, he slowly caressed her mouth, then plunged his tongue deep within to explore the inner recesses, while his hands massaged her buttocks. At her moan of contentment, he drew her closer to him and allowed her to feel how hard and hot she'd made him.

Every nerve ending in Rose Elizabeth's body tingled. Her skin felt scorched, and her nipples were so rigid she thought surely they would fall off if he so much as touched them. And there was an uncomfortable throbbing between her legs that wouldn't stop, even when she pulled her thighs together tightly.

"I'll go fill the bathtub," she croaked, sounding not unlike Lester.

Alexander caressed her cheek tenderly. "You do that, sweet. I'll be there in a moment, and we'll finish what we started."

As she gazed at Alexander reclining in the tub, Rose Elizabeth thought she had never seen a more perfect man. His arms had grown even more muscular from his work on the house, and his chest was deeply tanned from the hours he'd spent shirtless in the sun.

He looked so contented lying there, his eyes closed, his arms hanging loosely over the sides, that she hated to disturb him. But she was still so very aroused by his kisses and caresses that she decided to meet their bargain right away.

"Alexander." She poked his forearm, and his eyes flew open. The smile he flashed made her heart pound anew.

"I thought I was dreaming. How long have I been soaking?"

"Long enough to shrivel any working parts." She blushed when he laughed and pointed to the bedroom door.

"Wait for me inside. I won't be a moment."

"And will you be wanting your back rubbed? I need to fetch the liniment."

"Madam, there are many parts of me that I intend to have you rub, but my back is not one of them."

Her face flaming redder, Rose Elizabeth scurried into the bedroom and slammed the door behind her.

Alexander found her moments later, cowering beneath the bedcovers, which were pulled up to her chin. "Do I need to check for animals before I come to bed?" He gave a cursory glance around the room.

She shook her head. "I've already put them out."

"Excellent. Now there'll be nothing to spoil our afternoon." He untied the towel around his waist and let it drop to the floor, and Rose Elizabeth's eyes widened to the size of silver dollars.

Alexander's member jutted out like the ridgepole supporting the roof, and it looked every bit as long and hard. She swallowed. "You're naked!"

"Indeed. And so will you be soon, my sweet." He yanked back the covers and climbed onto the bed, leaving Rose Elizabeth nothing to cling to but the front of her gown and her apprehension.

"Come now, Rose," he coaxed, pulling her into his embrace. "There's no need to be nervous. You know I would never do anything to hurt you, don't you?"

Her eyes fixed on his member once again, and she wasn't quite certain how to answer. Surely she'd be rent asunder if he attempted to stick that large protrusion inside of her. "I'm not a petite woman, your grace, but your maleness will never fit. I think we'd better forget this whole thing." She attempted to rise, but he leaned over and pushed her back down with his body, kissing her lips, then her neck.

"Relax," he crooned, grasping the hem of her nightgown. "You're much too beautiful to hide, Rose Elizabeth. Take off this thing. I want to look at you."

Mortified that he would find her less than pleasing, she turned her head away. "I'm not pretty like my sisters, Alexander. You're not going to like what you see."

"Because you're built like a woman and not like a thin stick of a girl?"

She tried desperately to push her gown back down. "My papa always called me his plump little partridge. I'm not pleasing to the eye, your grace."

"Nonsense." With one fell swoop he pulled the gown up and over her head, revealing her naked body to his view.

Rose attempted to cover herself with her hands, but he would have none of it and clasped both her hands in his large one. "You're beautiful, my sweet. Don't ever let anyone tell you any different." He lowered his head to lick at her protruding nipples. "Your breasts fill my hands," he palmed her mounds to demonstrate, "and I have very large hands." Those same hands then slid down her stomach to her abdomen, and he felt her muscles quiver in anticipation.

"Your stomach is womanly; your hips just the right size for a man to lose himself in."

"Alexander, stop. You're embarrassing me." Why had she chosen to meet their bargain in the middle of the day with the sun shining brightly? At least nighttime would have afforded her some modesty. "I appreciate what you're trying to do, but I can look in the mirror to see that I'm not the perfection you claim."

"Then you do not see what I see, Rose Elizabeth. I see a beautiful woman when I look at you. A woman who excites me, a woman who has the power to drive me insane with lust."

A woman who is driving him insane with her incessant chatter.

Rose Elizabeth shut her eyes tightly, unwilling to believe Alexander's flattery. For too many years she had viewed herself as plump and unattractive. The image Alexander had painted was not of Rose Elizabeth Martin but was a product of his lust and overactive imagination.

But as his hands continued their sweet caress, and his mouth found the center of her being, and his tongue began to glide over the surface of her womanhood, none of that mattered anymore to Rose Elizabeth. She was too caught up in the moment, in the exquisite sensations pouring over her, building inside her. . . .

"That's it. Just relax, my sweet." Alexander's mouth and hands trailed over every inch of Rose's body, kissing and caressing. He worshiped, communicating with his hands and body what he was unable to voice: that he loved her, desired her, as he had no other woman.

Rose lost herself in the wonderment of Alexander's lovemaking, and she began to respond in kind. Her tongue met his in a dueling battle of passion, and her hands explored his back, buttocks, the mystery of his very maleness, which she stroked tentatively at first, but then masterfully, making Alexander cry out in a strangled voice.

"You'll unman me if you continue on in that fashion."

"I like touching you, as much as I like you to touch me."

He kissed her again, wondering if he would ever again meet such an honest, unassuming woman. "Don't ever change, sweet Rose, for I cherish you just as you are."

His words brought tears to her eyes, but they quickly vanished as she felt him explore her most secret of places. All sensation centered in her womanhood, and the bud of her desire began to pound with unrelenting rhythm. "Holy—!"

He smothered her curse with his lips, pulled her legs apart, and entered her with one firm thrust, breaching the barrier of her virginity.

Rose felt only a moment of pain, and then there was only pleasure as Alexander took her to a higher plane of reality, ever up toward that intangible moment when the heavens thundered, a million stars exploded, and she cried out her climax.

Alexander spilled into her moments later, then collapsed in utter contentment, feeling totally replete for the first time in his life.

Wrapped in Alexander's arms, and the wonderment of her newly found bliss, Rose knew that she would never again feel as happy as she did at this moment, or quite the same way about a great many things. But mostly, she would never feel the same way about herself.

Alexander made her feel truly beautiful, but more important, he made her feel desirable. Seeing herself through his eyes, she could almost believe it was true.

The morning of the grand engagement party, which was how Euphemia was now referring to the celebration—because not only Seamus and Rebecca were being honored, but Marcella and Skeeter as well—found Rose Elizabeth busy preparing applesauce.

Alexander was still furious and barely speaking to her, for no sooner had their glorious afternoon of lovemaking ended than the bundling board had been put back in place, along with Rose Elizabeth's stern reminder that their bargain had been met.

The duke had used the most colorful expletives that Rose had ever heard. In addition to the usual "bloody hell," there had been "God's perdition, a pox on you, woman!" and a host of other swear words, which sounded far more eloquent when uttered with a British accent than an American one.

Rose felt conflicted about her decision to replace the bundling board to prevent any further lovemaking. Their afternoon together had been the most wonderful thing she'd ever experienced. But she was a practical woman, and she had vowed that she'd become no man's mistress, including the Duke of Moreland's, even if she did love him to distraction, much to her eternal disgust.

The apple peelings piled higher as she continued to contemplate her present situation. Though she knew Alexander cared for her, he didn't love her, had made no avowals to that end, and she had to protect herself against the hurt that was sure to come when he left.

If they continued making love, her feelings for him would deepen and intensify, and they would no doubt enter into a sordid affair in which she would come out the loser.

Men were permitted to sow their oats where they may, but a woman's reputation was a bit more tricky. Even though Rose might not be looked upon by her neighbors as a sterling example of young womanhood—she had been living with a man without the benefit of marriage, after all!—at least she had not fallen into that scurrilous position of whore, mistress, or, God forbid, prostitute!

The Martin name was still untarnished, as far as she could tell, and would remain so if she had anything to say about it. It was doubtful that anyone would be able to tell what had transpired yesterday afternoon . . . and evening . . . and night. No letter *A* would adorn her chest, as it had Hester Prynne's. Maybe the letter *S*, for stupid, silly, simpleminded twit who would trade her body for a dilapidated soddy.

But she would never regret it.

For one precious, ecstasy-filled day, Rose Elizabeth had felt like a real woman—a well-loved woman, a woman in love.

She had made enough memories to last a lifetime, maybe two, and she had Alexander James Warrick to thank for them.

There would be no regrets. Only sweet memories of the man she loved, of the man who would surely leave her one day.

"Why, Rebecca!" Rose Elizabeth stared wide-eyed at the lovely woman, admiring her blue and red taffeta dress and wondering at the transformation of her normally conservative friend. "You look truly beautiful. But why aren't you wearing your usual garb, if you don't mind me asking? Was this Seamus's idea? Or worse, Euphemia's?" Rose wouldn't put it past the interfering woman to dictate dress styles to the Mennonite girl.

Standing in a secluded corner of Euphemia's large, attractively furnished, if overly ornate, parlor, Rose Elizabeth was enjoying her third glass of champagne punch. The alcohol, which Skeeter had provided, unbeknownst to Euphemia, who was zealous in upholding the state's prohibition statute, seemed to lessen the effect Alexander had on her emotions, and it definitely took the edge off her annoyance at his unreasonable attitude and surly behavior.

"It was my idea to wear something colorful, Rose Elizabeth. I have decided to try a different way of living."

Rose took a gulp of her drink. "Can you do that? I mean—isn't it against the rules of your church or something?"

"Yes. It goes against everything I was taught. But I don't care. The church was not there for my father when he needed it, or for me either, and I do not wish to belong to such an uncaring community."

Noting the anguish on her friend's face, and knowing what a painful decision this must have been for Rebecca to make, Rose changed the subject quickly. "Congratulations on your upcoming marriage to Seamus. I know you'll be very happy. He's a wonderful man."

"Yes. And it is the most practical thing for us to do. Miss Bloodsworth made it quite clear that people would talk if we continued living together without the benefit of marriage."

Rose frowned in annoyance. "I wouldn't worry about what that woman says, Rebecca. If Euphemia isn't butting in to somebody else's life, she isn't happy. Anyway, her opinions are usually contrary to everyone else's. She's told me the same thing about my living with the duke. But quite frankly, I don't give a hoot and a holler what she says or thinks. I never had much of a reputation to begin with. And I certainly don't want to live my life like Euphemia Bloodsworth." *At least I've eliminated the dried-up old virgin part.*

"You're a very strong woman, Rose Elizabeth, and I envy you that. I wish I were more like you."

"No, you don't. I'm considered as common as good old Kansas dirt by most. My speech is usually peppered with cursing, and I never mince words when it comes to speaking my mind. You're much better off being the sweet, gentle woman you've always been. Folks respect that in a woman."

A soft smile crossed the blond woman's face, and she wrapped her arm about Rose's waist. "Perhaps all that you say is true, Rose Elizabeth, but that doesn't make me want to be any less like you. It is women like you who have made this country what it is today. You possess the spirit and the strength to succeed. Don't ever devalue yourself."

Rose was stunned and extremely touched by her friend's sentiments. No one had ever admired her before or paid her so grand a compliment. "My mama was the true pioneer woman. She carved a life for herself out of nothing, helped build our soddy with her own two hands. Neither wind, prairie fires, nor tornadoes could defeat her, so it makes me proud to hear that I might have turned out a little bit like her."

She smiled reflectively. "Though my sister Heather might take exception to that. She always said I was lazy."

Having heard most of the conversation, Alexander was

filled with pride and compassion. Rose Elizabeth was a rare breed, and it was good to know that someone else recognized her best qualities. "You are about as unlazy a human being as ever I've met, Rose Elizabeth. I'll be happy to debate that point with your sister, if the matter should happen to arise."

Rose's cheeks flushed at Alexander's unexpected compliment. She swallowed with some difficulty, trying to regain her composure as he stepped forward, looking devastatingly handsome in his somber black suit and blue satin waistcoat, which matched his eyes exactly.

His words touched her heart, and his smile brought forth glorious memories best forgotten, but she could not let those words and memories show on her face. Euphemia's eyes were trained on her and the duke, and she had the look of a hungry dog waiting eagerly for scraps to be thrown.

Determined not to give the older woman any grist for the gossip mill this evening, Rose Elizabeth replied, "Thank you, your grace. The next time I write to my sister I'll mention it."

"Everyone come into the kitchen now," Euphemia ordered with a clap of her hands, clearly disappointed that she would have nothing new to report to the Garden Club and Ladies Sewing Circle come Monday. "We're going to cut the coconut cake that Rebecca provided for this auspicious occasion." She marched off to the kitchen, expecting everyone to follow.

"Thank God we won't have to be eatin' any of Euphemia's desserts," Skeeter declared after she'd gone. "My stomach's still reeling from that prune pie she baked last week. I must have run to the privy over sixteen—"

"Skeeter!" Marcella shook her head. "Euphemia might hear you. And it was very generous of her to include us in this engagement party."

"Hmph! She just did it so she wouldn't miss any gossip. You know how Euphemia likes to have her hand in things. She probably figured that if she couldn't drag me to the altar, having me to this engagement shindig was the next best thing. Wait and see—she'll probably insist on coming on our honeymoon."

"Well then, you'd best get yourself a hotel room with one of those double-sized brass beds, Skeeter," Rose Elizabeth suggested with a grin, "'cause Euphemia's put on a few pounds in the last month."

Seamus burst out laughing. "Lord have mercy, lass, but you truly are a stitch. The man who marries you is sure to have laughter the rest of his days."

Rose and Alexander exchanged an uncomfortable look before strolling into the kitchen to watch the cutting of the cake.

"I guess you were hoping that this was going to be your engagement party, Rose Elizabeth." Peggy took a bite of cake, a sip of punch, and another bite of cake without so much as taking a breath. "But I can tell you firsthand that you're probably lucky it's not."

Feeling the urge to smear Peggy's smirk with a generous amount of white confectioner's frosting, Rose set down her plate, her appetite suddenly lost.

"I'm sure I don't know what you mean, Peggy. I've no intention of marrying anyone." She stared across the room at Sven, who smiled back, and her heart grew heavy.

"I found my trip to Omaha extremely enlightening. Alexander Warrick isn't quite the man I expected him to be." The woman's secretive smile bore straight into Rose's heart, for it was obvious that Peggy spoke from experience. But just what the extent of that experience was, Rose had no idea.

"Come to think of it, Alexander did mention that he had spoken to you and your father while he was there."

"Oh, we did much more than talk." She licked the gooey frosting off her fingers in a manner that could only be construed as suggestive. "At least we tried to."

Rose's expression hardened, but she did her best to maintain her composure. She had no intention of giving Peggy the satisfaction of knowing how much she irritated her. The woman was worse than a case of chicken pox. "I got the distinct impression from Alexander that he wasn't at all happy about the turn of events in Omaha. He said he found the *tarts* bitter and overdone. I wonder what he meant by that." Her smile as innocent as a baby's, Rose licked the sweet icing off her fork with a great deal of relish.

Peggy slammed her plate down on the table with such force that she nearly cracked the delicate china. Fortunately, the other guests, including Alexander, were absorbed in laughter and conversation and did not hear her outburst.

"The Duke of Moreland can go straight to the devil for all I care. He's not even a man, and I don't intend to waste another minute of my time on him." She stalked away, leaving Rose to wonder about her odd comment.

Alexander not a man? Whatever did Peggy mean by that?

Rose had firsthand knowledge that Alexander was all man—more man than most women experienced in a lifetime. But perhaps Peggy had never really gotten the chance to find that out.

That thought restored Rose's appetite, and she helped herself to another piece of cake, which was almost as huge as the grin on her face.

An hour later, Sven approached, looking like he had a great deal on his mind, and Rose Elizabeth dreaded the thought of what that might be.

Engagement parties and weddings gave folks fanciful notions, and Sven already had ideas about matrimony that made Rose feel uncomfortable.

"Good evening, Rose Elizabet. It is good to see you out and enjoying yourself."

"How have you been, Sven? How are the boys?"

"Good . . . good. But they miss you. They are always asking, When is Rose Elizabet going to come over for a visit?"

Rose felt heat creep up her neck. She was very fond of the Anderson boys, but she had been neglecting them of late, and she knew how much they craved a woman's attention. "I've been meaning to bring over some oatmeal cookies for Wilhelm and Peter, but I've just been so busy with the farm."

"You have been too busy for many things. You did not attend church last Sunday."

"I wasn't feeling well," she lied, unable to tell the truth that would surely wound him—that she had made love with another man, a man whom she loved more than life itself.

"You look healthy. There is a glow about you, Rose Elizabet. You look happy, but yet there is a shadow behind your eyes. Is anything wrong? I vill be happy to help, if you are having problems."

She patted the astute Swede's arm, wishing with all her might that she loved this generous, kindhearted man, but knowing in her heart that she did not. She loved Alexander, and therein lay the problem.

"You're too kind to me, Sven. I don't deserve your friendship."

"I told you once before, Rose Elizabet, that vill never change. We vill always be friends. I love you, Rose Elizabet. I always have and I always vill."

His admission brought tears to her eyes, and Rose was not a woman given to crying. "I love you too, Sven—as a dear, dear friend. I'm sorry it cannot be more."

"I am a patient man, Rose Elizabet."

She shook her head. "Don't wait for me, Sven. Go and find yourself a nice woman and marry her. There are plenty of ladies in Salina who would be proud to be your wife."

"But not you?"

"I don't think I'll every marry, Sven. I'm too independent . . . too set in my ways. I like my life just the way it is."

Sadness filled the Swede's eyes, and he patted Rose Elizabeth's hand before saying softly, "Maybe the right man has not asked you yet, Rose Elizabet."

Sven walked away, leaving Rose to ponder his words and to wonder if the "right" man ever would.

CHAPTER 15

As the knife sliced through the pig's throat and its blood poured onto the ground, the Duke of Moreland's stomach heaved twice, then its contents poured out as well.

Rose Elizabeth stared at the nobleman with complete and utter disgust. "Oh, for heaven's sake, Alexander! Haven't you ever watched a pig being killed before?"

Wiping his mouth with a clean linen handkerchief, then passing it across his perspiring forehead, Alexander shot her a scathing look. There was no understanding or compassion in her eyes, only condemnation. "No. I have never before participated in such a barbaric custom."

Hands on hips, her look incredulous, Rose Elizabeth shook her head. "Barbaric? How in hell do you think those hams and pork chops you eat get on your plate? The hogs have to be butchered first, your squeamishness. You're already sick and we haven't even gotten to the good part yet."

He slid her a look that said more clearly than words that he didn't believe for a second there could be a good part. "It gets better? What do we do next—drink the blood?" His stomach began to churn again.

Rose tapped her chin as if considering the suggestion, then smiled as Alexander's skin became greener. "We have to scald the pigs in boiling water, then scrub down their hides with brushes before we can begin the actual butchering."

She pointed to the large, cast-iron caldron bubbling furiously over the open fire, and Alexander couldn't help but make the comparison to a witch's brew. "Why don't we just hire someone to do this, Rose Elizabeth? I've plenty of money. And a lady shouldn't be involved in something so disgusting."

"For your information, your dukeness, I have never been accused of being a lady. And we have been killing hogs on this farm in November since I was knee-high to a grasshopper. Just because you've got a weak constitution doesn't mean we're going to stop that practice."

"Weak! How dare you! I've never in all my life had a weak constitution."

She laughed. "That's good. Because after we're done with the scraping of the hides, you're going to get a chance to carve the pigs up with a knife. The head and feet will have to be chopped off first, then boiled to make head cheese, then the . . ."

But Alexander wasn't listening anymore. He was splayed on the ground at Rose Elizabeth's feet, passed out colder than a frozen pond in January.

Dearest Rose,

With the Thanksgiving holiday just around the corner, I am reminded of how much I miss you and Heather. Things have not gone as planned, and my life here in Denver is disappointing to say the least.

Due to circumstances that I will not elaborate on now, I have left the saloon and Mr. Rafferty's employ to join the Denver Temperance and Souls in Need League, which is part of the Women's Christian Temperance Union. Chance's saloon is at the top of my list for reformation. Hortensia Tungsten, our leader, assures me that I have the talent and the ability to change lives and save souls.

Pausing halfway through her sister's letter, Rose's eyes rounded. *Laurel, saving souls?* She shook her head in disbelief. Was this the same Laurel who cringed if someone so much as said an unkind word to her? Who hated to hurt someone's feelings by telling the truth?

And did her sister really think that Chance Rafferty was going to sit back while she ruined his saloon and gambling business?

Rose Elizabeth concluded that her problem with the duke paled in comparison.

"Good grief, Laurel!" Rose declared with no small amount of ridicule, staring once again at the scented stationery. Laurel had always been naive, but Rose had never thought her stupid, until now.

Rose Elizabeth decided that she wasn't one to talk. She was clearly not the smartest human being on the face of this earth: She was hopelessly in love with a man who didn't love her; she had traded her body for a miserable soddy; and the only man who had ever professed interest in marrying her had turned his attention elsewhere, at her suggestion.

Sven had recently been calling on Hannah Whitaker, an attractive young widow with two small girls, who lived on the outskirts of town. She was a kind, vivacious woman and would be a good match for the quiet Swede.

Though she was pleased with Sven's selection and the prospect of his happiness, she was disappointed that he and the boys would not be spending the Thanksgiving holiday with her and Alexander. With Heather and Laurel gone, it would have been nice to have some semblance of family and tradition.

The holiday was the day after tomorrow, but Rose decided that she had little to be thankful for. Unless she counted the stalks of wheat blowing in the wind and the fact that Alexander hadn't returned to England yet.

She hadn't the courage to broach the subject, but the possibility of his leaving was always on her mind. Whenever a note arrived from Seamus, or an official-looking letter from Sussex, she broke out in a cold sweat, thinking that this was the missive that would drag him back home.

The object of Rose's thoughts was at the moment staring quite apologetically at the large turkey Rose had picked out for their Thanksgiving dinner. Alexander had been assigned the distasteful role of executioner, and the bird, which eyed him warily, seemed to sense that.

"This is going to hurt me far more than it'll hurt you, my friend," he said to the bird. Boomer barked twice, as if agreeing with Alexander's assessment.

"No need to put your two cents' worth in, you mangy mutt, or you might find yourself on that platter Thursday, too."

A bolt of lightning stabbed the sky, followed by a loud crack of thunder. The dog howled piteously, then took off for parts unknown, leaving Alexander to face his task alone.

"Coward," Alexander said, unsure whether he was referring to Boomer or to himself.

Holding the hatchet tightly in his hand, he stared at the bird and suddenly despised the age-old tradition of turkey with all the trimmings. In England, the turkey was presented golden brown and roasted to perfection atop a sterling silver tray. One didn't have to stare into its sorrowful eyes before eating the blasted thing.

"If you had the least bit of intelligence, you stupid thing, you'd fly out of this pen and never return." A gobble, accompanied by a slight ruffling of feathers, was the only reply he received, and Alexander breathed deeply to fortify himself for the task.

Why he allowed Rose Elizabeth to force him into these unsavory duties was beyond his ken. After all, he wasn't getting any personal benefit out of doing them. It wasn't as if he could go in after a hard day's work, take a hot bath, and crawl into bed and make love to the woman he loved.

Oh, no! Rose had put that damnable board back up quicker than he could say "bloody hell!" And she'd been firm in her convictions. Nothing he could say, had said, had made a bit of difference to her. She would not succumb to his overtures. And he'd made plenty! All she continued to say was that she would not become any man's mistress, and that to do the deed more than once constituted becoming a mistress.

Damn, but the woman was stubborn, obstinate, irrational, and irritating.

But he loved her, and that was the hell of it. And the reason why he remained on the farm and did her bidding, no matter how distasteful that bidding was.

Gobble-gobble-gobble.

"Don't remind me, you stupid, featherbrained creature." Maybe the turkey would just drown itself, Alexander thought hopefully, glancing up at the black clouds. Turkeys were known to do that in rainstorms, or so Rose Elizabeth had informed him.

Droplets of rain hit his face and soon the deluge started. Alexander cursed, holding the hatchet up over his head, and wondered if he shouldn't just use it on himself.

No man should have to be so miserable.

But then he thought of Rose Elizabeth's sweet smile, the way her hair fanned out over the pillow while she slept, her slightly off-key voice as she sang hymns at church, and he knew he wasn't really that miserable.

He was horny. The bulge in his pants gave testament to that, and he planned to rectify the problem immediately.

Right after he killed the poor, defenseless turkey.

Damned if he wasn't miserable!

*   *   *

The front door slammed shut, and Rose Elizabeth turned from the pie dough she was rolling to see a wet and bedraggled Alexander standing there. Moaning loudly, he was clutching his lower back with one hand and in the other holding what had once resembled a turkey. It now looked like some mutilated creature from another planet.

"Is that my nice fat Thanksgiving turkey?" Rose asked, horrified.

Alexander nodded. "He wasn't too cooperative, and it took several swipes of the hatchet before I could fell him. But I accomplished what I set out to do."

There was such pride in his voice that Rose didn't have the heart to tell him that the turkey's head was the only thing he was supposed to have cut off, not the feet, wings, and a good portion of the breast.

Apparently Alexander had performed his executioner's task a bit too zealously.

Rebecca and Seamus were having Thanksgiving dinner with them on Thursday, and Rose Elizabeth had no idea how she was going to serve them such a disastrous-looking bird. She considered herself a damn good cook, but she wasn't a miracle worker.

"Just set it in the sink. I'll pluck it after I'm finished with the pumpkin pies."

The entire room smelled wonderful. Cinnamon, nutmeg, and the tantalizing aroma of boiling pumpkin filled the air, making Alexander's stomach rumble. He was about to ask for something to eat when he remembered what sustenance he really craved.

Heaving the bird onto the counter, he cried out, "Oh . . . oh, my back!" while clutching at it and doing his best to look pitiful.

Rose glanced up again, and this time there was genuine concern in her eyes. "What's wrong? Are you injured?"

He shrugged, then winced. "I must have strained my back again when I was killing that bird. I'm sure it'll be fine in a few days."

She wiped her flour-covered hands on her apron. "Nonsense. You're drenched to the bone, and your back muscles have probably stiffened up again. You need a soak in a hot tub."

Alexander was smiling on the inside, but he nodded gravely. "You're probably right. I'll go get it."

"You'll do no such thing. Now get into the bedroom and strip out of those wet clothes. I'll get the tub and fill it with hot water."

He was about to argue, then thought better of it. If he was going to play the role of invalid, then he might as well play it to the hilt. Besides, Rose Elizabeth would no doubt thank him later, after he showed her what she'd been missing all this time.

The steaming tub stood near the stove when Alexander entered the kitchen area a short time later. Rose was once again at the table preparing her pies, and the rain beat a steady cadence on the roof and windows.

The atmosphere was warm and cozy. Just right for an afternoon of lovemaking, Alexander decided with a grin, lowering himself into the tub. *"Aaah,"* he crooned, leaning back against the end of it. "Thank you, Rose Elizabeth. You don't know how wonderful this feels."

His ardent moans of ecstasy went straight to Rose's midsection and lower, and she knew exactly how good it felt. She had peeked at Alexander's naked body while he was lowering himself into the tub, and the sight had excited her imagination and her memories.

She had made it a practice to keep her eyes shut tightly all the other times Alexander had disrobed, knowing that to put temptation before her would be extremely foolish. But today, knowing he was naked and only a few feet away, she hadn't been able to resist the urge to glimpse his glory.

"Your face is all flushed, sweet Rose. Is the steam making it too hot in here for you?"

She shook her head, wiping the sweat from her forehead

with the back of her hand. "I'm fine," she said. "Don't bother about me, just enjoy your soak."

But he was bothered. And so was Rose, if he wasn't mistaken. She was flushed to the tips of her ears, and she kept shifting her weight from one foot to the other, as if she couldn't stand still.

"Would you mind washing my back? The pressure of your hands might ease the soreness out of my muscles."

Their eyes met, and there was a slight hesitation on Rose's part before she said, "I'll fetch a washcloth."

"I'd rather you use your hands. I think it would be far more beneficial that way."

She stopped in her tracks, swallowed, and moved cautiously to the side of the tub. "You'll need to bend at the waist."

He scooted forward a bit instead, disturbing the water, and she could see his rigid manhood quite clearly. He grinned at her surprised expression. "Sorry, but your nearness always has that effect on me."

She blushed. "You behave yourself, Alexander, or I'll be forced to push your head under water to clear away your obscene thoughts." His grin was purely erotic.

Rose lathered the soap in her hands and began to massage Alexander's smooth, muscular back. The sounds of contentment he made were torture, as was the feel of his hot skin beneath her hands.

"God, that feels wonderful. But the pain is a bit lower, if you don't mind."

She paused, staring down into the water, then dipped her hands to his waist and below. "Yes, that's it. Just a little bit lower. *Aaaah . . .*" he said, then suddenly clasped her wrist and pulled her into the tub with him.

"Alexander!" she screamed. "What on earth—"

He silenced her with a kiss, settling her more firmly on his lap. Her dress was sodden and heavy, and he moved his hands beneath it to caress her.

There was only a moment of protest before Rose Elizabeth

succumbed to the desire that had been building inside her for weeks. Her need for Alexander ruled supreme over common sense and good intentions. "Alexander." His name came out as a sigh, as surrender.

Not waiting for any further invitation, Alexander tried to take off Rose's dress, but he fumbled with the wet, unyielding buttons. "Bloody hell!"

"Let me," she said, pushing his hands away and unbuttoning her dress with great efficiency. She removed it and her underclothes and tossed them onto the floor.

Naked, she reclined atop Alexander's chest and lap. "I doubt you'll ever complain about this old tin tub again," she said with a soft smile, caressing his cheek.

"I doubt you will either." He slipped his hand between them to her womanhood and began to rub his finger against the bud of her femininity.

"I should be furious with you." She moaned. "But I'm not." She moaned again, pulling his head toward her. She kissed him thoroughly, thrusting her tongue into his mouth just as his finger slid into her.

Moments later he entered her, filling her with his hard, hot shaft, and they climaxed almost instantly.

"God, I've missed being inside you like this," he admitted when they'd both recovered their equilibrium.

She nestled her cheek against his chest and listened to the rapid beat of his heart. "We shouldn't have done this. I can't allow it to happen again."

"How will you resist, my sweet Rose? I have only to do this," he tongued her nipples, "or this," he palmed her crotch, rubbing it slowly, seductively, "and you grow hot and wet with need. Why deny what we both want?"

Lifting her head, Rose gazed into his eyes. "And if our coupling results in a child, then what will I do?"

His look was like that of a wounded animal, and his voice was filled with sorrow, apology, and bitterness as he said, "It won't. I'm unable to sire children."

Was he telling the truth? Or was this merely a man's ploy

to have his own way? Rose Elizabeth wasn't certain, but it didn't matter anyway. Fear of a child wasn't the reason why she couldn't continue making love with Alexander. It was fear of losing her soul.

She had already lost her heart, and she'd learned that it was a devastatingly painful experience.

Extricating herself from his embrace, she climbed out of the tub, gathering up her clothes and hugging them to her breast. "This will not happen again, Alexander."

"But it will, Rose Elizabeth. And you know it."

She did. And she hated herself for her weakness.

"Your dinner was truly delicious, Rose Elizabeth. Was that something new that you did with the turkey? I don't recall ever seeing one shaped like that before."

Rose bit back her laugh and handed Rebecca another dish to dry. "Thank you. If the turkey looked odd, it was because Alexander has not yet learned how to kill one without hacking it to death." Fortunately, the bird had tasted much better than it looked.

Rebecca laughed, nodding in understanding. "It is like Seamus with the doughnuts. The first time he made them I could have donated them to Salina's new baseball team. They were that hard."

"Men don't know everything about everything, like they seem to think they do."

"It's true. Even my papa thought he knew more about baking than I did. He was forever making suggestions about the recipes, the way I baked my bread. . . ." Her eyes filled with sadness and her voice quivered. "I miss him."

"Of course you do. But now you have Seamus," Rose reminded her, pulling out a chair from the table and urging her to sit. "When are you two fixin' to marry, anyway? I haven't been to a wedding in ages."

Rebecca toyed nervously with Rose Elizabeth's best lace tablecloth. She didn't want to appear presumptuous, but Rose was the only real friend she had in Salina. "That is what I wanted to talk to you about, Rose Elizabeth. Seamus and I would like you and Alexander to stand up for us. We didn't want to set a date until we knew if you would."

Like a small child who has just been gifted with a grand present, Rose Elizabeth clapped her hands excitedly and squealed. "I'd be honored! I've never been a maid of honor before. And I'm sure Alexander will agree to be Seamus's best man." She remembered all the times the duke had referred to Seamus as "his man."

"I'm sure Seamus is outside right now asking him that very question. He felt a little awkward because Alexander used to be his employer, but I reminded him that the duke is his friend first."

Before Rose could reply the door flew open and the two men entered. Both were grinning like schoolboys, and Rose supposed that the question had been posed and answered in the affirmative. Either that, or they'd found her papa's old cache of corn liquor hidden in the barn.

"Alexander said yes, Rebecca," Seamus announced proudly, his arm wrapped around the duke's shoulders.

Rebecca beamed. "So did Rose Elizabeth."

The prospective maid of honor and best man exchanged smiles at the couple's exuberance, then Alexander winked. "Indeed, we'd be delighted. And I have suggested to Seamus, who has just taken a tour of *our* new house, Rose Elizabeth, that the wedding take place there. Pastor Bergman can come to the farm to perform the ceremony, then we can host the reception. What do you say?"

Three sets of eyes turned to stare at Rose Elizabeth, but it was the brilliant blue ones that set her teeth on edge. Though she'd known it was an impractical notion, Rose had hoped never to set foot inside Alexander's new home. From the triumphant gleam in his eyes, she could see that he was elated to thwart her plans.

Rebecca and Seamus's faces filled with hope, and Rose knew that she could not disappoint them. But she would find a way to deal with Alexander's underhandedness, of that he could be certain.

"I think it's a wonderful idea." Ignoring the duke's surprised expression, she added, "I'll get some of the ladies in town to help with the cooking, and Alexander can attend to furnishing the house and decorating it.

"You do intend to furnish the house, don't you, your highness?"

Rose was piqued, just as he'd known she would be. She had called him "your highness," which was a dead giveaway, and her nostrils had flared slightly, but Alexander remained determined that she would accept his home as her own. "Of course I intend to furnish it. Delivery of the furniture will be made next week. If we plan the wedding for the third week of December, that should give us plenty of time to arrange everything."

Everyone agreed that Alexander's plan was brilliant.

Rebecca's eyes filled with tears of joy.

Seamus's grin was so wide you could have driven a hay wagon through it.

Alexander radiated so much arrogance that he could have passed for one of the roosters in the hen house.

As Rose Elizabeth smiled, nodded, and seemed in perfect agreement with everyone, she formed a mental picture of Alexander as a bull's-eye and proceeded to shoot arrows straight into his conniving heart.

CHAPTER 16

Rose had been keeping an eye on the goings-on at the new house for the better part of the morning. She knew that her curiosity was about to get the best of her.

There had been a steady stream of wagons coming down the dusty lane, carrying various pieces of furniture and accessories. While hanging out the wash, she'd caught a glimpse of a huge four-poster being unloaded, and her heart had tripled its beat. Never before had she seen so large a bed, so soft and fine a mattress, and she had easily imagined herself lying upon it, nestled in Alexander's arms.

As the clacking of wagon wheels diverted her thoughts once more, Rose looked out the window and decided that her geraniums needed watering immediately. Grabbing her fleece-lined jacket, she headed outside.

The air was cold, the sky gunmetal gray; the promise of winter was not far off. Rose huddled deep within her warm coat, still able to discern the familiar odor of the pipe tobacco that her father had used for so many years.

A sense of longing washed over her. For what, she wasn't

certain. Perhaps for her youth, her innocence, for what could never be again. Or perhaps for something else she wanted but knew was unattainable.

"Hopes and dreams are fine, Rose Elizabeth," her mama used to counsel, "as long as your feet are planted firmly in reality."

With a dispirited sigh, she reached for the watering can, then caught sight of a tall, burly man she had never seen before. He was carting a lovely maple rocker up the front steps of the new residence, and her eyes widened in appreciation. It was by far the grandest rocker she had ever seen, with bright red cushions and a back so high a body could get lost in it, and it wasn't hard to picture herself seated in it before a roaring fire. . . .

"Stop it, Rose!" she scolded herself. "Alexander is just trying to lure you with all those fancy geegaws." *Damned if he isn't doing a good job of it, though!* she thought, fighting the urge to cross the yard and see the rocker up close.

The geraniums' leaves had turned brown and were drooping quite pitifully. Rose realized that no amount of water could cure what ailed them, so she tossed the watering can aside and started toward the barn. A nice chat with Elvira and Elmo was sure to take her mind off that damnable house.

She had taken only three steps before a loud, grating voice halted her in midstride: *"Yoo-hoo! Rose Elizabeth!"*

She cursed inwardly before turning about. "Why, Euphemia, I had no idea you were planning to visit today."

Inflated with self-importance, the spinster floated forward like a hot-air balloon, shaking a chastising finger at Rose Elizabeth. "Why aren't you over at the new house helping his lordship, young lady? A man needs a woman's help at times like these. It's clear to me why the duke has asked for my assistance in decorating the house. Of course, my excellent taste is known far and wide." She pursed her lips in what was supposed to be a smile.

Rose's mouth dropped open at the spinster's less-than-welcome news that she would be decorating Alexander's new house, especially considering the fact that Euphemia's purple and red floral dress looked like it belonged on one of Madame Rousseau's girls over at the House of Delights in Abilene.

Looping her arm through the spinster's, she led her toward the soddy. "I didn't want to tell the duke, 'cause I was saving it as a surprise, but I've already begun sewing curtains and such for his new residence. I appreciate your offering to help, Euphemia, but I've got everything under control." It was only a small lie—considering that she was at least planning to fashion curtains for the new house—and a lie told very convincingly, in her opinion.

Disappointment etched the older woman's face. "If you're sure . . ."

"Quite sure. Now come inside and warm up. I'll fix tea. And I've got some apple pie left over from last night's supper." Entertaining Euphemia was a small price to pay for saving Alexander's home from garish ostentation, and Rose wondered if the duke would appreciate the gesture.

"You'll keep my little secret, won't you, Euphemia? I'd hate to spoil Alexander's surprise."

"My dear, you know that I am the soul of discretion when it comes to keeping secrets."

Rose rolled her eyes heavenward. The only thing faster than a tale spinning from Euphemia's mouth was the locomotive of the Kansas Pacific Railroad, and even that was a toss-up, Rose decided. "I knew I could count on you."

"Why, of course, my dear. Now why don't we go over the plans for Miss Heller's wedding to Seamus O'Flynn. I'm sure if we put our heads together, we can make this the social event of the year."

A lump of apple pie lodged in Rose's throat, and she did her best not to gag. She had already dodged one bullet today, but it appeared that the spinster's gun was loaded and ready for bear.

*   *   *

Later that day, while Alexander had gone to Sven's to pick up a table the Swede had built for the new house, Rose Elizabeth's curiosity got the better of her.

Alone, with nothing but her imagination for company, she had plenty of time to wonder about the house and what it looked like inside.

Once, she had glimpsed a fine staircase, and she had seen the grand wraparound porch encircling the structure, but the rest of the residence remained a mystery.

Figuring that she had at least an hour before Alexander returned, Rose grabbed her jacket and hurried across the yard. She paused on the porch steps to admire the attractive exterior.

Alexander had chosen a soft gray paint with white trim, and the shutters were the color of ripe cherries. Her hand caressed the smooth newel post as she ascended the stairs and crossed the porch, which had a shiny gray floor and white trim as well. If she'd been asked to choose the colors herself, she would have selected the very same ones, she decided.

The oak front door had a set-in leaded glass rectangle, which looked like a work of art from one of those fancy big-city museums. Her finger traced the intricate floral design, then she opened the door and paused in the hallway.

The house exuded warmth, from the shiny oak parquet floors to the colorful oriental rugs covering them. Wandering from room to room, she oohed and aahed over the walnut and mahogany furniture, at the brass lamps and light fixtures, at the crystal chandelier that was suspended over the long dining room table with chairs to seat eight people.

As she entered the kitchen, she pulled up short, her eyes widening at the lovely rocker situated near the stone fireplace; it looked every bit as welcoming as she'd imagined. The cookstove was magnificent, and she ran her hand over the top of it reverently. It was black as coal, with shiny silver trim. Pots and pans of copper and cast iron hung over it, seeming to wait for a woman's touch.

Wide pine planking graced the floor, and there was a red,

white, and blue oval braided rug near the window, which, she suspected, would be placed under the table that Alexander had gone to fetch.

Sven was something of a craftsman when it came to his woodworking hobby, so she knew it would be of high quality as well as attractive.

She stared out the large bay window and wondered what it would be like to sit at that table and look down the lane leading up to the house, or sit in the rocker on a cold winter's day and peel potatoes for a rich meaty stew.

Red gingham curtains would look just perfect at the many windows. And there was even a small window in the door that led out to the rear of the house.

Upstairs she found three bedrooms. Two were small, as if designed for children—the thought filled her with sadness, for she knew that Alexander was incapable of siring any—and the large one was obviously the master bedroom.

The massive four-poster she had seen earlier rested against the back wall, and she had only to close her eyes to envision one of her colorful quilts spread upon it. Maybe the starburst, or perhaps the double wedding ring . . .

"I see you couldn't resist the temptation, my sweet Rose. I'm glad."

Spinning around to see Alexander standing in the open doorway, smiling at her, she felt like a child caught with her hand in the cookie jar, and her face reddened. "I thought you had gone to Sven's."

"I did. But I'm back, as you can see. Much to your surprise, I gather, from your shocked expression."

"The house is beautiful. You've done a wonderful job with it. And the furnishings are finer than any I've seen."

He stepped forward and gathered her into his arms. "I did it for you, sweet Rose. Each piece of furniture, lamp, rug, and mirror was chosen with you in mind. I envisioned you standing in every room . . . in this one, just as you are now."

"But I told you I wouldn't live here, Alexander. Why would you go to so much trouble?"

"Why indeed?" He captured her lips and tried through his kiss to communicate that he loved her. "You've given me a great deal, Rose Elizabeth. I can only repay you with monetary means, so I wanted everything to be very special."

His words wounded, though she knew that wasn't his intention. But Rose also knew that Alexander was incapable of loving her, and so had gifted her with material treasures instead of the love she so desired.

"You are too generous for your own good, your grace. As I've told you many times before, I'm suited to simpler things. This house is far too grand for a farm girl like me."

"Nothing is too grand for you, Rose Elizabeth. Nothing on this earth. And don't you ever forget that."

She caressed his cheek, noting the blond stubble. Alexander had been working very hard these past weeks, and the strain was beginning to show. "I'd best be getting back to the soddy. I've supper to fix, and Boomer's probably scratching to get out."

"I hoped we could have supper in the new house tonight. Sort of break it in before the wedding."

What she wouldn't give to cook supper on that shiny new stove and eat before that magnificent picture window. But Rose knew that if she did, she might be tempted to move into the house permanently, and that was something she'd vowed to herself never to do.

Not without a declaration.

And that was about as remote a possibility as Alexander's staying on the farm.

"Dearly beloved. We are gathered here in . . ."

"I'm so nervous I'm sweating like a pig in a summer drought," Rose whispered to Alexander, who was staring straight ahead and trying not to smile. "I've never done this before. What if I mess up?"

"You only have to stand there and look beautiful, Rose Elizabeth. You'll be fine. I promise." He gave her elbow an encouraging squeeze before resuming his stiff, somber posture.

Gnawing her lower lip, Rose listened with half an ear as the pastor droned on about cleaving, love, and duty. Though Alexander's words were comforting, they didn't erase a smidgen of her nervousness, though the idea that he thought her beautiful was some consolation.

She did feel rather pretty in the blue satin gown he'd purchased those many months ago. Though he'd offered to buy her a new one, she'd protested, saying it was silly when she hadn't worn all the new off of this one yet.

Trussed up again in that miserable corset—at his insistence—she'd told Alexander that it would be on his head if she fainted dead away during the wedding ceremony. And she doubted if Rebecca and Seamus would appreciate that occurrence.

Both looked splendid in their new finery—Seamus in his well-tailored suit of black superfine, and Rebecca swathed in yards and yards of cream satin and lace, looking every inch the fairy-tale princess.

Rose Elizabeth stole a peek at the duke, who was standing very solemnly, taking his duties as best man quite seriously. She knew she should be taking her duties seriously, too, but she hadn't quite figured out just what those duties were.

As far as she could tell, she was supposed to stand like a statue, hold her bouquet of flowers, and keep her trap shut, while Pastor Bergman pontificated on every subject known to God and man. Brevity had never been the good pastor's strong suit.

"What God has joined together, let no man . . ."

The end was near. Thank God for that! Rose thought, her toes curling painfully beneath her. Her feet were killing her, her ribs felt crushed, and she had to go to the privy.

There was one good thing about Alexander's new house: it had indoor plumbing!

*   *   *

The last champagne bottle had been uncorked, the remaining slice of cake eaten, and the newly wedded couple was at last ready to depart for home.

Nobody's smile was as wide and eager as Seamus's, nobody's face redder than Rebecca's as she heard the ribald comments directed at her husband.

"Never marry a woman with the kind of looks you'd like to see on another man's wife, Seamus," Skeeter jibed, elbowing the bridegroom in the ribs before letting loose with a drunken howl.

"Hush, Skeeter, you're embarrassing me," Marcella warned, smiling apologetically at the couple. "I'm afraid Skeeter has had a few too many glasses of champagne."

Wrapping his arm about his fiancée's shoulder, Skeeter planted a sloppy wet kiss on her cheek. "Now, Marcie, don't you be frettin' none. We're going to get hitched real soon. Maybe the duke will have us a real fine shindig like this one."

Alexander smiled reassuringly at Marcella. "Of course, Skeeter. Rose Elizabeth and I would be delighted. Wouldn't we, Rose?"

"Drunks sober up. Fools remain fools," Euphemia declared, though no one had asked for her opinion. "I think you should take Mr. Purty home now, Marcella. A man who can't hold his liquor is depraved and disgusting. And by the way, your grace," she turned her self-righteousness on Alexander, "Kansas is a dry state. You could get into trouble for having that champagne."

Funny, the spinster hadn't thought to complain the whole time she was drinking it. "I'll take my chances, Euphemia." Considering that Sheriff Covington had had more to drink tonight than almost anyone except Skeeter, Alexander didn't think he had much to fear from the law.

Rose too had consumed a few too many glasses of champagne, but rather than make her talkative and bubbly, they had had the opposite effect, rendering her quiet, almost morose.

She guessed her mood came from observing the love shining brightly on the newly wedded couple's faces, and knowing that for Seamus and Rebecca life was just beginning. A life with happiness, disappointment, unbelievable joy, and unbearable heartache. But a lifetime shared by two people who were very much in love.

Her eyes welled with tears. Damn, she hated weddings!

"What is it, my sweet? You look as if you're ready to cry." Alexander drew closer, but rather than feeling comforted, she felt even more miserable.

"Too much champagne and wedding sentimentality, I suppose."

"The bride and groom are about to leave. Why don't you dry your eyes, so we can make our farewells."

Rose followed Alexander across the wide hallway, where Rebecca and Seamus were waiting to depart. "I can't thank you enough, Rose Elizabeth . . . Alexander, for your generosity. Seamus and I are very grateful."

Rose kissed her friend on the cheek. "Be happy, Rebecca."

Alexander pumped the Irishman's hand. "You take good care of this fine woman, Seamus, or you'll have to answer to me."

Seamus laughed, hugging Rebecca to him. "That's an easy promise to make, your grace. And I might say the same to you." He winked at Rose Elizabeth.

Before she could respond, someone at the window shouted, "There's a buggy pulling up."

Rose Elizabeth wondered who could possibly be calling at such a late hour. Perhaps Sven had decided to come to the reception after all. Wilhelm had broken his arm this morning, forcing Sven and Hannah to cancel their plans to attend. It seemed unlikely that they would come, but then . . .

"Are you expecting someone else, Rose Elizabeth?" Alexander asked. "It's rather late for callers."

She shook her head. "No. Everyone we invited is here, except Sven and Hannah."

"I wonder who—"

The knock on the door interrupted Alexander, and Rose Elizabeth strode forward to answer it. She didn't recognize the blond woman standing alone on the porch, but she smiled politely. "Can I help you?" she asked. "Are you lost?"

The woman practically sneered as she sized up Rose Elizabeth from head to toe. "If this is the residence of the Duke of Moreland, then I am not lost," she replied in a haughty manner. "I insist on seeing the duke at once."

A sense of foreboding tightened Rose's stomach, and she suddenly felt uneasy.

"Who is it, Rose Elizabeth?" Alexander asked as he stepped to the door. Then his face whitened, as if all of the blood had drained out of it.

"Jessica! What the hell are you doing here?"

The woman smiled, but it wasn't friendly or kind. "Why, Moreland, is that any way to greet me after so many months?"

"Who is this woman, Alexander?" Rose slid the duke a sidelong glance, noting his irritation and anger.

Sweeping regally into the house past the two startled hosts, the tall woman faced the small assemblage and removed her cloak with a flourish to reveal a belly swollen with child.

"I am Jessica Kentland, the future Duchess of Moreland."

CHAPTER 17

"You said your fiancée was dead."

Alexander could not answer her statement, so he said nothing and continued to pace the small sitting room of the soddy.

Jessica had ensconced herself in the new house as if she belonged there. Within ten minutes of her unexpected arrival, the wedding guests had cleared. The bride and groom, only one of whom knew the devastating consequences of Jessica's arrival, had departed for town, and Rose had fled to the soddy, accusation and hurt clouding her eyes.

And who could blame her for being upset? Alexander had led her to believe that Jessica was dead. He'd certainly had no idea she was pregnant . . . with Edward's child.

Hard to believe that the sniveling bastard was capable of such a thing. It made his own failure to father a child all the more bitter. But, of course, it wasn't necessarily Edward's get. Jessica had many lovers. Edward was merely the most recent, though one could never be certain if he was the only one who could have done the deed.

"Your fiancée is pregnant. I thought you said you couldn't sire children."

The accusations kept coming. Finally Alexander halted his agitated steps and turned to face her. "I can't. It's not my child."

"But she is your betrothed?" Rose Elizabeth did everything in her power to maintain her composure. But it was damned difficult. She felt like screaming.

She had known, when she'd first seen the elegantly dressed woman standing on the porch, that something dire was about to happen. Like Alexander, Jessica had the look of prosperity about her. She and Alexander fit together like two peas in a pod . . . like the two small figures decorating the top of Rebecca and Seamus's wedding cake. It was painfully obvious that they belonged together.

"Jessica was . . . is my fiancée." The wounded look Rose flashed him pierced his chest. "But I have every intention of setting her aside once I return to England."

"How is that possible? She's your fiancée. You've promised to marry her, spend your life with her."

The things he loved best about Rose—her naiveté, her generous heart—now came back to smack him right in his principles. "I don't expect you to understand, Rose Elizabeth, for the kind of life you lead is honest and pure. But there are those in this world who do not share those values."

"I don't understand."

"Life in England isn't as straightforward as it is here. Nobles marry for different reasons—property, convenience, continuation of the line. Marriages are often arranged, or one is pressured into it, as in my case.

"Jessica and I don't love each other. We are to marry for the sake of expediency, to please my mother. Jessica wants financial security, and my family covets the Kentland property, which borders ours." His laughter was self-deprecating. "Unfortunately, I find myself unable to contemplate marriage to my deceitful fiancée. We've looked to others for comfort, and she found many men to accommodate her, including my brother. I suspect it is his child that she carries."

Rose Elizabeth gasped, her hand flying to her throat to hold back the bile that rose quickly there. "I'm very sorry. This must be terrible for you." She understood that for such a proud man, the humiliation would be unbearable.

His shoulders sagged, and he stopped before her, holding out his hand. She took it and rose. "I'm not proud of the things I've done, Rose Elizabeth. When I found out about Jessica and my brother, I tried to kill them in a drunken rage." He ignored her sharp outcry. "If it hadn't been for Seamus, I probably would have succeeded."

She caressed his cheek in an effort to comfort him. "Why did she come here, do you suppose?"

"With Jessica one can never be certain. I haven't yet had a chance to ask her that question." But he had his suspicions, knowing Edward as he did. And the dowager duchess no doubt played a part.

"You'd best go to her, Alexander. She is still your fiancée. And she's pregnant. Those facts cannot be changed, no matter what happened between you in the past."

"I want you to know, Rose, that I never loved Jessica, nor do I now. What happened between you and me had nothing to do with her."

His reminder of what had transpired between them made her flinch, and her heart grew heavy with remorse and despair. "I should hate you for the way you misled me, Alexander, but I don't. What happened was as much my fault as yours, maybe more. But I want you to know that had I known you were promised to another, I would never have come to your bed. I would never have entered into that bargain."

"I know that, Rose. You are far more honorable than I. But I can't honestly say that I'm sorry it happened, or that I don't want it to happen again."

"It won't." The glacial vow hung heavily between them, like a cold, misty fog that chilled to the bone. "Only a fool or a dimwit makes the same mistake twice. I don't happen to be either."

"I never meant to hurt you. Please believe me when I say that." Turning, he walked out into the cold night air.

And I never meant to be hurt, Alexander. But I am. Oh, God, I am.

The front door slammed, rattling the windows and light fixtures, and Alexander tore through the house like a madman with a mission.

"Jessica! Dammit, Jessica. Where the hell are you?"

He found her moments later, seated in the kitchen rocker he had purchased especially for Rose Elizabeth. Seeing Jessica in it was somehow a violation, an intrusion into his relationship with Rose and the new life he had made for himself in America.

Her smile was poised, practiced, artificial, just like the woman he knew her to be.

"What are you doing here, Jessica?"

"Just trying out your provincial furniture, Moreland. It's so terribly quaint, like this house and all your new friends." Malice peppered her laughter. "Really, Alexander! Were you so bored in England that you had to stoop to such depths?"

He balled his hands into fists, the veins in his neck pounding furiously, as he sought to restrain himself from wiping that supercilious smirk off her too-beautiful face.

Jessica was indeed beautiful—blond hair like spun gold, eyes the color of sapphires—but that beauty rested only on the outside. There wasn't a speck of it within the comely package she presented to the world.

"At least the people here are genuine, Jessica. They have morals, which is more than I can say for you. I am accepted for who I am and what I accomplish, not just for what I can give them. Unlike those fawning cronies you surround yourself with back home."

"Really? Even your new mistress? How utterly charming. But I didn't think your taste ran to stout, Moreland."

Alexander took a menacing step toward her, and the rocker stilled; he was gratified to see fear clouding her eyes. "Shut your vicious mouth. Rose Elizabeth is not my mistress, merely the former owner of this farm."

A finely etched eyebrow arched. "Why do I find that hard to believe, Moreland?"

"Because you equate every woman's morals with your own depraved ones, madam."

"You're not still sulking about Edward, are you? You know it meant nothing."

"No, I suppose it didn't. There's little that means anything to you, aside from expensive baubles and gowns. But it does seem that you got more than you bargained for this time, Jessica."

She stared down at her swollen belly with disgust. "By the time I discovered the nature of my malady, it was too late to do anything about it. The physician refused to accommodate me. But you can be sure I did everything in my power to get rid of the little bugger." She would have disposed of it herself, had she not been afraid that the act might kill her, too.

Alexander stepped away as if she were contaminated with some vile, communicable disease, and there was loathing on his face as he said, "You and my brother deserve each other. Why aren't you with him now? It's where you belong. You're certainly not welcome here."

Tears came easily to Jessica. Crying on cue was only one of her many accomplishments as a lady of leisure. She dabbed her eyes with a lace handkerchief as she said, "I had nowhere else to turn. When Edward found out about the baby, he left for an extended trip to India. I couldn't bear to face the scandal alone."

"And no doubt my mother suggested that you come here and beg my forgiveness."

Jessica indicated that she had, sniffling once or twice for

good measure. "Beatrice was very cruel, Alexander. She said terrible things about me. And about you, I might add."

"What a surprise." He frowned in disgust. "You've made your bed, Jessica. And as far as I'm concerned you may go back to England and lie in it. I don't really give a damn about you, my mother, Edward, or anyone else I left behind. I want you gone from here and from my life."

She rose slowly from the rocker and approached him, reaching out to touch his arm. "We were good together once, Alexander. We could be again."

With a look of disdain, he removed her hand from his person. "You sicken me. Did you really think I would take you back after the humiliation you caused me? Do you think I'm so dedicated to preserving the family reputation that I would take my brother's child and pass it off as my own? No doubt that was Mother's suggestion." She blushed, and he knew at once that his suspicions were correct: The dowager duchess would do everything in her power to sweep the whole sordid affair under the carpet so that the precious Warrick name would not be tainted.

"You loved me once."

The fire in the hearth crackled and spit, and the glow from the flames cast Alexander's visage in a demonic light. "No, Jessica, you're wrong. I never loved you. Besides, no one could love you more than you love yourself. You've always been a perfect bitch, self-centered and full of self-importance. No man could love a woman like that."

A knowing light entered her eyes, but rather than take insult at his words, she threw back her head and laughed. "You're in love with the plump farm girl, aren't you, Moreland? And because you're committed to me, you can do nothing about it."

Dread filled him. If Jessica suspected his true feelings for Rose Elizabeth, she would do everything in her power to use that knowledge in the cruelest of ways against the woman he loved. Alexander would not let that happen.

His laughter was contemptuous. "Really, Jessica! Your

imagination is working overtime. I love no woman, including you." At her flinch, he added, "Rose and I are merely friends. She has taught me a great deal about wheat farming, and I respect her knowledge. But to think . . ." He snorted disdainfully, an affectation he'd acquired from the old duke. "I am a lord of the realm, or have you forgotten? After our engagement is broken, I do not intend to—"

"You're planning to break our engagement?" Her face paled, and she slumped back into the rocker, clutching its arms until her knuckles turned white.

"Indeed, madam. As soon as I return to England, you will be branded the whore that you are, and our affiliation will be no more. The Duke of Moreland has a responsibility to the Crown. I do not pass off tainted goods, or uncouth Americans, as my equal."

Long, tapered fingers went to her throat. "But . . . but what of the child, Alexander? It will be branded a bastard."

"Like his father?"

"But I am a lady. I have a position in society to maintain."

"Not for much longer. Your reign will soon be at an end." He stalked out of the room, leaving an ashen-faced Jessica staring after him and plotting a way to thwart his threats.

Sitting smack in the middle of her bed, Rose Elizabeth drew her knees up to her chin and gave in to the tears that had threatened to spill all evening. For someone who rarely exhibited such unrestrained emotion, Rose thought, she was doing a damn fine job of soaking her flannel nightgown.

Boomer whined and drew closer to her, and she wrapped her arms about him for comfort. "We are a pair, aren't we, Boomer boy?" She wiped her tears, and his wet kisses, from her cheeks with the back of her hand.

"Alexander has a fiancée. Did I bother to mention that? She's beautiful, too. Even carrying a child she looks thinner than me. Of course, that wouldn't take much. Her skin's so pale it looks like newly churned cream. And did you notice how she carries herself so regally?"

If she didn't stop thinking about Lady Jessica Kentland's more-than-adequate assets, Rose knew she'd soon be in a state of full-blown depression. Besides, there wasn't a blasted thing she could do about the woman's looks. And though she was pretty, her disposition certainly wasn't anything to brag about. For a lady of quality, Jessica had the manners of a pig.

Actually, Elvira and Elmo were much better behaved. Rose made a silent apology to her pigs.

Tomorrow she would have to face that woman again. And though she was no coward, and was used to her fair share of ridicule, Rose Elizabeth had the distinct feeling that Alexander's fiancée was going to take great delight in pointing out the obvious differences in their stations.

"With her ladyship's nose stuck so high in the air, it's a wonder she can breathe, Boomer." The dog barked, as if agreeing, then licked her hand, and Rose sighed, petting the faithful animal's head.

At times she had envied her sisters' departure, thinking about the wonderful adventures they were having in the big city with their new and exciting careers, while she remained at home, living the mundane, sedate life of a farmer.

But her life had turned out to be anything but dull, thanks to the arrival of Alexander Warrick. And now, with the addition of his fiancée, she had a feeling that life in Salina was going to prove interesting, if not downright disagreeable.

"Poor Rose Elizabeth!" Euphemia shook her head, her double chins nearly colliding with her porcelain teacup. "I just knew no good would come of that duke coming here." Her tone was as tart as the lemon she squeezed into the hot liquid.

Sarah Ann's mouth fell open, and her cup clattered noisily in the saucer. Euphemia's change of heart about the Duke of Moreland seemed to go right along with the new, garish Louis

XIV red brocade settee now decorating her parlor. Euphemia was forever changing things, including her opinions.

"The man is obviously a cad," Abigail concurred. "Imagine him knowing all along that he was engaged to marry and never breathing a word about it to anyone. I doubt Rose Elizabeth would have allowed him to stay if he had."

Peggy snorted loudly. "Alexander does own the farm, in case you've forgotten. And Rose Elizabeth has no one to blame but herself. She practically threw herself at the duke."

"Peggy!" her mother admonished with a shake of her head, "that's an unkind thing to say about a friend."

Peggy had the grace to blush.

"It's not unusual for a woman Rose Elizabeth's age to be thinking about finding a husband, and the duke would have made an excellent catch." She pinned her daughter with a knowing look that seemed to say, *He could have been yours.*

"Well, that lecher might as well pack his bags and return to England immediately," Euphemia declared. "No decent family in this town will receive him again, if I have anything to say about it."

Marcella cleared her throat nervously. "What about the duke's fiancée? She's the one in the . . . the family way, and he ran out on her."

"He said the child wasn't his," Abigail reminded her. "Can you imagine any decent, moral man denying a child's birthright. And him a duke and all. I say Rose Elizabeth is well rid of that bounder."

Euphemia nodded. "As much as my heart goes out to any woman in that predicament, my—our first loyalty must be to Rose Elizabeth. She is one of our own, part of this community, and we must stand by her now. She'll need all," she looked pointedly at Peggy, "of our support."

"I need your help, Rose Elizabeth."

Rose didn't acknowledge Alexander's arrival, but instead

continued rolling out the cookie dough she had prepared for Christmas baking.

She'd used cooking and baking to keep herself occupied since the arrival of his fiancée a week ago. Unfortunately, her plan had succeeded only in making her plumper.

Alexander stepped closer and laid his hand on her shoulder, and she tried not to notice how wonderful it felt to be touched by him. "Rose?"

"I told you that I've much to do with the Christmas baking, Alexander." Her voice was filled with impatience. "I can't very well go to Seamus and Rebecca's house empty-handed, now can I?"

His midsection tightened as Rose's words punched an unexpected blow. "You're not staying here for the Christmas holiday? But I thought . . ." His voice was filled with disappointment.

Rose stopped what she was doing and looked up, leveling her gaze at him. "Under the circumstances, Alexander, I didn't feel it proper to intrude on you and your fiancée at such a special time." She certainly had no intention of pretending that Jessica's arrival hadn't changed everything between them. Even if she had foolishly entertained thoughts about a permanent relationship between them, which admittedly she had, the appearance of a fiancée—*his fiancée*—had changed all that.

"Jessica can't stand the sight of me. The few times I've spoken with her, she's gone out of her way to let me know that my presence isn't wanted."

Actually, Lady Kentland had gone out of her way to let Rose know that she was only a fraction smaller than a cow, not much smarter than a jackass, and uglier than warts on a frog. At least that was Rose's interpretation of the woman's unflattering remarks.

"Her feelings matter not in the least, Rose Elizabeth. I'm in charge here, not Jessica."

She sighed, unwilling to debate the subject of his fiancée a moment longer. "What is it you need help with, Alexander? I told you that I would take over the chores from now on. I'm sure you have your hands full with her ladyship."

That was the understatement of the century, Alexander thought miserably. Jessica had been an immovable object since her arrival. Without the assistance of her maid, who had elected to stay behind in New York, he had been forced to play lady's maid, cook, and nurse to her many ailments, and he couldn't tolerate one more second of it.

Unfortunately, the doctor's arrival this morning had precluded his plans to force Jessica out of the house. And he now suspected that the dark cloud hovering over his head was taking on gargantuan proportions.

"The doctor was here this morning."

Rose's eyebrow shot up in surprise. "Doc Spooner? Whatever for?" She looked him over from head to toe. "You're not sick, are you?"

He shook his head, though he had been feeling rather ill of late. "Heartsick" was the diagnosis he had come up with. Incurable and deadly.

"It's not me, it's Jessica. It seems that there's some type of complication with her pregnancy. The doctor says she can't travel until after the baby is born."

Rose couldn't hide her disappointment and dismay. "I see. Well, it looks as if you've got a houseguest for a few months."

"At least two, by the doctor's calculation. I'm not sure I'll be able to stand it."

"She's your responsibility. And the child is innocent of her doings." She wiped her hands on her apron, as if to dismiss his excuses. "It wouldn't be fair to jeopardize the health of the baby because you can't stand being around its mother."

"But there's more to it than just that, Rose Elizabeth. You know I can't cook anything edible. And there are things she requires that I feel uncomfortable assisting with." His stare hooked hers. "Personal things."

She shut her mind to the images stabbing at her—images that filled her with jealousy and envy. "Perhaps Euphemia or one of the other ladies in town can come out here to help."

"I've already inquired. No one wants to travel at this time of year because of the weather. Even now there's a threat of snow." He looked out the window, and his frown deepened at the black clouds forming. "They don't want to risk being kept from their families over the holiday. And I can't blame them."

"I find it hard to believe that Euphemia didn't jump at the chance to ingratiate herself with her ladyship."

"Euphemia's gone to visit her brother in Kansas City. She's not expected to return until after the New Year." At least that was the excuse the spinster had given him before slamming the door in his face. Obviously, the woman believed Jessica's child to be his. Probably the entire town believed it; he'd been receiving the cold shoulder of late.

A sinking feeling formed in the pit of Rose's stomach. "Why do I think that this is leading up to something? You can't honestly believe that I would be willing to play servant to your fiancée. Pardon me for saying so, but she's got the tongue of a viper and the disposition of a cantankerous mule."

Her honesty made him smile. "Jessica's a bitch. You don't need to mince words, Rose Elizabeth. I would never ask for your help, if there were any other way. I'm at wit's end."

Understanding his frustration, she felt herself weakening. "Don't you think it would be rather awkward having me care for her, considering that you and I . . . ?"

"Though Jessica may suspect something, I have convinced her that—" his face reddened, "that I would never be interested in an American, especially a commoner."

Now it was Rose's turn to blush, but it wasn't embarrassment that caused her high color, it was anger. "You've got a lot of nerve, your dukeness! You know that? I think you'd better leave."

He held out his hands beseechingly. "Rose, I'm sorry. I didn't mean to offend you. I just made up that story so Jessica wouldn't suspect anything. If she thought I cared for you, she'd make your life a living hell."

Her arms crossed over her chest in a defensive posture,

Rose harrumphed loudly. "Well then, I guess it's a good thing that you don't care for me, isn't it?"

He reached for her, but she pulled back, and his arms fell dejectedly to his sides. "You know I care for you, Rose Elizabeth. How could you think otherwise?"

Though she ignored his avowal, it did lighten her heart just a bit. "Don't you dare touch me, your highness. I wouldn't want my *commonness* to rub off on you."

He ran agitated fingers through his hair and sighed audibly. "Bloody hell! I'm not only cursed with one unreasonable woman, now I'm cursed with two."

She held open the door, letting in a blast of air that was as frigid as her words. "Go home, Alexander. I have work to do."

"But what about my situation with Jessica? Aren't you going to help me?"

She shrugged. "I'll think on it and let you know."

As soon as he stepped outside, she slammed the door behind him. "Arrogant jackass fool!" she shouted at the door, wiping at her tears, which fell more freely these days. "I hate you, Alexander Warrick."

But she knew that was a lie. She loved him. And because she did, she would do as he asked. Even if it meant abasing herself to that snooty bitch, the future Duchess of Moreland.

CHAPTER 18

Rebecca snuggled close to her husband's warm body and allowed the glow of contentment to wash over her after their lovemaking. Even now, she couldn't believe her good fortune in having Seamus for a husband.

He made her feel beautiful, womanly, and, most of all, loved.

Her life was good. He had made it that way. But she worried that something or someone would come to snatch away her newfound happiness.

She still had not finished grieving for her father, still was not able to embrace her religion, but her heart had softened, and grown more accepting, thanks to the love of her husband.

"Your fierce frown is bruising my ego, lass," Seamus whispered, kissing her brow, her cheek, and finally her lips. "Didn't I please you? I'd be happy to try again." He smiled suggestively, wiggling his brows, bringing a bright blush to Rebecca's cheeks.

Shaking her head, for she was growing used to his antics now, she patted his stubbled cheek. "You know that you please me very much, husband. It is just that I feel selfish for feeling so happy, when I know that my friend Rose Elizabeth is miserable."

Seamus hugged his wife to his chest, combing his fingers through her mass of honey-blond hair, and thanked the Almighty that he'd found such a treasure. Never before had he felt so needed, so useful. Never before had he loved a woman so totally and unashamedly with his heart and soul as he loved Rebecca.

Which made Alexander's plight that much sadder.

"'Tis a sorrowful thing that happened, lass. And knowing the duke's fiancée as I do, both Rose Elizabeth and Alexander are surely suffering from her presence."

At the mention of Alexander, Rebecca frowned. "It is my opinion that Alexander deserves the misery he gets. He should not have deceived such a trusting, kind woman as Rose."

"If you knew the whole of it, lass, you might not judge the duke so harshly."

"I know it is not my place to pass judgment. That is up to our Lord. But Rose Elizabeth is my friend, and I cannot bear to see the sadness on her face. Christmas Day she did not laugh or joke, as is her way. Why did that awful woman have to come?"

A red eyebrow arched. "You're perceptive to have seen through Lady Kentland so clearly, lass. And you just making her acquaintance briefly."

"You don't have to drink the whole glass of milk to know it is sour. Rose taught me that."

"The sprightly lass will have her patience tested, that's for sure. Alexander confided that Rose has agreed to tend Jessica during her confinement."

Rebecca's head shot up, her eyes wide with disbelief. "Surely you are funning with me, Seamus. Please tell me that the duke wasn't so callous and inconsiderate as to put Rose Elizabeth in such an awkward position. It is unforgivable!"

"Alexander suffers guilt of his request, Rebecca, but his

hands are tied." Seamus empathized with the duke and understood why he didn't want to touch Jessica.

There was nothing he would put past Jessica Kentland, including the purposeful seduction of Alexander Warrick.

Or Alexander Warrick's servant.

Seamus knew firsthand. He had nearly succumbed to the beautiful woman's advances—her practiced kisses, her bold caressing hands on his body—but he had realized in the nick of time that her visit to his room above the stables those many months ago had been calculated to coincide with the duke's return from London.

Her motive had been revenge . . . spite . . . malice. . . . Whatever the reason, it was undoubtedly the same one that had prompted her to seduce that gullible, spineless bastard Edward.

There was no telling what drove the vengeful woman. But she wreaked havoc on those she encountered.

"What will happen, do you suppose?" Rebecca asked, a concerned frown marring her fine features. Seamus smoothed the worry lines with his thumb.

"You know I'm not much of a churchgoing man, Rebecca lass, but I think I'll be praying for Alexander and Rose Elizabeth while her ladyship remains in their home. They're going to be needing all the help they can get from here on out."

"You're scalding me, you stupid cow! Watch what you're doing."

Having offered to wash Jessica's hair, Rose Elizabeth now decided that she'd much rather yank it out. She held the water pitcher aloft and counted silently to ten. Her hands shaking with the force of her anger, it was all she could do not to bring the vessel down upon the ungrateful woman's head.

It was damn tempting!

"Aren't you going to rinse it? I'm getting chilled sitting here with my hair wet."

"It must be the draft you're creating with all your screaming. But this should warm you up." With unrestrained glee, Rose Elizabeth dumped the remaining water over Jessica's hair and delighted in the gasps of outrage spewing from her mouth.

A mock show of concern registered on her face. "Oh, dear! Did I pour too much at once?"

Jessica groped blindly for the towel on the washstand. "You did it on purpose and you know it!"

"Feel free to get someone else to assist you, your ladyship." *Anyone else*, Rose prayed.

Jessica was stunned by the suggestion. Alexander had already warned her that Rose Elizabeth was her only choice. It was either the plump farm girl or no one. And she had no intention of managing alone. "You know there is no one to help but you, Rose Elizabeth. That is your name, is it not?"

"It is. But you may call me Miss Martin, if you like. It's far more preferable than 'stupid cow.'"

The haughty woman didn't bat an eyelash and continued toweling her hair. "No need to take offense. 'Tis the way I speak to my servants at home."

Rose bristled at being referred to as a servant. "You're not at home, Lady Kentland. And I am not the hired help. I'm here as a favor to the duke. And because you are with child.

"Let me assure you that I have plenty of chores on this farm to keep me occupied. I'm not here out of boredom."

Donning a blue satin bed jacket, Jessica eased herself back into bed, ignoring the rebuke. "The doctor says I'm to avoid excitement."

Gathering up the dirty clothing that the spoiled woman had carelessly discarded about the room, Rose thought ruefully that she might not actually be a servant, but she certainly felt like one at the moment.

"Why don't you come downstairs and have dinner? The exercise will do you and the baby good."

Jessica looked aghast. "I'm much too frail to climb up and down the stairs. You just want me to injure myself, so you'll have Alexander all to yourself. Well, I can assure you, your ploy won't work. He might be angry with me right now, but I know he loves me. We're alike, you see. You would never fit in to his world. Never in a million years."

Jessica Kentland was about as frail as a plow horse, in Rose Elizabeth's opinion. But the rest of what she'd said had a ring of truth to it. Jessica and Alexander were alike, at least in the breeding department. They were two attractive Thoroughbreds, while she was just a plain old work horse.

"I suggested the exercise for your own good, but if you're determined to remain in bed, I'll fetch your dinner. However, I wouldn't get too used to this treatment. I'll humor you today, but tomorrow you'd best get on your feet and down the stairs, or you'll be starving for something to eat."

The woman's mouth dropped open. "Why . . . Alexander shall hear of your rudeness, you insolent piece of baggage!"

Shutting the door firmly behind her, Rose Elizabeth held back the scream of frustration she felt and prayed that Jessica's two-month confinement would go by quickly.

Considering that this was only her first day to cater to her ladyship's whims, two months seemed an eternity.

Alexander was waiting at the kitchen table when Rose Elizabeth entered, an expectant look on his face. Outside the bay window behind him, snow was falling rapidly.

"Was it awful?" he asked, looking sheepish and ill at ease. "Was my . . . Was Jessica rude?"

Rose crossed to the stove and began ladling chicken soup into two ceramic bowls. A good portion of it sloshed over the sides and onto the stove top because her hands were shaking again. "Your fiancée is a spoiled brat, your dukeness. But I guess you already know that." She set the two bowls of soup on the table none too gently, followed by a basket of hot rolls fresh from the oven.

The only thing joyful about the whole horrible experience, as far as Rose Elizabeth was concerned, was getting to use the wonderful cookstove. She cast it an affectionate glance—far more affectionate than the one she turned on the duke. "I'll prepare Jessica's dinner tray and bring it up to her today, but I'm not waiting on her hand and foot. She's pregnant, not sick. And in my opinion the exercise will do her good. I told her as much, but of course she ignored the suggestion."

"I'm sorry, Rose Elizabeth. If there was any other way . . ."

"Eat your soup before it gets cold," she ordered, not wishing to hear his apologies or enter into another discussion about "his fiancée." Changing the subject, she remarked, "The snow's piling up. We'll have to shovel a pathway between the two houses."

He took a bite of roll, then suggested, "Or you could stay here. It would be—"

Her fist came down hard on the table, nearly upsetting her glass of milk. "No! I have my own home. I won't stay in the same house with you and your betrothed." How could he even suggest such a thing! To live in the same house with his fiancée, after what they'd done . . .

The rest of the meal was eaten in silence, then Rose Elizabeth prepared Jessica's dinner tray. "I'll take this upstairs before I go home."

Alexander sighed with pure frustration and combed his fingers through his hair. "I'll take it up. I know you don't like being around Jessica any more than you have to." He could hardly blame her. No doubt Jessica had treated Rose to a display of her bitchy, short temper and tactlessness.

The look of relief on Rose's face was almost pitiable. "I do have more chores to attend to."

He reached out to caress her cheek. "I won't be a minute, Rose, then I'll walk you over to—"

"Alexander! Moreland! Get up here this instant. My fire is going out and I need you to bring more wood. And have that woman bring up my food! I'm starving to death."

An enchanting idea. Rose noted the disappointment on Alexander's face. "You'd better go. I'll be fine by myself." She'd better be, Rose decided, for it looked as if she would be by herself for a long while to come.

*   *   *

The knock on the door made Rose's stomach tighten, then she remembered that Alexander wouldn't announce his arrival, he'd just walk in. Setting aside her sewing, she went to answer it. There stood Sven, shivering and covered with snow, his face red from the cold, his battered felt hat pulled low on his head.

Rather than relent, the inclement weather had worsened, and there was talk about a full-blown blizzard materializing from this latest storm.

"Come in, Sven. You look plumb froze. What brings you out in this terrible weather? Is it the children? Is Hannah all right?" Sven and Hannah had married two weeks before, but Rose Elizabeth had been unable to attend the ceremony because of her responsibility to Jessica.

Alexander had offered to tend his fiancée so that she could go to the wedding, but Rose had recognized the suggestion for what it was—a supreme sacrifice—and she just couldn't put him through it. More fool, she.

The big man shook his head. "No, Rose Elizabet, they are all fine and send their love. I came to see for myself that you are all right. I haven't seen you at church, and you were not at my wedding." He lowered his frame onto the slat-backed chair at the table, warming his hands on the hot cup of coffee Rose gave him.

"I sent word that I was unable to come. You know . . . because of her ladyship."

He studied her closely, then frowned deeply. "I have never seen you looking so tired, Rose Elizabet. You have black smudges under your eyes that were not there before. If you do not take care, it vill be you who is forced to stay abed, not just Alexander's fiancée."

That word still made Rose wince; even though she should have become used to the idea that Alexander had a fiancée— that he was promised to another—she hadn't. "You know how incapable Alexander is when it comes to the chores and such?" she asked, and Sven nodded. "He is ten times worse about caring for a pregnant woman. He seems to have this revulsion about it." Or about Jessica; she wasn't certain which was the case.

Understanding and sympathy lighted his eyes. "Perhaps that is because she carries another man's child."

"That's what he says, but her ladyship is careful to avoid the topic. When she does speak of it, it's to say that her and Alexander's family will soon be complete." That conversation had resulted in three pieces of broken dishware.

"I have not met this woman, but I do know Alexander, and I believe him to be telling the truth. He is an honorable man."

You wouldn't think so if you knew of the bargain we made.

Rather than voice that thought, Rose refilled Sven's coffee cup. "I've missed you, dear friend. Have Hannah and the children adjusted to their new situation? Is everyone getting along?"

Sven's smile was thoughtful. "They fight like all children do. But I think in time all vill be fine. I vill have it no other way."

She squeezed his hand. "I'm glad you're happy, Sven. You deserve to be."

"There have been times," he confessed, looking at her with a sad smile of regret, "that I have questioned if what I have done is right. But then I tell myself that you are in love with another man, and I . . ."

"I'm not!" she stated emphatically, almost launching herself out of the chair.

His gaze leveled Rose back down. "I have eyes, Rose Elizabet. There is no need for deception."

She blushed, wishing that Sven were not always so perceptive. "Well, maybe I do love Alexander, but a lot of good that does me now. He's engaged to marry someone else. And I'm sure he'll be going back to England as soon as Jessica has the baby and can travel."

"Has he told you as much? He has said nothing to me about this." But Sven suspected that was because Alexander did not yet know what he was going to do. Sven knew that the duke loved Rose, but he also knew that their situation was impossible. A man couldn't be bound to two women, unless he lived in that place called Utah.

"Perhaps you could become Mormon," he joked, bringing a smile to Rose's lips.

"I'd rather die an old maid than live under the same roof with that harridan who calls herself a lady. She's called me a stupid cow so many times I'm half inclined to moo at her."

Sven smiled, despite his best intention not to. "She is not a nice woman, I take it?"

"Nice? She's the devil personified. Jessica Kentland makes Kate in *The Taming of the Shrew* look like an angel."

"You speak of the English poet Shakespeare?"

She nodded. "I have bathed her body, washed her hair, picked up her dirty clothing—she's an awful pig—and even played cards with her to pass the time, and not once has she thanked me or said a kind word."

The Swede looked clearly appalled. "And what does the duke say about this?"

Her shoulders lifted, then sagged, and there was a look of resignation on her face. "He apologizes profusely, tells me not to wait on her, and makes excuses for her ill behavior because of the pregnancy. His constant explanations are almost worse than her verbal attacks. At least with those I can fight back. Alexander looks so wretched, I can't bear to take him to task."

"You are too soft-hearted, Rose Elizabet. You always have been."

"There's no one else to help her but me."

"She sounds like a woman who has known great unhappiness in her lifetime and strikes out at everyone because of it."

Rose's brow wrinkled in confusion. "Unhappiness? She's a lady of quality, for heaven's sake! She's rich, has a wonderful fiancé who she's treated like dirt, and is expecting a child." Her face softened. "What I wouldn't give to be in her place."

"I thought you were content to remain as you are." Sven smiled as her face turned red. "Do not apologize for wanting what all women want, Rose Elizabet. You just wanted it with a man you could love. I understand."

"You don't know how many times I wished it was you I loved and wanted to marry, Sven. My life would have been so much simpler and happier."

"If you marry the wrong person, then you are never happy, Rose Elizabet. Look at the duke and his betrothed. They planned to marry for all the wrong reasons. Surely it has not been easy for either of them. If the woman is mean-spirited, maybe it is because she knows she is tied to a man who vill never love her. I'm sure it was a great blow to her vanity not to be able to win Alexander's love."

Rose thought about Sven's words long after he had gone. Perhaps his insights were correct, and Jessica was just taking out her misery on everyone else. It couldn't be easy for a woman like her to be saddled with a child she didn't want and a man who didn't want her.

Rose vowed once again to try to be a little more understanding of the future Duchess of Moreland.

"You look like hell, Moreland."

Alexander scratched his stubbled chin, realized he probably did, wished that's where he was, and shrugged his shoulders. "You don't look so wonderful yourself, Jessica."

She realized a long-suffering sigh and continued to rock back and forth in the rocker, which Rose Elizabeth had insisted he cart upstairs for his pregnant fiancée. Though it had galled him to do so, he'd done as she asked, wondering if Rose knew he had purchased the lovely piece of furniture specifically for her.

"I feel as big as a cow. I can't wait for all this to be over, so we can return home where we belong."

He was tempted to correct her assumption, tempted to tell her that she would no longer be welcome at Moreland House, but because of her condition he thought better of it.

The doctor had cautioned against upsetting Jessica. He

worried that in her advanced state of pregnancy, she might lose the child, or even her own life, and every precaution to prevent that from happening had been instituted.

Jessica remained bedridden most of the day. She did not venture downstairs, had to be carted to the bathing room at the most inconvenient times, and played her role of invalid to the hilt.

"Your color seems a bit better today. You don't look quite as pale," he offered, trying his best to be civil.

She patted the overstuffed chair next to the bed. "Please sit down. We really haven't had a chance to talk lately, and I do get bored with just Rose Elizabeth's company."

His brow shot up. "I would think you would be more gracious, Jessica. Rose has gone out of her way to treat you with kindness."

"Because she loves you. Don't think I don't know that."

He shook his head. "You're a fool if you believe that. She hated the very sight of me when I first arrived. Now, at best, she only tolerates me."

"I can't blame her for that, Moreland. You're not the easiest person to get along with."

"How would you know? You never found my company all that compelling."

She did her best to mask her annoyance. Honesty had always been one of Alexander's greatest strengths and biggest flaws.

"You didn't really desire my company either, Alexander. It was quite clear from the beginning that ours was not a love match."

"You seemed agreeable."

"As did you."

"Touché. Now, don't you think you should get back into bed before you overtire yourself? The doctor was very specific about your getting enough rest."

"Your solicitation is surprising, Alexander. If only it stemmed from your heart and not your sense of duty. 'Duty above all,' that is the Moreland creed, is it not?"

He pulled back the covers for her and sighed, already weary of the verbal duel. If it weren't for Rose Elizabeth's constant admonishments that they keep Jessica from overtiring herself, he would not have bothered with his "solicitation," as Jessica called it. But his sense of duty was strong, she was right about that.

No matter what had transpired between them in the past, he could not bring himself to punish Jessica in her present condition. He was not that heartless and cold, despite what she might think.

"I've decided that God has already given you considerable punishment for your transgressions, Jessica, so it's not necessary for me to continually harangue you."

She held out her hand so that he could assist her to her feet. When they were standing face to face, she reached up to caress his cheek. "Alexander, do you think you could ever forgive me for what I have done?"

He grasped her hand and held it, staring into blue eyes that begged for an absolution he was unable to give. "What game do you play now, Jessica? I told you that whatever was between us is over."

"I will never accept that, Alexander. Never, as long as I live."

"Which will not be long, madam, if you do not climb back into bed and rest."

"Is that what you desire, Alexander? My death? Will it take that to atone for my sins?"

Like his heart, his face hardened, and he dropped her hand. "You may find this difficult to believe, Jessica, but I don't care whether you live or die." With those cutting words, he marched out of the room, forgetting his vow not to upset her, remembering only the pain and humiliation she had caused.

CHAPTER 19

Dearest Rose,

It is with a heavy heart that I pen this letter, as my life has taken some unexpected turns, and I know not when or how I will recover from this latest predicament I find myself in.

I cannot bring myself to reveal my humiliation, but can only say that I am no longer employed by the temperance league because of it.

I've come to a crossroads, not knowing which way to turn, but I knew that writing you to unburden myself would somehow make me feel better. And it does.

I had such high expectations when I arrived in Denver, but the career I so fancied turned sour. The man I love is not inclined to share my feelings, and I despair of ever having a normal life, such as Mama and Papa shared.

241

Rose felt her eyes fill with tears. Laurel's letter could just as easily been written about herself as her sister. The Martin sisters seemed doomed to love the wrong men, save for Heather, who had apparently found true love in the arms of Brandon Montgomery. But Rose had not heard from Heather since Christmas, so she knew not whether Heather and her arrogant newspaper publisher were enjoying matrimonial bliss.

She glanced out the window and saw that the snow had not abated, and she cringed at the idea of venturing out to the barn to check on the animals. Just the thought made her shiver, and she chafed her arms briskly.

February was not conducive to chores. It was a cold, dismal, quiet month, in which reading mail and catalogues lent excitement to a period that for the most part was void of visits and parties.

Sven and Hannah had called a few times, their close proximity made visiting possible. Doc Spooner was the only other frequent visitor. He came once a week to check on Jessica's progress, and his frown deepened each time he emerged from her room.

"It doesn't look good, your grace," Rose had heard him tell Alexander the last time he'd visited. "Your fiancée continues to bleed, and there is no guarantee that she won't lose the child."

Rose's heart had grown heavy at that. No woman, not even Jessica Kentland, deserved to lose her child. Not after carrying it all those many months beneath her breast, wondering if it would be a boy or a girl . . .

Rose released a heartfelt sigh. If only she had gotten pregnant with Alexander's child. At least she would have had something to remember him by when he left.

And Jessica assured her daily that he would be leaving. Let there be no doubt that the Duke of Moreland would be escorting his fiancée home, along with her child. On that Rose Elizabeth could place a wager, Jessica had stated emphatically.

Rose had gotten over her jealousy and dislike of Alexander's fiancée. The most important consideration now was the child's well-being. And if she had to bite her tongue a thousand times a day to keep from upsetting Jessica, she would. The baby's survival depended on the mother's health.

Stuffing Laurel's letter into the pocket of her denim overalls, Rose pulled the heavy sheepskin coat off the hook and donned it, making a mental note to answer her sister's letter as soon as she completed her chores.

Alexander's house might prove a haven for Laurel's troubles, and Rose Elizabeth intended to offer her the opportunity to come for a visit. Besides, when Alexander left it would be lonely at the farm, and Laurel's presence would help ease that loneliness.

"What are you doing outside in this weather, Rose Elizabeth? You should be inside where it's warm."

Startled by Alexander's arrival, Rose jumped, and the sack of grain she held almost slipped through her fingers. She turned narrowed eyes on him. "Don't ever sneak up on me like that again, Alexander. You almost made me spill this feed, and I've got no great desire to drive into town to fetch more, as terrible as this weather is."

Even in the baggy overalls and man's jacket, Rose Elizabeth looked beautiful. Flushed from the cold, her cheeks flowered bright pink, and her brown eyes flashed sparks of indignation. Alexander stood mesmerized by the sight of her.

God, how he missed her. Missed being with her every day and night. Missed their talks, even their fights. And he definitely missed having her in his bed.

Rose Elizabeth noted the change in his expression and immediately took a step back. There was hunger in Alexander's eyes, hunger and longing, and it mirrored her own passionate feelings.

"Your horse could use some grooming while you're here," she stated, hoping to take her mind, and his, off matters they had no right to consider.

He stepped closer, and she caught the spicy scent of his cologne. Mingling with the distinctive odors of hay and leather, it created a totally masculine effect. "Rose, I . . ."

She thrust the sack of grain at him so hard that he grunted. "Take this. You can finish feeding the animals. It's cold, and I'm anxious to get back inside."

He studied her for a moment, recognizing the determined glint in her eyes, the stubborn tilt to her chin. "Avoiding the subject won't make it go away."

"There is no subject to discuss, as far as I'm concerned. I think I've made my feelings quite clear on everything."

"Your feelings show on your face, my sweet Rose, despite your words to the contrary. I know you want me as much as I want you."

Though it took an enormous effort, she threw back her head and laughed. "Your conceit continues to astound me, your dukeness. I don't recall panting after you like a bitch in heat."

His eyes darkened. "No. You're good at hiding your emotions. You've been doing it most of your life, haven't you? But I know what you're feeling just the same. I feel it, too."

She shook her head. "You're wrong! Besides, you belong to another, so anything I may or may not feel is irrelevant at this point."

Lowering the sack of grain to the earthen floor, he reached out and pulled her to him, and was relieved when she didn't resist. "I've never wanted any woman as much as I want you. Never cared for any woman as much as I care for you."

Tears filled her throat, making it difficult to speak. "You're making this hard on both of us, Alexander. Please don't say anything more. What happened in the past must be forgotten."

"I will never forget it." Though his words were hard, his touch was gentle as he caressed her cheek. "If circumstances were different—"

"But they're not. And I will not . . ."

Alexander never gave her a chance to finish. Instead, he captured her lips beneath his own, as he'd been dreaming of doing for weeks.

Rose seemed to melt into him. She had no defense against this man, not when he kissed her, not when he held her so tenderly in his arms, as he was doing now. She wanted him with a desperation that was alien to her. And she thought that if she didn't have him inside her soon, she would die from want.

But then honor reared its head. And Rose Elizabeth, being a very honorable woman, knew she would not act on the impulse her heart dictated.

Wresting free of his embrace, she tried to reason with him. "We mustn't do this, Alexander. It isn't fair to Jessica."

He looked clearly astounded and frustrated as hell. "Jessica! Why should I be fair to her? She's had so many men in her bed I've lost count. And I don't love her."

"She's your fiancée and as such deserves your fidelity and my honor. If the shoe were on the other foot, I wouldn't want another woman messin' with my man."

"Jessica deserves nothing but my loathing and contempt. Her liaison with my brother made me the laughingstock of Sussex. I owe her nothing."

"Then think of the child. It will be your niece or nephew, a part of your bloodline and family."

He sneered. "It will be a bastard."

She did her best to control her temper, but Alexander's obstinacy made it damned difficult. "You remain a thick-headed dolt, your dukeness, for the child will be innocent, even if his mother is not." She tried to walk away, but he grabbed her arm.

"I want you, Rose Elizabeth. Only you."

"There can never be anything more between us, Alexander. You and I are from different worlds. I have accepted that. What we shared was a mutually fulfilling passion. Lust, I guess you could call it. It's over and done with, and it's time that you owned up to the responsibilities of your title."

He stiffened, but said nothing, allowing her to continue.

"The Duke of Moreland isn't a farmer or a philanderer. He's a good, honest man who's been hurt and deceived and who ran away to lick his wounds and heal. Now it's time for you to go back to England and face the music. You have a fiancée. And now there is a child to consider. Your brother doesn't sound like he'd make a good father, but I know you would, Alexander. I feel it in my bones."

His visage darkened like thunderclouds. "You forget yourself, madam," he stated in his most imperious voice. "I am the Duke of Moreland, and as such, I don't need an interfering young woman dictating what I should and should not do.

"In case you have forgotten, this is still my land, and you are merely a guest here."

She reeled back on her heels as if slapped. "If this is the way you treat your guests, then I'd hate to see how you treat the hired help. I've pulled my fair share of the load around here, not to mention service to her ladyship. So don't even think you're going to intimidate me with your noble threats. I'm not buying it, Alexander."

Rose stalked out of the barn, leaving him staring after her. "If only things could have been different between us, Rose," he whispered.

The bloodcurdling scream ripped through the stillness of the night, jolting Alexander awake. Bolting upright, his heart pounding loudly in his ears, he reached for his pants and the lamp by his bed almost simultaneously.

A glance at the window told him it was the middle of the night; the piercing wail, that Jessica was in distress.

Barefoot, he hurried to the door, stubbing his toe on the foot of the wing chair. "Bloody hell!" he cursed, stumbling into the hallway and down to her room.

Alternately screaming and moaning, Jessica lay writhing in pain in a pool of blood. "Jesus! God!" He stared, almost dumbfounded.

"Help me, Alexander. The baby is coming."

He shook his head as if to deny what she was telling him. "It can't be. The doctor said—"

"I don't give a damn about the doctor!" Jessica shouted. "Get Rose Elizabeth. She'll know what to do."

With a nod, and a mountain of uncertainty about leaving her alone, he returned to his room and put on his boots, then raced downstairs, grabbed his jacket, and ran out into the foot-deep snow.

"Rose Elizabeth! Rose Elizabeth!" he screamed at the top of his lungs as he approached the soddy.

Boomer barked several times at the noise, and Rose Elizabeth came instantly awake. Hearing Alexander urgently calling out to her, she knew that the midnight call could only be attributed to Jessica and the baby.

Fear gripped her insides like a vise, and she grabbed her wrapper and hurried to the door to find a disheveled Alexander standing there.

"Come quick. Jessica's bleeding all over the bed, and she says the baby's coming."

"Damn, damn, and double damn!" Rose Elizabeth didn't know a thing about birthing babies, only pigs. "We'll have to fetch the doctor. You stay with Jessica, and I'll ride Percival into town."

He shook his head. "I'll go. You'll be more help to Jessica. You're a woman. And I can ride faster than you."

Rose Elizabeth hated to point out that just because she was a woman didn't mean that she knew anything about bringing a new life into the world. "I've never delivered a baby before, only pigs."

He seemed surprised by the revelation. "That's more than I know, Rose, and I doubt Jessica's going to ask for your credentials. She asked expressly for you."

"I'll get dressed."

"There's no time. Just grab your coat and boots and head over to the house. I'll bring back Doctor Spooner just as soon as I can."

"But that could take hours."

He patted her shoulder. "Just do your best. Childbirth is

natural to a woman. I'm sure Jessica will be just fine with your help."

Standing by the side of the wailing woman's bed, Rose observed the great abundance of blood and knew that Alexander's confidence had been misplaced. This would be no ordinary delivery.

Jessica's blood was pouring out at a rapid rate, and Rose Elizabeth didn't have the skill or the knowledge to stop the flow. The woman's skin was ashen, and she was sweating so profusely that her hair was matted to her head and her nightgown clung damply to her body.

Rose knew in her heart that Jessica Kentland was not long for this world.

"Please help me, Rose Elizabeth," Jessica whispered. "I am dying, and the baby is trying to be born."

With soothing fingers, Rose brushed back the damp curls from Jessica's forehead. "Hush now, you hear? You're not going to die. Childbirth is as easy as falling off a horse. My mama always said so. This baby will arrive when it's ready and not a moment sooner. I know you're in pain, but it'll end soon. You'll see." There was water in the basin by the bed, and she wrung out a washcloth and mopped Jessica's face with it.

"This is my punishment," Jessica said, crying tears of genuine remorse. "God will take my life so that I may atone for my sins, but I hope he will spare the child. The baby should not be punished for my transgressions."

"My ma always said that God was a forgiving sort. He doesn't punish folks for their sins, if they're truly sorry for them."

"I am," she admitted between gasps of pain. "More than you'll ever know. I've made a mess of my life here on earth. I hope the next one is better."

"Lie still as you can. I'm going to fetch some towels from

the bathing room and see if I can stanch the flow of blood until the doctor gets here."

Rose moved to leave, but Jessica, frail as she was, grasped her wrist with surprising strength. "I know I've been wretched to you, Rose Elizabeth. And you've treated me with nothing but kindness. I hope you'll forgive me for the things I said. It was only jealousy that motivated my words."

Rose stared at her in disbelief. "Why would a beautiful woman like you be jealous of me? I have nothing, and you have everything."

Pain that had nothing to do with childbirth etched deep lines into Jessica's face. "You're wrong, Rose Elizabeth. You have Alexander's love. It was the only thing I ever wanted, and the one thing he denied me."

"You mustn't say such things. Alexander and I are only friends. There is nothing between us." The lie came easily to her lips. Jessica had enough to contend with at the moment, Rose decided.

"He loves you, and I know you must love him back. Alexander is a very lovable person despite all his faults. I only wish I had tried harder to make him love me."

"You must rest now and not upset yourself. I need to fetch the towels. When you're well again, we'll finish this ridiculous conversation."

"I'm not going to get well, Rose Elizabeth. We both know that. I can feel my strength slipping away even as we speak. I need you to promise me something before I go. Please don't deny my last request."

"You mustn't talk like this, Jessica. It isn't good for you or the baby. You must rest, save your strength for the delivery."

"Promise me that when the child is born you will not let Alexander abandon it. The child deserves a home and family. Alexander could provide that for him."

Rose Elizabeth turned almost as white as the sheets covering Jessica's frail body. Alexander would never recognize this child as a Warrick. He'd made perfectly clear what he thought of Edward's get. "You know I can't speak for the duke, Jessica. He can be a very difficult man. You, of all people, know that."

"That is why you must reason with him, Rose. You are kind and smart. He will listen to you."

"If he had listened to me, Jessica, he would have left this farm when he first arrived. He doesn't take advice easily. Nothing I've ever said to him has made an impression."

"You're wrong again. I see the change in him. He's more open to his feelings now and not nearly as pompous and full of himself as he once was. It was good for him to get away from England and his domineering mother. You're good for him, Rose Elizabeth."

Rose could have debated that point for hours, but she feared they had little time left, and she wanted to ease the dying woman's mind. "You are asking a lot of Alexander after all that has happened, Jessica."

"I know that. But he is twice the man his brother is, and I know Edward would never recognize this child as his own. If Alexander doesn't agree to raise him as a Warrick, the child could end up in a foundling home."

Rose Elizabeth was horrified at the prospect. "Surely Alexander's mother would never allow her son's child to be abandoned."

"Beatrice cares only for the Warrick name. The scandal of my giving birth to Alexander's brother's child would prevent her from accepting the baby. She will want to do away with it and pretend it never existed."

"She would harm a baby?"

Jessica shrugged. "There's no telling with the dowager duchess. She was never much of a mother to Alexander or his brother. I doubt she has an ounce of maternal instinct. And though I'm hardly one to talk, after having considered getting rid of the child myself"—Rose gasped aloud at this admission—"I think I would have made a better mother than Beatrice Warrick."

Rose Elizabeth would never allow anyone to harm an innocent child. "I'll do my best to convince Alexander that the child belongs with him."

Jessica reached out her hand and Rose clasped it tightly. "If I am gone when Alexander returns, tell him that I am truly sorry for all the pain I caused him. I know he'll never forgive me, but you must promise to tell him."

Rose promised, and then spent the next few hours in the most horrifying nightmare of her life.

Alexander heard the baby's cry as soon as he burst through the front door, with Doc Spooner close behind him. Wet and covered with snow, he didn't bother to remove his outer garments but took the stairs two at a time, urging the portly doctor to hurry.

At the doorway to Jessica's room, he paused, trying to make sense of everything he observed. Jessica lay very still on the bed, not uttering a sound, while Rose Elizabeth sat in the rocking chair, cuddling the newborn to her breast and chanting soothing sounds in an effort to quiet him.

"We came as soon as we could," he said.

Rose looked up, and there was deep sorrow in her eyes. "It's too late, Alexander. Jessica is dead. She wasn't strong enough to hold on. She died shortly after the baby was born. I couldn't stop the bleeding."

The doctor rushed in to assess the lifeless body, then pulled up the bloodied sheet to cover Jessica's face. He turned to Alexander. "I'm afraid Rose Elizabeth is correct, your grace. The woman is dead." Taking the infant from Rose's arms, he examined it carefully, his large body shaking with relief as he proclaimed, "The child is fine. It's a boy."

Alexander appeared stunned. He stared first at the lifeless body on the bed, then at the infant. "Jessica's dead?" He shook his head. "How typical of her to abandon her problems to others without a thought to the mess she created."

At his callous words, Rose Elizabeth exchanged a horrified look with the physician, then stepped forward and clasped

Alexander's forearm. "You're overwrought and don't know what you're saying."

Without a word, or a thought to the now sleeping baby, the duke spun on his heel and retreated to his room, leaving Rose alone with the doctor.

"He's upset, Rose Elizabeth. His reaction is natural, considering the . . . uh . . . unusual circumstances and all."

She nodded. "I'm sure he'll be fine in a few days, after he adjusts. Are you sure the baby is all right? I didn't do anything to harm him, did I?" It had been her greatest fear that she would lose the child as she had the mother. Though she'd done everything in her limited powers to save Jessica's life, her efforts had proved futile. The woman had hemorrhaged to death—a common enough fate for a woman in childbirth, especially in the West.

Handing the infant back to her, Doc Spooner patted Rose on the back. "You should be proud of yourself, Rose Elizabeth. This little tyke will grow up to be a strong lad because of you."

She hugged the small bit of humanity to her breast, already forming an attachment she had no right to feel. "I did my best."

"That's all we can ever hope to do." He glanced back at the bed and shook his head sadly. "I'll take the body back to town with me. Tell his grace that as soon as he decides what to do about his fiancée, he's to let me know. The body will keep for a while, because of the bitter cold, but we don't have an indefinite amount of time before we'll need to put her into the ground."

Rose shivered, nodded, then looked away as the doctor wrapped Jessica's body in the blankets and removed it and himself from the room.

She thought about going to Alexander to offer him solace, to tell him of Jessica's parting words, but she decided that he'd be better left alone to his grief.

Tomorrow would be soon enough to sort out the new set of problems that Jessica's death had created, not the least of which was the baby she held in her arms.

CHAPTER 20

A baby!

Even now Alexander could hear his pitiful cries, and Rose's soothing voice as she tried to quiet him. But the infant's wail grew louder, rasping sharply over Alexander's frayed nerves, and he covered his ears to block out the sound and his own responsibility in the matter.

Clutching the neck of a crystal brandy decanter, he poured himself a stiff drink—one of many he would need before this night was through.

"It isn't my child," he murmured before belting back the amber liquid.

It isn't my child!

He wasn't Rose Elizabeth's child either, but you'd never know that to watch her with him. The baby had become an integral part of her life in the past twenty-four hours.

She had remained in the house because of the infant, knowing that the soddy was far too cold in winter and might prove harmful to the baby.

Food had become her first priority, and when the child was sleeping, she had gone to the soddy to fetch feeding bottles that had been stored away from her own infancy, as well as blankets and old linen sheets that she could fashion into diapers.

A search of Jessica's trunk had revealed nothing but fancy clothing totally inappropriate for Kansas. There had been no baby clothes, no crocheted blankets, nothing to indicate that the woman had been expecting a child. But then Rose suspected that the baby had never quite been real to Jessica until right before he was born.

Thinking of Jessica brought Alexander to mind. He'd been holed up in his room since her death, and as far as Rose Elizabeth knew he hadn't emerged to eat, tend to chores, or inquire about the child's welfare.

His overt reaction to his fiancée's death had somewhat surprised her, since Alexander had professed such a strong dislike of the woman. But death had a strange effect on people, and folks reacted to it in different ways.

Rose Elizabeth cast an eye toward the fireplace and the wooden apple crate she had converted to the baby's bed. She had a similar arrangement in the bedroom, only there she had used an empty dresser drawer as a bed. Resting before the hearth, the child seemed snug and warm in his new environment.

The cow's milk she had warmed on the stove was nearly the right temperature. She had tested it on her wrist, as the Farmer's Almanac instructed, and poured it into the bottles she had previously cleaned and boiled.

There was a lot more to this motherhood business than she had ever considered, and Rose wondered how she would be able to keep up with her chores and the baby's needs as well.

The odor of brandy reached her before the sound of Alexander's footsteps, and she turned to see him leaning unsteadily against the doorjamb. He was unshaven and smelled of sweat, and there were dark circles beneath his eyes, as if he hadn't slept. But then, neither had she.

She hadn't been able to bring herself to sleep in the bed where Jessica had died, so she had spent a miserable night in the rocker. She'd been so uncomfortable, she was sure that her spine was permanently curved.

"Are you hungry?" she asked, unable to mask the disapproval in her voice. Alcohol, she knew, had been the bane of many a good man.

Bleary-eyed, he sat down at the table. "No, but I'd like some coffee, if you have some made."

"I do." She filled a mug and set it before him. "Have you done the chores yet? I'm not sure I can handle everything with the baby and all."

He glanced toward the hearth, noted the sleeping child, and frowned. "The child is not your responsibility."

"I know. It's yours. But you don't seem inclined to take it."

He flinched at her words, and his voice thickened with an unfathomable emotion as he said, "It's not my child."

"But he is your nephew, and as such he deserves to be raised as a Warrick. It's what Jessica wanted."

His fist came down hard on the table, upsetting the mug and spilling the hot coffee to the floor. "No! The child is a bastard. It will never be raised as a Warrick."

At that moment the baby began to cry, and Rose Elizabeth balled her hands into fists at her sides. "There's only one bastard here, as far as I'm concerned, Alexander Warrick. And that bastard is you."

Over the next few days they fell into a routine of sorts. Rose Elizabeth continued to care for the baby, and Alexander continued to absent himself. She wasn't sure whether he was avoiding her or the child or both.

On the third day after Jessica's death, Seamus and Rebecca arrived. Winter's grip had eased a bit, and the sun shone brilliantly, melting some of the snow and making travel somewhat easier.

Rose Elizabeth hoped this was a portent of good things to come.

"How are ye, lass?" Seamus asked, stomping the snow off his boots before entering the house. "And where is Alexander? I thought he'd be about tending to the chores on such a sunny day, but I didn't see him when I pulled up."

Rose sighed as she ushered her guests into the kitchen. "The duke is upstairs in his room. He doesn't do chores anymore. He only drinks brandy and feels sorry for himself."

Rebecca's eyes widened, and Seamus asked, "What's this I'm hearin'? The duke is pining for his dead fiancée? That don't sound right to me, lass. There was no love lost between the two."

Rose set a cold pitcher of milk and a platter of freshly made doughnuts on the table. "To tell you the truth, Seamus, I've been so busy with the baby, I haven't had time to worry about Alexander's problems. He's been extremely stubborn and inconsiderate, and I'm washing my hands of him."

Rebecca cast Seamus a worried look before crossing to the makeshift cradle to peek at the baby. "He's beautiful, Rose Elizabeth," she said, and there was a wistfulness in her voice that Rose did not miss.

"Your time will come soon enough, Rebecca."

"It ain't for lack of trying, lass. I'll give you that," Seamus said with a naughty grin.

"Seamus O'Flynn!" Rebecca's hands flew to her flaming cheeks, and Rose Elizabeth laughed for the first time in days.

"Thank goodness you two have come. I've been at wit's end trying to figure out what I'm going to do about Alexander and this baby. He refuses to recognize him as a Warrick."

Seamus studied her for a moment. "And do you really want him to, Rose Elizabeth? For it would mean that he would take the child away from here and raise him in England."

Tears filled her eyes. "No, it's not what I want. It's what

Jessica wanted. It was her dying wish that her son be raised as a Warrick."

"A mother's concern should be for her child," Rebecca counseled. "I'm sure Jessica would have wanted what is best for her son." She took Rose's hands in her own. "I believe you are what is best, Rose Elizabeth."

"Me? But I never truly considered keeping the child. I mean . . . I'd love to, but . . . I'm not married, and a child should have two parents. And I just assumed that once Alexander snapped out of his maudlin state, he'd be taking the baby back to England with him."

"And to the dowager duchess?" Seamus grimaced. "The woman is a harridan."

"So Jessica indicated." Rose frowned. How could she possibly turn over an innocent child to someone as ruthless and uncaring as the dowager duchess was said to be?

"Let me talk to Alexander, lass. Perhaps I can find out what his intentions are, remind him of his responsibilities. He seems to have forgotten his duty in this matter, but I intend to remind him."

"I've tried that, Seamus. He won't listen."

He clenched a fist and shook it threateningly. "Then perhaps I'll have to be a bit more persuasive with his grace."

"Seamus!"

He smiled at his furious wife. "Just kidding," he said, before disappearing up the stairs.

Seamus found Alexander in his room, staring into the flames of the fire, a brandy snifter in his hand. He wasn't at all surprised by the duke's behavior.

Alexander had always had difficulty facing problems head-on. As with the situation of Jessica and Edward's betrayal, he was choosing to flee, to hide his head in the sand and hope that things would miraculously rectify themselves.

"Alexander, what the hell is going on with you? Why have you sequestered yourself up here like a Benedictine monk?"

The duke didn't bother to turn around. "Leave me be, Seamus. I've got a lot on my mind. I just want to be left alone."

"When pigs fly, your grace. Now get your arse downstairs. Rose Elizabeth needs you, as does the wee one."

Alexander's face was a mask of fury as he turned to his former servant, but Seamus wasn't the least bit intimidated and stood his ground, ready to do battle if necessary.

"What are you doing here, Seamus? Can't you see that I wish to be left alone?"

"What I see, your grace, is that you've shirked your duties to the sprightly lass, leaving her to perform all the chores and tend to the child, too. You should be ashamed of yourself. I never took you for a coward, Alexander."

Guilt flushed the duke's face. "I'm . . ." *Running away again,* he finished silently, unable to voice the awful truth. There was much to be faced—the child, the dowager duchess, Jessica's burial, Rose Elizabeth—but he hadn't wanted to deal with any of it. Seamus was right—he was a coward.

The duke stared at the snifter in his hand, at the empty brandy decanter on the nightstand, then threw the glass into the fireplace, where it shattered into the ashes. "Bloody hell! I feel worse than horseshit."

"You smell worse than it, too, if you don't mind me saying so, your grace."

"What day is this?"

"Wednesday. And by your stench I'd say you haven't bathed in a few days."

Alexander had the grace to blush beneath his recent growth of beard. "Why have you come, Seamus?"

"Rebecca and I came to pay our respects, and to see the child, but I find you are due no respect, only contempt, your grace."

Regret and shame filled Alexander's being, and he shook his head forlornly. "I don't know how to deal with it all, Seamus, with the child Jessica's forced upon me—my brother's child."

"Not dealing with problems won't make them go away, Alexander. It only makes things worse in the end."

"I know you're right, Seamus, and I also know that I've made a bloody mess of things. Rose must surely hate me."

"I guess she's got good reason. You left her with no help and a wee one to care for. I doubt the poor lass knew much about babies and such."

"I just naturally assumed . . ."

"Not all women are cut out to be mothers just because they're women, Alexander. Your own mother is certainly living proof of that. Jessica would have made a horrible mother, but Rose Elizabeth has taken to the role like a duck to water."

A thoughtful smile lifted the corners of Alexander's mouth. "She's a nurturing woman."

"Aye. And that child would be well off with her."

That statement sobered the duke up quickly. "What makes you think she would want it?"

"She wants him, all right. I've seen the love on her face when she gazes at him, heard the tenderness in her voice when she speaks to him. Rose Elizabeth is a born mother."

"This bears careful consideration." If Rose Elizabeth took the child, it would relieve him of all obligation to it, not to mention his ne'er-do-well brother, who knew nothing of taking responsibility for his actions. It could very well be the solution to a very difficult problem.

Seamus nodded. "Aye, it does. And perhaps you'll give the situation your full and undivided attention, as well as serious thought to providing Rose Elizabeth with the security she'll need to care for the child."

"You talk as if I'm leaving here."

Seating himself beside the duke, Seamus wrapped a comforting arm around his shoulders. "You've got to return to England, your grace. Jessica's body must be returned for burial. It wouldn't be right to deny her that. And you've got to face the questions her death will surely raise. Though you loved her not, she was your fiancée, your responsibility, and you must take charge now and do what is right for all concerned."

What Seamus said was valid, and the pain of that reality

seared deep within Alexander's chest, filling his heart with sorrow. "I know what you say is true, Seamus, but I don't know if I can bear the separation from Rose Elizabeth. I love her with all my heart and soul. What will I do without her?"

Seamus rose slowly to his feet, staring sadly at the man before him. Alexander Warrick was the perfect example of how money and power couldn't bring happiness. In fact, at the moment, it was the cause of a great deal of misery, to judge by the pitiable look on his face.

"You'll have time to sort out your feelings for Rose Elizabeth and the child while you're gone, your grace. Think long and hard on the matter, for if you make the wrong decision, you'll regret it the rest of your life."

"But how will I know what that is, Seamus? I've not made good choices up till now. Jessica was a perfect example of that."

Seamus squeezed the duke's shoulder in a display of support and affection. "You'll know what to do when the time comes, Alexander. Trust your heart. It won't guide you wrong."

It was a very different Alexander who appeared in the kitchen a few hours later. Clean-shaven and smelling of his spicy cologne, he stood in the doorway, an uncertain, sheepish look on his face.

Rose Elizabeth was oblivious to his presence. Seated by the fire, she held the baby close to her breast while feeding him his evening bottle.

But Alexander was definitely aware of her. A Renaissance painting of the Madonna and Child could not have been more poignant or beautiful than the scene before him. And it made his heart ache.

Rose's face, as she stared down at the baby, was aglow with love and wonderment, and Alexander wished only that she looked upon him with half the love he saw directed at the infant.

Feeling somewhat like a voyeur, Alexander cleared his throat nervously, not quite sure what kind of reception he would receive after his unconscionable behavior.

She looked in his direction, her expression unreadable. There was neither surprise nor acceptance, nor an indication that she was glad to see him after so many days. "Supper's on the stove if you've a mind to eat. The stew should still be hot."

"Rose, I . . ." Nervously he toyed with the belt loop on his pants.

"Was there something else you needed, your grace? As you can see, I'm quite busy at the moment." She lifted the baby to her shoulder and burped him gently, then resumed the feeding.

It was a good thing there was a fire in the hearth, Alexander decided, because Rose's words were as cold as icicles. "I've come to apologize."

"Really? And is that supposed to make everything you've done and said these past few days all right? That's not how it works, your dukeness."

Alexander took a few tentative steps farther into the kitchen. The hair shirt he wore was deuced uncomfortable, but there was no help for it, if he was going to settle things between them before he left. "I know I've been a fool and an idiot—"

"You forgot horse's ass."

He tunneled exasperated fingers through his hair. Rose was not going to make this easy on him. "I'd like to explain, if you'll let me."

"You don't owe me any explanations, your highness."

"I owe you everything."

The admission took her aback, and she gazed into blue eyes full of sadness and remorse. She'd always been a sucker for an apology. More fool, she.

Placing the sleeping child in his bed, she rose from the chair and faced Alexander. "Just because we slept together doesn't mean that you owe me, your grace. We made an honest bargain; you kept your part and I kept mine."

"You know it was more than that."

"I know nothing except that you lied to me about having a fiancée, acted less than noble about an innocent child, and behaved in an abominable fashion, wiling away in self-pity. I expected more from you, your grace. I guess I thought living and working here on the farm had changed you. But you're still the self-centered, arrogant man I met those many months ago."

If her words had been bullets, they could not have pierced him more deeply. "You're wrong, Rose Elizabeth! I'm nothing like that man. If circumstances had been different . . ."

But they weren't. He had to return to England. Duty dictated that he must. And Rose Elizabeth would never be happy living there, even if they married. Like her namesake—Prim Rose—she would wither and die from being forced into a society and way of life she knew nothing about.

Rose belonged on the land that she loved, and that was so much a part of her.

Jessica's death had forced him to see how destructive his selfish wants and needs could be. He would not put Rose Elizabeth through that, no matter how much he loved and desired her.

And there was the very important matter of children. She desperately wanted them, and he could not fulfill that need; but he could leave her with Jessica's child to cherish.

"When will you be leaving, your grace?" Rose asked. Though the very words burned bitter in her throat, she had to know.

"I've instructed Seamus to purchase a ticket for me on Friday's noon train heading east. From New York I'll secure passage on a ship bound for England."

Friday! It was too soon, too soon, Rose thought. There was so much that hadn't been said, so much that had, but not the words from her heart. Not the words that said how much she loved him, wanted to be with him, wanted him to stay.

But like the panic that lodged in her throat, so did the words that could bind him to her. And she knew that for them it was too late. "I guess that will be best." She tried to keep her voice even, but it was very, very hard.

"I'm not sure anymore what's best or what isn't. I only know that I have responsibilities waiting for me at home, and I must return Jessica's body for burial."

The question she feared most came out as a whisper, and she suddenly felt chilled all over. "And the baby?"

"You were right about the child. He is innocent of all that has happened. But I do not think that returning him to England would be the wisest thing. My mother would no doubt reject him because of the circumstances surrounding his birth. And it's obvious by my brother's unchivalrous behavior that he has no intention of becoming a true father to the child who could well be his." He cast another look at the baby, and his features softened.

Rose Elizabeth held her breath, watching Alexander pace back and forth in front of the stove as she waited for his decision.

"I had considered adoption, or placing the child with Seamus and Rebecca. I know they would make excellent parents."

She nodded in agreement, unable to deny that truth, but her heart grew heavy with despair. "They would."

He stopped before her and reached for her hands. "But I want to leave the baby with you, Rose Elizabeth. I know you'll care for him as if he were your own. And I think Jessica would be pleased by that decision over any other. Would you consider taking him?"

Her face lit with relief and happiness, and she squeezed his hands to communicate her thanks. "I will love him like he was my own child, Alexander, on that you have my word.

"But what will you tell your mother and brother? Won't they wonder what happened to the baby? He is a Warrick, after all."

"I will inform them that the child died. They won't question that, knowing that Jessica succumbed during her delivery."

It would be a lie, but a worthwhile one, in Rose Elizabeth's opinion. "A lie told to protect others is forgivable." Her mama's words made perfect sense now. "I will do my best by him. I know it'll be hard, since I'll have to find a job to support us, but—"

"That won't be necessary, Rose Elizabeth." He pulled an official-looking document from his shirt pocket and handed it to her. "I am turning your farm back over to you. It should never have been sold in the first place. No one but a Martin should own the Martin homestead. Don't you agree?"

She gazed at the deed and could scarcely believe her eyes. "But . . . but I can't afford to pay you back all the money you've spent on this house, on the improvements you've made to the farm." She thought back to the shower stall, the many fights they'd had over it, and felt silly and small.

Alexander caressed her cheek. "As I said before: You've given me everything. I have more money that I'll ever need, and building this house was purely a labor of love."

The word made her catch her breath, and there was an awkward silence between them before she said, "You're very good with your hands."

His smile was full of regret and something she could not fathom. "I hope you'll always remember that about me."

She pressed her cheek against his chest and hugged him about the waist. "I'm not likely to ever forget anything about you, your grace. Especially your conceit."

He laughed. "Are we friends, then?"

She swallowed her sadness and gazed up at him. "Always."

CHAPTER 21

The ormolu clock on the mantel ticked away the seconds and minutes, all the while keeping time to the pounding of Rose Elizabeth's heart.

It was the middle of the night, and she had lain awake for hours, every tick and thump a reminder that the time for Alexander's departure drew near.

Was he thinking of her, too, as he lay in his bed across the hall? she wondered. Would he think of her even half as much as she would miss him? Would he think of the hours they'd spent toiling with the wheat and the pigs? Would he remember the blissful moments they'd spent wrapped in each other's arms in the sagging bed of the soddy?

Memories could sustain a body. She remembered her mama saying so before she died. But those memories had to be special, poignant, each bringing forth a joyous moment in time.

And if those memories were fresh, then surely they'd be remembered and treasured for a long time to come.

Rose Elizabeth eased herself out from under the heavy quilt and tiptoed to the fireplace, depositing several more logs onto the fire. The embers ate greedily, and the flames leaped suddenly to life.

The baby slept contentedly in his bed-drawer and wasn't likely to awaken for several more hours.

There was still time to make memories with Alexander, if her courage didn't fail. Time to make love with him once more before he left.

And there was time to etch him into her heart and her soul, where he would remain for the rest of her days, and where no one else would ever reside.

The knob turned easily beneath her trembling hand, and she padded on bare feet into Alexander's room. Shivers overtook her, but not because the fire in his hearth had burned down. The audacity of what she was about to do made her fearful and euphoric, sending shudders of excitement up and down her spine, like a feather tickling her skin.

Turned on his side to face the wall, Alexander snored softly, oblivious to her presence. She could barely make out his outline in the dimly lit room, though the full moon shining through the window helped her make her way stealthily to his bed.

Standing there in her faded flannel nightgown, Rose wished for one of those scandalous gowns she had read about in books. The kind you could see clear through, leaving little to the imagination.

Then, on second thought, she wasn't sure she'd want Alexander to see her dressed like that. She was no *Venus de Milo*, for heaven's sake! Though the duke hadn't seemed to mind, the few times he had seen her naked.

That thought gave her courage, and she eased back the covers and slid in beside his warm body. Inching closer, she pressed herself against his back, hoping the feel of her taut nipples and eager body would be enough to arouse his interest.

It wasn't.

Damn, damn, and double damn! The man was as dead to the world as a resident in a funeral home. Just her luck, she had to pick a night when he was exhausted. But it couldn't be helped. This was the only night she had left, and by God she was going to make the most of it.

Brazenly she wrapped her arm about his middle and reached for his flaccid member. Fortunately, he slept in the nude, which facilitated things, and it took only a moment and a few well-placed strokes to gain his attention.

Alexander hadn't realized he'd been dreaming, but damned if he wasn't harder than a brick. He hated opening his eyes, hated losing the sensation of being fondled and caressed, but if he didn't do so soon, he was going to explode right in the middle of his all-too-realistic fantasy.

He flipped himself over, his eyes and mouth popping open at the same time, and he blinked several times to make sure that what he was seeing was real. "Rose Elizabeth?" Then louder: "Rose Elizabeth!"

She smiled in a way she hoped looked seductive, and her voice trembled slightly as she said, "Yes, Alexander, it's me. I hope you don't mind, but I thought it would be nice if we could share one last night together before you left." One last night to cherish and keep close to her heart.

He grasped the hand that held his organ, in an attempt to still the torturous stimulation. "I thought I was dreaming."

"Was it a good dream?" she asked.

"Good? Bloody hell! I thought I was going to explode and then some, woman."

Her eyes widened. "Oh!" It didn't sound at all good, but she hoped it was.

Pulling her into his arms, he cuddled her to his chest. "You will always remain a mystery to me, my sweet Rose. You always do the unexpected."

"Life should never be dull," she retorted.

"With you, my sweet, that is an impossibility." He reached down to slide his hand up her leg, and Rose moaned contentedly, caressing his cheek.

"I will miss you, Alexander."

He covered her lips with his own, not wanting to hear the words that might make him stay and forget all about duty and honor and years of tradition.

Alexander's kiss sang through her veins, and Rose plunged her tongue deep inside his mouth, mating it with his. He made short work of the gown she had worried over, and soon she was gloriously naked.

"God, Rose!" he said, worshiping her breasts with his mouth and tongue. "You taste as sweet as cotton candy. I can't get enough of you."

"And what do you taste like, Alexander?" She trailed an inquisitive finger down his flat stomach and beyond. Though the question was innocent, the look in her eyes was pure siren, temptress, and it made the breath catch in his throat.

"Oh my God!" Alexander cried out as she lowered her head.

"Salty, not sweet," she proclaimed a short time later.

Flipped onto her back, Rose offered no protest when he returned the favor, placing his mouth on her womanhood and caressing her most intimate area with his tongue.

The result was instantaneous, and she writhed beneath him, urging him to satisfy the burning hunger and longing he'd created.

He entered her quickly, plunging his hard shaft deep within her. Their mating was frenzied, furious, each knowing that this would be the last time to taste, to feel, to experience the joy of their lovemaking.

Higher and higher they climbed to that mystical, magical place where hearts collide to become one and time stands still as souls embrace.

Locked in each other's arms, they said nothing, for there was nothing more to say.

Tomorrow Alexander would depart, and Rose Elizabeth would have her memories to sustain her through all the days of her life.

CHAPTER 22

Spring burst upon the prairie like a comet splintering the earth. Doves, redbirds, and meadowlarks made ready for their young. The cottonwoods would soon blossom with white flaky leaves to snap in the wind like the crack of a whip, and the wheat swayed tall and majestic, glistening and bending in the sunlight.

Colorful wildflowers graced the earth for as far as the eye could see, dispelling the myth that the land was barren, and blue gama grass nurtured and provided for the creatures, as it always had.

It was a time for rebirth, and it had always been Rose Elizabeth's favorite season.

"See the fluffy white clouds, Duke?" Rose pointed skyward, and the child in her arms gurgled happily. "See all the pretty shapes they make? There's a dog just like Boomer, and a magical unicorn."

Two-month-old Duke Warrick Martin, as Rose Elizabeth had named Jessica's child, seemed more interested in the shiny curls falling over Rose's shoulder than in the splendid formations above, and was intent on stuffing the hair into his mouth along with his chubby little fist, much to Rose's consternation.

After weeks of motherhood, Rose Elizabeth had a new respect for the difficulties of the job. The infant depended on her for everything: nurturing, love, sustenance . . . its very existence.

It was an awesome responsibility and rather intimidating to someone who had much preferred to shovel pig manure than to play dolls with her sisters.

Rose took the baby's hand and kissed it. "There're better things to eat than that, Duke." They were seated on the swing, and the warm sun beating down on her face felt welcome after the long, harsh winter. Spring had come to Kansas, and she was grateful.

"I'll just be another minute, then we'll go into the house and I'll feed you something yummy."

The house she referred to was the new house—Alexander's house—for that's where she now lived. She felt a closeness to Alexander there, taking comfort in every wooden plank of the floor, every beam in the wall and ceiling, which he had put in place with his own two hands.

"You look like your uncle, you know," she told the baby, and he smiled and cooed. Duke's hair was blond, like Alexander's, and like his mother's, but the blue eyes were unmistakably a Warrick trait. The baby was a constant and sometimes painful reminder of the duke, who was far away and out of reach.

Alexander had been gone seven weeks, and she missed him terribly. There wasn't a day that she didn't think of him, yearn for him. She had a lot to keep her busy—her chores, the baby, the wheat fields—but they weren't a substitute for Alexander and never could be.

He hadn't written, but then, she hadn't really expected him to.

But she wasn't alone. Sven and Seamus made it a habit to drop in on her every week. They helped out with the more difficult chores, and Sven had built a beautiful cradle for the baby. Seamus always brought bread or other baked goods, and sometimes he brought Rebecca with him, which was always such fun and a welcome intrusion into her routine.

Rebecca was pregnant now, so she found Duke increasingly fascinating to observe. Rose remembered the day when Seamus had proudly informed her of Rebecca's condition, much to the woman's mortification. The memory still brought a smile to Rose's lips.

"We've done it, lass. Our efforts have not been in vain. Rebecca's got a bun in the oven, and I'm not talking about the kind we make at the bakery. She's going to have me child."

He'd said "me child" with so much pride and pleasure, it made one think that Seamus's child would be the only one in existence.

"Uncle Seamus is a silly man, isn't he, Duke?" Rose muzzled the baby's downy cheek.

Rather then reply, Duke turned red in the face, then grunted and groaned, and by the familiar odor wafting up, Rose knew that her idyllic afternoon had come to an end.

"Well, well, if it isn't Rose Elizabeth. Where have you been hiding yourself? But then, I guess you've been rather busy—too busy to visit old friends."

Rose handed the postal clerk the letters she had written to Heather and Laurel, informing them of her new status as unmarried mother and sole owner of the farm. She had found great solace in writing to her sisters and vowed to keep in closer contact with them.

Adjusting Duke a little more comfortably in her arms, Rose gave a soft sigh of frustration. Peggy Mellon was the last person she wanted to talk to today.

She had hoped to run a few errands, drop in on Seamus and Rebecca, and buy a few items of clothing for the baby. She hadn't come to town to socialize, and she certainly hadn't come to spar with Peggy. And to make matters worse, the annoying woman wasn't alone.

The pimply-faced Frederick Farrell was standing next to her, totally enamored of the older woman and hanging on her every word. If one judged by the blush on his face, which made his blemishes even more apparent, Freddy was smitten.

"I'm not sure I would use the term 'old friends' when referring to our relationship, Peggy. But yes, I have been rather busy, as you can see."

"Playing mother to a dead woman's child. What you've done is scandalous, Rose Elizabeth. The whole town's talking about it."

Rose shrugged, finding it odd that someone with Peggy's less-than-sterling reputation would be concerned about scandal. "I've never been concerned with what other folks think or say. I do what I do to please myself and no one else."

"I guess you didn't please the duke, since he ran back to England without you or the child. Folks think it's odd that a man would run off and leave his own flesh and blood behind to be raised by an unmarried woman."

"I'm sure the duke had his reasons," Rose Elizabeth replied, unwilling to offer any details.

"England. That's across the ocean, isn't it, Miss Peggy?" Frederick asked, and Rose Elizabeth wanted to vomit. The boy was still wet behind the ears and apparently dumb as a stump.

"Hush, Frederick! Can't you see that Rose Elizabeth and I are having a discussion. It's very rude to interrupt."

"But you said you'd show me your—"

"Frederick, that's quite enough! Now run along and look at the merchandise while I finish talking with Rose Elizabeth. I won't be very long." The disgruntled young man flashed both women an indignant look before heading to the other side of the store, where the fishing tackle was located.

"I wouldn't want you to disappoint your new beau, Peggy. Feel free to run along and show him whatever it is you promised to show him. After all, every other man in town has seen your attributes."

"Including your duke, but that's another story," Peggy retorted, ignoring the thinning of Rose's lips. "Why are you content to be saddled with a child who isn't even your own flesh and blood, Rose Elizabeth? It's very unnatural. My mother even says so."

Then it must certainly be gospel, for Sarah Ann was second only to Euphemia in the gossip department. No doubt the entire Garden Club and Ladies Sewing Circle was talking about Rose Elizabeth and the new addition to her family. And no doubt they had plenty of disparaging comments to make on the subject. But then, they always had when it came to her, Rose Elizabeth reminded herself.

"I appreciate your mother's concerns, but I'm perfectly happy to raise this precious boy as my own." She kissed the sleeping baby's cheek. "He's an angel most of the time." Unless one counted all those episodes during the middle of the night when he woke up screaming. Irritated bowel, Doc Spooner called it. Rose Elizabeth dubbed it hunger and had added cereal to his nightly feedings, which seemed to pacify him.

"A child should have two parents. And what man in his right mind is going to want to marry a woman who already has a baby?" Peggy shook her head in disgust. "You'll never find a husband now."

"I'll leave marriage to you, Peggy. I'm not as desperate to marry as you seem to be." She cast a disdainful look at Frederick, who was now attired in an absurd-looking hat adorned with a pheasant feather and a too-large fishing vest.

"Mama thinks Frederick will make an excellent husband. His family is well off, and he's obedient as a puppy."

Rose Elizabeth was shocked. "You're not going to marry that sniveling whelp, are you? I thought you had better taste than that."

Peggy's cheeks turned red. "I find that I'm not in a position to be too choosy at the moment."

Her eyes widening as the realization dawned, Rose Eliza-

beth slapped her hand over her mouth and stared at her childhood acquaintance as if she'd lost every ounce of sense she'd
been born with. "Does your mother know?"

"Of course she does. It was her idea that I marry Frederick.
He's been pining over me for months, and Wolf already has a
wife."

"You're carrying Wolf Turlock's child?"

"Sssh. Not so loud. I wouldn't want Freddy to get wind of
it before we're hitched."

"You haven't told him yet? That's the most despicable
thing I've ever heard, Peggy Mellon." She poked an angry
finger into Peggy's arm, wishing she could as easily punch
some sense into the selfish, conniving woman. "Bearing a
married man's child is one thing, but passing that child off as
another's is unconscionable."

"Freddy will never know. We've been . . . Well, you
know."

"And you have the nerve to take me to task over performing my Christian duty to mother this innocent babe! I will
never understand you, Peggy. Never in a million years."

"That's because you've always been such a goody-goody,
Rose Elizabeth Martin. You're happy as a lark living in this
godforsaken place, while I've been just miserable. I'm destined for greater things. In time, and with Freddy's father's
money, I'm going to leave Salina and move to the big city."

What are you going to do there, Rose Elizabeth wanted to
ask, *open a brothel?* Peggy's talents did seem to lie in that direction.

"I hope your dreams come true one day, Peggy," she said
graciously, realizing that there was little point in arguing with
the woman. It took too much energy, and energy was not in
great abundance these days, as Peggy soon pointed out.

"If you don't start fixing yourself up better, Rose Elizabeth, no man is ever going to look your way. Why, those bags
under your eyes are just awful. And your hands look worse
than a plowman's. It's no wonder the duke took off for civi-

lization. He was obviously used to a more genteel type of woman."

Though the words blistered her soul, for Rose Elizabeth thought there was a great deal of truth in them, she didn't flinch or show any emotion. "I really must be going now. Seamus and Rebecca are expecting me."

Peggy harrumphed loudly. "Seamus O'Flynn is a fool, if you ask me. He could have married me instead of that simpering Rebecca Heller, but he chose her instead."

"Perhaps he had a hankerin' for fresh, unspoiled goods. I hear men like to marry virgins when the time comes for them to settle down." *Which doesn't bode well for me,* Rose thought.

"Freddy doesn't seem to mind."

The corners of Rose's lips twitched. "Maybe that's because there was already one virgin in the family." Before Peggy could fire a retort, Rose Elizabeth sauntered out, feeling quite proud of the rejoinder.

For once, Peggy Mellon hadn't had the last word.

Rose listened to Seamus with half an ear while he regaled her with details about the new oven they'd just purchased for the bakery. Business was booming, and the O'Flynns could now afford to add a few modern conveniences.

They had even discussed installing a telephone, so that the customers could phone in their orders, but Rebecca had judiciously pointed out to Seamus that no one else in Salina presently owned such a device, so it would be useless for them to have one. Rebecca, despite her new clothing, was still uncomfortable with things not Plain.

Rose Elizabeth had never cared for the idea of telephones—they seemed so impersonal—but she knew that they were becoming more prevalent in the big cities.

"Why do you let that woman get to you, lass? Everyone in town knows that Peggy Mellon is a tramp." Seamus had suddenly changed the subject, and Rose returned her attention to the frowning Irishman. Since Alexander's departure, Seamus had assumed the role of protector of Rose Elizabeth and the baby. And though it was flattering and terribly sweet, he took that role a little too seriously at times.

Setting down her glass of milk, Rose decided that in the future she needed to be more circumspect in her discussions about Peggy. It was obvious that Seamus didn't understand how it was between the two women.

"Peggy and I have been sparring for years, Seamus. As a former pugilist, I'm sure you can appreciate a worthy opponent. Life will most likely grow dull around here once Peggy takes off for parts unknown."

"I can't believe how much the baby has grown, Rose Elizabeth," Rebecca commented, oblivious to the ongoing conversation. "He has put on weight, and his hair has gotten thicker." Rebecca made cooing noises at Duke, and he responded with a smile.

Grateful for the interruption, Rose replied, "He eats like a horse, but unfortunately everything that goes in comes right back out. I'm constantly washing diapers."

Rebecca giggled. "Seamus says he will not change the baby's dirty diapers when it arrives. I told him that was not a fair attitude, and that the father should share equally in the chores with the mother, whether they be good or bad."

Seamus wrinkled his nose in disgust. "I've shoveled my share of manure, Rebecca lass, but I can't be bringing myself to change dirty linens." He shuddered, making Rose Elizabeth laugh.

"You get used to it after a while, though I imagine Alexander would have felt the same way as you."

There was an awkward silence at the mention of the duke, then Seamus asked, "Have you had word from him, lass?"

Though she did her best to conceal it, Rose couldn't disguise her pain. "Not a word, Seamus. But that's all right. I'm not expecting to ever hear from him again."

Seamus had received a brief note from the duke, informing him and Rebecca of his safe arrival in England and the details of Jessica's funeral. The dowager duchess had apparently shown little emotion when informed of her future daughter-in-law's demise and had not asked a thing about the child. Edward had not attended the funeral and would remain in India for an indefinite period of time. "Hopefully forever," Alexander had written.

Wondering whether to reveal the missive, Seamus searched his wife's face and found approval there. Nervously he cleared his throat. "Rose, lass, I've had a brief note from the duke, and he's well."

Hope lit her face. "Did he ask for me?" Then it faded quickly as Seamus shook his head.

"I'm sorry, lass. I know how much you care for him. But you mustn't vex yourself over it. Men are not known for being considerate sorts. I know for a fact that Alexander abhors letter writing." He clasped her hand. "And I also know for a fact that he cares for you, Rose Elizabeth. Never doubt that."

She pushed herself up from the chair and forced a smile. "His consideration overwhelms me, Seamus. And you can stop trying to make me feel better. I'm a grown woman, and I've known from the beginning what I was letting myself in for. Alexander made no promises."

She held out her hands for the baby. "We've got to go now, Rebecca. I want to get home before dark."

"Why don't you stay the night, Rose Elizabeth? You and the baby can stay in Papa's old room. It isn't safe for you to make that long journey by yourself."

"Rebecca's right, lass. Stay and I'll escort you home in the morning. I'll even prepare you one of my special breakfasts."

Rose Elizabeth laughed and shook her head. "You two are worse than broody hens. I've been making this trek into town and back for years. Nothing's ever happened before. Why should it now?"

* * *

Rose Elizabeth had plenty of time to ponder that question as she stared down at the bent wagon wheel and frowned deeply.

"Damn, damn, and double damn!" she cursed, then admonished herself for swearing in front of the baby, who was fortunately still asleep in his basket in the back of the wagon.

Alexander had always said that the rickety old wagon would collapse one day. Too bad he'd been proven right when she was still at least two miles from home.

Glancing at the sky, she knew that she didn't have much daylight left, and traversing the road in the dark would be too dangerous with Duke in tow. Knowing that she had little choice in the matter, Rose took the baby and a blanket from the wagon, and tied it around her neck and waist papoose fashion, fitting the baby against her chest and stomach.

If Indian women could walk miles hauling their young with them, she guessed she could too, and she set about to prove it.

Rose's boots were sturdy, but they weren't made for walking great distances, and her feet were starting to notice that fact. Swollen, and probably redder than a July strawberry, they ached with every step she took.

Duke had taken all the adjustments in stride, but it was closing in on his suppertime, and he'd soon be making his hunger known.

The sky grew darker by the minute, and the sun was only partially visible as it sank lower to the horizon. The evening air nipped at her skin; once the sun disappeared for good, it was going to be downright chilly.

"We'll make it, Duke," she assured the child, who was already showing signs of hunger. Rose suddenly craved a big bowl of beef stew chocked full of vegetables and several dumplings to go along with it. "Stop it, Rose," she chided herself. She tried to stop thinking about food, knowing that was almost as useless as wondering why Alexander had never written.

"Spilt milk . . . water under the bridge," her mama would have said. "No use worrying about what can't be changed,

Rose Elizabeth. You got more important things to worry over."

Rose repeated the adages, hoping they would take her mind off her feet and her heartache. But nothing did much good in either case. Her feet would no doubt be callused for weeks, her heart bruised much, much longer.

"Rose Elizabet! Rose Elizabet!"

Sven's voice came out of the darkness, and Rose thanked the Almighty for hearing her prayers.

"Over here." She was seated by the side of the road, trying to comfort the screaming baby and praying that she would have the strength to go on.

The wagon halted a few feet from her and Sven dropped down to the ground. She had never been so glad to see anyone in her life. "Thank God you've come, dear friend."

"Are you all right? Is the baby vell?" Worry and fear shone clearly on his face, and he rushed forward to assist her, taking the infant from her and holding him against his chest, despite the fact that Duke was soaking wet and immediately rendered Sven the same way.

"Hush, little baby. Sven has come to help."

"How did you know where to find me?" Rose asked, once she was seated on the wagon bench next to Sven. Duke quieted, content to suck her finger for a while.

"I came to your house to bring the ice but found it empty. When I saw your wagon was gone I grew worried. I knew you vould not stay in town for the night. Not vith the animals to care for. When it started to grow dark, I decided to come look for you."

She squeezed his arm. "You don't know how grateful I am that you did. I'm not sure I could have walked the rest of the way home.'

Sven's voice took on a note of censure. "Now that you have a child, Rose Elizabet, you cannot afford to make such foolish decisions again. You either leave for home earlier, or you remain in town for the night. Did Seamus approve of your plan to drive home alone?"

When she blushed and shook her head, he heaved a sigh. "I thought not. You are too stubborn and independent for your own good."

"Please don't take me to task, Sven. I think I've learned my lesson."

His second sigh indicated that he only half believed her. "Where is the wagon?"

"It's back down the road a ways. The wheel broke."

"I vill fix it in the morning and bring it back to the farm for you."

"Thank you."

"When Alexander returns I vill tell him of your foolishness."

She winced, but he couldn't see her reaction in the dark. "He's not coming back, so you'll not be able to tattle on me."

"Did he tell you that he would not be back?"

"No. Not in so many words. But I know he won't. Alexander wrote to Seamus, but made no mention of me or the baby. He has washed his hands of us." Speaking that truth drove a stake through her heart.

Sven pondered Rose's words, the agony in her voice, then replied, "It takes more than miles and months to make a heart forget that it loves, Rose Elizabet. You have not forgotten, have you?"

"But Alexander is not in love with me, Sven." What would it take to convince this kindhearted man of that fact? Not every man was as honorable or as giving as Sven Anderson.

He snapped the reins with the same conviction that colored his words. "We vill see, Rose Elizabet, who is right in this matter. We vill see."

CHAPTER 23

At the sound of wheels crunching on the drive, Rose Elizabeth set aside the bowl of peas she'd been shelling and glanced out the kitchen window to see Euphemia alighting from her conveyance.

Boomer rushed to greet the older woman and was rewarded with a stern shake of the spinster's finger and an admonishment about being a bad dog. Tail between his legs, he slunk away in disgrace.

Rose chuckled at the antics and went to answer the soft knock. "You are the last person I expected to see at my door, Euphemia Bloodsworth," Rose said, ushering her inside and along to the kitchen. "I know how much you hate driving your buggy alone."

Sighing, the older woman removed her bonnet and gloves. "I do hate driving alone, but I decided it was time that I came by to see how you and the child are doing." She looked about the room. "Where is the baby? I hope I haven't come at his nap time."

Rose pointed to the caged pen on the far side of the kitchen.

"I got the idea from Elvira and Elmo's pigpens and asked Sven to build me something I could keep the baby in. He's content to play in it while he's awake."

Euphemia's eyes widened. "How very unusual, but clever of you, my dear. May I hold him?"

Now it was Rose's turn to look surprised. Euphemia had never shown much interest in children, other than to scold them when they trampled her flower beds, and Rose was dumbfounded that she would want to hold a small baby.

What if the child soiled her dress? The thought was too hideous to consider.

"I don't mean to be rude, Euphemia, but I didn't think you liked children." The Martin sisters had never been treated to any overt displays of affection from the spinster. Quite the contrary. Euphemia used to take great delight in tattling on them to their parents.

"Just because you and your sisters received tongue-lashings from time to time, Rose Elizabeth, does not mean that I don't like children. I just don't like unruly children." She cast Rose a measured look.

"And just because I'm a spinster doesn't mean that I desire to live my life this way. The good Lord just never chose to provide me with a husband, though I came close once."

Lifting the baby out of his pen, Rose handed him over to the older woman, then settled into the chair next to her and listened with interest as she detailed the events of her life.

Euphemia Bloodsworth's love life had long been the cause of much speculation among the townsfolk, but no one had ever been privy to the truth, until now.

"You had a beau?" Rose hoped she didn't sound too surprised by the revelation.

The spinster's smile was wistful. "I had many beaus when I was younger, I'll have you know, young woman. But one in particular, Lionel Farnsworth, was the man of my dreams—the one I thought I'd spend the rest of my life with." She sighed. "Unfortunately, Lionel could not accept my ailing mother into his family, and I was forced to turn down his marriage proposal.

"And you know better than most, Rose Elizabeth, family always comes first."

Rose felt compassion for the older woman, whose tart, often sour disposition now seemed to have a foundation. "I'm sorry, Euphemia. I had no idea."

Euphemia cuddled Duke to her breast, and a faraway look entered her eyes. "I always wanted a child of my own," she confessed, then looked up at Rose with sadness in her eyes. "I hope you don't end up like me, Rose Elizabeth. There's nothing fun about living your life alone."

Duke started to fuss and none of Euphemia's efforts to quiet him worked, so Rose put him back in his pen, placing a small rag doll she had made next to him for companionship.

"I'm content to remain as I am, Euphemia. There is no man here that interests me."

A knowing look surfaced, and the spinster's eyes filled with pity. "I know we've been at cross purposes many times, my dear, but if there's anything you need, you just let me know. Life's hard enough without having a baby to care for and all the responsibility that goes along with it.

"I know you probably won't believe me when I say this, but I admire you for doing what you've done. That baby is far better off with you than he would have been with that floozy he had for a mother and that philandering Duke of Moreland."

Rose was quite surprised by Euphemia's unexpected show of support. Though the spinster had professed a motherly interest in her over the years, Rose had never taken her seriously, had never looked beyond the surface of her unwanted interference and advice. Perhaps she had misjudged her.

"Thank you for your kind words, Euphemia. But you must not judge Alexander Warrick too harshly."

"*Hmph!* Well, you're too soft-hearted by half. And my goodness but you've lost a lot of weight! Your cheekbones are prominent, Rose Elizabeth. Are you eating enough?"

Rose wanted to laugh. Euphemia had always chided her for

being overweight, and now she was being taken to task for having lost some. There was no pleasing the woman. "I thought you said I was too plump."

"Well, now you're too skinny. We need to get some meat on your bones, young woman. It wouldn't do to have you come down sick when you have a baby to tend. Besides, I've decided that full-figured women are a bit more appealing." Preening, she smoothed her black taffeta dress over her own generous curves.

"I've never been accused of being skinny, and I'm not now. If you could see me in my drawers, you'd know that I'm as well rounded as ever."

Euphemia looked aghast at the prospect. "I really don't think that will be necessary, my dear." She rose to leave. "Before I forget to mention it—that fool Skeeter Purty has finally decided to put Marcella out of her misery. They are going to be married a week from Saturday."

Rose's face lit with pleasure. "That's wonderful! Marcella must be beside herself with glee."

"Wait until after she marries the man, then she'll find out what I've been telling her all along: Skeeter Purty is a wastrel and an imbiber of alcoholic beverages."

"Are you sure you won't stay for dinner, Euphemia? I'm making a ham. And I've fixed a chocolate cake for dessert."

Euphemia smacked her lips, but shook her head. "Thank you, but no. I've got to get back to town. But before I go . . ." She reached into her reticule, extracted two envelopes, and handed them to Rose Elizabeth. "These were at the post office, so I told Beauford Pugsly that I'd deliver them to you. I thought it might save you a trip to town."

Rose scanned the letters quickly; they were from her sisters, not from Alexander, and she did her best to hide her disappointment. "They're from Heather and Laurel." She pasted on a smile. "I've been writing to keep them apprised of my situation here on the farm."

"Yes, I know, dear. I took the liberty of looking them over to see if the duke had written." She squeezed Rose's shoulder in commiseration. "Don't ever give up hope, Rose Elizabeth. That man may come to his senses yet.

" 'Hope springs eternal.' Isn't that what someone once said?" Euphemia added.

But hope was not in Rose Elizabeth's vocabulary any longer. Or in her heart.

> *Dearest Rose,*
>
> *I am increasingly concerned by the despondency I sense from your letters and wanted to reassure you that all will be well if you just have faith.*
>
> *There were times when I despaired of working things out with Brandon, but those days seem a distant, unpleasant memory now, and we are very happy.*
>
> *You must remain strong for the baby you now mother and know that things will work out for the best, as they always do. Remember what our beloved mama said: "If it is meant to be, it will be."*
>
> *Your loving sister,*
> *Heather*

Tears fell upon the ink, smearing her sister's words of comfort, and Rose took another sip of hot chocolate and cursed herself for the maudlin state she'd been in for months now.

It was no wonder that her sister was concerned. She had poured out her heart to Heather in her last letter and had probably alarmed the woman half to death. Heather was the worrier of the family.

Self-pity had never been Rose Elizabeth's style. She had always prided herself on being strong, self-reliant, resistant to despair. But damn, it was hard getting over a broken heart.

Laurel's letter lay unopened, and Rose pondered whether to open it. She didn't need any more advice or platitudes, well meaning or not. Between Sven, Euphemia, Seamus, and now her sisters, she'd had more than enough.

Dear, dear Rose,

Snap out of this horrible mood you are in and get on with your life. You are making me feel horribly guilty for finding happiness with Chance, and utterly miserable that you are not equally as happy as I am.

Find solace in the child that you love so much. He will be a great comfort to you in the months ahead. Remember what mama always said: "Life is what you make it." So make yours wonderful and fulfilling, as I have.

Love and hugs to Duke,
Laurel

Rose was not altogether convinced that Laurel's time spent with the Women's Christian Temperance Union had not been an utterly wasted effort. It certainly hadn't taught her sister humility. But then, Laurel had always been more concerned with her own desires and happiness than with others'. Her attempt at becoming an opera singer had proven that. If Laurel had only listened to herself sing, she would have known that she had no talent.

Crumpling the letter, Rose's tears began anew, and she hated herself for being petty and jealous of her sisters' happiness. Laurel and Heather deserved to be happy. Both had experienced their share of heartaches and lived to talk about it. Rose guessed she would, too.

"Twirl your lady round and round. Sweep her feet clear off the ground . . ."

Rose tapped her toe and clapped her hands in time to the lively music, wondering how Duke was faring in the special room that had been set aside for the children attending Skeeter and Marcella's wedding reception. The last time she'd peeked in on the little angel, he was fast asleep.

The honored couple grinned at her from their position on the dance floor, and Skeeter waved, then twirled his ladylove around. Marcella's face glowed with happiness, and it made Rose Elizabeth's heart swell with joy for the newly married couple, who almost hadn't made it to the altar.

Skeeter had confessed right before the ceremony that he'd gotten cold feet and wanted to back out. And even Euphemia's stinging rejoinders hadn't persuaded him to go through with it. It wasn't until Rose Elizabeth took him aside and spoke gently from her heart about the dismal prospect of spending her life alone that Skeeter had decided to go through with the ceremony.

"You'll never find another woman as gentle and giving as Marcella, Skeeter," she'd told him. "If you walk away from her now, you will lose all the sparkle and joy from your life. Don't be afraid to commit your heart and soul. Being with someone you love is worth more than a million days of footloose freedom."

Looking at them now, smiling and laughing like children, Rose knew she'd been right to lay bare her most private feelings to the confirmed bachelor. Skeeter had given her a kiss on the cheek, along with his wishes for her own lifelong happiness, then had gone to the altar with only a hint of a hesitant smile.

"You're looking awfully pleased with yourself, lass," Seamus said as he approached with Rebecca on his arm. "Are you taking all the credit for this wedding, then?" Rose blushed, and he laughed. "Aye. I can see that you are."

"Why don't you go dance with your wife instead of bothering me, Seamus O'Flynn," she suggested. "Rebecca has to put up with your sassy ways, but I don't."

His grin was infectious, and it made Rose smile. "Rebecca won't dance with me. She says she's too tired because of the wee one."

Rebecca patted her softly rounded tummy. "I don't have the energy that I used to, Rose Elizabeth," she confessed, seating herself on the bench next to her friend. "It's as if this baby saps all my strength."

"No doubt he'll grow up to be bossy like his father," Rose quipped, making Rebecca smile.

"No doubt." She winked at Seamus.

"It ain't fair for you ladies to be ganging up on a poor defenseless gent who's outnumbered. I think I'll fetch you both some punch. It might sweeten up your dispositions."

Once he was out of earshot, Rose said, "Seamus is going to make a wonderful father, Rebecca. You're very lucky to have found such a fine man."

A wistful smile crossed the pregnant woman's face. "I pray to God every night and thank him for my good fortune, and for this child I carry. I never thought to be so truly blessed. I only wish Papa could have been here to share in my joy."

Rose nodded in understanding, then turned as Seamus approached with the two promised glasses of punch. "Here you go, ladies." He handed each woman a glass. "Now, Rose Elizabeth, I'll be expecting you to dance with me to make up for your many insults." He held out his hand expectantly, and there was a challenging grin on his face.

"You'll be sorry, Seamus O'Flynn, for I'm a terrible dancer."

He hauled her to her feet. "I'm so proficient at it, lass, that no one will pay you the least bit of mind. Just follow me lead."

Forming two parallel lines for the reel, Rose Elizabeth faced her partner, smiled, and curtsied. But as they started to move in and out of the row of dancers and twirl about, she began to feel lightheaded and strange. The lights above seemed overly bright and looked as if they were swaying in time to the music, and she felt the floor beneath her feet begin to give way. Then suddenly everything went black.

"I just knew she wasn't eating enough," Euphemia declared, wringing her hands and shaking her head, as she and the O'Flynns waited nervously in the waiting room of Doc Spooner's office.

Seamus paced back and forth, while Rebecca was content to sit and chew her nails. "She seemed fine while we were talking," the pregnant woman said. "I don't know what happened."

"It's my fault. I shouldn't have insisted that she dance."

"It's nobody's fault but Rose Elizabeth's, Seamus. No doubt she's been eating poorly. And she tries to do the work of six men on that farm of hers. And with the baby to care for . . . I just think it all became too much for her. I'm sure she'll be just fine in a day or two. She needs rest and plenty of it. I think I shall insist that she come stay with me for a while, until she regains her strength."

Seamus and Rebecca exchanged worried looks, knowing exactly how Rose Elizabeth would feel about that prospect.

"I think we should wait until we hear what the doctor has to say," Rebecca suggested, looking expectantly at her husband, who nodded vigorously in agreement.

Doc Spooner stared down at the young woman seated on the edge of the examination table and frowned. There was just no telling how Rose Elizabeth might react to the news he was about to impart.

"What is it, Doc? Why are you staring at me so strangely? I'm not dying of some rare disease, am I? 'Cause if I am, I want you to be square with me and tell me. Don't keep any secrets from me. I have Duke to think about." She waited anxiously, rubbing her sweaty palms on the skirt of her dress.

Rose had never fainted before in her life, and that gave her cause to worry that something was terribly wrong. Though she had been under a great deal of strain lately, it was no more than she could manage. Her mama had always said that the good Lord never gave a body more than they could handle. She sure hoped her mama was right this time.

Doc took a deep breath and removed the stethoscope from

around his neck. "Your fainting wasn't caused by any rare disease, Rose Elizabeth. It was caused by something a whole lot more common."

"I knew it." She shook her head in disgust. "I should never have worn this damn bustle. It squeezes my insides until I can't breathe right."

He swallowed his smile. "You'll be happy to know that the wearing of bustles is definitely out of the question for the next few months, as is plowing fields, lifting sacks of grain, and all the other unsuitable chores you have set for yourself."

She stared at the old man as if he'd lost this mind. "What are you talking about, Doc? I've got to do all those things. That's what wheat farming takes. If I don't do them, who will?"

His gruff voice gentled as he said, "Rose Elizabeth, a woman in your condition must be more circumspect in her behavior. I can't guarantee what will happen if you're not."

"My . . . my condition?" A suspicion began to grow in the pit of her stomach.

"You're pregnant, Rose Elizabeth. You're going to have a baby in about six months' time, give or take a week or two."

Her mouth fell open, her eyes widening in disbelief. "Pregnant! But that's impossible. That can't be."

Doc Spooner's eyebrows lifted nearly to his hairline, like they'd done when she was a small child and had told a whopper of a lie.

"To the best of my knowledge, Rose Elizabeth, there's been only one immaculate conception, and I don't believe you're it."

CHAPTER 24

"That bastard told me he was sterile!"

Rose Elizabeth's eyes flashed fire as she made the announcement to the group waiting anxiously in Doc Spooner's outer office.

Seamus and Rebecca shared a horrified look, while Euphemia turned various shades of red, her eyes bulging slightly. Then she put her hand to her throat and said, "Whatever do you mean, Rose Elizabeth?"

"I mean . . ." Rose stared at the trio of shocked faces and decided then and there to take them into her confidence. The truth would be known sooner than not anyway, she concluded. Something as scandalous as this would surely become the topic of discussion at every barbecue and church social in Salina.

"I'm pregnant!"

Euphemia gasped, then dropped down on Doc Spooner's well-worn leather sofa, which was as creased by the years as his face was.

Rebecca covered her mouth to hold back the curse she knew would not be proper or Plain.

Not so Seamus, who let loose a string of expletives that had the women blushing in mortification, including Rose Elizabeth, who was not usually prone to embarrassment.

"That goddamn liar!" he shouted, the veins in his neck bulging. "If I could get my hands around his noble throat, I'd—"

"Seamus, that is enough!" Rebecca cautioned. "Your anger will not help Rose Elizabeth. And she is going to need our help."

Realizing the truth of her words, and looking quite sheepish, Seamus quieted.

Rose sat beside the spinster on the sofa. "I've taken you into my confidence, Euphemia, and I hope you will not reveal the news of my condition to anyone."

Hurt and surprise washed over the woman's face. "I may have a big mouth, my dear, but I know when to keep it shut. Word of your condition will not come from me. On that you have my word."

She shook her head. "I was afraid something like this was going to happen. You being such an innocent about the ways of men, Rose Elizabeth. And that duke . . ." She pursed her lips. "How dare that wretched man take advantage of your navieté. He's nothing more than a rake and bounder . . ."

"Euphemia." Rose's softly spoken voice stopped the spinster in midsentence.

Euphemia clasped Rose's hand in her own. "What on earth are you going to do? How will you manage with a baby to care for and another on the way?" She *tsk*ed several times. "This is terrible. Just terrible."

"Sven and I can divide up the chores on the farm, so you needn't worry about that, lass."

Rebecca squeezed her husband's hand. "And I will prepare bread every week, so you won't have to toil in that hot kitchen."

"And I," Euphemia offered with a pleased-as-punch expression, "can assist you with the baby. I'm not very experienced, but I'm sure I can learn. And I—"

"Whoa, everybody!" Rose Elizabeth held up her hands to

stop the onslaught of good intentions. "I'm pregnant, not sick with some dread disease.

"Though I'm touched by your concerns, I'm perfectly capable of handling most of the chores at the farm, although I'll welcome your help from time to time, Seamus. And may I remind you, Rebecca O'Flynn, that you too are carrying a child and so will not be baking bread for me. And dear, dear Euphemia, I appreciate your kind offer of help, and will welcome it on occasion, but you know that I like doin' for myself. Duke and I will be just fine."

"But, Rose Elizabeth," Euphemia cautioned, "it's obvious from your fainting spell that you've been overdoing. You're going to need help. Tell her, Doc."

Doc Spooner, who'd been leaning against the wall with his arms folded across his chest as he listened to the entire exchange, nodded sagely. "I'm afraid Euphemia's right, Rose Elizabeth. You're going to need help. At least until your body adjusts to the changes taking place. There's no shame in asking for it. That's what neighbors and friends are for."

For most people, Rose wanted to say. But she had never been comfortable asking for help, had always been too prideful and stubborn to admit when she needed it. To her, asking for help was admitting weakness. She'd spent most of her life trying to prove that she was just the opposite, and it didn't set well that she was expected to change her ways now. Baby or no baby.

"I appreciate your concerns, but this baby," she patted her stomach, suddenly charmed by the idea of bringing a new life into the world, "and I will be fine. If I need assistance, you'll be the first to know."

Seamus cast her a skeptical look. "I don't believe you for a minute, Rose Elizabeth, and I'm going to telegraph the duke and let him know of the predicament he's placed you in."

Rose paled momentarily, then her nostrils flared wide with anger, and her voice grew strong with conviction. "No, you will not, Seamus O'Flynn. Because if you do, I'll never speak to you again. This child I carry has nothing to do with the

Duke of Moreland. It's mine. And I will raise it as a Martin, not a Warrick."

"But, lass . . ."

"But, my dear . . ."

"Rose Elizabeth, please . . ."

She shook her head. "The Almighty has seen fit to bless me with two precious children, who I will raise to the best of my ability and love with every fiber of my being.

"If you are truly my friends, you will heed my wishes."

There were many times over the next few weeks when Rose Elizabeth wished her friends had not heeded her wishes quite so stringently.

Like the time Boomer ran through the yard chasing a jackrabbit, knocking over the wash barrel and causing dozens of Duke's clean diapers to be scattered by the wind. Or when the loaves of bread she'd spent most of the morning preparing had burned to a crisp when the baby's cries for attention had made her lose track of the time.

But solitude had its rewards, too. Especially in the evenings when she and Duke were alone in front of the fire, and she would sing him softly to sleep, or they would play a rousing game of peek-a-boo. He would laugh joyfully at her antics as she covered her head with his blanket, then popped out of it unexpectedly to his squeals of delight.

Love filled her heart as she stared at the child playing contentedly in the pen, which she had moved outside this morning so that he could enjoy the warmth of the sun while she tended the wash and kept an eye on him at the same time.

Her lower back ached as she bent over the washboard and scrubbed diligently at Duke's diapers. Her mind wandered back to the times she had washed Alexander's shirts in the same manner, and a feeling of sadness crept over her.

"What's done is done, Boomer," she told the dog, who lay at her feet, lapping at the soap suds overflowing the barrel.

Boomer responded with a bark, and Rose Elizabeth wondered if he was actually starting to understand what she was saying, until she glanced up and saw Sven's wagon coming down the drive.

Sven and Hannah were frequent visitors, but others from town had not been so generous. She'd been sneered at, shunned, branded a fallen woman by people she'd known all her life—good Christian folk. But she could put up with their gossip and snide remarks, for she still had close friends who cared about her—friends who didn't judge too harshly.

"I should have figured you weren't that smart, Boomer," she finally chided the dog. "Animals aren't supposed to eat soap suds, you know."

"Hello, Rose Elizabet." Sven helped his wife, Hannah, to alight from the wagon. "We have come to visit."

Rose dropped the half-washed diapers back into the barrel to soak, drying her hands on her apron. "I welcome the interruption. Washing dirty diapers is not my idea of a pleasant way to spend the day."

Hannah, a fine-boned woman with light brown hair, sparkling green eyes, and a sunny disposition, stepped toward Rose, holding a bundle of clothes. "I've brought some things that the children have outgrown, Rose Elizabeth. I hope you can use them."

A glance at the pile of well-worn but clean clothing brought an appreciative smile to Rose's lips. Conserving money had become an absolute necessity. And though Alexander had left funds at the bank on which she could draw, her pride would not allow her to touch a cent of it. Instead, she had opened up a savings account for the two children, which they would share when they were older.

Rose was determined to succeed on her own, but she still welcomed small gestures of kindness such as Hannah's.

"How very thoughtful of you. I'm sure Duke will grow into these in no time." She held up a child's-size pair of breeches.

"If he grows as quickly as my Peter and Wilhem, it will not be long before you need to buy more," Sven said, then added, "I vill tend to the stock while you ladies have some refreshment. It vill not take me long."

"Elvira is in the family way again, Sven. I'd appreciate it if you'd have a look at her. She was feeling a mite poorly this morning."

"*Ja,* I vill do that. And you vill go inside and rest, *ja*?" His look was searching, making Rose's cheeks blossom with guilt. She hadn't taken Sven into her confidence yet, unable to face his disappointment with her.

"Is he always that bossy?" Rose asked as she led Hannah into the kitchen, having checked to make sure Duke was still content in his pen, playing with the silver rattle Euphemia had recently purchased for him.

The spinster was turning into a regular fairy godmother! *If only she could conjure up a wish or two for me,* Rose Elizabeth thought.

"Sven is overprotective, but I find I like it. After being without a man for so long, it's a comfort."

"I'm happy Sven has you, Hannah. He needed a good woman to make his life complete. And the boys are very fond of you."

The woman smiled thoughtfully. "I know Sven was in love with you, Rose Elizabeth. He told me as much. But I think he truly loves me now."

"That's as obvious as the glow that washes over his face every time he looks at you, Hannah Anderson." The petite woman blushed, and Rose, hoping to remove the niggling doubt she saw flickering in her eyes, added, "Sven and I have always been dear, dear friends, and I hope that will never change. But I don't believe he loved me in a romantic way, despite the fact that he might have thought so at one time.

"Our relationship was too comfortable to let loose of, like a good sturdy pair of shoes that don't fit anymore, but you hate to part with them because they're so darn comfy. Do you understand?"

Hannah laughed, then nodded. "Sven would be insulted to know you compared him to a pair of shoes, but I thank you for the explanation. I admit, I still had fears."

"We all have fears. But it's how we face them that makes

the difference." Rose was still trying to decide how she would face hers.

Her mama had always said, "Face fear head-on, and it will disappear." But Rose had so many fears—the responsibility of the babies, the working of the land, the loneliness that lay ahead—that she was afraid if she faced them squarely, she'd become so overwhelmed that she would be plowed under like dirt beneath a tractor, buried under her own mountain of insecurities.

It was easier, she found, to chip away at them a little bit at a time. Easier, but not the least bit comforting.

Rose Elizabeth had just bidden Peggy and her pimply-faced husband goodbye at the train station, and suddenly she felt bereft by the woman's departure. A strange reaction, considering all the arguments and invectives they had exchanged over the years. Still, they had grown up together, shared childhood secrets and plans, and those memories of happier times blotted out the more recent, injurious ones.

"You take care of that baby now, you hear, Rose Elizabeth? And once you spruce yourself up a bit, you might actually find yourself a husband." With a laugh and a brief, awkward hug, Peggy had had the last word before pushing her husband onto the train and waving a triumphant goodbye.

The funny thing was, Rose Elizabeth had pretty much convinced herself that spinsterhood was now her destiny, so she hadn't taken offense at the remark. Besides, if Peggy had said anything kind, it would have been out of character.

Skeeter rocked forward in his chair. "Don't know who you'll be scrapping with now, Rose Elizabeth. Now that that sharp-toothed hussy has up and left town."

"Well, it's good riddance, I say." Euphemia bounced Duke gently in her arms. "This town is much better off without the likes of her. Isn't that right, my precious?" she asked the baby, who responded with a giggle and a swat of his hand to the side of her head.

"Duke!" Rose Elizabeth admonished in a stern voice,

bringing tears to the child's eyes. "You mustn't swat Aunt Euphemia like that. You might break her new spectacles."

Not the least bit upset by the child's antics, Euphemia beamed at her new status in life. She had proclaimed aunthood upon herself, and no one, especially Rose Elizabeth, had had the heart or the temerity to dispute the claim.

"He's perfectly fine, Rose Elizabeth. I don't mind at all."

"You spoil him outrageously, Euphemia." As did Skeeter and Marcella when they came to visit, and Rebecca and Seamus, who always had a special baked treat for "little Duke," as they called him. "Everyone indulges his every whim, then I'm left to discipline him after the damage has been done."

Skeeter laughed. "One thing's for sure, Rose Elizabeth, you'll never be without godparents and caretakers as long as you live in this town." He slapped his knee, then spit a large wad of tobacco into the brass spittoon near his feet.

Euphemia looked aghast. "Really, Mr. Purty! You are nothing if not disgusting." She attempted to shield Duke's eyes. "I don't want this child picking up your dirty habits."

Rose bit back a smile. Euphemia and Skeeter's bickering had grown even more pronounced over the last few weeks, due to the practical joke Skeeter had played on the older woman.

Arriving home late one Sunday afternoon after visiting Rose Elizabeth, Euphemia had found her unmentionables strung up for public display across her front yard. Her red satin corset—an impulsive, secret gift to herself, which she had recently ordered from the Montgomery Ward Catalogue—had been wrapped around the trunk of a stately elm tree, like the arms of a lover embracing her mate.

Euphemia had been so humiliated and outraged, she'd not shown her face in public for two weeks. When she finally discovered who the perpetrator of the awful trick was, she had marched down to the railway station and unceremoniously dumped the entire contents of Skeeter's spittoon on top of his head.

"Now, Euphemia. I already done said I was sorry about the corset. And Marcie did bake you that delicious apple pie."

"Your wife's kindheartedness is the only reason I even speak to you, Skeeter Purty."

The three-fifteen roared into the station, belching black smoke. Glad to have been reprieved, if only temporarily, Skeeter jumped to his feet, shouting out to anyone and everyone the news of the train's arrival.

Rose Elizabeth, realizing the lateness of the hour, took the baby from Euphemia's reluctant arms. "We've got to go home now. I'm not taking any chances on getting stuck in the middle of nowhere again."

"That's a wise decision," the older woman agreed.

Turning about, Rose was just about to step off the platform when out of the corner of her eye she caught a glimpse of an elegantly dressed woman stepping down off the far end of the train.

She wore a large, wide-brimmed hat that obscured her face, and was accompanied by two small children, a boy and a girl, and a distinguished, very handsome dark-haired gentleman, who did not look at all impressed by his surroundings. The woman's attire bespoke money and refinement, as did her companions', and Rose couldn't help but stare at the attractive family.

When she finally turned to face her fully, Rose Elizabeth's eyes widened in recognition, and she nearly dropped the squirming child in her arms.

"Rose Elizabeth! Rose Elizabeth!" the smiling woman shouted, waving frantically at her.

"My God!" Rose whispered, blinking twice to be sure her eyes hadn't deceived her. Her big sister, Heather, had come home.

CHAPTER 25

The farm kitchen buzzed with activity. Heather Montgomery set the table for supper, while her husband, Brandon, seated comfortably in the rocker by the hearth, did his best to amuse Duke with a reading of the *Salina Sentinel*'s most recent editorial on the need for a town garbage-collection service.

The twins, Jenny and Matt, were plopped on the floor at their father's feet, drawing pictures with the paper and pencils that Aunt Rose had provided.

"I wish I could have taken a photograph of you today, Rose Elizabeth," Heather said, folding a blue napkin and placing it by a plate of the same color. "Your mouth dropped open so wide when you first saw me, I thought your chin was going to hit the railway platform."

Rose smiled at the memory of rushing into her sister's outstretched arms and nearly knocking her over in her excitement. She still couldn't believe Heather had come all the way from San Francisco to visit her. Even now she had to pinch herself to make sure it was real.

"You might have let a body know you were comin'. I'd

have fixed something special for supper. Now you'll have to be content with squirrel stew."

"Is that going to be anytime soon?" Brandon inquired as he looked up from the paper, casting a wary eye at the pot boiling furiously on the stove. "I'm quite famished. The food on the train was atrocious. You did say—squirrel stew? Is that edible?" He shot a questioning, somewhat horrified glance at his wife, who laughed at his squeamishness.

"As our cook, Mr. Woo, would say: Squirrel stew make dang good grub." She winked reassuringly at Brandon.

Rose Elizabeth's eyes widened. "You have a cook? My goodness! That's not something to shake a stick at. I suppose you have a maid, too?" Apparently, Brandon Montgomery was wealthier than Rose had realized.

Her sister shrugged, as if material possessions were of little importance. "We did. But Mary-Margaret got married. And now that Peter has been promoted to city editor, she wants to stay home with Jack—that's her son—and concentrate on having more children." A wistful sigh escaped Heather's lips before she continued.

"Harriet, Brandon's mother, still lives with us. She was recently married to a wonderful man, a widower by the name of Frank Burnside, who's vice president of Brandon's newspaper. Anyway, our home is so large that it was stupid for them to live anywhere else, so I insisted that they stay with us. Harriet's a big help with the children."

"Grandmother bosses Grandfather Frank around sometimes," Matt told his aunt, and his earnest expression made Rose smile. For a child of seven, Matt seemed very mature and serious, like his father.

"But he doesn't seem to mind much," the child continued. "Grandfather Frank says that's what women do."

"She isn't bossing him, Matty," Jenny corrected, looking quite put out by her brother's misinterpretation. "Grandmother is merely showing Grandfather the error of his ways, like Mother shows Father sometimes. Isn't that right, Mother?"

All heads turned to Heather, who nodded weakly, her cheeks filling with color. Rose Elizabeth burst out laughing.

Brandon shot his wife an indignant, exasperated look. "I hope this isn't what you've been teaching the children, Heather. A man deserves a certain amount of respect from his own family members."

At that moment Duke decided to make his feelings known on the subject by throwing up all over Uncle Brandon's brand-new navy pinstriped suit.

Horrified, for he had a weak stomach, Brandon stared at the mess on his lap, held the now-screaming child at arm's length, and remarked, "So much for respect."

Later, after the children were abed, Rose, Heather, and Brandon enjoyed coffee and doughnuts at the kitchen table. Outside the large bay window, crickets chirped their nocturnal greetings, and the persistent wind moaned, rustling the tall stalks of ripened wheat in the fields.

"You really should get Rose Elizabeth to give you the recipe for these doughnuts, Heather." Brandon bit into a large jelly-filled one and licked his lips. "They're delicious."

"I didn't bake them," Rose confessed. "They're from Heller's Bakery. Rebecca and Seamus brought them yesterday when they came to visit. But I'll be sure to tell Seamus you liked them. They're one of the few things he's learned to bake that are actually edible."

"Isn't that the man who used to work for the duke?"

Rose nodded at her sister. "The very same."

Dabbing at the sugar on his face with his napkin, Brandon's expression suddenly chilled. "I'd like to get my hands on this Duke of Moreland. I can't imagine any self-respecting man leaving a defenseless woman alone with a small child who's not even her own flesh and blood."

Rose swallowed, wondering how her brother-in-law and sister were going to react to the other, more pressing news she had yet to tell them. Tolerance did not appear to be Brandon's strong suit. His next words confirmed her opinion.

"The man should be strung up, drawn and quartered. For a nobleman, Moreland has very little that's noble about him."

"Well, I'd like to pin his aristrocratic backside to the wall, I can tell you that." Heather's violet eyes flashed fire. "Just look at you, Rose Elizabeth. You're exhausted. And your face looks puffy. I was really hoping that—"

"I am putting on weight, but it's not from overeating." Rose took a deep breath, deciding that now was as good a time as any to break the news. "I'm going to have a baby." She held her breath, waiting for the outburst. She didn't have long to wait.

"A baby!" Heather paled. "You're pregnant?"

Brandon's fist hit the table with such force that Rose nearly jumped out of her chair. "That damned scurrilous bastard!" The veins in his neck and temples pounded ominously.

"I didn't want to tell you in a letter. I didn't have the words to explain how it all came about."

"I think we can figure that out," Brandon said snidely, and Heather tossed him a fulminating look before kneeling down by her sister's chair.

"You poor thing." She gathered Rose to her breast. "And here you've been shouldering this pain all by yourself. No wonder your letters sounded so despondent."

Rose toyed with the folds of her skirt. "Not exactly. I shared my problem with a few people. Euphemia Bloodsworth knows, as do Rebecca, Seamus, and Doc Spooner."

"Euphemia Bloodsworth!" Heather looked aghast. "Then the whole town must be aware of your condition."

"Who is this Euphemia person?" Brandon wanted to know.

"Only the biggest gossip in town."

"She's not quite as you remember, Heather. Euphemia's turned out to be a good friend to both me and Duke. She's helped us out on several occasions when others were not as generous." Rose had grown quite fond of the older woman.

"Are we talking about the same Euphemia Bloodsworth— Old Beaknose? The one with vinegar running through her veins? The one who pursued poor Papa until he was afraid to go into town for fear of being dragged to the altar by that persistent spinster?"

"I admit, the change in her took me by surprise at first. But perhaps we misjudged her. She's really grown quite motherly."

Heather didn't look at all convinced, and it took her a moment to digest all the new, startling information. "Unfortunately, Euphemia Bloodsworth is not our biggest problem at the moment, Rose Elizabeth. You are. The fact that you're pregnant and unmarried is going to become fodder for the gossip mill, and folks will not be forgiving of that. You'll be considered a fallen woman, no better than a prostitute."

"I thought you came here to cheer me up. So far, you're doing a lousy job."

"Rose Elizabeth is right, Heather. There's no use dwelling on what cannot be changed. We need to set our thoughts to what can."

Heather slumped dejectedly in her chair. "You're a big help, Brandon. Rose Elizabeth is in the family way, with no family, and I don't see how we're going to fix that."

"We've remedied far more difficult things in the past." The painful reminder made her cheeks color.

Rose knew that Brandon referred to the incident that had occurred after their marriage, when Heather had become involved in illustrating for Brandon's newspaper behind his back. He had almost lost his wife and children to his ex-fiancée's vengeful machinations, and Heather had almost lost her life and husband to divorce.

"I don't mean to be rude," Rose interjected, "but I don't particularly want a remedy. I'm content to raise this child on my own. And I don't give a tinker's damn about what other folks say."

"Watch your language, Rose Elizabeth," Heather admonished.

Brandon stopped pacing and ground to a halt. "That is out of the question. Heather is correct in saying that you'll be branded a whore. The only solution to your present predicament is to find a husband, and quickly."

Rose Elizabeth and her sister exchanged surprised looks, then Rose said, "Maybe you didn't hear me the first time, Brandon: The father of this child is gone for good. There will be no husband."

His look was intractable. "Young woman, no sister-in-law of mine is going to be treated with contempt and disdain. If I have to take out a full-page advertisement in every newspaper in this country, we will find a suitable husband for you, and a father for your unborn child."

Rose stared aghast at him, then did something that shocked not only Heather but Rose Elizabeth herself: She burst into tears.

"Now look what you've done, Brandon! Do you always have to be so overbearing?"

"Overbearing! I was merely trying to help. Your sister is obviously not thinking clearly." That statement brought another round of sobs, and Brandon stared helplessly at his sister-in-law, wondering what he'd said to provoke such a reaction.

Heather's look of pure disgust had Brandon clearing his throat nervously. "I'll go up and check on the children." He paused by the door. "I'll wait up for you, Heather."

The promise in her husband's voice made Heather's pulse quicken. They'd had little opportunity on the train to share intimacies, and she was looking forward to making love with Brandon and continuing her efforts to get pregnant.

Sadly, their efforts thus far had produced no results, but Brandon continued to point out how much fun they were having in the attempt, and vowed to persevere for however long it took. Heather smiled, remembering his erotic grin when he'd said that.

"I'm sorry to have behaved so badly, Heather. I hope Brandon isn't too upset with me."

"He'll get over it. He's always upset with me and the children about one thing or another, but I've grown used to his quicksilver moods. Besides, making up is the best part of arguing."

Rose squeezed her sister's hand. "You love him very much, don't you?"

"Yes. Brandon and the children are my whole life. The only thing that would make it more complete would be if I had a child of my own." She'd thought once that she wanted a career, but now she realized that there were far more important things in life.

Rose's hand went unconsciously to her abdomen, and she rubbed the swelling mound softly. "It's wonderful to be with child." She sighed. "But it would be even more wonderful if there was a husband to go along with it."

"Is there no chance for you and the duke? Perhaps if you wrote him, explained your condition . . ."

Rose shook her head. "Alexander and I come from different worlds. We had a passionate interlude, which was more wonderful than words can express, but now it's over and done with, and I have to get on with my life. I have two children to consider."

"Children who are his responsibility." Heather didn't bother to hide her contempt.

"He left money for Duke's upbringing, but I've not touched a cent of it. I won't be beholden to any man, especially one who deceived me."

Her sister's forehead wrinkled in confusion. "Deceived you? How so?"

Rose explained about the duke's supposed sterility, and Heather gasped. "The cad! The man really is a bounder."

"Just my luck to have fallen in love with him, huh?"

"Never you mind, Rose Elizabeth. You have your family here now, and you needn't spend another moment thinking about Alexander Warrick. You have a baby to consider, and that must take first priority."

Aloud, Rose agreed, but deep in her heart, she knew that what Heather suggested would be impossible. Not a day went by that she didn't think about the man she loved, that she didn't worry about raising two children by herself, and she felt terrified and terribly alone, despite her brave facade.

* * *

"I'm so worried about Rose Elizabeth," Heather confided to her husband, snuggling closer to him in the large guest bed, her fingers toying with the thick mat of hair on his chest. "What if she's unable to handle things here on her own?"

"I thought you were of the opinion that women could handle anything, love. Have you changed your mind?" He nuzzled her ear, and gooseflesh rose over her arms and neck.

"No. Of course not!" Heather's heartbeat had suddenly grown irregular, as had her breathing. "It's just that . . . that Rose is all alone now, and I feel guilty that I can't do more to help her."

"Your sister is a grown woman and seems content with her lot. But if she needs help, you know she need only ask. I'd be happy to give her money or hire someone to assist her with the farm." His hand crept up her thigh, resting perilously close to her heat, and Heather flooded with wanting.

"I'm trying to talk seriously, Brandon. You're making that very hard."

"You're making me very hard, love." His tongue traced circles around her ear. "I want to make love to you."

Heather wanted that too, more than anything, but she felt uncomfortable even contemplating such a thing in her sister's house. She guessed she'd been the mother figure too long to abandon that role altogether.

"The children might wake up."

"That's doubtful, since they're sleeping down the hall. It was most considerate of Rose Elizabeth to appreciate our pressing situation and suggest the spare bedroom for them."

Heather laid a caressing palm against her husband's stubbled cheek and smiled softly. "Perhaps it was the hunger she saw in your eyes, or the fact that you haven't been able to keep your hands to yourself since we arrived. And still can't."

"Are you complaining, love?" The hands in question crept up to cup her breasts, caress her turgid nipples, and Brandon moaned like a man in pain. "These past few days of not making love to you have been torture. I've missed touching you, kissing you. . . ."

Heather released a deep sigh of surrender. "Then stop talking and kiss me."

Brandon didn't need a second invitation.

The ruby stickpin the gambler wore flashed brightly in the summer sunshine, and Chance Rafferty didn't bother to hide his disdain as he stepped off the train in Salina and looked around.

"They don't even have a saloon here, angel. What kind of place did you bring me to anyway?" He shook his head.

Laurel Martin Rafferty rubbed at the small of her aching back and sighed wearily. "I'm the one who's pregnant, Chance. If anyone should be complaining, it should be me."

"I told you it wasn't wise to make this trip in your condition."

The familiar argument stressed Laurel's already frayed nerves. "Please, Chance. I don't have the energy right now to debate this with you."

"Now, angel, don't get your corset all in an uproar. It isn't good to get upset in your condition. I told you I'd bring you to see your sister, and I have. I'm a man of my word."

"Only because Bertha and Jup bullied you into it, and you know it. You had no intention of bringing me to Salina. Even though my sister needs me. I could sense Rose Elizabeth's despair in her last letter and just knew I had to come."

He wrapped a possessive arm about her expanded waistline. "Doesn't sound like this Duke of Moreland is nearly as chivalrous as I am. At least I came to my senses in time and married you."

She caressed his cheek, smiling at the memory of his gallant efforts to woo her. "My Prince Charming."

"Not every man would chase the woman he loved across the plains. That horse ride nearly broke my butt, I can tell you that."

"Yes, my love. So you've said many times. Now, why don't you fetch the baggage so we can be on our way."

"For someone who's only been married a few months, angel, you're getting downright bossy." He chucked her chin. "I guess I'm just going to have to take you in hand and teach you who's really in charge."

Laurel leaned in to him and smiled seductively. "Perhaps you can show me tonight. There's nothing more romantic than making love in a barn on top of a mound of soft hay."

"A barn?" His eyebrow shot up. "Jesus, Mary, and Joseph! Doesn't your sister own a bed, like normal folks? I haven't done it in a barn since I was fifteen. That sounds damned uncomfortable."

"Crystal and Flora Sue assured me it's not. They said varying our lovemaking would keep the spark in our marriage."

"Jesus, Mary, and Joseph! Why would you be taking advice from a couple of former prostitutes? If you want sparks, angel"—his hand moved up to touch her breast—"I'll give you a raging inferno." Her cheeks flushed bright red, and he grinned rakishly. "Now, let's get ourselves to the Martin homestead. The more I think about the barn, the more I think I'd like to try it out."

"You're here! You're really here!" Rose Elizabeth wept into her hands, then crushed her sister to her breast, wrapping her arms about Laurel and squeezing as hard as her condition allowed. "I can scarcely believe my eyes."

"My heavens, Laurie!" Heather chimed in. "You're as big as a house." A stab of envy filled her at the sight of her other, very pregnant sister, while her heart seemed about to burst with joy. "I can hardly believe my eyes. Come and give me a hug."

Laurel grinned. "I'm going to have twins, that's why I look so fat." She rushed into Heather's outstretched arms, kissing her cheek.

Brandon and Chance sized each other up, found they had

much in common—both being married to a Martin sister—
and shook hands in greeting.

"I think the men of this family better stick together," Brandon remarked, and Chance laughed.

"From what I see here, I'd place a wager on that."

Rose Elizabeth made the rest of the introductions.

Laurel oohed and aahed over the children, kissing their
cheeks, then plopped down in the kitchen rocker, holding her
swollen feet aloft in front of her. "I'm wore out. The train ride
was awful."

"You slept most of the way," Chance reminded her.

"It was still awful." She smiled at Rose Elizabeth. "Don't
worry about putting us up, Rose. Chance and I can rent a
room at the hotel. We had no idea you had so many guests
staying here. But your new house is lovely, and so much
larger than the soddy."

"Don't be silly. You're not guests, you're family. Duke and
I will move out to the soddy. The weather's warm, and it
won't be a problem. You and Chance can have my room."

Chance shot his wife an erotic look. "We can sleep in the
barn. Laurel has a mind to—"

"Your room will be just fine, Rose Elizabeth," Laurel interjected quickly, before her husband could embarrass her further. "But we don't want to put you out."

"I'd sleep outside on the ground for a chance to have my
family home with me again. I've missed you and Heather so
much. . . ." Tears sprang to her eyes again, then Laurel and
Heather followed suit.

"Jesus, Mary, and Joseph! I hope the roof doesn't leak. It
looks like we're going to have another flood."

The children giggled, the sisters sobbed in renewed joy,
and Brandon shook his head.

"Women!"

Chance nodded. "Amen to that!"

CHAPTER 26

Alexander Warrick, the Duke of Moreland, was afraid. It was silly, he knew, to be afraid of the unknown, but he was bloody terrified.

New York was just a distant memory now, as was Sussex. And as the train chugged along, bringing him ever closer to his destination, the knot in his stomach tightened considerably, the pain in his chest growing more acute.

There were so many variables with the unknown. What if Rose Elizabeth despised him for leaving as he had? What if she'd found someone new to love? What if she didn't want him back?

His breath grew short, and as he moved his hands to his chest to still the rapid beating of his heart, he suddenly realized that his palms were sweating.

So much depended on Rose Elizabeth's reaction to his return—his sanity, his title, his very will to live.

He was nothing without her. His life had no meaning without her in it.

It hadn't taken him long to realize that upon his return to

England. After Jessica's burial, and after attending to his affairs and vast estates, there hadn't been much to occupy his time or his thoughts.

Except for Rose Elizabeth.

Memories of making love to her had almost overwhelmed him. And the image of her beautiful face, or the sound of her infectious laughter, swept over him at the most inconvenient times, like during church service, and he'd been unable to hide his body's yearning for her, which had proven most embarrassing on more than one occasion.

Not a day went by that he didn't wonder what she was doing. Had she brought the wheat harvest in yet? And had it been bountiful? He hated not being there for it. For her. The farm had become a part of him now. As had Rose Elizabeth.

England wouldn't miss him for a while, and he wouldn't miss England. He had trained his people well. They were competent, capable of handling all the affairs of his domain. And despite the constant haranguing from the dowager duchess, who couldn't understand why he moped about and "acted very queer," he knew she would miss him least of all.

Of course, he would have to return. His responsibility to his estates and title, and to the family name, could not be ignored, as he'd tried to do in the past. But neither could the strong pull of Rose Elizabeth's love be ignored, which was what had brought him back to Kansas.

Life without Rose Elizabeth, he'd discovered, was meaningless, and he had come back to persuade her to come to England with him, if only for a visit. He knew she would be loath to leave the farm, but he had to make her understand how much he needed her, loved her.

After all that had transpired between them, that would be no easy feat.

"You've made enough potato salad to feed an army. How many folks did you invite to this barbecue anyway?"

Rose Elizabeth grinned at Laurel, shrugged, then took another taste of the salad to check the seasonings, and added more salt and pepper. "Just a few close friends: Sven and Hannah, Rebecca and Seamus, Euphemia . . ."

"Euphemia! You haven't really invited that spinster to join us, have you? Heather told me you two had become friends, but I just couldn't believe it."

"She's not so bad. Just a bit opinionated."

"Opinionated!" Laurel's blue eyes widened. "That's putting it mildly. If Euphemia told me once, she told me a hundred times: 'Laurel, dear, don't forget to wear your bonnet and gloves. It isn't seemly for young ladies to be out and about without them.' "

Laurel's voice rose to a falsetto pitch as she did her best to mimic Euphemia, and Rose burst out laughing. "You did that rather well."

Heather entered the kitchen with Duke riding her hip. "What's so funny?"

"Rose invited Euphemia Bloodsworth to our barbecue today, but I hardly think it's reason for hilarity."

"Now, Laurie, Rose assures me that Old Beaknose has changed her ways. I guess we'll have to give her the benefit of the doubt." And Heather had some serious doubts about the spinster.

"As Hortensia Tungsten, the esteemed leader of the Denver Temperance and Souls in Need League, was fond of saying: 'The leopard does not readily change his spots.' Of course, she was referring to Chance at the time." Laurel smiled at the memory. Hortensia had her faults, there was no denying that, but she and the temperance league had been there for her when she'd needed them, and Laurel would always be grateful for that.

Not so Chance, who still despised the older woman, usually referring to the overweight matron as "old blubber guts."

"Oh, that reminds me, Laurie." Heather shifted Duke to a more comfortable position. "Chance wants you to meet him in the barn. He says there's something he wants to show you."

Knowing just what that "something" was, Laurel's cheeks

crimsoned, and Rose Elizabeth couldn't resist the opportunity to tease her. "Maybe it's his spots he wants to show you, Laurel. I don't think all of them have changed yet."

Heather and Rose exchanged amused grins, then laughed, and Laurel pushed herself out of the chair and waddled to the door. "I'll have both of you know that Chance has changed considerably. He no longer operates a gambling parlor, but a restaurant and theater club.

"Rooster Higgins, our manager, has already staged some wonderful productions. Just last month we performed Shakespeare's *The Taming of the Shrew*. Rooster's wife, Flora Sue, and I take turns starring in the lead roles."

Laurel didn't bother to add that Chance had remarked she'd been born for the role of Kate. Instead, she smiled proudly and said, "The Aurora Borealis has become Denver's most respectable gathering place."

"And they say a good woman can't change a man," Heather quipped, delighted that her sister had found such happiness. *One down and one to go,* Heather thought.

"You should know better than anyone the truth of that, big sister," Rose told Heather with a playful wink. "You took an impossibly autocratic mountain lion of a man and turned him into a tame pussy cat."

At the mention of the word *cat*, Boomer, who'd been asleep in front of the hearth, raised his head and let out a halfhearted bark.

Heather was grateful that Brandon wasn't within earshot to hear Rose's opinion, for she knew that a man's ego was a fragile thing.

She remarked to her younger sister, "You be careful walking out to the barn, Laurie. In your condition you could fall and hurt not only yourself but the babies."

Laurel didn't feel it proper to point out that she faced far more danger inside the barn than out. "Rose is pregnant, and I don't hear you warning her about such things."

"Rose Elizabeth isn't as far along as you are, Laurel. And she's not expecting twins." Heather's violet eyes widened in question as she looked at Rose, who shook her head emphatically.

"I certainly hope not! Two babies is quite enough, thank you very much."

Laurel patted her growing belly. "Chance is quite pleased at the prospect of my having twins. He struts around the Aurora like a cock-o'-the-walk, bragging about his virility and other manly things. Jup and Bertha, the older couple who work for us, say he's gotten too big for his britches and needs to be taken down a peg or two." She paused. "And they say women are conceited."

"It doesn't take a genius or perfect vision to see that Chance is crazy in love with you, Laurie. It shows every time he turns those intriguing green eyes on you."

"He'd better be. It took that gambling man long enough to realize that marriage to me wasn't going to be a death sentence."

Rose grew increasingly quiet as she listened to the exchange and busied herself with the cooking chores.

Laurel slipped out the door, and the eldest Martin sister heaved a dispirited sigh. If she ever got her hands on that stupid duke, she would . . . Heather wasn't quite certain just what she would do. But it would be something ghastly for the way he'd made Rose Elizabeth suffer. Something downright gruesome.

Alexander Warrick's character was a popular topic of conversation among the men at the Martin barbecue.

Brandon thought the man should be torn limb from limb. He'd said as much between sips of hard cider. Chance concurred with his brother-in-law's bloodthirsty opinion as he sucked on his cheroot, adding that a good tar-and-feathering would be just the ticket for the cowardly nobleman.

Even Skeeter, who normally didn't have a vindictive bone in his body, chimed in that the Duke of Moreland was a great disappointment to him and Marcella, and that the man should be horsewhipped for running out on such a caring woman as Rose Elizabeth.

Sven and Seamus were the only two who remained relatively quiet during this exchange. Sven because he still had no doubt that Alexander would one day return, and Seamus because loyalty to the duke, however misguided it might be, was still deeply ingrained in him.

"You mustn't be judging his lordship too harshly now, lads," Seamus cautioned. "I too wanted to bloody Alexander's face when I first heard about Rose Elizabeth, but I know in me heart that the duke had little choice but to leave. And had he known she was pregnant . . ."

Sven and Skeeter exchanged shocked looks, then Sven stepped forward. "Rose Elizabet is carrying the duke's child? I did not know."

"It's best to keep things like that quiet," Seamus said, noting the wounded look that crossed his face. "Women are touchy about such matters, Sven. I'm sure Rose was just too embarrassed to tell you."

"And it's not as if Rose Elizabeth wanted her condition broadcast to the world," Brandon reminded the Swede.

"Does Alexander know of her condition? Because if he did, I know that he vould not have left. He loves her."

Chance threw his cheroot down to the ground and stomped on it, wishing it were the duke's noble head. "Yeah? Well, if he loved her, how come he ran out on her? Answer that question."

Brandon thought that Chance sounded a bit hypocritical for a man who had recently considered marriage and respectability a one-way ticket to hell, but he refrained from saying so. His brother-in-law had promised to teach him how to beat Heather at strip poker, and he couldn't afford to alienate him at the moment.

"It's hard to say why a man makes the decisions he does." Brandon's eyes filled with memories better forgotten. "We've all made mistakes, decisions we've regretted. Perhaps the duke will come to his senses one day."

Skeeter spit a wad of chewing tobacco at the ground, narrowly missing the toe of Chance's snakeskin boot. He smiled apologetically at the frowning gambler. "Rose Elizabeth is as stubborn as a mule. Even if the duke was to return, she's not going to take him back. I'd wager a can of my favorite chewin' tobacco on that."

The gambler's eyes lit at the prospect of a game of chance. "Perhaps you'd consider wagering something a little more substantial than chewing tobacco?"

"I thought you gave up gambling," Brandon reminded his brother-in-law. "Laurel won't like it."

"A gambler never gives it up entirely, Brandon old boy. That would be like giving up sex and liquor." He shivered at the thought, bringing laughter to every man's lips, including Sven's.

"I vould be villing to wager one of my new calves that Alexander vill return for Rose Elizabeth and that she vill take him back."

"A cow? Jesus, Mary, and Joseph! What the hell am I going to do with a cow?"

Sven shrugged. "I am a farmer. That is all I have to wager. Besides, I do not think you vill vin."

"I'm still willing to bet my tobaccy that Rose Elizabeth says nay to the duke."

The wagers were placed, and since Brandon had opted not to join in the betting, he was placed in charge of the bets and declaring a winner.

"I trust you men will be discreet." Brandon cast an uncertain look at his wife and the other ladies who were putting dishes on the long picnic tables across the yard. Heather would skin him alive if she found out he had participated in wagering on her sister's happiness. "Our wives will not be happy to discover our harmless venture."

Seamus looked over at Rebecca, who was swollen with child and prone to temperamental moods of late, and swallowed the lump in his throat. There'd be no living with the lass if she found out that he'd bet two dozen jelly doughnuts on Rose Elizabeth's future with Alexander.

All the men wholeheartedly agreed that discretion was in order, and locked their hands together in one large handshake to seal the bargain, knowing that if one breached the trust, all were likely to suffer the consequences.

It was a frightening thought, to say the least.

"Those men are up to no good. I can feel it in my bones," Euphemia declared, staring narrow-eyed at the assemblage under the cottonwood tree. "I can smell their guilt from here."

Old Beaknose was at it again, Heather thought. "I'm sure they're just talking man-talk, Euphemia. You know how men are when they get together."

"Worse than women, I think," Rebecca said with a smile. "At least women don't need to brag so much." Seamus's chest had been inflated with sinful pride lately, due to the impending birth of their child, which he considered all his doing.

"*Hmph!* The only thing worse than a group of men plotting is a group of drunks singing. Wars have been started over much less."

"My husband much prefers to make love, not war, Euphemia," Laurel declared.

Marcella covered her mouth and giggled. "Mine too," she confessed.

"You always were a ninny, Marcella Purty. And that was never proved more correct than the day you up and married Skeeter. And you, Laurel, have always been a little too free with your speech. You should learn to be more subdued, like your sister Rose Elizabeth. Especially now that you're expecting."

Laurel's eyes widened at the rebuke, and she shot Rose Elizabeth a questioning look that clearly said: *I thought you said Euphemia had altered her ways.*

Rose's smug grin replied that she liked being the preferred

one for a change. It was certainly a novelty not to be the Martin sister in disfavor.

"Whether or not the men are plotting is not going to make a lick of difference if our dinner is ruined," Heather pointed out wisely. "And I for one am starved."

"Me too." Laurel eyed the roasting side of beef that Sven had provided, and her stomach growled loudly. "I swear I could eat that entire steer by myself."

Rose glanced down at her slightly swollen belly, pleased for once that Laurel was fatter than she was. Maybe it had taken twins to make her that way, Rose conceded, but the end result was the same.

"You know something, Laurel? You're finally fatter than me."

Laurel looked down at herself, then at Rose, and her mouth formed an O. "Well, you're right about that, little sister. I'm presently fatter than just about anyone. But there is a dividend to being fat," she declared with a huge grin. "I finally have a decent pair of titties!"

Afternoon gave way to twilight, and the last of Rose Elizabeth's guests had departed for home. Having accepted her sisters' offer to clean up, Rose had gone upstairs to nap.

Brandon and Chance used the opportunity to sit on the front-porch rockers and relax over a brandy.

"It sure is flat here in Kansas. Don't think I'd like living in a place like this. I'd miss the Rocky Mountains too much," Chance said, inhaling his cheroot.

Brandon refused the offer of a smoke and mopped at the back of his neck with a handkerchief. "It's too blasted hot. I much prefer the coolness of the coast. I like the smell of the ocean when I wake in the mornings. We can hear the pounding of the waves right outside our bedroom window, and I'd miss that."

"Folks are always comparing wheat fields to the waves of the ocean," Chance pointed out, staring at the fields ready to be harvested. "Guess Rose Elizabeth is going to need some help with the crop this year."

"I've already spoken to her about it, offered to pay whatever it takes to hire a crew to get it done."

"I bet that didn't set too well. She's an independent sort of gal."

Brandon snorted. "All the Martin sisters are. I don't think old Ezra did his girls any favors by instilling all that independence in them. Of course, my mother's all in favor of it. Says women in this day and age shouldn't be dependent on a man."

Chance reflected on that for a moment, and was about to comment, when he looked up and saw a rider coming down the lane. "Now who do you suppose that is?" He indicated the approaching visitor with a nod of his head. "Think someone forgot something?"

"Not likely. Everyone who came today arrived in buckboards or buggies. This one's on a big black stallion, and he's riding like his life depends on getting here."

They rose to their feet simultaneously and walked down the steps to find out for themselves who the stranger was, now halted in the yard.

The stallion was lathered, indicating that it had indeed been ridden hard; the rider, covered in his own sweat, hadn't fared much better.

"Howdy," Chance said to the man. "Looks like you're in a mighty big hurry to get someplace."

The man dismounted and removed his hat to reveal a shock of golden hair. Despite his obvious exertion, he was neatly attired in a black suit and tie, now covered with dust.

"I've come to see Rose Elizabeth Martin. Does she still reside here?"

The clipped English accent was a dead giveaway. Brandon and Chance glanced knowingly at each other, then moved shoulder to shoulder to close ranks around the man.

Finally, Brandon said, "I guess that depends on who's coming to call."

Tired, anxious, and agitated, Alexander had no patience for

interference or games. And these two men, whoever they were, looked like they were in the mood to play. "I am Alexander Warrick, the Duke of Moreland."

His suspicions confirmed, Chance's eyebrow shot up and he remarked, "There goes the cow," and Brandon laughed despite himself.

Alexander stared at the two men as if they'd lost their minds. "Who the bloody hell are you, anyway? And where is Rose Elizabeth?" He tried to step forward, but they refused to move out of his way.

"Not so fast, your highness." Chance tossed aside his cheroot, then poked a ringed finger in Alexander's chest to still his forward movement. "We've got a few things we want to settle with you first."

"Settle with me? I don't even know who you *gentlemen* are." And he used that term loosely.

"That's right, Warrick, you don't," Brandon agreed, unable to mask his disdain. "But we know all about you."

CHAPTER 27

At the older man's threatening tone, Alexander held up his fists and assumed the stance of a boxer, just in case the gentleman decided to make good on the murderous gleam in his eyes. "I should warn you—I've had experience as a pugilist."

"And are you also experienced as a sniveling, cowardly bastard, Warrick?" Brandon wanted to know.

"I can't believe you ran out on Rose Elizabeth like you did." Chance shook his head, disgust written all over his face. "Even I'm not that big of a heel." Though he'd come close, as he recalled.

"What's between Rose Elizabeth and myself is our business. And you have still not had the decency to tell me who in the bloody hell you are."

"We're the men who are going to beat you to a *bloody* pulp, your highness." Chance shrugged out of his jacket and hung in on the newel post. "Right, Brandon?"

Brandon? Alexander studied the dark-haired man. Might this quarrelsome chap be Brandon Montgomery, the newspaper magnate about whom Rose Elizabeth had spoken? The Brandon Montgomery who was now her brother-in-law?

Contemplating that possibility, Alexander never saw the fist of the green-eyed man until it was too late. It connected hard with his jaw, knocking him unconscious as he fell flat on his back.

Brandon yelled out his approval, slapping Chance on the back and raising quite a commotion, which brought two of the Martin sisters rushing out of the house to see what was happening.

"What on earth is going on here?" Heather hurried down the steps, Laurel close on her heels.

They arrived in time to see Chance standing over the stranger, who lay as still as a corpse, and looking inordinately pleased with himself despite his bloodied knuckles.

The duke had a chin of granite, Chance had decided.

"Chance Rafferty, stop fighting at once!" Laurel waved her arms wildly in the air, moving as fast as her increased girth would allow.

Chance's smile turned sickly.

"And you, Brandon Montgomery! What kind of example are you setting for your children by settling a disagreement with your fists and not your brains."

He held out his hands in supplication. "I didn't hit anyone. It was Chance." He pointed at his brother-in-law, who frowned fiercely at him.

Just then Rose Elizabeth emerged from the house, and Boomer flew past her, rushing down the stairs and growling ferociously. He stopped before the injured man, then began to lick his face. The action seemed to revive him.

"What's happened?" Rose asked as she continued to move toward the group circled around the prostrate form.

Concerned that the dog might harm whoever it was lying on the ground, she quickened her steps, shouting, "Boomer! Stop that, you naughty dog! Boomer, you mustn't . . ." The circle parted, and she ground to a halt, her eyes widening as recognition hit her square between the eyes. She felt her heart twist inside her chest.

"Alexander!" she cried, unwilling to hope what his arrival might mean, and concerned that her brothers-in-law would kill him before she had a chance to find out.

Heather and Laurel shared concerned looks, hoping that their sister, who looked as pale as bleached muslin, was not about to faint.

Alexander moved his chin back and forth, making a quick assessment to find that none of his teeth had been broken, then gave a pitiful smile. "Hello, Rose Elizabeth. It's nice to see you again. Would you mind calling off this damn dog?" Boomer was presently gnawing on the duke's ear. "And those other two animals behind you?"

She looked over her shoulder and saw Chance and Brandon backing away toward the house, sheepish smiles on their faces. The irate looks Heather and Laurel wore as they followed their husbands told Rose Elizabeth that her brothers-in-law would be having their comeuppance shortly. She almost felt sorry for them. Almost.

Dispensing Boomer to the barn with a firm command, Rose Elizabeth held out a trembling hand to Alexander. "I'm sorry you were greeted in such a hostile manner, Alexander. But . . . well, my brothers-in-law are a bit protective of me. And they've already formed their own opinions about you—not at all flattering, I'm afraid."

"Aided by you, no doubt." He brushed himself off.

"Actually, no. I've done my best to defend you. But you know how men are—always jumping to conclusions."

He devoured her with his eyes, wondering what madness had made him leave such a beautiful, courageous woman. It was then he noticed that she had lost a considerable amount of weight, making the soft rounding of her stomach more prominent, and her hands and feet were slightly swollen.

Alexander felt as if his heart had been ripped from his chest, the pain was so severe. "I'm too late. You've already married another."

Her eyes widened, and she wondered where on earth he had gotten such a bizarre idea. "I haven't married anyone, Alexander. What would make you say such a thing?"

He looked her over again from head to toe, more carefully this time, and his frown deepened considerably. "I guess it's the fact that you're standing before me looking quite pregnant.

"Who is he, Rose Elizabeth? Who is the bastard? Do you love him? Because if you do . . ."

Rose Elizabeth knew she should be outraged, should be contemplating the Duke of Moreland's murder, but the abject misery on his face and the ridiculous conclusions he had formed made her laugh instead.

Holding her sides, she laughed until tears rolled down her face, then she said to the duke, who was looking quite confused and very affronted by her attitude. "You're the bastard, Alexander! The child I carry is yours."

He rocked back on his heels, disbelief etched clearly on his face, and then Rose knew that he had told her the truth. Or at least the truth as he believed it. Her heart lightened.

"How can that be? That's not possible."

"You really didn't lie to me, did you, Alexander? You really thought you were unable to father a child?"

"I *am* unable to father a child. The doctor confirmed it."

Taking hold of his hand, she placed it on her abdomen. "Here is the proof that you're not sterile, your grace. You are indeed very potent. The doctor was wrong." And she silently thanked God for that.

It took a few moments for everything she'd said to register. When it did, his eyes filled with tears as unbridled joy filled every fiber of Alexander Warrick's being.

"You have made me the happiest of men, my sweet Rose." With uncertain but gentle fingers, he explored the growing mound that was his child, and grinned hugely when it moved beneath his hand, as if recognizing him as its father. "It knows me."

She caressed his cheek and smiled softly. "Intimately, your grace."

He pulled her against his chest and kissed her with all the pent-up longing within him. He kissed her so long and hard, Rose Elizabeth thought she might die of pleasure. Or suffocation. Or both. When he finally released her, she nearly toppled over.

"I love you, Rose Elizabeth. I should never have left. I realized it was a mistake as soon as the train pulled out of the station, but I was too stupid, too wrapped up in my honor and duty, to come back."

"You did what you had to do, Alexander. I realize that. But I never stopped loving you, never stopped praying that one day you'd come back to me." She moved toward the swing to allow them more privacy, drawing him with her, and they sat.

"We'll get married right away. You will marry me, won't you, Rose Elizabeth? It'll mean living in England for part of the year, but I promise we'll always come back here."

"Of course I'll marry you, Alexander. I love you with all my heart and soul." She smiled impishly. "And I've always had a hankerin' to be a duchess. But we'll have to wait until after the wheat harvest is done."

The swing rocked gently to and fro, and as Alexander glanced out at the unbroken sweep of golden grain, his chest tightened. He hadn't missed the harvest after all. It had waited. As Rose Elizabeth had waited. A lump rose in his throat.

There was something about this vast, windswept slab of prairie. Something Rose Elizabeth had tried to convey those many months ago. And now he understood. He had become one with the land. And now he would become one with the woman he loved.

"I'm surprised that you don't hate me, Rose, for everything I've put you through."

"That would be like hating myself, Alexander. I never thought to love anything or anyone more than I love this land, as I love your nephew and our child growing within me. But

I do, Alexander. I love you more than life itself. And this is something that will never change as long as I draw a breath."

He stood and pulled her to her feet. "You'll never be sorry for loving me, Rose Elizabeth. I'll make damned certain of that." Sweeping her off her feet and into his arms, he carried her toward the house.

"I want to show you just how much I love you."

Rose's heart was beating so fast at the idea of making love with Alexander again that it made what she had to say that much more difficult. "Uh . . . uh, Alexander . . . the house is a bit crowded at the moment."

He ground to a halt. "Bloody hell! I forgot. Does marrying you mean that I'm going to have to become related to those two savages I met earlier?"

She smiled. "Chance and Brandon are really quite sweet, as are my sisters Heather and Laurel, who you glimpsed briefly.

"And wait till you see how Duke has grown. You won't believe how big—"

"Duke?" His eyebrow shot up. "You named Jessica's child Duke?"

"He's my child, Alexander. Jessica might have given him life, but I have nurtured and cared for him and made him my own. And now I will share him with you. And yes, I named him after you. He looks just like you, you know."

Alexander's chest swelled with pride, as did another appendage, and he shifted Rose's weight in his arms. "Is there somewhere we can go to have some privacy? And not the barn. I know those damned cows will not be happy to see me again."

Rose nodded happily and pointed at the soddy. "It's where it all began, your dukeness."

"Bloody hell!" Alexander cursed, but he quickened his pace just the same.

EPILOGUE

Moreland House
Sussex, England
May 1885

   My dear Euphemia,

   There is so much to tell you since last I wrote, I hardly know where to begin.

   Adelaid was the best Christmas present Alexander could have given me—though I didn't think so when I was in labor. We're both thrilled with our darling girl, especially Alexander, who's become the doting daddy and spoils both Addy and Duke outrageously.

   Duke continues to ask for his "Aunt Oophie," and will no doubt shower you with kisses upon our arrival in two weeks. I can hardly wait, and have been marking the days off the calendar!

   How are Skeeter and Marcella? I hope they are taking good care of Boomer. I was distraught at not being able to take him with us to England, but I doubt he would have liked the ocean voyage all that much. It made me heave a time or two, I can tell you that, and Boomer's never been partial to water.

Rebecca wrote that she and Seamus are thinking about expanding the bakery and their family again. I would think they would have their hands full with little Sean, who Rebecca describes in her letters as a miniature version of Seamus down to his mop of red hair and mischievous smile. I can't wait to see him.

You'll be as happy as I was to hear that Heather finally finds herself with child. The waiting's been hard on both her and Brandon, but by year's end they'll be blessed with a child of their own. She writes to say that Jenny and Matt are overjoyed at the prospect of having a baby brother or sister, and Brandon's grin "seems permanently etched in his face," was how she put it.

Laurel and Chance are planning to come to Salina for another visit this summer and will arrive in time for the harvest. The twins, Augusta, named for that reverend she's so fond of, and Crystal Kathleen (Katy), in honor of her best friend, are thriving. Chance has become quite the family man and insists on pushing the baby carriage when they take the children for an outing.

Their business continues to flourish, and Chance is thinking of purchasing the building next to his and making a small hotel out of it. Laurel doesn't mind, as this will provide her with more of an audience when she gets the urge to sing, which is often, according to Chance. He's offered to pay for singing lessons, but our Laurie won't hear of it, saying that God blessed her with natural talent! That might be, but I don't think it had a thing to do with her voice.

Your last letter informing me that Peggy Mellon had left her husband and child and had run away with a traveling shoe salesman left both Alexander and me astounded. I could understand her need to leave Frederick.

But her child? I suppose the responsibility of raising it will fall upon Sarah Ann's shoulders. Mama always said: "As you sow, so shall you reap." And it was Sarah Ann's idea for Peggy to deceive Freddy in the first place.

I would never think of leaving Alexander, or my darling children, but I could certainly envision running away from that harridan, the dowager duchess. Beatrice doesn't bother to hide her dislike of me. And she's far from being grandmotherly to the children. She told Alexander after Adelaid's birth that it was just like him to deprive the Warrick name of an heir. He looked so hurt I wanted to flatten her, but he assured me that his mother doesn't have the power to wound him as she once did.

When she mentioned how Duke favored Alexander in appearance, we lied and told her that he was my child from a previous marriage. I can take no chances where my child's welfare is concerned.

Anyway, she's been moved to the dower house, which is a goodly distance from here, and very rarely comes to visit. Thank heavens!

Time cannot go quickly enough for me, Euphemia. I miss all of you so much. And though I love Sussex—Moreland House is a dream come true!—I can't help but yearn for the farm and all things familiar. Alexander understands this, and I believe he's as anxious to return to Kansas as I am. Maybe more so.

Please give our love to everyone. And tell Skeeter that I'll expect to see his smiling face when the train pulls into the railway station. Until then,

I am yours,

Rose Elizabeth, Duchessship of Moreland

Please Turn the Page

for a Preview of

DESPERATE

Book One of The Lawmen Trilogy

Available from Warner Books

July 1997

PROLOGUE

Misery, Texas, Summer 1879

"I ain't seen you this nervous, little brother, since we got the drop on that Mex bastard Juan Corrola down San Antonio way, and he nearly shot your cajones off. You look like you're fixin' to attend a funeral, not a wedding."

Rafe Bodine shot his brother a look that would have withered a lesser man, then wiped away the sweat on his upper lip with the back of his hand. The pristine white clapboard church, the town's newest edifice, loomed in the distance, and his heart kept perfect time to the clanging of the bells, which announced his upcoming marriage to Ellie Masters.

Even if he was marrying a woman he'd known all his life, a woman he considered his best friend, a man still had a right to be nervous. And he shouldn't have to apologize about it to anyone, especially someone like Ethan, who'd made it perfectly clear years ago that he'd sooner be shot dead than married.

"Man's got a right to be discomforted on his wedding day,

Ethan," Rafe said, reeling in his jangled nerves and sitting just a little taller in the saddle. The sun blazed brightly, adding to his discomfort, and he tugged at the stiff collar encircling his neck like a hangman's noose. There was nary a cloud in the sky to mar the blue perfection, and it seemed evident that his upcoming wedding had been blessed by a higher authority than Texas Ranger Ethan Bodine.

"I suspect Lorna Mae Murray and her four hulking brothers are still waiting for you to show up in Nogales and do right by her." Rafe swallowed his smile as Ethan shifted uncomfortably in his saddle. The worn leather creaked despite Ethan's judicious use of saddle soap.

"Heard the Murray boys were still looking for that no-good Ranger who sweet-talked their little sister outta her virginity, then up and left her a brokenhearted, fallen woman."

Ethan smoothed down the corners of his mustache, and a faraway look lighted his eyes, as if the memory he'd conjured up was a pleasing one. "Sampling Lorna Mae's ample charms was like dipping bare-ass naked into a hot tub of water— slick, easy, and mighty pleasurable. There weren't nothing to impede my enjoyment, if you follow, but those poor misguided fellas who were trying to defend her so-called honor. Don't think Lorna Mae had much honor left by the time I met her, having already shared it with half of Nogales."

Rafe chuckled, but his laughter was short-lived, for Ethan continued on in the opinion he'd been voicing for weeks. "There's still time to back out, Rafe. You can change your mind about marrying Ellie, about quitting the Rangers. Can't believe you'd want to do such a foolish thing anyway. We've been rangerin' all our lives. It's who we are, all we know."

"It's who *you* are, Captain Bodine. I never wanted all that guts and glory in the first place. I'm thirty-five years old. It's time I settled down and got married, started that ranch I've been thinking about for years. I don't want to end up a lonely, miserable old coot like you, with nothing to show for myself but a tin star and a passel of memories."

"Nothing wrong with memories. And I ain't too old to

make new ones. Once you hogtie yourself to that pretty little filly, your memory-making days are over, little brother. You'll be hobbled. And you'll only be unfettered when it's time to service your mare. Damn shame to turn a wild mustang into a tame gelding."

"Your concern, not to mention your vivid prose, is touching, Ethan. But nothing you can do or say is going to make me change my mind about marrying Ellie. We're a comfortable match. She's a good woman who'll make me a fine wife."

"Ellie's the best. There ain't no problem conceding that point. But marrying her's gonna be like marryin' your little sister. You grew up together. She's like family. And it ain't natural to be marrying family, is all I'm saying."

Ethan's concerns were no greater than the ones Rafe harbored himself. Rafe loved Ellie in his own special way. It wasn't an all-consuming, hearts on fire, romantic kind of love that novelists wrote about, but a genuine, caring, dependable kind of love—one that promised contentment and friendship. That was more than most couples shared in a lifetime.

And Rafe knew without a doubt that Ellie loved him.

Ellie Masters had loved Rafe Bodine from the time her mama and his had set them down on the same tattered quilt to play beneath the spindly cottonwood tree growing next to the stream on Ben Bodine's ranch.

It was Ellie with whom Rafe had shared his first pet bullfrog and his first defeat at the fists of Ethan; and it was Rafe whom Ellie had confided in when her breasts began to bud and when her woman's time came and she feared she was bleeding to death from some rare disease.

If there were two people better suited, Rafe hadn't encountered them yet.

"No offense, big brother, but you are hardly the one to be handing out marital advice. For a supposedly fearless Texas Ranger, you are scared of anything in calico. You're afraid that one day you're gonna meet some woman who's going to turn your insides to mush and make mincemeat pie outta you. Admit it, Ethan, you're afraid of women."

Ethan's spine stiffened as straight as the Winchester rifle slung next to his saddle. His blue eyes, a shade deeper than Rafe's, darkened to cobalt. "There's nothing in this world that scares me, Rafe, except maybe your stupidity. Go ahead and marry that girl. But don't say I didn't warn you."

Rafe gazed affectionately at his brother. It was hard to stay mad at a man who had only your best interests at heart. Ethan had been looking out for Rafe, whether or not Rafe wanted him to, since Rafe had smiled in toothless adoration at his older brother. And despite the fact that they were now grown men, nothing had changed much.

"I appreciate your concern, but I know what I'm doing. It's about time I grew up, don't you think? I can't be Ethan Bodine's baby brother all my life." He grinned. "Besides, you've still got Travis to boss around."

The Ranger snorted, shook his head in disgust, and spurred his horse into a gallop. Rafe, an expert horseman in his own right, kept pace. When they reached the churchyard and dismounted, Ethan grabbed Rafe's arm and dragged him toward the building without saying a word.

To the casual observer it looked like the disgruntled Texas Ranger had come to make an arrest rather than perform the duties of best man for his younger brother.

There wasn't a soul in all of Taylor County, Texas, who didn't think that the sun rose and set on Ellie Bodine, née Masters. Sweeter than sorghum and prettier than a Texas bluebonnet, levelheaded Ellie was well suited for Ben Bodine's wild, impetuous son. Or so Ben thought. She would settle Rafe down, have a calming effect on him, and Ben had been only too happy to give his blessings to the union, as well as offer his ranch as the proper locale for the wedding reception.

Patsy, Ben's first wife, had predicted that Rafferty, which is what she'd always called Rafe, and Ellie would wed one day, even going so far as to place a ten-dollar wager on it some years back. Ben still had the gold piece tucked away safely in the drawer of his desk, and planned to present it to Rafe's firstborn on the occasion of the baby's christening.

Rafe's sudden decision to wed had come as a great relief to Ben, who'd always had a hankering for grandchildren and had about given up hope that any of his three boys would tie the knot.

It was damn doubtful that any woman would put up with Ethan's surly disposition and independent ways, and Travis seemed content to remain hitched to his lawyering profession, though the boy had come close to marrying that judge's daughter, Hannah Barkley, but something had soured him on the idea before they could make it to the altar.

The music ended and Travis moved off the dance area, his stepmother's gloved hand tucked securely in the crook of his arm as he traversed the short distance to where his father stood. Brightly colored lanterns strewn across the yard on long lengths of ribbon hovered over his head, illuminating the effusive and somewhat inebriated grins of the guests attending the reception.

"Been doing a little sashaying, huh, son?" Ben grinned at Travis's flushed face, then winked rakishly at his wife before bowing gallantly before her. "Lavinia, darlin'."

"Lavinia is complaining, Pa, that you haven't danced one dance with her yet."

"That's right, Ben." Lavinia's soft brown eyes twinkled. "I'm bound and determined to dance with the handsomest man at this reception."

Ben beamed down at his wife of five years. With her thick auburn hair gently sprinkled with gray and a flawless complexion unmarred by time and the elements, Lavinia was a handsome woman. But it wasn't her looks that had first attracted widower Ben Bodine, it was her smile—a smile that had warmed the old man's lonely heart and won over his three sons with little problem.

Staring at the older couple, Travis wondered if he'd ever

find the kind of happiness he saw reflected in their eyes, and he sighed at the memory of how close he'd come, once.

Across the yard, his older brother two-stepped with his new bride. Rafe had never been what one would call graceful, but he was doing a fair job of keeping up with energetic Ellie. Travis smiled, genuinely happy that Rafe seemed content with his new lot in life.

"What are you grinning at, little brother?" Ethan sidled up next to him. "You look like an imbecile with that crooked grin on your face."

Travis had been a member of the Bodine family too long to let a little good-natured teasing rile him. And from the smell of Ethan's breath, it was most likely the whiskey talking. Though Ethan had no trouble being outspoken and opinionated when the situation warranted, the Texas Ranger was not known for his subtlety or tact.

"Sounds to me like you're just upset because you couldn't keep Rafe from quitting the Rangers and settling down." At Ethan's wounded look, Travis squeezed his brother's shoulder affectionately, knowing full well that Ethan would miss Rafe's companionship. The two men had been closer than ticks on a hound their whole life, and the younger Travis had often felt left out because of it.

"Don't take it so hard, Ethan. The life of a Ranger's not for everyone. Rafe grew tired of the killing and the nomadic life. He wants to put down roots, get some permanence in his life. I know you want him to be happy."

The tall man's conflicting emotions played across his sun-beaten face—a face most women found irresistible and many men feared. "It ain't normal for a man to go against his natural inclination. Rafe was born to rangerin', same as me. A woman can't give you the same feeling of camaraderie as a camp full of men bent on the same mission."

"Since I've never been a Ranger, I can't comment on that, but I have been in love and—"

Ethan snorted, slapped his brother none too gently on the back, and said, "And you never saw fit to hitch up with that filly neither, 'cause you had more sense that that, boy. Whatever happened to that sour-pussed woman you was sweet on? I never could figure out who dumped who."

Travis masked the pain in his voice. As a lawyer he'd learned many things—the most important being: never reveal a weakness—and Hannah Louise Barkley was definitely a weakness. "Hannah's gone East to live with her mother." And that was all he was going to say on the subject.

Pulling a silver flask from his inside coat pocket, Ethan took another swallow of whiskey, then offered the bottle to his brother, who shook his head in refusal. "Too bad Rafe couldn't have had the same good luck as you did, Travis. You always was the luckiest of the three Bodine brothers."

Travis's glance drifted to the groom once again. Rafe was smiling down at his bride, looking happier than Travis had seen him in a long, long while. "I'd say Rafe would dispute that opinion 'long about now, big brother."

"I'm so giddy I feel like I've had twenty glasses of Mama's wine punch, Rafe. Pinch me and tell me that we're really, truly married." Ellie's ebullient smile radiated warmth as she hugged herself around the middle and swayed in time to the music.

A fiddle and a banjo plunked out a lively tune, but they could just as well have been a washboard and a jew's harp, for all the attention the new bride paid them. Ellie's fondest desire had just come true: She had finally managed to get Rafe Bodine to the altar.

Laughing at her childlike exuberance, Rafe chucked his wife under the chin. "No one is more surprised than me, Ellie darlin'. I can assure you."

Her smile melted quickly, the brightness in her eyes dimming slightly to be replaced by self-doubt. "You're not sorry, are you, Rafe? Sorry you decided to make an honest woman out of me?"

The absurdity of her statement amused him. "You've always been honest, Ellie. You're the most honest woman I know."

"And I'm still a virgin, Rafe. I've saved myself for you all these years. I didn't want to give myself to anyone but you." She leaned in to him, and there was promise in her eyes and a wealth of love for this man she had loved all her life.

Her confession made Rafe swallow with some difficulty. He'd always figured Ellie for a virgin, but to have her confirm it . . . A virgin was a big responsibility. And though most men wanted virginity in a bride, at the moment Rafe would have settled for the opposite.

Ellie's state of virginity made him feel guilty—guilty that she'd waited for him all these years, when she could have had any of a dozen beaus, all more prosperous than he, guilty that she'd married a man whose life had been filled with mayhem and killing, and who didn't know if he possessed the gentle side she was sure he had.

Guilty that he wasn't madly in love with the woman he now called wife.

Dear Reader,

I hope you enjoyed PRIM ROSE, and the other two books of the "Flowers of the West" trilogy, WILD HEATHER and SWEET LAUREL.

The Martin sisters of Salina, Kansas were sterling examples of the independent and courageous women who settled the American frontier and paved the way for generations of women to follow. Though their stories were fictional, they were based on the struggles women faced in a male-dominated society.

Depicted as a sleepy prairie town in the novels, Salina, Kansas was in actuality a bustling community in 1883 and boasted almost 4,000 inhabitants. The Kansas-Pacific Railroad put it on the map, and its many flour mills and granaries made it prosper.

There is always a sense of loss when an author has to leave her characters behind. I've grown attached to these people. They are as real to me as any friend or family member, and I hope after reading the books you feel the same way, too.

I would love to hear your comments and opinions on the books of the "Flowers of the West" trilogy. Please write to me in care of Warner Books, Time & Life Building, 1271 Avenue of the Americas, New York, NY 10020.

Best Wishes,

Millie Criswell